"Slick high-finance melodrama and dizzying technical speculation lift Edelman's SF debut, the first of a trilogy. Centuries in the future, humans rely less on machines than on upgrading their own nervous systems with nanotech bio/logic programs. Natch, a gifted young code programmer-entrepreneur obsessed with clawing his way to the top, jumps at the chance to merchandise a major new technology, MultiReal, even though he doesn't know what it is. Natch soon becomes a target for not just his business rivals but also totalitarian governmental agencies and more mysterious groups. Natch's being a borderline sociopath makes him extremely creative in business tactics and personal manipulation (and thus fascinating to read about). The world in which he operates is also fascinating, with awesome personal powers being sold on a frantic open market. Edelman, who has a background in Web programming and marketing, gives his bizarre notions a convincing gloss of detail. Bursting with invention and panache, this novel will hook readers for the story's next installment."

—*Publishers Weekly*

"*Infoquake* is a rare beast: a future history that is simultaneously convincing and wondrous. David Louis Edelman takes no shortcuts to a destination quite unlike any visited before—and we are richer for it."

—Sean Williams,
New York Times best-selling author of *The Crooked Letter*

"David Louis Edelman's *Infoquake* may be a new subgenre unto itself: the science fiction business thriller. Set in a fully realized future world, the narrative is more interested in the economic impact of future technologies than in the technologies themselves. The suspense derives entirely from politics and economics, and the most exciting moments (and they are exciting!) surround new product launches. Edelman doesn't resort to any of the typical tricks to keep the reader turning pages, but I found that I still couldn't turn them fast enough."

—Chris Roberson,
Sidewise Award–winning author of *Here, There & Everywhere*
and *Paragaea: A Planetary Romance*

INFOQUAKE

DAVID LOUIS EDELMAN

INFOQUAKE

VOLUME I OF THE JUMP 225 TRILOGY

an imprint of **Prometheus Books**
Amherst, NY

Published 2006 by Pyr®, an imprint of Prometheus Books

Inquiries should be addressed to
Pyr
59 John Glenn Drive
Amherst, New York 14228–2197
VOICE: 716–691–0133, ext. 207
FAX: 716–564–2711
WWW.PYRSF.COM

10 09 08 07 06   5 4 3 2 1

Library of Congress Cataloging-in-Publication Data

Edelman, David Louis.
    Infoquake / David Louis Edelman.
        p. cm.
    ISBN 13: 978–1–59102–442–2 (alk. paper)
    ISBN 10: 1–59102–442–0 (alk. paper)
    1. Corporations—Fiction. I. Title. II. Series: Edelman, David Louis. Jump 225 trilogy ; v.1.

PS3605.D445I54 2006
813'.6—dc22

2006009272

Printed in the United States of America on acid-free paper

CONTENTS

The product of an engineer is technically at a higher pitch of perfection than a product of nature.
—Karel Čapek, *R.U.R.*

I

NUMBER ONE ON PRIMO'S

(((|)))

Natch was impatient.

He strode around the room with hands clasped behind his back and head bowed forward, like a crazed robot stuck on infinite loop. Around and around, back and forth, from the couch to the door to the window, and then back again.

Behind him, the window was tuned to some frantic cityscape that Jara didn't recognize. Buildings huddled together at crooked angles like the teeth of old men, as tube trains probed the cavities. Singapore, maybe? Sao Paulo? Definitely a Terran city, Jara decided. Every few minutes, Natch would look in that direction and inhale deeply, as if trying to draw energy from the thousands of manic pedestrians ensconced within the four corners of the window canvas.

Natch stopped suddenly and wheeled on his apprentice. "Why are you just *sitting* there?" he cried, punctuating the question with a snap of his fingers.

Jara gestured to the empty spot next to her on the couch. "I'm waiting for Horvil to show up so we can get this over with."

"Where *is* Horvil?" said Natch. "I told him to be here an hour ago. No, an hour and a *half* ago. Can't that lazy bastard learn to keep a calendar?" Around and around, back and forth.

Jara regarded her employer in silence. She supposed that Natch would be devilishly handsome to anyone who didn't know he was completely insane. That casually athletic physique, the boyish face that would never know gray, those eyes predictably blue as sapphires: people like Natch just didn't exist on this side of the camera lens. Nor did they spout phrases like *trouncing the competition* and *creating a new paradigm* without a trace of irony or self-consciousness.

Natch shook his head. "I can only *hope* he remembers we've got a product launch tomorrow."

"I don't know why you're so uptight," said Jara. "We do twenty or thirty product launches every year."

"No," whispered Natch. "Not like this one."

Jara let it go. As usual, she had no idea what Natch was talking about. NiteFocus 48 was a routine upgrade that fixed a number of minor coding inconsistencies but introduced no new features. The program had an established track record in the marketplace, built on the well-known optical expertise of the Natch Personal Programming Fiefcorp. Unless Natch expected them to rework the rules of bio/logic programming overnight—and she wouldn't put that past him—the NiteFocus product launch would be a pretty routine affair.

"Listen," said Jara. "Why don't you let Horvil sleep for another hour? He was up all night tinkering on this thing. He probably just got to bed. Don't forget that out *here*, it's seven o'clock in the morning." *Here* was London: a sane place, a city of right angles. The city where both Horvil and Jara lived, and some six thousand kilometers away from Natch's apartment in Shenandoah.

"I don't fucking care," Natch snorted. "I haven't gotten *any* sleep tonight, and I didn't get any yesterday either."

"Might I remind you that *I* was up all night working on NiteFocus too?"

"I *still* don't care. Go wake him up."

For the third time that week, Jara considered quitting. He always had this condescension, this mania—no, *lust*—for perfection. How difficult would it be to find a job at another fiefcorp? She had fifteen years in this business, almost three times as much experience as Natch. Certainly PulCorp or Billy Sterno or even Lucas Sentinel would take her on board. Or, dare she think it, the Patel Brothers? But then she considered the three agonizing years she had spent as Natch's apprentice, and the scant eleven months to go before her contract expired. *Eleven months to go until I can cash out! I should be able to keep it together that long.*

So Jara didn't quit. Instead, she gave her fiefcorp master one last bitter look and cut her multi connection. True to form, Natch had already turned his back on her, probably heading into his office to do more fine-tuning on NiteFocus. *You need to watch yourself*, Jara thought. *Natch's brand of insanity just might be contagious.*

She slid into nothingness.

• • •

The hollow sensation of a mind devoid of sensory input. Those blessed two and a half seconds of free time after one multi connection ends, but before the next begins. Emptiness, blankness.

Multivoid.

Then consciousness.

Jara was back in London, but not at Horvil's place, as she had expected. Horvil must have refused her multi request, so the system had automatically stopped the feed of sensory information flowing through her neural cortex. She stood now on the red square tile that was her apartment's gateway to the multi network, staring at the walls she had never had time to decorate. She stretched her calves, slightly sore from five hours of multi-induced paralysis, and walked down the hall to the living room.

Jara's apartment insulted her with its desolation: a featureless space, a human storage chamber. She resisted the urge to blow off Natch's little summit and go shopping on the Data Sea for wall hangings. *Eleven months, eleven months, eleven months*, Jara told herself. *And then I can cash out and start my own business and it won't matter. In the meantime, I'd better wake up Horvil.*

If Horvil wasn't answering her multi requests, he was either asleep or ignoring her. The engineer was not known for being an early riser.

In Horvil's parlance, *early* meant any time before noon, and to a global professional who hopped continents with barely a thought, *noon* was a slippery concept. Jara gritted her teeth and called up Confidential-Whisper 66, the program de rigueur for remote conversation. If Horvil wouldn't see her, maybe he would at least *talk* to her.

The engineer accepted the connection—solid evidence he was, at least, awake.

Jara waited impatiently for an acknowledgment, a response, *something*. "Well?" she complained. "Are you coming over to Natch's apartment or what?"

Jara heard a number of fake stretching and groaning noises from Horvil's end of the connection. ConfidentialWhisper was strictly a *mental* communication program, not an oral one. "I *could* pretend I'm still asleep," said the engineer.

"If *I* have to be at this idiotic meeting, Horv, then *you're* not getting out of it."

"Tell me again why he wants to hold a meeting this early in the morning."

"Come on, you know how it works. Apprentice in a fiefcorp, work on the master's time."

"But what's this all *about*?"

Jara sighed. "I have no idea. Probably another one of his stupid schemes to take over the world. Whatever he's up to, it can't be good."

"Of *course* it can't be good," said Horvil. "This is *Natch* we're talking about. I ever tell you about the time in school when Natch tried to form a corporation? Can't you just picture him trying to explain laissez-faire capitalism to a bunch of nine-year-old hive kids—"

"Horvil, I'm *waiting*."

The engineer sounded unconcerned. "I'm *tired*. Call Merri. Call Vigal."

"They're not invited."

"Why not? They're part of this company too, aren't they?"

The question had occurred to Jara as well. "Maybe Natch trusts us more than he trusts them."

Horvil chuckled and made a sound like he was spitting out pillow lint. "Right, sure. Maybe he knows *we're* too cowardly to stand up to him." And before Jara had a chance to respond, the engineer cut the 'Whisper connection, leaving her alone with her empty walls.

How dare he call me a coward! she fumed silently. *I'm not afraid of Natch. I'm just practical, that's all. I know I only have to put up with him for eleven more months.* She called up her apprenticeship contract for the thousandth time and reread the clause on compensation, hoping as always to catch a glimpse of some previously unknown loophole. But the letters floating before her eyes hadn't changed: Jara would receive nothing except room and board until the end of the four-year term, at which time her shares matured. She blinked hard, and the illusory text on the surface of her retinas vanished.

Jara gave one last wistful glance at her apartment and stepped back down the hall to open another multi connection. Multivoid swallowed her empty walls and regurgitated Natch's metropolitan windows. The fiefcorp master was nowhere to be found, but Jara was in no mood to track him down. He had to be here somewhere, or she would have never made it into the building. Jara threw herself down on the couch and waited.

Five minutes later, Horvil materialized in the room wearing the same mixture of bonhomie and bafflement he always wore. "Towards Perfection," he greeted his fellow apprentice amiably as he plopped down in Natch's favorite chair. It was actually a chair-and-a-half, but still barely wide enough to accommodate Horvil's considerable bulk. "Who's ready to wallow around in the mud? I know *I* could use a good wallow right about now."

Jara frowned, wondering whether Horvil had concocted some algorithm to make even his virtual clothes look disheveled. "That makes *one* of us," she said.

The engineer yawned and sat back in his chair with a smile. "Stop being so *dramatic*, Princess. If you don't want to be here, go home. What's Natch going to do? Cancel your contract? Fire you?"

Jara extended her finger into an accusatory position by reflex. She lowered it when she realized she had nothing to say.

And then Natch returned.

Neither apprentice saw the fiefcorp master come in, but now there he stood with his arms crossed and his eyes glaring. For once, he was not pacing, and this made Jara nervous. When Natch chose to focus all that kinetic energy on some concrete goal instead of stomping it into oblivion, mountains moved. Jara examined the gorge in her stomach and came to a sudden realization: she *was* afraid of Natch.

"We're going to the top of the bio/logics market," he announced. "We're going to be number one on Primo's."

Horvil put his feet up on the coffee table. "Of course we are," he said breezily. "We've been over this shit before. Market forces, fiefcorp economics, blah blah blah. It's inevitable, ain't it?"

Natch closed his eyes and took a deep breath. When he opened them, his gaze fixed on a spot of nothingness hovering midway between the two apprentices. Jara suddenly felt transparent, as if the world had gained presence at her expense. "You don't understand, Horvil," he said. "We're going to be number one on Primo's, and we're going to do it *tomorrow.*"

(((2)))

The two apprentices sat stiffly, afraid to move. Jara wondered if she had stumbled onto the set of an old-fashioned drama by mistake, with Natch playing the part of the Mad Capitalist Who Went Too Far. Or maybe the fiefcorp master was starring in a farce instead. Number one on the Primo's bio/logic investment guide *tomorrow?*

"Impossible," said Jara. "You can't just press a button and *will* yourself to the top of Primo's. It's all impartial, rules-based. They've got strict formulas that nobody knows except the senior interpreters."

Natch regarded her with a stare he might have given a less-evolved subspecies of humanity. "And?"

"Don't be ridiculous, Natch. They sift through ten thousand bio/logic programs a day, and every decision they make affects the hierarchy. You can't predict Primo's rankings. And don't give me that look—you can't rig them either. People have tried." She turned to Horvil, aiming her index finger at his bulbous nose. "Come on, Horvil—*you* know about Primo's as well as I do. They're not accountable to anyone."

The engineer stretched his arms out over his head, suspended them there momentarily, then sent them crashing down onto his commodious lap. *"Primo's: impartial because we have to be,"* he quoted the company's official slogan. *"Your bio/logic systems depend on us, from hearts and lungs to stocks and funds."*

Natch might well have been a video clip in pause mode. He gave no outward sign he had even been listening to his apprentices' exchange.

"All right," spat Jara, anxious to break the tension in the room. "I suppose you have some brilliant plan to make this happen."

The fiefcorp master began to pace once more. "Of course I do," he replied, stone-faced. "Now, as you know, today we're scheduled to release NiteFocus 48, our biggest—and best—product this year."

Jara thought about debating the *best* portion of his statement, but changed her mind and leaned back in the sofa. Horvil was one of the *best* engineers in the business, but Jara knew from experience he got sloppy when he worked long hours. NiteFocus 48 would have its share of bugs and inconsistencies, like any program bred of human thought.

"Well, guess who *else* is planning a product launch this week?" continued Natch.

Jara's heart skipped a beat. "Don't tell me the Patel Brothers are finally releasing NightHawk 73," she said.

The fiefcorp master nodded. "The same."

Jara frowned and crossed her arms over her chest. With that kind of competition, how in the world did Natch expect to top the market *this* week of all weeks? The Patel Brothers had dominated the number one rating on Primo's for the past two and a half years. They were widely perceived to be unbeatable. Of course, this hadn't stopped Natch from confronting the Patels head-to-head on a variety of programs over the past few months—on the contrary, the challenge spurred him to new heights of competitive frenzy. He plotted their release schedules on graphs of three, four, and five dimensions. He hunted down even the deadendingest rumors about Frederic and Petrucio Patel.

And now, it seemed, after feeling the occasional prick of Natch's jabs on the Primo's battlefield—a loss of a point here, a preempted product launch there—the Patel Brothers had finally accepted the challenge of their younger rival. Releasing NightHawk in the same week as NiteFocus was a direct assault.

Horvil was unperturbed by this latest turn of events. "Why are you two so worried?" he said, trying unsuccessfully to stifle a yawn. "We've put a lot of work into NiteFocus. It's good code. I'm not afraid to go up against the Patels."

"So then, what do we do?" asked Natch. His tone of voice indicated it was a rhetorical question.

Jara scowled. She knew where this was heading. "If anybody but *you* asked me that question, I would say, *We both launch our products on the Data Sea, and may the best company win.*"

The fiefcorp master gave her one of his wolfish grins, the kind that had little to do with humor. On some alternate plane of existence, Natch's audience howled in gleeful anticipation. "You think I'm afraid to go up against the Patels."

"I just don't like pulling these dirty tricks of yours. We're number six on Primo's, in a field of thousands. Why can't you be happy with that?"

Natch stopped in midstride and gave his apprentice a piercing look. "Happy with failure?" he said incredulously, as if she had suggested joining one of the creeds and devoting his life to poverty. "Happy with *this*?" He gestured wildly around him at what seemed to Jara to be a pretty nice flat. Natch's apartment had enough space for both living and working quarters, with room left over to entertain. Not only that, but it boasted real *and* programmable windows, as well as a lush garden of daisies right smack in the middle of the place. Maybe Natch's apartment paled in comparison to the Lunar estates of the big tycoons, but at least it was decorated.

Jara composed herself. "Natch, number six on Primo's isn't failure," she said. "Most programmers spend their whole *lives* trying to crack the top ten. We've gotten here in thirty-six months. *Thirty-six months*, Natch! Primo's has been around for almost seventy *years*, and nobody's ever done it as fast as we have. Horvil, where were we a year ago today?"

The engineer focused his attention inward for a split second, the telltale sign of a brain angling for information on the Data Sea. "Sixty-two," announced Horvil momentarily. "The year before that, four hundred nineteen." Jara threw up her hands as if to say, *See what I mean?* "And the year before that, we didn't—"

Natch cut his apprentice off in midsentence. "Does this shit have a point?"

Jara stood her ground. "I'm not suggesting we quit trying, Natch. I'm just saying we'll *get* to the top eventually, *by the strength of our products*, without dirty tricks. The Patel Brothers are getting older, and we're gaining on them all the time. In a couple of years, when all the tax breaks dry up, they'll sell out and dissolve their fiefcorp. That's what happens in this business."

Natch grimaced, rocked back and forth on his heels, and let out a restless sigh. He looked like the little boy who had been scolded by his proctors for staying out past curfew. Despite all his frantic motion, every chestnut-colored hair on his head remained perfectly in place. Jara met his stare, but she was disappointed to see Horvil struggling to stay awake. *Thanks for backing me up, Horv!*

"All right," said the fiefcorp master, with a look on his face that said, *I'll go through the motions of considering your worthless ideas, but only for form's sake.* "Let's take a look at NiteFocus 48 in MindSpace. Let's see how *strong* our products really are."

Jara and Horvil followed Natch into his office. The room was short and sparsely decorated and functional, but still quite a bit nicer than Jara's workspace. Artificial daylight, streaming into the room from two square windows, showed a hectic market square somewhere in Beijing. *That's one way to keep working through all hours of the night*, Jara thought sourly. *Pretend it's day.*

Natch walked up to the squat workbench that sat in the center of the room and waved his hand to summon the virtual programming bubble known as MindSpace. He was instantly surrounded by a clear holographic sphere about two meters in diameter, along with an assortment of interlocking geometric shapes and connecting fibers.

The program loaded in MindSpace looked like a dense pyramid carpeted with spikes. It wasn't any code that Jara recognized. "What's that?" she said.

"Nothing," grumbled the fiefcorp master, banishing the display with a flick of his wrist. A more cohesive structure appeared in the layer beneath, shaped like a lopsided donut and colored in soft grays and blues. Strands of purple and white formed an intricate net through the center. Jara could have traced those supple curves with her eyes closed. NiteFocus 48.

Natch took one look at the mass of bio/logic code floating in front of him and gave a snort of disgust. His dissatisfaction grew as he rotated the donut slowly along its z-axis. *Imperfect!* Jara could hear him thinking, a fourth-act soliloquy to his invisible audience. *Unsatisfactory! A mocking reminder of all the projects I've left unfinished, all the goals I've left unattained.*

"Well, what are we waiting for?" said Horvil. "Let's fire this baby up."

Jara gave her internal system a silent command to activate Nite-Focus, and then waited a few seconds as the program disseminated its instructions to the microscopic machines floating in her bloodstream. She tried to detect the millions of calculations going on inside her brain, the logical handshakes extending thousands of kilometers from her virtual body here to cellular structures standing stiff on a red tile in London. But she knew that even if she were here in the flesh, the chemical reactions in the retina and the electric pulses along the ciliary muscle would be completely undetectable. Bio/logic programs had not been that crude since Sheldon Surina invented the science some 360 years ago.

"I think it's working," said Jara. A hopeful statement.

Horvil puffed up his chest and clapped a virtual arm around Natch's shoulder. "Of *course* it's working. What'd I tell you?"

The fiefcorp master said nothing. He turned off the Beijing scene on the left window, leaving a view of the real darkness outside. Natch squinted, shook his head, and marched through the other room to the balcony door. Horvil and Jara followed him as he stepped outside into the coal-dark Shenandoah night, about half past three now. A platform promptly slid under their feet from the side of the building.

The three fiefcorpers stood at the railing and gazed into the distance, looking for a suitable object on which to test their enhanced vision. Flashing lights were still evident in the rowdier quarters of the city, but out here in the residential district, things were relatively quiet. "There," said Horvil, pointing towards a viewscreen that stood several blocks down the road, its lights dim now that there was no foot traffic. Jara found she could read the advertisement clearly.

DRINK CHAIQUOKE
Because the Defense and Wellness Council Still Lets You.

Beneath the print, the smart-alecky ChaiQuoke pitchman suckled on a neon purple bottle while a Council officer looked on with overt disapproval.

Horvil danced a clumsy jig of triumph. "Looks like the Natch Personal Programming Fiefcorp will still be in business tomorrow," he crowed. "Oh yeah!"

Jara breathed a sigh of relief. Why had she been nervous? NiteFocus 48 had worked fine yesterday too, and the day before, and the day before. She hadn't seen a major glitch in the program since version 43 or 44. "So what do you think?" she asked Natch. "Ready for launch?"

"Does it *look* like it's ready for launch?" the fiefcorp master replied brusquely. "The color resolution needs a lot of work. And from the look of those blueprints, this program uses *way* too many cycles. You think we can just release a product that sucks up all the computing resources on the Data Sea and crashes people's systems? No, it's not fucking ready at *all*."

Jara reacted as if he had slapped her. There was a sudden fermata in Horvil's dance, which he tried to pass off as intentional. Why had they slaved through so many nights if they were going to get this kind of treatment?

"Can't either of you see what I'm trying to do?" asked Natch, his tone suddenly quiet and contemplative. "I'm just pointing out the same inadequacies that Primo's is going to find tomorrow. Primo's doesn't care if you spent all night coding. They only care about two things: success and failure. Success means more sales. It means more respect. It means moving up to the next level of the game. Everything *else* . . . is failure." Natch rubbed his forehead and gave a yearning look out towards the horizon.

Jara couldn't help but roll her eyes at his histrionics. *Doesn't Natch ever stop to wonder if he's taking himself too seriously?* She wanted to screech obscenities at the invisible audience, to throttle his knowing smirk. She wanted to get him out of those breeches somewhere quiet and instruct him in low, sibilant tones about the things that *really* mattered.

The fiefcorp master turned. He gave Jara a long, penetrating stare of amusement and contempt while Horvil shifted awkwardly from foot to foot behind them. "Now come inside," Natch said, "and I'll tell you my plan."

Jara lowered her eyes. "I thought you said no more dirty tricks," she whimpered.

"I never said that. I said I'd *take a look* at NiteFocus 48, which I just did. And it's awful. Besides, why do you keep using those words, *dirty tricks*? I don't do dirty tricks. It's called *business*."

(((3)))

The sun crept up the early-morning sky, pantherlike, reminding Jara she had managed to last another twenty-four hours without going crazy or quitting or killing someone. She flushed with accomplishment. All she needed to do for the next eleven months was pace through the days with her head bowed low, like Natch in one of his moods, and she would survive. That was how you killed a stretch of time: stick around long enough to outlast it.

She told the others she needed a few minutes alone in the cool night air. Natch and Horvil disappeared inside.

Jara stayed on the balcony and watched the city of Shenandoah shake itself awake. Buildings that had automatically compressed themselves overnight to conserve space began puffing up like blowfish as their tenants awoke. The balcony outside Natch's apartment floated upwards, almost imperceptibly, as residents on the lower levels claimed their living space for the morning. A river of pedestrian traffic wended from the poorer districts to the public multi facilities, ferrying half a million workers to offices around the globe, or to Luna, Mars, or one of the orbital colonies. Others flooded into the tube stations where sleek trains would whisk them across the continent at exorbitant speeds. A privileged few used the teleportation stations, still shiny and unspoiled and mostly empty.

Jara had witnessed the same morning transformation many times in London, but until now, she had never seen it in Shenandoah. She felt a momentary pang of envy for the people who lived and worked in the smooth, low curves of a modern city. They had never scrabbled to work over ancient brick or weedy cobblestone, nor taken a circuitous tube route around yet another corroded abbey that had been given perpetual right-of-way for the sake of history. *Stop feeling sorry for yourself*, Jara thought. *You could live in Shenandoah if you really wanted—even though all you could afford here is a room in one of the old skyscrapers.* She gazed off to the east, where the faint broken towers of Old Washington thrust above the mist. The towers were all that remained now of the variegated American empires that had flourished in the years before the Autonomous Revolt. One lone tube track snaked out in that direction from Shenandoah and disappeared into the fog like the fossilized tendril of some long-dead beast.

Stop delaying, Jara thought. *Go inside and get this over with. Then you can go home and sleep. Whatever idiocy Natch is planning can't be much worse than what you're already doing.*

• • •

She was wrong.

"You want me to *what?*" Jara shrieked, sounding even to herself like some farcical harpy from the dramas. The Unbeliever, the sour-faced One Who Doubts Our Hero's Prowess.

Natch gloated at his apprentice's reaction. "I want you to spread rumors," he said calmly, midpace, "that the Data Sea is about to be bombarded with a crippling black code attack."

"A crippling black code attack."

"By the Pharisees."

"The Pharisees. And what good is this going to do?"

"It's going to cause the Patel Brothers to delay their product launch."

Natch's orders were such an affront to common sense that Jara couldn't help but laugh. An emboldened Horvil let out a guffaw of his own. "Great plan," cheered the engineer mockingly. "While we're at it, let's *cause* the Patel Brothers to put a million credits in our Vault accounts and give us all neck massages."

Jara wondered fleetingly if Natch really *had* lost his mind. What connection was there between a respectable bio/logics company selling programs to improve the human body, and a group of superstitious fanatics who had walled themselves off in a far corner of the globe? Then she looked at Natch's condescending smirk and realized he was utterly serious.

Insanity.

The analyst took a seat on the sofa next to her fellow apprentice. "All right, start explaining," she said.

Natch nodded and gave another one of those self-absorbed looks into the distance. "What's tomorrow?" he said at length.

Horvil tilted his eyes upwards in thought. "November first."

"November first. A day like any other, right? For us, yes. Products launched, products sold, business as usual. But for the Pharisees, tomorrow is the Day of the Dead." He waved his hand at the closest viewscreen, which happened to be showing an early landscape by Tope. The painting's sharp blues and greens morphed into an old Prime Committee video about the Day of the Dead. *Technology has marched onwards*, announced the narrator, *but in the mythology of the Pharisees, ghouls and goblins still come out at night.* The three of them watched as a band of brown-skinned Pharisees bowed low in dusty robes and began chanting in an archaic guttural tongue.

The Pharisees hate the civilized world, continued the nameless documentary narrator. *Using bio/logic programs to manipulate the human body is "ungodly," they say. And to implant tiny machines in the blood, to let some programmer's code actually broadcast images into the brain . . . Unnatural! A sin!*

Natch paused the display and snapped for emphasis. Onscreen, a youth was frozen in midscowl, his sunburned fist raised in defiance at some unseen foe. "Remember the program that started raising blood pressures in all the orbital colonies?" said Natch. "That was just two years ago. Twenty-three hundred dead, and a harsh military response from the Defense and Wellness Council. But do you think they've had their fill of bloodshed? Of course not! The Pharisees haven't been idle since then. They've been plotting and scheming and studying programming techniques, just waiting for the perfect opportunity to strike.

"When do the Pharisees tend to attack? On days of religious significance, of course. Like the Feast of All Saints. Like Jesus Joshua Smith's birthday.

"Like the Day of the Dead.

"Think about it! Couldn't the Pharisees have figured out a way to disrupt the financial markets or Dr. Plugenpatch or the multi network by now? Couldn't they have chosen *tomorrow* to launch their opening salvo in the next holy war against us 'connectibles'? Isn't it possible the Defense and Wellness Council is shoring up its defenses *right now* to prepare for a major onslaught by some frightening new breed of black code?"

Horvil was totally captivated by Natch's little narrative. He leaned forward on the edge of the sofa, shifting his attention nervously between the wildly gesticulating Natch and the ominous figure on the viewscreen with the unkempt hair and dirty robe. "It *is* possible, isn't it!" he gasped.

"And if all this is true . . . wouldn't November first be a very unlucky day for the Patel Brothers to launch a product upgrade?"

Jara felt Natch's plot snap into focus, and for one sickening instant she saw the world through the fiefcorp master's warped lenses. Colors faded away, blacks and whites dissolved into a miasma of indistinct gray. "So you want us to tell people *our friends at the Defense and Wellness Council say something big is about to happen*, and wait for the rumors to clog up the gossip networks?"

"I don't want anything *clogged up*. I want fucking bedlam."

"And you think the Patel Brothers will catch wind of all this and postpone their product launch to a day with a slower news cycle."

Horvil shook off the jitters and sat back in thought. "So *that's* why you've been pushing us so hard on NiteFocus 48," he said. "A near-perfect program . . . launched on a day where there's no competition . . . That just might cause Primo's to edge us up a notch or two in the ratings."

Jara frowned. She now gleaned why Serr Vigal and Merri had been excluded from this early-morning rendezvous; they would never participate in such a scheme. In fact, now that Jara thought about it, Natch had been excluding them from a lot of ethically shady errands like this lately. A thought slithered through the back of Jara's mind. What did that say about Natch's opinion of *her*? She purposefully let it go.

Natch restarted the video. They watched a squad of Defense and Wellness Council officers execute a coordinated strike on a crowd of restless Pharisees standing on a hilltop. The Pharisees fired laser rifles wildly at the white-robed figures materializing all around them. But the figures they hit were nothing but ghostly multi projections, spotters for the real strike force lining up behind them. A volley of needle-sized darts flew through the air, lodging themselves in the flesh of their adversaries and unloading their deadly cargo of toxic chemicals and molecule-sized machines of war. Within seconds, the fight was over and the Pharisees lay motionless on the ground.

"It's a nice theory, Natch," Jara said, "but I doubt one new program could cause us to jump five slots on Primo's overnight."

"No," said Natch with a sudden diabolical grin, "but *four* programs just might."

The apprentices simply stared at him, unable to summon any coherent words in response.

"What do you think I've been doing these past few weeks while the two of you plugged away on NiteFocus 48? I've been *working*, that's what. Getting DeMirage 52 and EyeMorph 66 prepared for launch."

Horvil counted ostentatiously on his fingers. "That's only three. What's the fourth program?"

"Mento Calc-U-Later 93.9. That's been ready for weeks now."

"*What?* You told me that program was unlaunchable."

"I lied."

• • •

As the morning wore on, Natch stubbornly resisted all objections to his plan, though Horvil and Jara tried their best.

"This all sounds so *nebulous*," protested Jara. "Who's going to believe *we* know anything about terrorist attacks? We're not spies—we're *businesspeople*."

"We've got good connections. People will believe *them*. Besides, we don't need to come up with any specific information—a rumor of a rumor, that's all."

"What if it doesn't work?"

Natch shrugged. "If it doesn't work, then what's the harm done?"

"The Council will deny the rumor," interjected Horvil.

"And knowing the Council, they'll deny it so forcefully that people will remain suspicious. Nobody ever accused High Executive Borda of being subtle."

I could say the same thing about you, Natch, Jara thought to herself. "I don't understand this at all," she said, throwing up her hands in exasperation. "If we have four programs ready to launch on the Data Sea, why don't we just launch them now? Why do we need Pharisees?"

Natch shook his head. "First off, the programs *aren't* good enough yet," he replied. "We need at least another day to polish them up. And second, the Patel Brothers have been watching our every move for weeks now. They know we're eyeing their number one spot on Primo's. Unless we catch the Patels unaware for a few hours, they'll immediately fire off a barrage of their own upgrades so they can stay on top. But if we have enough of a cushion, we just might be able to grab number one for a few hours."

"What if someone catches us spreading rumors?"

"Like who?"

He's right, the fiefcorp analyst reflected bitterly. Truth on the Data

Sea was like the light from an ancient kaleidoscope: tinted and scattered and refracted on all sides. Especially in the bio/logics trade, where everyone was an interested party. Fiefcorps and memecorps spread rumors about their competitors all the time. So did the capitalmen who funded them and the channelers who pushed their wares. Jara remembered the recent case of a woman who planted rumors of incompetence about her own son to drive him out of business. Or the case of the fiefcorper who cornered the market on gastrointestinal programming by sabotaging his competitors' sales demos. No charges had been filed in either case.

And who stood in Natch's way? The Meme Cooperative—a fumbling bureaucracy.

Jara thought back to those interminable childhood lectures from the hive. *So if the Meme Cooperative is so incompetent*, she had once complained, *who's looking out for the little guy? Who's keeping things fair?*

Nobody, her proctor had replied ruefully.

Nobody? Jara had screamed in youthful outrage.

Oh, I could tell you what the headmaster wants me to tell you, the proctor had replied. *All that bullshit in the official hive curriculum. "The fluidity of information on the Data Sea ferrets out weak struts in the economy." "The independent writers, pundits, and watchdogs known as the drudges are very effective at rooting out corruption." "We rely on the Local Political Representative Associations of Civic Groups—the L-PRACGs, our governments—to keep the free market in check." But you read the news, Jara. Do any of those statements sound like the truth to you?*

They had not. But those discussions had all taken place half a lifetime ago, back when a career as a Meme Cooperative bureaucrat or an L-PRACG policy maker had seemed like an attractive option. Fiefcorps were a place to build up a nest egg until something *real* came along. How quickly everything had changed after the hive! All it had taken for her to sell out her governmentalist ideals, Jara thought with bitterness, was the flattery of handsome, intelligent men like Natch.

Jara rubbed her eyes and came back to the present moment, but she could not dislodge Natch's obfuscating lenses. *The plan might work because it's so ridiculous*, thought Jara. *Who would suspect the industry has sunk so low that one of its finest is willing to sow panic in the streets with Pharisee terrorism rumors? Who would suspect Natch has anything to gain by it?*

And if someone *did* find out—if the Council or the Cooperative or the drudges or the Patel Brothers caught wind of the true source of these rumors—Primo's would probably still crown them number one. An independent valuation system couldn't afford to be swayed by the vagaries of law or politics.

Natch stopped pacing, making Jara uneasy. "I only see two potential problems," he said. "One, the rumors might not generate enough flak in the marketplace to faze the Patels. They might still launch NightHawk on schedule. Two, Primo's might find some undiscovered flaw in one of our programs and penalize us for it."

"What about the other fiefcorps?" asked Jara.

"Who? Lucas Sentinel? PulCorp? Prosteev Serly?" Natch gave a dismissive flip of the hand. "I've already checked their launch schedules. Nothing."

Horvil frowned. He had been silent for some time now, listening to Natch's maddening logic and making quiet calculations of his own. Jara wondered if he had enough functioning brain cells this early in the morning to fully comprehend the magnitude of Natch's scheme. "There's one more problem," said the engineer.

"Which is?"

"What if these rumors spook more than just the Patel Brothers? The Pharisees have *killed* people with these terrorist attacks before. What if we spark too much panic? I mean, we're all connected"—the engineer waved his hands around in the air as if he could scoop up molecule-thick multi bots and subaether transmissions with his fingers—"and so we're all vulnerable. There *could* be another black code attack any day now. Everyone knows that. The Council might *really* be gearing up for another assault. What if we cause too much panic? There might be a rush on the Vault. People might stop trading. The whole financial system could collapse."

Natch grinned as if he relished the possibility. "Small chance," he said. Was that a note of disappointment in his voice? "Come on, Horvil! A few rumors shut down the financial system? People aren't *that* gullible. Besides, the Council will quash the rumors long before that happens."

"And what—what if the Pharisees *do* actually launch an attack that day?"

"Horv," laughed the fiefcorp master, "*I'm* not responsible for what those lunatics do. The only one I'm responsible for is *me*. Let them do their worst. No matter what happens, the markets will still be there on November second. *Trust* me."

(((4)))

Jara stared gloomily at the three-dimensional flowchart she had constructed on the coffee table. The flowchart towered mightily over her head, information layered on top of information like a ziggurat. She sat back and surveyed her handiwork. The names of people Jara had known all her life were lined up on a tier of data labeled GULLIBLE. Other names—friends, relatives, old lovers, and companions—were skewered on holographic arrows labeled HARD SELL and SOFT SELL. Her own mother's name stood on an out-of-the-way parapet with the caption UNTRUSTWORTHY.

This is what you've always wanted to do, isn't it? Jara told herself. *Strategic analysis for a bio/logic fiefcorp. Managing timetables, scheduling product launches, assigning resources . . . right?*

Monday was nearly over, and she still hadn't gotten any sleep. Jara suddenly realized she had been staring at the flowchart without moving for at least an hour. Any minute, she expected the ziggurat to come crashing down on her in a virtual avalanche of data. And then she would die here, buried under the weight of Natch's lies.

If you don't want to be here, Horvil had told her, *go home.* She thought about the engineer, sweating inside a MindSpace bubble at the other end of London. The fact that Horvil was also forgoing sleep was small consolation to her.

Shortly after sundown, Jara felt the mental *ping* of an incoming multi request. Natch.

The fiefcorp master emerged from nothingness, gave her a cheerful wave in greeting, and began scrutinizing the flowchart. Jara hadn't seen him since this morning's meeting in Shenandoah, and his transformation was truly eerie. Gone was Natch the petulant schoolboy, seemingly shut off with the touch of a button. In his place stood Natch the slick entrepreneur, Natch the salesman, Natch the emblem of positive thinking.

"So you think we'll achieve maximum penetration if we start spreading the rumors tonight," he said with one hand pensively rubbing a chin that may have never known stubble.

Jara nodded wearily. "I've categorized all our acquaintances on three axes: credibility, connections, and sphere of influence. Then I've traced the likely flow of rumor from person to person, and plotted out the percentage chance the rumors hit critical mass." She pointed to the pinnacle of the tower, a place of convergence. "I figure we need to start with our most influential friends tonight and work our way to the bottom of the list by tomorrow morning."

"Why not the other way around?"

"These rumors have to have some foundation before they'll take hold. One carefully planted source is worth more than a hundred pieces of idle gossip. That's why I'm going to have Horvil talk to his family connections at Creed Élan later tonight. How can you get more credible than a creed?"

Natch began a fast-paced circuit around Jara's apartment, but this time it was less an obsessive march than a confident strut. "I'm impressed, Jara," he said. It was the first time he had praised her work in months. "Why the long face?"

Jara scowled. "Wouldn't *you* have a long face if you had just called your own mother 'untrustworthy'?"

Her sarcasm ricocheted off him like light off a mirror. "You really are something, Jara," he said. "I don't know how you manage to stay so detached through all this. My emotions have been all over the place the past few weeks. I've been irritable and demanding, I know . . . but that's just because I can't seem to find your level of *professionalism*. In fact, Horvil said to me the other day that you're really the glue holding this fiefcorp together. . . ."

On and on it went, and Jara found herself responding to his abject flattery in spite of herself. She had a secret weakness for a handsome face and a sugary voice, and Natch could be devastating when he turned on the charm. *How does he do that?* she cursed silently. Didn't she know by now that Natch's apologies were never sincere, that the honeyed words were just another weapon in his arsenal?

Nevertheless, his strategy worked. Somehow he had discovered her weakness for praise and exploited it. Jara found herself responding to the low, erotic pulse Natch stirred up in her—that he could stir up in *anyone*, male or female, at his discretion—and hated it. Hated it and hungered for it like she had never hungered for any of the hundred sexual satisfaction programs she had tried in the thirty years since initiation.

Or are you just jealous? she asked herself. *He's still in his twenties and he's ready to take over the world. You're past forty, and you're still working as an apprentice.*

"We're going to be number one on Primo's tomorrow, Jara, and we couldn't have done it without you," said Natch with a hand on her shoulder. It was a firm hand, not inappropriate, but still pregnant with possibilities. "The capitalmen are going to remember this in a few years, when you finally get sick of working for me and venture out on your own again. They're going to beg you to accept their money."

The analyst ran three fingers self-consciously through her curly mountain of hair. She wished there were an easy way to turn off the sensation of Natch's virtual grasp, but the multi network didn't allow that level of customization. "Yeah, well, maybe," she replied lamely.

And then, seconds later, he vanished. His smile remained burned on her retinas.

Jara tiptoed down the hall to make sure Natch had indeed cut his multi connection and not just ducked into the next room to deceive her. *You're so paranoid, Jara,* she told herself. *This is* your *apartment. Nobody can multi here without your permission.* Still, she breathed a sigh of relief after determining that her boss was not in the flat. Natch had been known to perform miracles before.

She glanced back at the ziggurat and nearly retched. There it sat, in three dimensions—the evidence of her final degradation in the bio/logics trade. *I have to find some way to stop this from happening.*

Jara stood at her window and watched the London evening crowd go about its business. Of course, it wasn't a *real* window; Jara couldn't afford an apartment with exterior walls on her meager fiefcorp stipend, and had to settle for flat viewscreens. But how easy it was to just tune in an outside view from the building and pretend. Down below, hundreds of people bustled around the public square, thousands maybe, casually perusing the Data Sea with hardly a thought to the bio/logic programs that ran their lives. Bio/logics regulating their heartbeats, bio/logics keeping their appointment calendars, bio/logics pumping sensory information into their skulls every second.

Jara's mind buzzed with evil possibilities as she fell into the familiar game of *what's the worst that could happen.* What would happen if panic overtook the market tomorrow and people started pulling money from their Vault accounts? What would happen if Horvil's trepidations became reality and the Pharisees really *did* launch a black code attack? Or what if—perfection postponed!—some unconnectible lunatics figured out a way to sabotage Dr. Plugenpatch? Jara's eyes darted to some anonymous pedestrian making his way across the cobblestones below, and suddenly he was no longer anonymous. . . . He was an important businessman who would wake up tomorrow in Beijing or Melbourne or one of the orbital colonies, Allowell maybe. . . . He tries to grab a batch of stock reports off the Data Sea while he drinks his morning nitro, and *nothing happens.* . . . His blood pressure starts rising; he's supposed to close a big deal today. What the heck is he going to do now? . . . The OCHREs in his body frantically ping the Plugenpatch medical databases for advice on how to keep his blood pressure down, and what to do about his congenital heart condition. . . . But Dr. Plugenpatch doesn't respond. . . . The room goes dark, the lights go out. . . .

Get a hold of yourself! Jara thought. *You're giving Natch way too much credit. One man can't bring the whole Data Sea crashing to a halt on a whim. The Pharisees* aren't *going to launch a black code attack tomorrow. What's the worst that could happen? A few fiefcorps will lie low for the day, that's all.*

She switched the window display to a peaceful Irish countryside and tried to get back to work. The three-dimensional flowchart on the table silently mocked her: GULLIBLE. UNTRUSTWORTHY. UNDEPENDABLE.

"Fuck fuck fuck!" Jara cried aloud, slamming her hand against the bare walls. She couldn't just sit back and let this happen. Natch had to be stopped. He *had* to.

• • •

"I'm telling you," said Horvil, "they're talking about it all over the gossip networks. I'm not making this up! Go check it out for yourself if you don't believe me."

The woman pursed her lips skeptically and regarded Horvil with a penetrating look. It was the kind of dubious stare that muckety-mucks from the creeds had been giving him his entire life, long before he was old enough to deserve them. Then she cast a spiteful glance at Horvil's apartment, which the engineer had carefully arranged in a tableau of dishevelment: half-eaten sandwiches mingling freely on the floor with dirty clothes, pieces of broken furniture, and the occasional bio/logic programming bar. The elderly woman sighed and turned back to smoothing the wrinkles on her purple suede robe. The state of the robe seemed more important to her than Horvil's dire warnings of enemy attack.

"Creed Élan has contacts in the Defense and Wellness Council," she said. "We have people in the Meme Cooperative. If everyone is panicking about Pharisee black code, why haven't we heard about it?"

"Heck, *I* don't know. I'm not a Council officer. Who knows how a wave of rumors like this gets started?"

"I don't care *how a wave of rumors like this gets started,*" she mimicked cruelly. "I'm more interested in knowing how *you*, of all people, end up on the crest of it."

The woman's name was Marulana—at least, Horvil *thought* her name was Marulana. These rich old crones from Creed Élan were all interchangeable. They scrapped amongst themselves to be the first to solicit your donation for their silly charity events, but when it came time for *you* to ask a favor, they were nowhere to be found. All Horvil knew for sure was that she was a bigwig in Creed Élan—one of the handful of minor bodhisattvas that ran the organization. She was also one of the women his Aunt Berilla frequently had over for lunch in that gaudy calcified estate of hers on the West End.

He could have verified her name in a heartbeat on the public directory, but it didn't really matter. Horvil knew this was going to be a short conversation anyway.

"You want to know how I heard about this?" Horvil gulped, looking for a quick way to foist Marulana's suspicions on someone else. "Natch told me." He gave her a conspiratorial shrug as if to say, *Crazy world. You never know when you're going to get swept up in another rumor or scandal. But what can you do?*

"Oh, *Natch* told you," replied the creed official with deepening suspicion. "Somehow that doesn't surprise me." Horvil had no doubt she would recognize the name. Ever since he had signed on with the fief-corp, Natch's name had been spreading among the Élanners like a virulent cancer. Aunt Berilla's influence, no doubt. "So you hear that a major black code attack is imminent, and your first instinct is to contact your spiritual mentors at Creed Élan. Is that it, Horvil?"

The sarcasm in her voice was palpable, almost a third participant in the conversation. "Listen, Your Holy Creedfulness," said Horvil. "I don't expect you to panic every time you hear a strange rumor. But this is *me* talking! You guys know me. My family's been shelling out credits to support Creed Élan since the beginning of time." *And I haven't paid any attention to your dumb creed activities since I was a kid. I don't even pretend to under-*

stand what kind of morals and values you people teach anymore. I'm not sure I ever did. "I'd just hate to see your fine customers—er, constituents—get sucked dry because some black code caught them unaware."

"I'm certain our *devotees* will be just fine."

The engineer lost his patience. "Why do you always have to look for ulterior motives? Do you think Creed Élan has a . . . a *monopoly* on good intentions?"

"No," Marulana replied drily. "We simply know from experience that the only people fiefcorpers care about are themselves." She threw a vulturelike frown in Horvil's direction. Then her multi connection winked out without even a good-bye.

Horvil collapsed back to the couch, frustrated, sending a stack of grubby pillows to the floor in the process. *So much for family connections,* he thought. At least he could be comforted that the state of his apartment would make it back to Aunt Berilla.

• • •

Jara stood in the atrium of the Meme Cooperative's administrative headquarters. All the other governmental and quasi-governmental agencies built their offices in Melbourne, under the imposing shadows of the Prime Committee and the Defense and Wellness Council complexes. Not so the Cooperative, which had chosen the lonely orbital colony of Patronell as its base of operations for no reason Jara could discern.

The building followed the same bland architectural recipe that all bureaucratic buildings used these days. Start with a base of stretched stone and flexible glass to provide that chic curved effect. Throw in a clump of rice-paper walls to show solidarity with the past. Add impossibly high ceilings. Coat every available surface with viewscreens, and auction off the advertising space to defray construction costs. Mix in a crowd of thousands. The result: instant nausea.

But Jara was not there to study architecture. She was there to do the right thing. She was there to report Natch to the Meme Cooperative and stop this insanity before someone got hurt.

The very idea was absurd, and it grew more ridiculous with each step she took. *Who are you going to tell? And what are you going to tell them?*

Jara didn't know; she just knew she had to tell *someone*. She tamped down that tiny voice inside suggesting she use the information as leverage to get out of her apprenticeship contract. *No, I'm not just doing this for myself. I haven't sunk to Natch's level yet.* Natch's plan wasn't just dangerous to the capitalmen who had grown fat off the fiefcorp boom, or the degenerate fiefcorpers like Natch and her old boss Lucas Sentinel, people Jara would just as soon see destitute. The plan also undermined the Primo's rating system that had served the public for seventy years. People trusted Primo's to uncover shoddy programs—programs that did not obey Plugenpatch specifications, programs that could theoretically overload bio/logic systems and cause fatalities. Primo's was not perfect by any means. Its interpreters could be petty and inaccurate and just plain spiteful. But who else was there to turn to, really?

If Primo's is that vulnerable, thought Jara, *then what in the world can you depend on?*

The fiefcorp analyst wasn't sure where her feet were taking her, but now she discovered they were heading towards a department called the Fraudulent Fiefcorp Practices Division. She could see the office now, just past the viewscreen hawking a program called Feminine Mystique 242.37a. Natch's fiefcorp had received its share of warnings from this office before, and Jara had walked these halls more than once to plead the company's case before an arbitration board. She could have filed a complaint from home, of course, but this was the only way if she wanted to remain anonymous. Without proof that the petitioners were real people, the office would be flooded with data agents from dishonest fiefcorps.

Judging by the long line of multi projections, there were plenty of disgruntled consumers willing to put in the extra effort. Jara scanned the queue and discovered a dozen people who had carefully scrubbed their public profiles to protect their anonymity. She herself had taken this prudent step before opening the multi connection to Patronell; anyone who pinged the public directories with Jara's image would see her name as Cassandra and her locality as Agamemnon's Palace. She doubted anyone here would get the joke.

A fine dust of boredom settled on the petitioners. Every minute or two, the line would shuffle forward. The silence of strangers, the doldrums of public spaces.

Forty minutes later, Jara reached the head of the line. An incoming message welcomed her to the Meme Cooperative and offered a map to guide her through the office to her designated inspector. She took a deep breath and dove into the labyrinth of cubicles.

"Come in, come in," urged the caseworker when she finally reached his cube. A slack-jawed fellow with Scandinavia in his eyes.

Jara walked to the metal chair opposite his desk and found herself ankle-deep in snow. The walls of the cubicle had disappeared—along with the rest of the Meme Cooperative building—and been replaced by a frozen tundra. *SeeNaRee*, Jara thought with distaste. She could practically hear the familiar SeeNaRee slogan she had seen on a thousand viewscreens: *If you can't go to the places you love, why not bring them to you?* At least it was good programming; her toes were already starting to freeze.

"I am required by the charter of the Meme Cooperative to inform you this is an anonymous conversation," began the official in a tired voice. "To ensure your confidentiality, neither I nor any of my colleagues can see you or otherwise identify you, your gender, or any of your distinguishing characteristics without your express permission, except to confirm your presence on the multi network. A sealed recording of this conversation will be stored in our archives for a period of no less than . . ." The nondescript official droned on for another minute as he gazed myopically in the direction of his visitor's chair.

"I'm here to report a crime in my fiefcorp," said Jara when she was finally given the chance to speak.

"The nature of the crime?"

"Inciting rumors with the intent to mislead."

The Meme Cooperative official gave her a patronizing nod. "That may or may not be an actual crime," he said nonchalantly, drawing circles in the desk condensation with his index finger. "Do these rumors concern a business rival?"

"Well, not exactly, they're more just . . . general rumors. . . ."

"About your industry?"

"You mean, are they about bio/logics? In a roundabout way, I suppose."

With smooth strokes, the man connected two of the circles on his desk, forming the mathematical symbol for infinity. "Do you have any evidence of these alleged rumors that can be presented before an arbitration board?"

I knew this was a mistake, thought Jara bitterly. *I haven't been here for five minutes, and we're already talking about "alleged" rumors.* The Meme Cooperative official was obviously more interested in enjoying his SeeNaRee than in listening to the grievances of some ghostly, genderless voice from the outside world. "Listen to me!" she said. "Something terrible is going to happen, and someone's got to stop it. It's a matter of public safety!"

Again the placating smile. "This really sounds like it's outside our jurisdiction. Perhaps you might try contacting your L-PRACG. Or maybe the Defense and Wellness Council would be willing to take a statement. There's also the Fair Business Working Group of the Prime Committee. Have you tried them? Or the Creeds Coalition's Council on Ethical Fiefcorp Behavior . . ."

Jara shook her head. This was pointless. Even if she did manage to ram a complaint through the thick skull of this bureaucrat, it would get lost in the administrative morass. She pictured a colossal Rube Goldberg machine two hundred meters high, her complaint a pea bobbing back and forth on some remote conveyor belt hidden deep in the works. *What else can you expect when you trust an industry to police itself?* thought Jara bitterly. But the system had lined too many pockets over the years; no one else wanted the responsibility.

The analyst cut her multi connection without a word. The familiar walls of her London apartment appeared once more. Let the bureaucrat prattle on in his little winter retreat and make excuses for the Cooperative's inaction. Jara couldn't take another minute of it.

She flopped down on her couch and called up the holographic rumor flowchart. Another towering structure that obscured her very existence, only this one she had built herself. Jara rubbed her temples and prepared to send a ConfidentialWhisper request to the first name on her list.

• • •

Horvil whined and pulled his head out of the burrow of pillows he had created in his sleep. His internal calendar assured him it was indeed Tuesday morning, and he had slept for ten hours. But if the sun wasn't directly overhead, then it was simply too early for someone to wake him up with an urgent ConfidentialWhisper request.

"What?" groaned the engineer.

"I believe we owe you an apology," came a timorous voice.

Horvil bolted upright, capsizing a stack of nitro mugs. "Marulana?"

"You were right, Horvil," said the creed official, her voice a mixture of fear and chagrin. "Someone *has* launched a black code attack—and they're going straight for the Vault."

(((5)))

It took Jara almost ten minutes to get anything coherent out of Horvil. He had shown up at her front door in person, having run halfway across London with a threadbare pillow clutched under one arm. He was babbling about Creed Élan and losing his family's trust and what would happen if the Data Sea came crashing to a halt.

"All right, slow down," said Jara firmly, clasping his plump chin in her right hand. "What's happening?"

The engineer activated a destressing program and took a deep breath. A few seconds of Re/Lax 57b was enough to allow him to cram the panic back into the mental sideroom where it normally resided. "The world is coming to an end," he said earnestly.

Jara rolled her eyes. "Can you be *more specific?*"

"A bunch of lunatics are launching attacks on the Vault. Black code is sprouting like crazy on the Data Sea. The Vault keeps spitting out messages telling people to check their account balances. Nobody's heard a thing from the Defense and Wellness Council. Ergo . . . the world is coming to an end."

"Are you sure you're not just falling for the same dumb rumors we spread last night, Horvil? That was *fantasy*, remember?"

The engineer shook his head vehemently. "Look at *this*," he said, and Jara instantly felt the mental click of an incoming message. She projected the message onto a blank patch of air, where the holographic letters hovered menacingly like stingrays.

PLEASE PROTECT YOUR HOLDINGS

The Vault has detected a DNA-assisted decryption attack directed at your account. Your holdings have not been compromised, but it is advised that you periodically check the security of your Vault account. This advisory has been automatically routed to the custodian of records for your L-PRACG and, depending on your L-PRACG's policies, may also be forwarded to the Defense and Wellness Council.

"My Aunt Berilla sent me that message," said Horvil glumly. "Half the women in her creed circle have gotten them by now. This is just how the last one started. Remember all those warnings from Dr. Plugenpatch that kept—"

"Did you tell Natch? What did he say?"

Horvil nodded. "I finally caught him on ConfidentialWhisper about ten minutes ago. He just cackled something about *those crazy Pharisees* and went off to examine his accounts."

The two of them sat down in Jara's breakfast nook. She instructed the building to mix up a tall glass of ChaiQuoke for the engineer, while he quizzically studied the fetid pillow in his hand and tried to figure out how it got there. Jara decided to see if her own meager holdings were in order. Within a fraction of a second, Vault statements were floating before her eyes in stolid financial fonts. All was well: there were no unusual transactions, and access was still guarded by a long series of encrypted numbers derived from her DNA. Jara turned to the fiefcorp accounts next, and was relieved to discover no sign of mischief there either.

Horvil slurped down the glass of milky ChaiQuoke that had emerged from the kitchen access panel. But despite the soothing beverage and the destressing program, the engineer was still fidgeting like a teenager. "You might want to read this too," he said. "This just came five minutes ago."

Jara found herself looking at the latest editorial rant by the drudge Sen Sivv Sor.

THE COUNCIL ASLEEP ON THE JOB—AGAIN

The reporter's screed appeared in letters the size of her arm. An ugly white-haired face grimaced from the margin, daring her to mention the red birthmark on its forehead. *Sensationalist hack*, thought Jara as she rubbed her eyes and pushed the article back half a meter to a more readable distance.

Nobody has broken into my Vault account. Yet. Like many of you, faithful readers, I was awakened early this morning by an announcement from Vault security telling me to double-check the security of my accounts. I was pleased to discover that not a single credit had been touched.

But I may be one of the lucky ones. The scuttlebutt across the Data Sea is that unexplainable transactions are starting to pop up. A woman in Omaha informs me she lost a hundred fifteen credits this morning. A business on the colony of Nova Ceti claims it lost twenty-seven. You might be thinking that twenty-seven credits is not a lot of money, but multiply that by the estimated 42 billion people who hold accounts at the approximately 11 million financial institutions secured by Vault protocols, and you have the makings of a crisis.

Now the question on everybody's lips: Where is the Defense and Wellness Council?

Rumors that the Pharisees were planning a major black code offensive have been circulating for days in the drudge community. High Executive Borda must have heard them too. Certainly, he must have figured out that today is a major religious festival in the Pharisee Territories. And if that's the case, then why wasn't the public warned ahead of time?

"We haven't seen a successful black code attack on the Vault in years," a source inside the Defense and Wellness Council told me. "It's a totally distributed system running millions of different protocols and locked down on the submolecular level. How far do you think these fanatics are going to get?"

But is High Executive Borda naïve enough to think that the march of technology won't eventually . . .

Jara waved the scrolling text into oblivion. She could predict the rest of the article anyway. Sor would make his typical excoriations of the Council for being so secretive, and insist that Len Borda be held accountable for his inaction. Then he would segue into his standard rant about the moral decay of society.

"See what I mean?" moaned Horvil, head in his hands. "The world is—"

"Shut up," Jara barked.

Sen Sivv Sor had a devout following of several billion who hung on his every word. And he was but one among hundreds of thousands of independent commentators competing for readership. Now that the drudges were involved, Jara knew it was only a matter of time before panic whipped across the Data Sea like a tsunami.

And so it did.

While Jara sat quietly with Horvil in her breakfast nook, messages started rolling in to her mental inbox. Urgent warnings and sheepish apologies from the same friends and family members she had spoken with just last night. A letter from her L-PRACG administrator urging calm. Offers for useless "black code protection programs" from desperate fiefcorps that traded on unsavory bio/logic exchanges. Jara bristled at all the confusion.

"Listen to this," said Horvil with a nervous laugh. "There's a rumor going around the Data Sea that High Executive Borda is dead."

Jara snorted. "Maybe he got caught in that orbital colony explosion that just killed half a million people."

Half an hour drifted past like a thunder-laden stormcloud, full of bad omens. Jara tuned her viewscreen in to the public square outside, expecting to see thousands of Londoners rioting in the streets. She saw nothing but the usual Tuesday afternoon traffic. But could she detect an edge to the crowd, an impatience, a fear of the unknown? Or was that simply the everyday background hum of anxiety? Too many choices to make, too many consequences to consider.

"You know this couldn't possibly be a coincidence," said the analyst.

Horvil rested his cheek on the cool plastic of the table and sighed. Obviously, this thought had occurred to him too. "So you think Natch knew a black code attack was coming?"

"Maybe. You know that he's hip-deep in the black coding culture."

"Jara, I've *seen* those 'black coding groups' on the Data Sea that he follows. They're a joke. A bunch of kids talking about mods for bio/logic programming bars, how to boost OCHRE transmission frequencies, shit like that. If one of *those* people launched an attack on the Vault, then I'm a Pharisee."

"Well, it's either that or . . ." Jara let the sentence trail off.

The engineer leapt to his feet, face as pale as the droplet of ChaiQuoke piloting its way down the grooves of his chin. "Come on, Jara. There's no *way* he could've done that black code himself. I mean, yeah, Natch is one of the most brilliant programmers out there, but to break into the *Vault*? The Pharisees and the Islanders and who knows how many other lunatics have been trying to do that for *decades*. You think he just cobbled together some black code to crack open the financial exchange system in his *spare time*? He's not that smart. No one is."

Jara grimaced, conceding the point. Humans had limits. It was an axiom she felt she would be wise to remember. "Okay, okay. So what are the other alternatives?"

"Are the messages fake?"

"I don't think so. Marulana said her people ran a bunch of tests on them, and everything checked out."

"Maybe he's involved with the Pharisees. Maybe somebody warned him ahead of time. But wait—that doesn't make sense either. The Pharisees don't use ConfidentialWhisper or multi or . . . or *anything*. They'd have no way to get in touch with him." Jara could see Horvil sliding back down into the mental quicksand. He was flailing his arms around in increasingly wide arcs to match the mounting decibels of his voice. "You know Natch likes to ride those tube trains in circles for hours on end. Maybe he's going to the Pharisee Territories . . . or meeting the Pharisees halfway . . . or—"

"That's ridiculous. Natch is *not* holding secret meetings on the tube with a bunch of violent lunatics. He just *isn't*."

"Then maybe he has a source in the Defense and Wellness Council."

Jara snorted. "Horvil, we're getting nowhere. Natch doesn't have sources *anywhere*. The only people he talks to are you and Serr Vigal. Everyone else trusts him even less than *I* do."

They were both standing now, venting their inner turmoil at each other. Jara turned away from her fellow apprentice and stalked to the other side of the kitchen. Suddenly, the news began flooding into her consciousness once more, overrunning the hastily erected barricades she had put up so she could concentrate on her conversation with Horvil. Drudges of all political stripes were bickering in public about the sums of money that had vanished. The Council was maintaining complete silence about the situation. Jara's younger sister in Sudafrica sent her a panic-stricken message asking for advice. And then, without thinking about it, Jara opened a message from the Vault authorities.

PLEASE PROTECT YOUR HOLDINGS

The Vault has detected a DNA-assisted decryption attack directed at your account. Your holdings have not been compromised . . .

The fiefcorp apprentice smacked her hand loudly against the wall and stomped off to the next room. She instantly regretted it. Blank walls weren't so bad in the kitchen, but in living space they seemed like an accusation. She didn't want the world to come to an end before she had made *some* kind of mark on this place.

"You know what we have to do," Jara said grimly to the engineer, who had followed her out of the kitchen.

"What's that?"

"We have to go to the Council and tell them what we know. *They'll* listen."

Horvil's jaw dropped. He was too stunned to speak.

"Horvil, can *you* live with something like this on your shoulders?" she bellowed. She started to pace, Natch-like. "I mean, deceiving greedy fiefcorp masters is one thing. Even deceiving Primo's. But what about *those* people out *there* who are going to suffer the consequences?" Jara's sweeping gesture encompassed the London commuters visible from the window. The multied businesspeople hustling to meetings, the families scampering across the square looking for safety, the street performers in the midst of some apocalyptic pantomime at the foot of Big Ben. "What if the medical networks break down? What if the multi network collapses? What if this black code attack sparks a total panic? What if people *die*, for process' preservation?"

The engineer cocooned himself in a ball on Jara's couch, as if his voluminous stomach might provide some insulation against the calamities of the world. "But . . . but . . . I'm *sure* that Natch wouldn't—that he didn't . . ."

Jara refused to give any ground. "I don't know *how* he's involved in this. Maybe he heard a rumor on the Data Sea weeks ago. Maybe he had a hand in putting this black code together. But he knows *something*. We can't just ignore that, Horvil! We can't just let people *die*! The Council might need Natch's information to help stop the attack." *I know Natch has been your best friend practically since birth, Horv, but sometimes you've got to look out for your own ass. Do you think Natch cares one way or the other what happens to you?* "Horvil, there comes a point where we have to put this Primo's nonsense behind us and think of the *people* out there."

The engineer was starting to crack. "All I ever wanted was to be a bio/logic engineer," he whimpered, as if it were the most relevant statement in the world. "All I ever wanted to *do* was help people." He peered up at the pint-sized woman with the mass of curly hair standing over him, but there was no mercy forthcoming.

Can't you see that I'm trying to help you, Horv?

Don't you realize this could be just what we need to do to get out *of these miserable apprenticeship contracts?*

And then Horvil narrowed his eyes, puzzled. The color gushed back to his face all at once. He looked as if his tongue was struggling to catch up with the information in his head. Finally, the engineer shook his head violently, banished the display on the viewscreen with an outstretched hand, and summoned forth the craggy visage of Sen Sivv Sor.

BLACK CODE ATTACKS OVER
Defense and Wellness Council to Make Statement

• • •

Jara could afford only one outgoing multi stream at her apartment, and it would have taken too long for Horvil to physically traipse back to his place on the other side of London. So the engineer had to rush down the street to the nearest public multi facility, something he hated to do. He didn't care how many times the Council guaranteed the safety of these public connections and how many guards they posted; he didn't care about the automatic overrides that would bring him back to consciousness in a heartbeat if there was any danger. You could never really feel comfortable letting your body stand immobile in a room full of strangers while your mind was off elsewhere. Life in the world of meat and bone could be so *inconvenient*.

Apparently, word of the Council's impending statement had hit the streets. People started vanishing throughout the block as they slid into multivoid and prepared to open new connections. Horvil arrived at the public multi facility just in time to claim the last open red tile. He breathed a sigh of relief, and stepped into the space between a fat

Japanese businesswoman and a wiry Indian man who seemed to be a technician of some kind.

"We didn't *have* to multi over here," said an amused Jara when Horvil finally caught up to her in the crowd. "We could have stayed at my place and watched the press conference on the viewscreen."

Horvil sniffed. "How much fun would *that* be?"

They were standing in the Defense and Wellness Council's main auditorium, its public face. Everyone knew the Council had moved its *real* base of operations to a new compound of unknown location. The auditorium was a fat wedge that might have represented 20 percent on some vast pie chart—a number that roughly approximated the Council's public approval ratings.

Horvil had actually been here in person once, during his requisite tour of the Melbourne governmental facilities. He remembered seeing the entire city laid out before him during the descent of the arriving hoverbird craft. If he had the power to see through the dozens of hanging pennants to the west and the stretched stone wall behind them, he could have seen the Prime Committee complex and the Congress of L-PRACGs. To the east lay the headquarters of the Creeds Coalition and the chief lobbying arms of TubeCo, GravCo, and TeleCo.

Jara pinged the Council's multi information node. "A hundred and twelve million," she said, gazing around at the assembled crowd of multi projections.

Horvil whistled. This black code attack had shaken people up. It looked like only twenty thousand, of course; in situations like this, the network conveniently abandoned the illusion that multi projections inhabited Cartesian space. "Any sign of Merri? Or Vigal?" he said.

"Public directory says Merri's here somewhere," replied Jara. "But no word on Serr Vigal. He wouldn't come out here for something like this."

"And Natch?"

Jara looked at Horvil and shook her head with a frown.

At precisely three o'clock (London time), there was a decrescendo in the background chatter of the crowd. Lights that had been glaring at full intensity dimmed to candle strength. Horvil held his breath and watched the stage below for the towering form of High Executive Len Borda.

But the man who materialized on center stage wasn't him. A white-robed and yellow-starred figure approached the podium. The man, a pure-blooded Asian, was little more than half Borda's height, and had only a third of his girth. He stood patiently for a moment, dispensing that arrogant Council stare.

Borda's underling did not give his name or rank. He simply opened his mouth and began to speak in a dead monotone. "My word is the will of the Defense and Wellness Council," the man said, "which was established by the Prime Committee two hundred and fifty-two years ago to ensure the security of all persons throughout the system. The word of the Council is the word of the people."

Horvil shuddered involuntarily. Out of the corner of his eye, he saw Jara doing the same. They had heard this opening dictum thousands of times in dramas, news reports, and speeches, and yet it still had the power to send ripples up and down the spine. Horvil was convinced the effect was bio/logically enhanced.

"Today, rumors have circulated on the Data Sea that the Vault was under black code attack by Pharisees," continued the Council officer coolly, as if systemwide panic was an expected hazard; the total at the bottom of a spreadsheet column, the predictable outcome of a well-weathered formula. "Many irresponsible words have been written about the so-called vulnerabilities of the financial system and the supposed failings of the Defense and Wellness Council.

"High Executive Borda wishes it to be known that these rumors are completely without foundation. There *was* no black code attack this morning."

Even through the sound-deadening programs of the Council auditorium, Horvil could hear the murmur of a million raised voices. He remembered his pathetic sniveling at Jara's apartment, his panicked dash across London, and felt an embarrassed flush cover his face. The engineer risked a peek at Jara. Her nostrils were flaring.

The anonymous Council spokesman pressed on, either oblivious to or unconcerned by the crowd's reaction. "The attack this morning was not a product of bio/logic engineering, or of black coding skill. It required nothing more than the ability to make clever forgeries and the will to deceive.

"These forgeries of Vault security messages were designed to fool the public into believing their financial holdings were under attack. What the perpetrators hoped to accomplish with this ruse is unknown. High Executive Borda believes the forgers' goal was to sow panic in the marketplace. Suffice it to say these messages have been tracked down and eliminated."

Jara seemed disoriented. She took a step backwards and turned her focus away from the diminutive Council spokesman, who began to recite a numbing series of technical statistics. "I don't understand," she ConfidentialWhispered to Horvil. "You can't just *forge* a message from the Vault like that. You'd need DNA, atomic signatures, who knows what else."

Horvil tilted his head in thought. "That's not necessary, if you do it right."

"Horv, we *saw* those messages. They said they were from the Vault. They looked authentic. They had valid signatures."

The engineer smiled. The panic of the world coming to an end had already given way to the open vistas of a mathematical challenge. "Sure, they *looked* authentic," he explained. "It's not hard to make a forgery that looks official at first glance. You could probably find black code on the Data Sea that'll do the trick. The *hard* part is getting people not to take that second or third glance. I never bothered to verify those signatures—did you? I'll bet Marulana never got around to it either." Horvil summoned a virtual tablet in the air and began making sketches. "Now if you actually knew bio/logic encryption theory inside and out, you might even be able to create a fake signature. . . ."

Jara cradled her head in her hands and began rocking back and forth. She interrupted Horvil's musings in midsentence. "Horv, have you checked the dock at the fiefcorp in the past few hours?"

Horvil had already ventured far afield into chaos theory and fractal patterns, but Jara's question brought him back to familiar territory with a sickening thud. He shook his head.

"I can't believe we fell for this," Jara croaked. "Natch did it. He went ahead and launched all those programs onto the Data Sea this morning, when nobody was paying attention. NiteFocus 48, Eye-Morph 66, everything."

"A-and the Patels?"

"Pushed back their NightHawk release until tomorrow. *Routine last-minute error-checking*, their channelers are saying."

There was a very easy syllogism to follow here, even for someone who had not studied subaether physics and advanced bio/logic calculus like Horvil had. Natch had spread rumors of a black code attack. . . . There *was* such an attack, or at least a fake one. . . . The attack had created confusion in the marketplace. . . . Horvil didn't want to solve the problem. He wanted the whole thing to disappear, to vanish like the multi pedestrians on the street had vanished.

But the Defense and Wellness Council spokesman had no such hesitations. "The perpetrators of this crime may not have launched an actual attack on the Vault," he said, his voice preternaturally calm. "But nevertheless there *has* been an attack—an attack on the people's assumption of safety and security. And that is something the Council cannot abide."

On cue, a row of ghostly figures materialized behind the spokesman. Council officers all, adorned with the white robe and yellow star, steely dartguns holstered at their waists, the inexorable mastery of the Data Sea written on their brows.

"This disruption has been thwarted, as *all* attacks against the public welfare are thwarted," continued the small Asian at the vanguard of the officers. "To the perpetrators of this act, let me say this:

"The Council will not forget. The Council will not forgive. The Council will bring you to justice."

Jara looked at the man with his index finger pointing towards the audience, the implacable representative of Len Borda's will. She remembered Natch's statement barely twenty-four hours ago: *We're going to be number one on Primo's, and we're going to do it tomorrow.* It had been so easy. Natch's had not been a statement of intent so much as a prophecy, a foretelling of an event already preordained. When she looked into the Council spokesman's eyes, she could see the same force of will.

Insanity, Jara thought. *There's no other word for it.*

(((6)))

Jara awoke groggy the next morning, hoping the past two days had been some sort of paranoid hallucination. After yesterday's grim pronouncements from the Defense and Wellness Council, she had prived herself to the world and slunk straight off to bed like a wounded animal. Now she discovered she had slept for fourteen hours straight, a Horvilesque achievement.

Anxious for something familiar, Jara fell back into the morning routine she had been forced to abandon by Natch's crazy plan. The routine went like this: Sit up and project the news feeds on top of the plaid blanket. Tune one viewscreen to the morning commentary by Sen Sivv Sor. Tune the other to the editorial by his rival, John Ridglee. Order a steaming cup of nitro from the building. Fetch nitro from the access panel at the left side of the bed. Activate Doze-B-Gone 91.

A few minutes of peaceful routine were enough to convince Jara she was okay. Enough to convince her that a small niche had been carved out for her somewhere in this hardscrabble mountain called the bio/logics industry. *Almost* enough to convince her she would survive another eleven months.

Insanity, insanity.

The chatter about yesterday's "black code attack" had already slowed to a trickle. Everyone who had claimed financial losses in the panic had quietly recanted during the early-morning hours. Representatives of the assorted Pharisee tribes were tripping all over themselves to declare they had nothing to do with the hoax. Talk on the Data Sea had shifted focus from the attack itself to the Council's behavior during the crisis. Why had Len Borda sent an underling to face the crowd at Melbourne instead of appearing himself? How did the Council plan on pursuing the offending parties? Other drudges were bemoaning the fact that vast swaths of the public had been deceived by such a simple stunt. Technology had kept the world so secure for so long. Had society become slothful and complacent?

The speculation merely elicited a yawn from Jara. She moved past the mundane news about TubeCo's financial woes and deaths in the orbital colonies, waved away the parochial gossip from her L-PRACG and the solicitations from programming supply companies. The news feed on her blanket shifted in the blink of an eye to the bio/logic industry reports.

The lead headline:

PATEL BROTHERS UNSEATED BY RIVAL FIEFCORP
Natch Personal Programming Takes #1 on Primo's

• • •

Jara let loose a tidal wave of messages on her boss. She stood on the red square in her hallway sending multi requests and ConfidentialWhispers by the dozens, enough to cause a major headache. Anyone but a trusted associate would have automatically been cut off by the Data Sea by now. Still, Natch could have prived himself to her communiqués with the barest thought. *What are you waiting for, Natch?* Jara asked. *What are you afraid of?*

Finally, one of her multi requests got through. Jara took a deep breath and activated the connection. Multivoid whispered its sweet promises of oblivion for a scant few seconds and then abandoned her in Natch's foyer. A viewscreen right in front of her face broadcast one of the early nudes of Baghalerix.

Voices drifted into her ears before the connection was stable enough for her to process them.

"Ratings? Who really cares about ratings?" came the first voice, cool and butter-smooth and almost certainly enhanced with bio/logics. Natch.

"Well, *you* do, from what I've heard," replied the second. Jara stood for a moment, trying to remember where she had heard that scratchy growl. A male voice, at least twice Natch's age. And then suddenly she placed it: the drudge Sen Sivv Sor.

So the feeding frenzy has begun, thought Jara bitterly. *Everybody wants to talk to the new number one on Primo's.*

She wondered when her fiefcorp master was planning to bring her in to the conversation. Or did he just plan to keep her dangling at arm's length? She studied the ballooning belly of the woman on the viewscreen and tried to decide if her boss had chosen this particular painting to send a message.

"Of course it doesn't *hurt* to have high ratings," Natch was saying from around the corner. "It's good for morale; it's good for business. But I don't care if we're number one on Primo's or number one thousand, as long as we deliver the highest-quality programming. If I can look back at the end of the day and say we've done the best job we can do, then I can sleep at night." Yes, Natch had definitely modified his voice; Jara recognized the laid-back cadences of SmoothTalker 139.

"But the Patel Brothers managed to pull back ahead of you in only forty-seven minutes," said Sor. "Number one for less than an hour! Come on, Natch, tell me that doesn't rankle you."

Natch laughed the free and easy laugh that only the rich or the deranged possessed. "I give Frederic and Petrucio Patel a lot of credit. They didn't waste any time launching a counteroffensive. It's no wonder they've been number one so long. But I think we've proven our point: the Patel Brothers' days of dominating the Primo's ratings are over. From now on, they'll have to watch their backs."

Jara had heard enough. Obviously, Natch had no plans to include her in the conversation. She stalked towards the living room, her face a study in carefully controlled rage—and then stopped.

Perfection taint you! she screamed silently at her boss. The fiefcorp master had cordoned off the living room, blocking access as only the apartment owner could. It was an inhuman feeling, this sensation of just *stopping*, the inability to even make an effort to transgress. The designers of the multi network strove so hard to provide complete verisimilitude, and yet their method of access control utterly short-circuited human instincts.

"So what's next for the Natch Personal Programming Fiefcorp?" Sen Sivv Sor was asking.

Natch's grin was practically audible. "Kick the Patel Brothers out on their asses, of course." His imaginary audience let out a spirited cheer.

Jara gritted her teeth and fired off a terse ConfidentialWhisper. "This interview is *over*," she announced, "unless you want me to start bombarding *him* with all the evidence I've found about your little scheme."

There was a pause in the conversation. Jara could hear the rustling of clothing, a man arising from his chair. "I'm afraid I'm going to have to call it a day, Mr. Sor," said Natch. "Duty beckons. I've got a fiefcorp to run."

"Sure, sure!"

The analyst suddenly found the impenetrable barrier lifted, and swooped around the corner just in time to see Sor give Natch a final clap on the back. The drudge looked exactly like his pictures on the Data Sea; his craggy face, white mop of hair, and distinctive birthmark would be recognizable anywhere. A second later, he disappeared. Off to rebroadcast the interview and play the bit part Natch had assigned him in the drama of his life.

Natch displayed no sign of the fatigue a normal human being would feel after four days without sleep. He looked alive, focused, handsome. Jara felt the familiar twinge of lust stabbing through her abdomen and sneered it down.

And then, in the space between one breath and the next, Natch's demeanor completely shifted. A mask was silently discarded. Now his eyes held nothing but sullenness, and the once-over he gave her spoke more of dismissal than command. Natch didn't even offer his apprentice a chair to sit in, but instead marched straight into his office. Jara stormed after him, trembling, only to find him standing at his workbench in the midst of a MindSpace bubble. The donut-shaped code of NiteFocus 48—now NiteFocus 49, she supposed—surrounded him like a life preserver.

"*What* evidence?" grunted Natch.

Jara put her hands on her hips and mustered her best accusatory stance. "Evidence of what you did."

"And what exactly did I do?"

"You know exactly what you did, you son of a bitch! You launched that fake black code attack yourself."

If the analyst expected an angry outburst from her master, she was disappointed. She would have even been reassured by one of his contemptuous laughs. Instead, Natch nudged a periwinkle-colored chunk of code with his left hand while he probed its cratered surface with the fingertips of his right. "What makes you think I did *that*?" he said.

"Come on, Natch! There aren't many people clever enough to pull off that little fandango yesterday. There's even fewer who would have anything to gain by it. I've seen you tinkering around with strange programs over the past few weeks, stuff that doesn't look like anything in *our* catalog. And then, of course, there's the fact that the so-called attack happened exactly when our rumors said it would."

"A happy coincidence."

"And was it a *happy coincidence* you put *our* necks on the line instead of *yours*? Did it occur to you that when the Council starts asking questions, the rumors'll lead back to Horvil and me? Not you, of course. *You* didn't have anything to do with those rumors. *You* were busy getting our bio/logic programs ready for launch, as the MindSpace logs will clearly show."

Something she said finally penetrated Natch's thick skin. He worked quietly for a few minutes without speaking a word, the gears in his head clearly grinding away. The pause of a politician carefully phrasing a key platform. "If you really think I would do that to you and Horvil," he said at length, "then you don't understand me at all."

Jara studied the fiefcorp master's face carefully. Could he possibly be telling the truth? Could he be operating on a plane that far removed from everyday life? Or was this just another one of his acting jobs? She gazed into that unblemished, boyish face and wondered if there were any truths at all buried beneath its surface, or if truth for him was as mutable as programming code, subject to updates by the hour.

A minute rolled by, then two. Jara cursed her body as a turncoat, fired up Delibidinize 14a for the third time that hour. *Can't he at least give me the satisfaction of turning MindSpace off?* she fumed. Finally, she straightened her spine and looked him squarely in the eye. "I quit."

Natch gave her a sly look. "Fine," said the fiefcorp master blithely. "Quit."

A stunned silence filled the room. Jara didn't move.

"Stop being so fucking melodramatic, Jara!" Natch burst out. He grabbed NiteFocus 49 with one hand and violently spun the virtual code around like a wheel, himself stuck in the spokes. "You've got less than a year left on your contract, and after that you'll have the option to cash out. You're telling me you're going to give up all those shares and start from scratch someplace else? Room and board for another four years? I know you better than that, Jara. You're going to stay right where you are and get filthy rich with the rest of us."

"I could turn you in to the Council."

Natch didn't lose a beat. "Without hard evidence—which I *know* you don't have—where would that get you? Nobody wants to hire a whiner or a whistle blower. You'd be right back where you were when I found you: blacklisted by the major bio/logic fiefcorps, taking shit from second-rate imbeciles like Lucas Sentinel. And *don't* tell me the Council will get to the bottom of this, because they *won't*. Dozens of cases like this cross Len Borda's desk every week, and he's lucky if he can close a tenth of them."

"Then I'll tell the Meme Cooperative."

"Don't make me laugh."

"The drudges. I could send a message to Sen Sivv Sor and John Ridglee right now."

Natch shrugged, as if the effort of responding to such an inane proposition was beneath him. He caught the spinning donut of code with one hand and began studying its surface once more.

Jara let her hands drop inertly to her sides. *Is he right about me?* she thought. *Is that all I am—a whiner and a whistle blower?* She thought back to her days peddling bio/logic analysis to Lucas Sentinel, to all the times she had cursed her fate and threatened to quit. Wouldn't Lucas pull the same stunts that Natch did, if he had the guts or the foresight?

She hadn't really intended to quit, she realized now. Despite all the indignities, Jara couldn't bring herself to hate this cantankerous child. What she had wanted was the opportunity to deliver some kind of high-handed sermon about Pyrrhic victories and the value of interpersonal relationships. She wanted him to take her seriously. "People could have gotten *hurt*, Natch," Jara said quietly.

"They didn't."

"But they *could* have."

Natch finally capitulated and flipped off the MindSpace bubble around his workbench. The holographic donut melted back into the void. "Jara, everyone who invests in bio/logics knows what's going on. Things like this happen all the time. Do you think the Patel Brothers got to the top without getting their hands dirty? Or Len Borda?"

Jara snorted angrily. "Oh, I see, *the end justifies the means.*"

The entrepreneur narrowed his eyes, as if trying to adjust his focus to a shallower depth of field. "Do you really think number one on Primo's is the *end?* Then you don't understand *anything*, Jara. Getting to number one on Primo's isn't an end at all—it's a means. It's part of the process . . . just a step on the ladder."

"So what *is* the end? Where do all these means *lead* to?"

Natch stared out into the nothingness for a moment without speaking. She saw him for a brief instant unadorned, between masks. His jaw rocked back and forth, and in his eyes burned a hunger the likes of which Jara had never seen. That fire could consume her school-girl lust, swallow it without a trace. She shivered involuntarily.

"I don't have a clue," said Natch. "But when I find out, I'll let you know." And with a peremptory wave of his hand, he cut her multi connection.

Jara found herself standing once more on the red square in her London apartment. It was Wednesday afternoon already. In a few blessed hours, this entire debacle would be a distant memory. On the viewscreen, she could hear the crowds milling about in the public square, restless, impatient, disconsolate.

Jara sank to the floor and cried for a moment, then dragged herself back to her office. There was work to be done.

(((7)))

Sleep tore at him, shrieked at him, pummeled him without mercy. His traitorous body was only too happy to succumb, and it took a monumental effort of will for Natch to keep himself awake.

Sheldon Surina, the father of bio/logics, had once defined progress as "the expansion of choices." Natch wanted the choice to stay awake. So he switched on PulCorp's U-No-Snooze 93 and let the OCHRE machines in his body release more adrenaline. Within seconds, he was awake and alert.

He was on the tube headed north out of Cisco station, through the great redwood forests that carpeted much of the northwest, and up to Seattle. Natch had been on this route hundreds of times. The tube would shuttle back and forth between the two port cities all afternoon, hauling industrial supplies and a dwindling number of commuters. At this time of the morning, the passenger car was nearly empty. Besides Natch, there was an elderly gentleman who appeared to be killing time; two businesswomen who were probably accompanying their cargo in the trailing cars; and an Islander tugging uncomfortably at the copper collar around his neck. Fickle economics, which had once courted TubeCo with ardor, had moved on to younger and more acrobatic mistresses.

Natch had no business to transact in either Cisco or Seattle. He came to see the trees. To see the trees and to plot his next move.

Everyone in the fiefcorp knew about his ritual of tubing out to the redwood forests whenever he had something to mull over. Nobody understood it, least of all Jara. "You refuse to eat a meal sitting down because it's a waste of time, but you'll spend *three and a half hours* riding a hunk of tin across the continent?" she had once scolded him. "Why tube all the way out there when you can multi instead?"

"It's not the same as being there in person."

Jara rolled her eyes. He saw the incomprehension written all over her face: *This is the same kind of backwards logic that the Islanders and the Pharisees use. I thought you were smarter than that.*

"What about a hoverbird?"

"I don't like hoverbirds. Bad memories."

"Okay, then why don't you *teleport*? I know, it's expensive. But time is money, isn't it?"

Natch had had no reply. He was not very good at elaborate explanations. He simply knew he did his best thinking while in a tube car staring at giant sequoias. Teleporting or multi projecting out to the redwoods just wasn't the *right way to do it*. It was *wrong*, like an imperfect bio/logic program was wrong.

Maybe what he appreciated about the tube was that it was *done right*. TubeCo had an eye for perfection in everything they did. Their vehicles were not "hunks of tin," as Jara had accused. They were sleek and beautiful, the product of a business that had reached its awesome maturity. Transparent from the inside but breathtakingly translucent from the outside, the tube cars floated on a cushion of air just molecules thick and whooshed over slim tracks with quiet grace. Even the armrests on the chairs were sculpted from synthetic ivory and contoured for maximum comfort. Unlike so many technological marvels these days that blended into the background—microscopic OCHREs that regulated the human body, multi projections that were nearly indistinguishable from real bodies, data agents that existed only within the mind—the tube was a visible, palpable manifestation of human achievement. It was progress writ large.

The redwoods, in contrast, were nature writ large. Natch gazed through the transparent wall at the sequoias towering over the tube tracks. These trees had watched over this route long before the tube even existed. Most of them had undoubtedly seen the days of Sheldon Surina and Henry Osterman, the days of bio/logics' founders. Some of the trees had stood here since long before the Autonomous Revolt or even the First American Revolution. All of human history, in fact, was but a footnote to their tranquil and reflective existence.

The tube car completed its circuit through the redwood forest and slid to a graceful stop at the Seattle station, but Natch stayed on for another pass. Then another, and another. He watched the trees; he pondered the future; he formulated plans. Gradually, the effects of the U-No-Snooze program wore off. Natch let his guard down and drifted off to sleep.

• • •

In his sleep, he dreamed.

He dreamed he was standing in a grove of redwoods, dwarfed by their majesty. He felt small: a forgotten attribute in the great schema of the universe. He was trapped down here. The forest was endless. Tube trains whizzed by just over the next hill, powerless to do anything but circle around in vain looking for an outlet.

But Natch had found a method of escape. He had prepared for this moment. He was a bio/logic programmer, a master architect of human capability. He had studied in the Proud Eagle hive, apprenticed with the great Serr Vigal, gone up against formidable enemies like the Patel Brothers. And he had brought all his skill and learning to bear when he had crafted the ultimate program: Jump 225.

He stared at the canopy of leaves many kilometers up in the sky. It looked impossibly distant. But then he thought about the Jump program, the way it swirled and swooped in MindSpace with impossible grace. The sheer number of its tendrils, its connections. The geometric shapes that formed mathematical constellations beyond human perception.

Natch was confident. He started the Jump program, felt programming instructions flowing off the Data Sea and into the data receptacles built into his very bones. Felt the tingling of OCHRE systems interpreting the code and routing commands to the proper leg muscles.

He Jumped.

Natch propelled himself right-foot-forward in an elegant arc towards the sky. The code was grounded in one of the classic moves of natural law: the jump, a movement humanity had worked out through a hundred thousand years of constant iteration. Yet the program bore the indelible signatures of an artificial product: the curl of the toes at midleap, the triumphant arching of the back, the pleasing whistle where no whistle would otherwise exist. The sky drew nearer and nearer, the ground now but a distant memory. Breaking free of the redwoods was already a foregone conclusion, and Natch had set his sights on still loftier goals. Jump 225 would take him not only above the redwoods, but up into the clouds and out of natural law altogether. He would achieve freedom from the tedious rules that had governed human existence since the beginning of time. Down would no longer follow up. Autumn would no longer follow summer. Death would no longer follow life. The Jump 225 program would accomplish all this, and more.

Then, just when his straining fingertips struggled for purchase on the twigs hanging off the highest branches—when he could feel the feathery touch of the leaves—when he had just gotten his first whiff of pure, clean, unspoiled sky—the inevitable descent began.

Natch could see himself falling in slow motion, as if he were looking down from the pinnacle of the tallest redwood. He could see his arms flailing and feel his lungs bursting every second of the way down. The whistle of the Jump had become the screech of gravity's avenging angel. What mere seconds ago had been a triumphant Jump now turned into a horrible, agonizing Fall. How could he have been so blind? How could he not have seen this?

This was worse than not having Jumped in the first place: the force of the impact would surely crush him, flatten him, destroy him. And still he accelerated. Falling so fast now that he would actually crash *through* the ground, down through the pulverizing rock, down to the center of the Earth, where nothing could ever rise again. He yelled his defiance. He shook his fists. He railed at the trees, reaching out in a vain effort to pull them down with him.

A split second before impact, Natch awoke.

2

THE SHORTEST
INITIATION

$(((\; 8 \;)))$

Natch's forefather Hundible was an acquaintance of Sheldon Surina and one of the earliest investors in bio/logics. He was a gambler, a teller of tall tales, a drifter of unknown origin and unsavory character.

But above all else, Hundible was a poor financial planner. His get-rich-quick schemes sank like leaky boats, leaving him constantly floundering in a sea of fathomless debt. Where he found the money to invest in bio/logics, no one knew. Human biological programming seemed an unlikely venture for Hundible; Surina himself, with his prudish ways and supercilious attitude, seemed an unlikely partner. Naturally, everyone assumed the new discipline was destined to fail.

Yet it was Hundible who had the last laugh. His partner, the skinny Indian tinkerer with the big nose, went on to revitalize science and revolutionize history. The gambler's modest investment ballooned a thousandfold and generated a large fortune. Hundible retired at the seasoned age of thirty-three, took a high-society companion, and slid contentedly out of history. If he had any interest in the great flowering of science that his investment helped bring to fruition, there was no record of it.

Hundible eventually passed on. His wealth endured, for a while.

Natch's ancestor was not the only one to stumble serendipitously onto Surina riches. A host of rogues, early adopters, and cutting-edge investors were handsomely rewarded for their early backing of bio/logics. Lavish mansions and villas sprouted up around the globe to serve their owners' whims—places where they could escape the harsh moral strictures that had kept order since the Autonomous Revolt. The bio/logic entrepreneurs sought cities that had largely escaped the havoc of the Revolt: Omaha, Melbourne, Shenandoah, Madrid, Cape Town. Cities that yearned for the greatness of antiquity, cities whose local governments could be easily bought.

This change in the political landscape did not escape the attention of the old nation-states. The old governments might have been dilapidated and their halls of power decaying, but they still had plenty of resources at their disposal to fight this territorial encroachment. They vested much of their power in a centralized Prime Committee. The Committee turned around and bestowed ultimate martial authority on a single Defense and Wellness Council. Crusading high executives of the Council like Tul Jabbor and Par Padron made reining in the excesses of the bio/logic entrepreneurs their top priority.

Thus the battle was joined. Society split along ideological fault lines: governmentalists who favored central authority versus libertarians who sought power for local civic groups. By the time Natch's fief-corp ascended to number one on Primo's, this dichotomy had come to seem like the natural order of things.

Hundible's descendants grew fiercely protective of their fortunes. Not only were they fending off the Committee and the Council, but they were also under siege by an even greater enemy: time. The bio/logic entrepreneurs knew that theirs was not the immutable wealth of the Lunar land tycoons. Their money was not a tangible thing like terraformed soil that they could stick their hands into. No, for better or worse, the fates of the bio/logic entrepreneurs were tied to the bio/logic markets.

And markets, like all living things, are mortal.

• • •

Natch's mother Lora was fourteen when the Economic Plunge of the 310s hit.

Lora was schooled in the best hives, with the children of important diplomats and capitalmen. Her proctors were crisp, disciplined citizens who saw the hive as a petri dish in which to experiment with the latest academic fashions. Lora and her hivemates yo-yoed between pedagogical theories, learning much about politics but very little about government, finance, engineering, or programming.

But what did it matter? When Lora looked into the future, she saw nothing but the comfortable track her parents had laid out for her, with scheduled stops at initiation, loss of virginity, career, companionship, and motherhood. There would be plenty of time along the way to pick up any other skills she needed.

In the meantime, Lora worked diligently to become a Person of Quality. She developed a keen fashion sense and an eye for good beauty-enhancement programming. She sharpened her social skills at the regular charity balls held in the Creed Élan manors. She dipped her toes in the Sigh, that virtual network of sensuality, and learned a thing or two about the pleasures of the flesh. And when holidays rolled around, she retreated to her cavernous family mansion to dally with servants whose parents had not been blessed with the money for a hive education.

Then, one gloomy spring day, Lora and her hivemates awoke to find all the proctors riveted to news feeds off the Data Sea. *Marcus Surina has died*, they said. *An accident in the orbital colonies.* A few of the proctors wept openly.

For a while, Surina's death seemed like a distant event that had little connection to the girl's carefully structured hive existence: a supernova in a remote galaxy, visible only through powerful refractive lenses. Surina had been the master of TeleCo, a big and powerful company. He was a direct descendant of Sheldon Surina, the inventor of bio/logics. His death had been a terrible tragedy. What else was there to say?

But from that day forward, everything changed.

Lora's friends began checking out of the hive and disappearing, nobody knew where. One by one, Lora's parents cut back on subscriptions to the programs that gave her eyes that china-doll sparkle and her hair that reflective luster. The servants were let go. Nameless fears escaped from the demesne of adulthood and roamed the hive at night with impunity, whispering words the children did not understand.

Six months after Marcus Surina's death, Lora's parents unexpectedly showed up at the hive and told her to pack her things. They gave her a single valise and told her to take as many of the precious knick-knacks and gewgaws lining her shelves as she could carry.

Where are we going? she asked.

To Creed Élan, they replied.

The last time Lora had seen the great ballroom at the Élan manor, its railings had been festooned with purple flowers, and its marble floors lined with elegant revelers in formal robes. Now the ballroom was a shantytown of clustered cots and frightened children. Lora's parents deposited her on an empty bunk and kissed her good-bye.

There's an opportunity in the orbital colonies that we can't pass up, but it's much too dangerous for children, they said. *Don't worry, Creed Élan will take good care of you, and the family will be back on its feet in no time. Just wait here and we'll send for you.*

They never did.

During the next few months, Lora managed to string together what had happened from scraps of overheard conversation and bits of news footage on the Data Sea. Her parents had invested heavily in TeleCo, as had all of the absentee parents of the boys and girls moping the hallways at Creed Élan. It had seemed like a safe bet. No less an authority than Primo's had heralded teleportation as the Next Big Thing. And why wouldn't it be? The master of TeleCo was a *Surina*. Sheldon Surina's invention of bio/logics had propelled the entire world from chaos to a new era of prosperity and innovation. The emerging science of teleportation would surely do the same, with a handsome and brilliant and urbane pitchman like Marcus Surina at the helm. Yes, the economics were fuzzy and the technical challenges daunting, but TeleCo would figure it all out in time.

And that might have happened, if Marcus and his top officers had not been charred to ash by a ruptured shuttle fuel tank.

Marcus Surina's successors at TeleCo tried to pick up the pieces of his work, but it was a Herculean task. They soon discovered that the economics of teleportation weren't merely fuzzy; they were disastrous. The company quickly scaled back its ambitions from Marcus Surina's pie-in-the-sky dreams to more sober and subdued goals. TeleCo supplicated the Prime Committee for protection from its creditors, and soon all the manufacturers and distributors that had anticipated a teleportation boom went belly-up. The ripples spread far and wide, leaving dead companies floating in their wake. Eventually, the ripples touched even Creed Élan, that last bastion of noblesse oblige.

Years later, Lora wondered how much of a fight the rank and file put up when the bodhisattvas of Creed Élan decided to let the children go. The girl found herself shunted off to a small, private institution that was obviously destined for bankruptcy.

Within the space of two years, Lora had gone from a promising young debutante to a penniless member of the diss. Her quest to become a Person of Quality would have to be put on hold.

After exhausting the generosity of her family's remaining acquaintances and selling all her trinkets, Lora found shelter on the thirty-fourth floor of a decaying Chicago office tower. The furniture had long ago been stripped away, and the windows had no glass. *Every few years, one of these buildings falls down and kills everyone inside,* cackled one of the neighboring women, a wretched old hag who had never experienced high society and resented Lora for her all-too-brief tenure there. *Maybe this one will be next.*

Lora learned to do the Diss Shuffle, that ungainly two-step that had her feigning malnutrition on the bread lines one day and faking job experience during interviews the next. Employment was almost impossible to come by for a woman with no marketable skills, no work experience, and no references. She tried the sacred totems that had opened doors for her in the past—the name of her hive, the names of her parents, the name of the *fashionista* who had designed her ball gowns. But in this new world, those names had lost their magic.

And so several years slipped by in slow motion. Down in the realm of the diss, nothing changed. The same expressionless faces meandered down the street, day after day, neither angry nor frightened nor scared nor hurt, but just *there*: zombies of the eternal now chewing synthetic meats grown in tanks. The beneficent forces of government sent bio/logic programming code raining down from the skies, containing chemical nourishment and protection from disease and hygiene. Black code sprouted up from the lower realms, programs to stir the sludge of neural chemicals in their skulls and relieve the boredom.

Sometimes she had real flesh sex with strangers in trashed-out buildings. Other times, she and her roommates embarked on errands of violence against the crumbling city. Bio/logics had made it very difficult to seriously injure someone with a pipe or a rock. But buildings . . . buildings followed the natural laws of entropy, and could eventually be beaten down into dust.

And then one day, the rumors began. Len Borda, the young high executive of the Defense and Wellness Council, was giving out money to the bio/logic fiefcorps. *It's a massive program of military and intelligence spending designed to end the Economic Plunge,* they said. *Jobs will be returning soon.*

Lora had not hunted for work in nearly two years. She had rarely even made it around the block in that time. But the rumors stirred memories of her old life, of the comfortable track that prescribed career, companionship, and motherhood. Lora left the Chicago slums and tubed to the metropolis of Omaha in search of work.

Within a few weeks, Lora's search brought her to the attention of Serr Vigal.

• • •

Vigal had matriculated in one of the great Lunar universities and discovered an innate passion for neural programming. He settled in

Omaha the same week that High Executive Borda defied the Prime Committee and began handing out massive defense subsidies. Vigal founded a company devoted to the study of the brain stem, and went to the Defense and Wellness Council for funding. They approved his request almost without question.

The young neural programmer decided to incorporate as a memecorp instead of a fiefcorp. Vigal had to spend much of his time pleading for public funding from a patchwork of government agencies, but he felt this was time well spent if his employees were insulated from the pressures of the marketplace.

His choice of company structure also allowed him to make unconventional hiring decisions.

Lora was his first such decision. Vigal could see her qualifications were slim, yet her scores on the logic quizzes he routinely gave to applicants were astronomical, far higher than most of his pedigreed apprentices. Clearly the woman was full of untapped potential, and Vigal was intrigued. The field of neuroscience had moved far beyond the basic mechanics of forming neurons and positioning dendrites. If he was to succeed in this field, Vigal knew he would need creative thinkers to help decipher the hidden electrical order in the brain. He hired Lora.

Unfortunately, Vigal's first controversial decision sparked his first major conflict. Lora was a quick learner, but the work was difficult and the rest of the team unforgiving. Mistake piled on top of mistake while the apprentices were crunching to hit major deadlines. Once the project was completed, a group of Lora's fellow apprentices approached Vigal and demanded her dismissal. *It's impossible to work under these conditions*, they said. *We have friends with much better credentials who are still out there in the ranks of the diss.*

Vigal refused to terminate her contract, but he had selfish reasons. He had fallen in love with her.

Over the next year, Lora found a place in the company as Vigal's muse. The very sight of her fierce blue eyes inspired flights of fancy, flights that glided Vigal over distant mathematical lands few had seen. And yet, one touch of her hand on his shoulder was enough to ground him and bring a sense of direction to his wandering intellect.

The memecorp began to experience great success. Soon, Serr Vigal had become one of the world's preeminent neural programmers, a fixture on the scientific lecture circuit, and a much-sought-after expert on brain stem issues. The other apprentices in the company suspected that Vigal and Lora were lovers, but they looked at the company's accomplishments and decided to give their master some leeway.

Lora frequently accompanied Vigal to scientific conferences and fundraising pitches. One month, Vigal sent her to the remote colony of Furtoid to prepare for such a conference. Two days later, the entire colony was quarantined with a sudden epidemic. Whether the virus was deliberately engineered or simply an evolutionary fluke was never determined.

Portions of Furtoid remained quarantined for months. Four hundred forty-seven people died in those sections of the colony.

Including Lora.

• • •

Vigal went into a deep depression when he heard the news. The future had seemed so bright and his own ambitions so limitless. He was just starting to notice the void in his heart that men often discover in their thirties, a void that neither career nor accomplishment can fill. Lora had filled that void for Vigal. Now that she was gone, life seemed bleak and purposeless.

But when Vigal arrived at distant Furtoid to claim her body, he had a surprise waiting for him. Lora had left behind a child, ex utero, at the colony's hiving and birthing facility. The child had been there in the gestation chambers since soon after conception. Rumors abounded that Lora had taken a lover, but the hive had been unable to locate a father.

Suddenly, Vigal found himself standing on Lora's track, looking straight ahead at that long stretch of open country after the scheduled stop at career and before the end of the line. The distance seemed unimaginably vast. To Vigal, it did not seem to be part of the natural order of things for a man to travel such a long distance alone.

When the boy emerged from gestation, the neural programmer had himself appointed legal guardian. Then he transferred the child to a hive facility back on Earth, in Omaha.

He named the child Natch.

(((9)))

Many years later, Natch would say that his greatest skill was his knack for acquiring enemies. He was only half joking.

Natch made his first enemies before the age of five. He had not learned to speak until he was almost three—an eternity in an age of bio/logics—and this set him apart from the other children. The hive's larger boys took notice of his solitude and quiet demeanor, his propensity for sitting alone in corners. They decided to examine this odd child the only way they knew how: with their fists.

One morning, Natch emerged from his room and found five of his hivemates waiting. They were older boys, uglier than he, and sullen since birth. Natch instinctively knew what was about to happen and felt a split second of astonishment. *What did I do wrong?* he thought. Then the boys jumped him. The next few minutes were a tumult of kicks, punches, and scratches that left Natch reeling on the floor in pain.

He limped back into his room, having learned a valuable lesson: always be on your guard, because the universe needs no reasons to inflict punishment.

Perhaps the boys were merely looking for a cringe or a whimper of fear, something that would validate their nascent theories of power and weakness. But Natch refused to give them this satisfaction. The next morning, he emerged from his room as always and marched without hesitation towards the waiting band of thugs. They gave him plenty of opportunity to flee, but the stubborn child refused to veer off his determined path. Instead, he waited silently while the bullies had their way with him. The beatings continued the next day, and the next, and the next.

The proctors were not blind. Natch's floor in the hive could barely contain four dozen children; no space remained for privacy. But bio/logic technology did not work in Natch's favor. The OCHREs floating in his bloodstream had been battle-tested for generations in much more rigorous environments than a suburban hive; they could heal minor cuts and bruises within minutes. The bullies could inflict little real damage on him until they were old enough to pull black code off the Data Sea.

The proctors decided to let the conflict play itself out.

But how can we just sit there and watch the boy suffer like that? argued one of the proctors in a staff meeting. *We can't just let this go on forever.*

Her superior was unsympathetic. *We're not here to coddle these children. There are sixty billion people out there waiting to chew them up and spit them out.* The headmaster nodded towards the flexible glass window, as if the thin membrane could ward off the world's suffering. Outside, tree branches scraped greedily against the window like claws. *These children need to be tough in order to thrive.*

So we're trying to create a generation of martyrs. Is that it?

Long pause. *Have faith in the boy, Petaar. He's not getting hurt, is he? We* won't *let this go on forever, but let's give him a few more days to figure things out for himself before we intervene.*

Nobody ever explained this decision to Natch, however, and to him the proctors' inaction felt like indifference. This was a greater blow than any the young bullies could deliver. Didn't the proctors drill into the children's heads every day that the world was run by logical, impartial laws? Everything happened for a reason, they said. Every effect was traceable to a root cause. But this daily punishment had no rational basis that Natch could see, and though the proctors could tell he was suffering, they remained mum. The boy pondered his dilemma for days on end, and spent his nights wrestling with cognitive dissonance.

One night, Natch awoke before dawn with his mind on fire.

The world around him dimmed and blanked out until all he could see were his hands in front of his face. And then the room exploded with colors. A frenzy of lights burned far away up over his head, while strange hollow voices began speaking to him of things he didn't understand. Random phrases in imaginary languages. The names of dead kings. Algorithms and encrypted messages. Natch lay quietly in the dark, consumed by fear, and let the vision wash over him.

When dawn arrived, he knew what he had to do.

Natch missed roll call that morning. The proctor Petaar scrambled to his room, fearing the worst. She found the boy on the floor, trapped beneath a heavy bureau and struggling to breathe.

The hive descended into pandemonium. After tending to Natch, the proctors quickly rounded up the thugs who had been tormenting him. They grilled the boys behind locked doors for two hours and extracted a number of tearful confessions. But the bullies were unanimous in insisting they had nothing to do with burying Natch under the bureau. *And the toys missing from Natch's room?* thundered Petaar. *Did they run off by themselves?* The boys had no explanation. The proctors weighed the evidence against the five bullies for much of the afternoon, and then summarily expelled them.

When he heard the news, Natch felt a cold thrill run up his spine. It was his first taste of victory, and he found it an intoxicating brew.

The boys had actually been innocent of their crime; the entire incident had been a setup. Natch had contrived to trap himself beneath the bureau by propping it up with blocks and then slowly removing the supports. He had sketched out the details of his plan in the early-morning hours with the zeal of a master draftsman, until no flaws were visible to the naked eye. He had long since forgotten the source of his inspiration.

But Natch's ploy succeeded in totally unexpected dimensions as well. The proctors who had ignored his plight now walked around with looks of guilt etched on their faces. Petaar went out of her way to accommodate Natch's every whim. Word of the episode even leaked out to his hivemates' parents and caused the institution no end of grief. Natch was astounded. He had vanquished his enemies and exposed his proctors' fallibility with a single blow.

The incident drove home another valuable lesson: with patience, cunning, and foresight, anything is possible.

• • •

This was not the last hurdle Natch had to clear in the hive. Other children rushed to fill the void left by the departure of the bullies, and they were not so easily fooled. They tried to sabotage his homework, steal his belongings, and blame him for all their own mischief. Natch quickly realized he had made a tactical error hiding behind the proctors; by not dealing with his opponents directly, he had only reinforced the perception that he was weak.

He wondered if this would be a never-ending cycle. Was he doomed to spend the remainder of his life fighting battle after battle with a succession of enemies, each more capable than the last, until he finally met his match?

At the age of six, Natch decided that escape was his only option. He ran away.

Serr Vigal received a panicked ConfidentialWhisper from Natch's proctors that morning. They wondered whether the boy had hopped the tube and found his way to Vigal's apartment, but the neural programmer had not seen his charge in weeks. He cancelled the morning's staff meeting and set out for the nearest tube station. The tube whisked him across metropolitan Omaha to a squat semicircular building that did, in fact, look like a beehive.

What do you mean, he's missing? asked Vigal, perplexed, when he caught up to the anxious proctors. *I thought you monitored the children here twenty-four hours a day.*

The headmaster bowed his head. *We do.*

Vigal was not an excitable man by nature. *Are you sure he didn't just wander onto another floor?* he said, scratching the few lonely hairs on his head. *You have security programs, don't you? Certainly he couldn't have gotten out of the building without you knowing it.*

Theoretically, no, said the headmaster. *But it appears he did.*

Omaha was no place for an unattended boy. A curious soul like Natch could easily disappear in a cosmopolitan city of twenty-two million and never be heard from again. Broken families had been commonplace in the depths of the Economic Plunge, but even a recovering economy could not totally stem the trickle of missing children.

Natch was not oblivious to the dangers of the city, but he had already learned to discount fear as an unreliable emotion. Omaha seemed like a zoo to him; everywhere he turned, there were tantalizing new sights arrayed for his amusement. Buildings expanded and collapsed like breathing animals, often causing entire city blocks to shift a few meters this way and that. Tube trains crisscrossed the city like veins. And the streets were filled with millions of people holding silent conversations with acquaintances thousands of kilometers away.

Natch spent hours trying to figure out which of the pedestrians were real and which were multi projections. The proctors had taught the children about multi, of course; some of the proctors multied to the hive themselves from as far away as Luna. But children under eight were not allowed to project on the network, and thus they had very little firsthand knowledge of the subject. So Natch spent hours pivoting 360 degrees in the crowd, looking for people on the periphery of his vision who seemed fuzzy and indistinct until he focused on them. Then he would run up and toss a pebble. Those that the pebble bounced off were real (and sometimes irritated); those that the pebble passed through were multi projections. Natch discovered to his astonishment that he could not tell the difference at all.

Once the initial fascination of the city wore off, Natch's experiences in the hive began to infect everything he saw. The belligerent street vendor shouting down his customer's haggling, the timid woman walking two steps behind her companion like a housepet, the down-and-out businessman being pressed out of his apartment by white-robed Council officers—every interaction he saw was a substantiation of the eternal struggle between the Pushers and the Pushed.

Natch found a quiet corner in a public square and sat facing the wall. A viewscreen above him repeatedly screeched a popular footwear slogan every ten seconds. *No matter where you go, there will be bullies and victims*, Natch told himself. *Which do you want to be?*

Back at the hive, the proctors made a poor show of mobilizing to find Natch. The boy had been gone for most of the afternoon, and yet the headmaster had only just managed to circulate his name and description to the local L-PRACG security forces. Serr Vigal, for his part, was absorbed in solving the riddle of how Natch had made it through hive security. All simply gaped with astonishment when the boy appeared back in the hive that evening, seemingly out of nowhere. On his return, he had managed to elude their security apparatus as effortlessly as he had on his departure.

That was a nice trick you pulled, said the neural programmer with a hint of pride. And then, mindful of the proctors' angry stares: *Is there anything you'd like to talk to us about?*

Natch frowned, shook his head, and vanished into his room without a word.

The next day, a tangible change had come over the boy. He met the taunts and jeers of his hivemates with a cruel smile that made them uneasy. And then his enemies began to suffer from a series of unfortunate accidents.

One boy who had constantly maligned Natch for his good looks found himself tripping down a long flight of stairs. A girl who liked to capsize Natch's lunch tray found herself locked in a spare pantry for an entire evening. And so on.

Each humiliation was carefully crafted to reach maximum exposure among the hive children. Natch instinctively knew that the punishments he imposed should be both brutal and disproportionate to their crimes. This new brand of psychological warfare terrified the other children, who had not yet learned the art of subtlety, who still expressed their emotions with curled fists and running feet. Eventually, even the dullest child in the hive saw a pattern: if you bother Natch, you will pay for it.

Natch got his wish. The other children left him alone. He had learned another valuable lesson: perception is everything.

• • •

Natch quickly outgrew his hive. Even the absentminded Serr Vigal could see that, although it took an eye-opening conversation with the proctor Petaar for him to recognize it.

Children like Natch need something to focus on, she said. *You'd better make sure he's pointed in the right direction, or he'll focus on the wrong things.*

Vigal furrowed his brow. A man who spent his day working with the quadratics of neural science had little time for binary terms like "right" and "wrong." *This new hive you suggest—they'll give him something to focus on?*

Petaar nodded knowingly. *And then some. Natch will get ten years of study*—hard *study*—*and then a one-year initiation.*

Initiation? The hives still do *that?*

This one does.

The neural programmer scrolled bewilderedly through page upon page of starchy marketing material. *The tuition seems rather large . . . and I'm afraid my Vault account is rather small at the moment . . .*

Which is why he can apply for a Prime Committee scholarship.

Days later, after an awkward farewell sermon from Petaar (and an even more awkward farewell embrace), Natch was shepherded off to the Proud Eagle hive in Cape Town. The Proud Eagle had a reputation for doing things differently. Unlike most other hives, they had no gestation and birthing facilities, no counseling staff, and no social programs of any kind. Children came to the Proud Eagle because they had stretched beyond the boundaries of the traditional hive system and needed a challenge. The proctors delivered it to them in the form of ten-hour classes, six days a week. This left very little time for idleness, boredom, or mischief.

Natch did not miss the infantile games and simplistic moral lessons that had taken up his time at the old hive. Initiation lurked somewhere in his future, but he would deal with that challenge when it came. He took to his new surroundings like a fish to water and spent the next several years gulping down knowledge.

The history proctors taught him about the thinking machines that had nearly decimated humanity during the great Autonomous Revolt, about the dark times that had followed, and about the golden age of scientific reawakening that Sheldon Surina's discipline of bio/logics had brought into being. They taught him about the evaporation and consolidation of the ancient nation-states, the rise of the L-PRACGs, the establishment of the Prime Committee and the Council, the never-ending quarrel between governmentalism and libertarianism.

The ethics proctors taught him about the early religions, how their influence waned after the dawn of the Reawakening, and how the violent fanaticism of Jesus Joshua Smith drove most of their remaining adherents into seclusion in the Pharisee Territories. They taught him about the Surinas' philosophy of spiritual enlightenment through technology, and about the creeds that had sprung up during the modern era to preach community and responsibility. They taught him the tenets of Creed Objectivv, Creed Élan, Creed Thassel, Creed Dao, and many others.

The data proctors taught him about Henry Osterman and the Osterman Company for Human Re-Engineering (OCHRE), about the microscopic machines carrying Osterman's name that swarmed through his blood and tissue. They taught him how to summon data agents with a thought, how to run bio/logic programs that interacted with the machines and supplemented his body's natural abilities. They introduced him to the vast corpus of human knowledge available on the Data Sea. They explained to him how Prengal Surina's universal law of physics allowed scientists to turn grains of sand, droplets of water, and molecules of air into quantum computers of almost limitless strength.

The business proctors taught him the basics of bio/logic programming. They showed him the holographic method of programming, which had long ago supplanted language-based systems of logic. They discussed the difference between market-driven fiefcorps and publicly funded memecorps. They put a set of bio/logic programming bars in his hands and set him loose in MindSpace to demonstrate how to visualize and manipulate logical processes.

Given the grueling program of study, most of the children couldn't wait for long weekends and vacations to be with their families. But Natch had only Serr Vigal to go home to, and Vigal had never acted like family. The neural programmer treated him like a colleague instead of an adopted son. When they were not simply ignoring one another, they were having cordial conversations about current events. These conversations usually turned into Socratic discussions, with Vigal feeding him question after question, as if skepticism were a form of dietary fiber.

I wish I knew something about children, Vigal would chuckle absent-mindedly from time to time. But Natch was grateful he didn't. He looked forward to spending weekends alone at the hive, when all of the children were gone and Vigal was shuttling around the globe fundraising.

For a few years, the Proud Eagle seemed like paradise to Natch. He tore into his assignments with gusto and asked for more, afraid to take this opportunity for granted because he knew it would not last forever.

(((| O)))

The families started arriving at noon the day before initiation, and continued streaming into the Proud Eagle until long past sundown. From a corner, Natch watched his hivemates go off for private chats with fathers and mothers and uncles and cousins to hear one last bit of wisdom they could take with them to initiation. He conjured up a picture of Lora, the mother he had never met, and wondered what kind of advice she would be giving him right now.

Natch felt a hand on his shoulder. He whirled around expectantly, but it was only Horvil. Horvil, the most anxiety-prone child in the hive, not to mention the sloppiest and the largest. Horvil, Natch's only friend. "So do you think it's gonna be painful?" he said.

Before Natch had a chance to respond, an older boy stepped in. He was ruggedly handsome and knew it, with a face that could have been the Platonic Form of symmetry. "Of *course* it's going to be painful," teased Brone as he advanced on Horvil. "What's initiation without pain? What's *life* without pain?" He called up a static electricity program and tapped the other two boys on the side. Horvil yelped and scooted out of the way, but Natch quickly activated a grounding program to deflect the charge.

"I really hope it's not too painful," whimpered Horvil to himself. He turned on Analgesic 232.5 to soothe his aching side. "I don't think I'll be able to stand a lot of pain." Brone and Natch stared at one another icily for a few moments without speaking.

Horvil's and Brone's families arrived shortly thereafter, leaving Natch alone in the corner with his thoughts. Horvil disappeared into a gaggle of aunts and cousins who seemed determined to wedge their advice into him with a crowbar if necessary. Brone walked off with two picture-perfect parents, looking less like their progeny than a model from the same factory. He gave Natch one last evil grin before vanishing. "Horvil's not the only one who's going to feel *pain*," Brone fired off at him over ConfidentialWhisper.

Everyone knew what to expect from initiation, but the ramifications only seemed to multiply the closer the time came. The students would be separated by sex and put in the wilderness for a year, where the OCHREs in their bloodstreams would be deactivated. The bio/logic programs that regulated their heartbeats, kept their calendars, and maximized the storage space in their brains would be cut off. They would look at words without being able to instantly glean their meanings from the Data Sea. They would snuffle and sneeze and bruise and forget things. And the worst horror of all, they would wake up in the middle of the night with actual *shit* oozing through their intestines. . . .

"'Human beings are only subroutines of humanity,'" said a voice.

Natch must have drifted off, because he hadn't noticed the middle-aged man approaching him. The man's sand-colored robe was decidedly unfashionable (and poorly tailored at that), but his face was friendly: the nonspecific goodwill of the perpetual cloud dweller. His almond-shaped eyes betrayed a hint of the Orient. Natch smiled politely at the multi projection of Serr Vigal.

"Sheldon Surina said that," Vigal continued gently.

"What did he mean?"

"Well, if you believe your proctors, Surina meant that everyone should experience the struggle of humanity from darkness to light. They think that Surina would have wanted you to see what life was like before the Reawakening. Make you appreciate the modern world more."

"And what do *you* think?"

The man stared off into the distance and tugged at his peppery goatee. "I don't know. I think maybe Sheldon Surina just wanted everyone to keep an open mind and be nice to each other."

Natch tried to refrain from rolling his eyes. It was typical of the advice he received from Serr Vigal: pleasant, inoffensive, and mostly useless. "I thought you couldn't come," he said. "I thought you were speaking at a conference."

Vigal frowned. "Yes, that's right. But I convinced one of my apprentices to cover for me. At least, I *think* she said she would cover for me. . . ." Vigal's eyes searched the ground as if he might find answers woven into the Aztec patterns on the carpet. Finally, he gave a self-deprecating shrug. "Well, there's nothing I can do about it now."

Natch noticed the neural programmer's baffled expression and stifled a smile. It was impossible to get mad at Serr Vigal. He might be hopelessly out of touch, but at least he had a sense of humor about it.

"Come," said the older man, clapping a virtual hand on Natch's shoulder. "Let's take a walk in the garden, and I'll give you the last bit of sentimental nonsense you'll have to endure for the next twelve months."

• • •

The Proud Eagle's garden was the envy of metropolitan Cape Town. Gargantuan sunflowers sat alongside lush poppies and forbidding cacti, all growing in the shadows of redwoods, bonsai, and elm. Natch had been training himself for initiation by trying to identify things that would not exist without Sheldon Surina's science of bio/logics, and this improbable congregation of plants was one of them. It was easy to forget that bio/logics dealt not only with the programming of the human body, but with other organic structures as well.

Serr Vigal kept his silence for several minutes. Natch could feel the hair on the back of his neck standing at attention as his guardian gave him one of those world-weary stares. The boy put his hands in his pockets and did his best to ignore it.

Natch wondered for the millionth time what kind of relationship Vigal had really had with his mother. Had he loved her? Had they slept together? Would they be bonded companions now if Lora had not been infected by that epidemic in the orbital colonies? It was a pointless exercise. All Natch ever managed to pry out of Vigal was the skeletal structure of a life story. Sometimes Natch suspected the neural programmer was really his father, but Genealogy Sleuth 24.7 concluded that the differences in their DNA made such a relationship unlikely at best.

"I hear some of your hivemates are starting their own fiefcorps after initiation," said Vigal abruptly.

Natch nodded. "A few of them."

"Your friend Brone among them, I suppose."

A flurry of emotions washed through Natch's mind as he considered the visage of his hated rival. The two had spent most of their childhood warily circling one another like fencers, always testing and probing for weaknesses. Over the past year, Natch's competition with Brone had turned into full-scale war. "Brone is not my friend," he said through gritted teeth.

Natch's malice passed right over Vigal's head. "What about Horvil?"

"He doesn't know."

"And you? After the hive, after initiation, what then?"

There was a pause. "I've had . . . a few meetings."

Vigal exhaled softly and pretended to study a hanging grapevine. "I see."

Another period of silence followed. Serr Vigal seemed to be marshaling the courage to say something. Meanwhile, Natch could see through the hothouse windows that the commotion in the hive building was dying down. Families were giving their sons and daughters one last virtual embrace before cutting their multi connections. Natch and his fellows would be on their way to initiation in just eighteen hours.

"Listen, Natch," said his guardian finally. "I'd like to give you some advice before you head out to initiation. It's just . . . I'm not very good at this kind of thing. As you know, raising a child wasn't something I planned. It sort of fell in my lap by accident. . . . And now, after all this time, I'm not sure how to begin. . . ." Vigal stopped and collected his thoughts, aware he had not exactly gotten off to an auspicious beginning. "Natch, I have tried to give you the education your mother would have wanted you to have. She believed her hive did not adequately prepare her for the world. And now I wonder if the same thing will prove to be the case with you, here at the Proud Eagle."

"That's ridiculous," snapped Natch, instantly on the defensive. "Everybody knows that this is one of the best hives around."

"And how does one measure that?"

"Well, the capitalmen seem to think so. Do you know how many programmers from last year's class got funding for their own fiefcorps?"

"Too many, if you ask me."

Natch shrugged. He would not be lured into one of these pedantic Vigalish dialogues today. "Things are different now. The economy is exploding, and there's too much opportunity out there to waste time on an apprenticeship. Two years ago—"

The neural programmer shushed him with a raised hand. His face bore a pained expression. "I hear that nonsense from the drudges every day. I'm surprised that *you*, of all people, don't know propaganda when you read it. But it's not just you. Your hivemates, the proctors, Brone, Horvil—everyone is falling for this drivel." Vigal wrung his hands as if trying to cleanse them of a foul and noxious liquid.

Natch searched his mental catalog of conversations with the neural programmer, but this outburst of emotion from Vigal was unprecedented. Natch had never imagined that Vigal had given much thought to his education, much less held any passionate convictions about it.

"Brone believes he is ready to start his own business," Vigal continued firmly. "Let him. He is a vicious person headed for a vacuous career, and he will be sorry he turned down a few extra years of study without the pressures of the marketplace. But *you*, Natch, you're *better* than that. You are *not* ready to run your own company. If you jump into the fiefcorp world too quickly, you will regret it."

Natch reeled back, stunned, and sat on the edge of a stone planter. He had never received a reprimand from Serr Vigal, and now it stung like a jolt from Brone's static electricity program. "So, what would *you* have me do?" he spat out bitterly.

"Natch, I can't *have* you do anything," said Vigal. Already his concentration was beginning to dissipate, to fade into everyday melancholy. "Once you return from initiation, you'll be old enough to make your own choices. You can subscribe to your own L-PRACGs, pledge to whatever creeds you choose. You can solicit capitalmen for funds and start your own fiefcorp, if you want. But . . . if I could wish anything for you, it would be that you would take an apprenticeship somewhere close . . . somewhere I can keep an eye on you." His face turned an embarrassed red.

So that's what this is all about, thought Natch. He hadn't expected a sermon from his legal guardian—in fact, he hadn't expected Vigal to show up today at all. But now that the sermon had become a referendum on his parenting skills, things were starting to make sense.

Serr Vigal exhaled deeply and stretched his arms out behind his back, as if he had just removed a heavy weight from there. Natch realized his guardian had been rehearsing this speech for some time. "I can see the look in your face," said his guardian softly. "I've seen your scores on the bio/logics exams, Natch. Best in your class."

"*Second* best," the boy whispered venomously. Brone's smug face leered at him from the corners of his mind.

"It doesn't matter. The point is, I know you are expecting lots of offers from the capitalmen. No, you don't have to tell me about your meetings—I already know. I'm not asking you to make any decisions right now. We'll talk about it again in twelve months. All I ask for now is that you keep your eyes and ears open, and consider the idea of taking an apprenticeship—*any* apprenticeship—after initiation. And be *careful* out there."

The boy frowned and kicked at the moss growing between the

flagstones. "You don't have to baby me. I know how to take care of myself."

"Yes," sighed Vigal under his breath, "and sometimes I am afraid that is *all* you know."

• • •

Natch was used to prowling the hallways of the Proud Eagle alone at night. He had learned to move in total silence, not out of any fear of punishment, but so he could concentrate on the staccato language of settling floorboards and restless insects. The kinds of noises only heard in places built prior to the invention of self-compressing buildings.

On the night before initiation, the halls were packed. Teenagers roamed from room to room in blatant violation of curfew, saying tearful good-byes, pledging their undying love, settling old scores. Natch saw at least a dozen couples sneak behind closed doors for one last romp on the Sigh. Nervous giggles abounded. He took a furtive glance down the hallway to the proctors' wing. They were following the time-honored tradition of looking the other way and getting drunk.

Over the past week, Natch had been studiously reading the drudge forecasts of the bio/logic market. This year, the demand for fresh programming talent had reached a critical mass. The Meme Cooperative's rules forbade fiefcorps and memecorps from signing on apprentices or providing start-up capital before graduation from the hive. But Len Borda's post-Plunge economy was churning out opportunity much quicker than warm bodies, and so many companies were willing to risk the Cooperative's tepid penalties.

Natch had studied the laws of supply and demand. What better time to raise money for a fiefcorp than the night before initiation?

Downstairs, he stretched out on a sofa in the atrium to await the arrival of the capitalman Figaro Fi. It was the fifth late-night rendezvous Natch had arranged this week with the power brokers in the fiefcorp world, and the most important yet. The rich and eccentric Fi had bankrolled some of the most spectacular successes on Primo's. Lucas Sentinel and the Deuteron Fiefcorp both owed their laurels to Figaro's generous assistance, as did the Patel Brothers, the rising young stars of the bio/logic scene. Natch had been surprised to get a meeting with the capitalman at all, and readily agreed to his conditions—a meeting in the middle of the night, when Figaro was halfway through his working day in Beijing. Natch explained that the network was off-limits to students so late. He took it as a good omen that Fi agreed to multi to Omaha instead.

At three minutes after midnight, when the ruckus from the upper floors had settled to a low rumble, a multi projection materialized in the atrium.

The person who had coined the phrase *Don't judge a book by its cover* might have had someone like Figaro Fi in mind. The great capitalman stood almost a head shorter than any of the proctors on staff—shorter, even, than many of the students—and he was almost as wide as he was tall. His robe, of vivid gold, silver, and copper, made a bold proclamation of idiosyncrasy. Each stubby finger was adorned with a ring; some boasted three or four. Figaro endured the boy's respectful bow and gave a feeble nod in return.

Natch looked the capitalman straight in the eye. "I invited you here tonight," he said, "because I'm interested in your money."

Fi appraised him coolly, like a rancher surveying his lands. "Is that so?" His voice was a low rasp, rich with irony.

"If you're not prepared to open your Vault account, then you'd better cut your multi connection right now and not waste any more of my time. Otherwise, follow me." And with that, Natch wheeled around and headed down the hallway.

Natch did not look back until he had reached one of the plush dens that the Proud Eagle had set up for entertaining guests. It was the kind of dusky room that might have once been lined with leather books.

Natch wasn't sure whether or not the capitalman would still be there when he turned around, and he barely managed to restrain a grin of triumph when he saw that the little man had indeed followed him.

Figaro Fi planted himself in one of the overstuffed chairs. "You've got balls, and I like that," said the capitalman sardonically. He pulled a beefy cigar from his coat pocket and chomped on one end. "Go ahead," he grunted.

Natch launched into the presentation he had already given a hundred times in his own mind. It was short and to the point. There were holographs of Natch's programming work, a brief list of the accolades he had won in academic competitions, and the outlines of a fiefcorp marketing strategy. When he finished, he made no attempt at idle chitchat, but rather waited patiently for a reaction from his audience.

Figaro wore an almost lecherous grin. "I *like* this," he said. "You've been planning this whole thing for weeks, haven't you? Waiting until the last minute. The little scene in the hallway out there. Clever, boy, *clever*!"

Natch stood politely with his hands clasped behind his back and said nothing.

"Of course, you know what I came here to see," continued Fi. He apparently had no intention of lighting his cigar—a pointless act in multispace anyway—preferring instead to swing it between two fingers for emphasis. "You know I'm not here to see your test scores again. I'm not here to see you perform your programming tricks like some *monkey* or hear your little prepared speech about how you can *benefit society*." The capitalman leaned back and let out a hearty laugh, as if he had just told an extraordinary joke. The gold sequins on his belly jingled sympathetically.

"I'm really here to see how you comport yourself," continued Figaro. "To see if you really have that *killer instinct* I've heard so much about. So tell me, Natch, what makes you think I'm going to put up a single credit tonight?"

"Because if you don't," replied the boy, "someone else will."

"And you think I'm going to ruin my good name with the Meme Cooperative by giving fiefcorp money to a hive boy before initiation?"

"Oh, please. You have enough money to pay them off ten times over."

"True, true." Figaro seemed quite satisfied with himself, and Natch wondered if he was about to dispense a few nuggets of gossip about what it was like to live a life of privilege. Parties with the Lunar land tycoons, programmers catering to your every whim, teleportation on command.

But the capitalman was on a different tack. He wedged the cigar back between his molars and gave Natch a sly look. "I'm surprised you even asked me here today," said Fi. "If you'd really done your homework, you would know that I like to spread my investments around. It's not like me to risk my neck for *two* boys from the same hive."

Natch instantly felt the bottom drop out of his stomach. There was only one other boy at the Proud Eagle who could have possibly caught the attention of someone with Figaro Fi's clout. In his mind's eye, Natch saw the last horrible smirk Brone had given him earlier that evening. *Horvil's not the only one that's going to be feeling pain.* He clenched his fists behind his back until his fingernails carved bloody crescent moons into his palms.

"So why did you come here?" the boy snarled.

Figaro broke into a full-fledged smile. "Because it amuses me, of course."

Wild thoughts scurried through Natch's head, baring their claws with fiendish fury. If Figaro had been sitting here in the flesh, Natch might well have buried his fingers in the fat man's throat by now. He could feel the growling in his gut and summoned an antacid program, but it did nothing. The visions pranced around his mind. Brone's smug face and Adonic figure, sipping fancy wine in a Lunar villa. Brone sitting at the head of a very long conference table lined with adoring apprentices. Brone laughing at *Natch's* expense.

"And will it *amuse* you if I go to the Meme Cooperative and tell them you're giving money to a hive boy?" hissed Natch. The words came out of his mouth before he realized what he was saying. He let them vent. "Not just any hive boy—a spoiled rich one whose parents probably paid you off. Or what if I go to the drudges? 'Capitalman admits to bribing Meme Cooperative officials'—that sounds like a good headline for Sen Sivv Sor."

Figaro Fi did not seem angry or surprised at Natch's sudden outburst. If anything, he became more serene, which enraged the boy even further. "So now you're threatening me," said the capitalman matter-of-factly.

Years later, Natch would cringe when he thought of that evening, and wonder how he had fallen for such obvious bait. But caught in the moment, he found himself hurling all his adolescent rage at the capitalman until he hardly knew what he was saying. "It's your choice. You can invest in *him* and I'll turn you in to the Meme Cooperative and the Defense and Wellness Council. I'll tell the drudges. You'll be sorry you ever came here. Or you can invest in *me*."

The little capitalman actually seemed to be enjoying the boy's discomfort. His face bore the look of a mischievous child poking a frog with a stick. "All right, all right, sit down, boy," he said abruptly. His chubby hand delivered backhanded slaps through the air in Natch's direction. "You can keep your threats to yourself."

"And why's that?"

"Because you have nothing on me. Yes, I've already decided to give your friend funding. But I'm not foolish enough to do it before he returns from initiation."

Natch could feel nausea swelling inside him and beating a tattoo on the inside of his skull. He wondered if this was what it felt like to throw up. In a daze, he reached for the armchair behind him and collapsed into the waiting cushion.

"The recruiters all *told* me about you," said Figaro Fi, plopping his virtual feet onto an ottoman. "*Brilliant but narrow-minded*, they said. *Volatile. Unstable.* But I just had to see it myself. Those bio/logics scores of yours were too good to ignore.

"Now here's the good news, Natch. I *like* you. You've got that same look in your eyes that *I* did forty years ago. Hungry! Vicious! Uncompromising! And by the way, much better scores than I ever got, even in economics.

"No, I haven't changed my mind. I'm not giving you a single credit from my Vault account. But I'm going to give you something even more valuable.

"I'm going to tell you *why*."

The pudgy capitalman pulled his feet off the ottoman. He leaned forward intently and stuck his elbows on his knees until he had nearly curled himself up like a pill bug.

"Listen: all of us in the bio/logics industry, all the capitalmen, the programmers, the channelers, the drudges, the fiefcorpers and memecorpers and engineers and analysts . . . we're slaves, Natch. We're all slaves to *want*.

"*Want*. It drives the world! It moves mountains; it swallows cultures!

"You see it, don't you, Natch? *Want* is everywhere. It's in people. It's in programming. In politics. In nature. The universe just won't stay still. It *wants* to move; even its smallest particles *want* to be in motion. Take bio/logics. Aren't bio/logic programs in a natural state of incompleteness? We release version 1.0 of a program, and inevitably it is imperfect. Version 1.0s *want* a version 2.0, don't they? They practically *beg* for it. You toil for months on version 2.0, and you've still barely tapped into its bottomless reservoir of *want*. Version 2.0 *wants* a version 3, version 3.0 *wants* a version 4, and so on and on and on and on and on—forever!"

The antacid program wasn't helping. Somewhere in the back of his mind, Natch realized he would not follow through on his implied threat to Figaro. He would not spend his last few hours at the Proud Eagle shuttling desperately between second-rate capitalmen and seeking illegal handouts. *If only this interview could be over. If only I could shrivel up inside my shell like a snail and never see Figaro Fi or Brone or Vigal again.*

But the capitalman continued on mercilessly. "You ever heard that story about the bodhisattva of Creed Objectivv and Lucco Primo? The bodhisattva asks Primo what the key to success is. Primo says, *Three things: ability, energy, and direction.* You have the ability, Natch, and you definitely have the energy—maybe more ability and energy than I've ever *seen.*

"But where's your *direction?* I don't need forty-five minutes to see you haven't got any. You have endless *wants*, Natch! But *want* without purpose destroys a person. Those who can't master their *wants* are loose cannons. They bring companies down. They ruin lives. They may flare brightly for a while, oh yes! But in the end, Natch, loose cannons fail. They *lose money.*

"Now your friend Brone—"

"Please don't call him that," Natch croaked.

"Your friend Brone is a real sharp programmer, but I've seen better. He's got a way with people, and he's a handsome kid, which never hurts. But he's got one thing you don't. He knows *exactly* where he's going, and what he's doing.

"I've seen it all before. You'll get to the top quicker than Brone, but then you'll just get pulled down by some other kid who's hungrier and angrier than you are. That's just the way it works."

Figaro arose, looking well pleased with his little sermon. He put the chewed cigar in his coat pocket, leaving Natch to wonder why he had drawn it out in the first place. Just before cutting his multi connection, he turned back to the boy with an arched eyebrow.

"Now, about that story with Lucco Primo. . . . A couple years later, this drudge asks Primo, *So what's the most important element of success? Ability, energy, or direction?* Primo sits back and thinks about it for a minute. *Direction,* he tells the drudge. *Ability and energy you can buy.*"

Figaro started chortling obscenely and prepared to cut his multi connection.

"Good luck at initiation," said Fi. "You're going to need it."

(((| |)))

Some of the boys had heard their initiation would take place in the South Pacific, on the edge of Islander territory. There were hundreds of islands in the area that remained pristine and untouched by modern technology. Other boys countered that an island wasn't remote enough. No, they would be shuttled off to some orbital colony specially designed for this purpose, or maybe one of the lawless quadrants of Mars.

Horvil decided (based on no evidence whatsoever) that they were headed to the bottom of the ocean to live in one of the bubble colonies that the real estate developers tried to revive every twenty years or so. "I *knew* I should have studied up on hydroponics," he fretted to Natch as they filed out of the hive for the last time. "And I'm a terrible swimmer. Can't even hold my breath for a minute. You'll take care of me, right, Natch? You won't let me drown, will you?"

Natch hadn't spoken a word all morning. He found it pointless to speculate about their destination. Countless initiation compounds littered the civilized world, from Earth to Luna to the asteroid belt, and he had never heard that any one was better than another. Besides, Natch knew from long and painful experience that isolation has no geographic boundaries. Even if the proctors arranged to shuttle them out to the remotest orbital colony—like one of those experimental stations beyond Jupiter—that still wouldn't erase the shame he had suffered last night with Figaro Fi. And Brone would still be there with his insufferable smirk and the knowledge that he had bested Natch.

Horvil and Natch marched solemnly with the rest of the boys towards the sleek hoverbird that would carry them to their destination. The Falcon 4730 was the standard workhorse of the aerospace industry, used for everything from cross-city transportation to intercontinental cargo hops. This craft could get them anywhere on Earth, or maybe even to a low-hanging orbital colony—but not underwater, Horvil was relieved to note.

Sixty-four boys boarded the hoverbird and settled into their seats with little conversation. Some pressed their faces up against the glass for a last wistful look at the beehive-shaped building they called home. The hive windows were lined with the small noses of children curious for a glimpse at their future. Others waved farewells to the girls, who were standing across the courtyard awaiting the arrival of their own initiation shuttle.

"Good-bye, fucked-up childhood," sighed Horvil, waving manically at the children. "Hello, fucked-up adulthood!"

Natch wasn't listening. He was thinking about Figaro Fi's accusation: *Where is your direction?* The boy winced at the irony as the hoverbird levitated over the courtyard and winged away towards the unknown. Wherever Natch was going, he was headed there *fast*.

• • •

From liftoff to touchdown, the trip took only a few hours. They were not headed to some remote orbital colony after all, but to a nature preserve southwest of the Twin Cities. The initiation compound sat on a few hundred square kilometers of undeveloped country, completely walled off from the outside world. The hoverbird landed on a makeshift platform atop a dusty, windswept hill.

Natch saw the dust and instinctively reached out with his mind for a sinus-clearing program. He discovered that there was nothing to reach for.

They had been cut off from the Data Sea.

Most of the other boys had already realized this fact. They disembarked with grim looks on their faces, shouldering their packs and wondering what would happen next. The lone proctor who accompanied them on the hoverbird trudged behind a large boulder that served as a podium and began to speak. His words had the air of a speech honed and refined over many years of repetition.

"Two billion people died in the Autonomous Revolt," thundered the proctor, thumping his fist on the boulder. "Two billion! Approximately one-fifth of the world's population at the time. Entire cities and cultures and ethnicities wiped out forever."

He paused for dramatic effect. None of the boys so much as breathed.

"Why? They died because they had forgotten about *this*." The proctor swept his arm expansively at their surroundings. A thousand trees waved in the breeze like some rapturous congregation, while a small encampment down the hill served as the lone Doubting Thomas on the horizon.

"What you see around you is nature as your ancestors once lived it," continued the proctor. "Your ancestors did not have access to the Data Sea. They could not activate bio/logic programs to keep themselves warm in the winter, or fetch ten different weather forecasts with a thought. They did not have OCHRE machines working inside their bodies to shield them from injury and disease. Your ancestors learned to live this way during a hundred thousand years of trial and error.

"But when humanity decided to ignore its heritage—to place its trust in *living machines* instead of in *themselves*—the race nearly perished. And because humanity had forgotten the lessons of its ancestors, billions more were doomed to starve in the horrible decades that followed.

"We must never forget our heritage again.

"And so, during the next year, you will become acquainted with nature in a way you never have before. You will experience pain and frustration and injury. The things you see as entitlements will become hard-earned luxuries. Because of this, some of you will decide that nature is your enemy. Others will see nature as an impersonal and uncaring force.

"But if you lose hope, remember this: our bodies were built to survive the harshest punishments nature can give. Over a hundred thousand years, we conquered nature. So will you again.

"You have many advantages over your ancestors. You have generations of genetic engineering that has broadened your minds and strengthened your bodies. You have all the accumulated knowledge sixteen years of hive education has given you. You have your comrades. And when all else fails, you have the certainty that a hoverbird pilot will be back on this very spot in twelve months to take you back to civilization.

"So when someone asks why your parents sent you to initiation, why you spent a year of your life out in the woods instead of practicing your bio/logic programming skills, you tell them this: I came to initiation to fulfill my responsibility to humanity. I came here to ensure the continuation of the human race.

"The Proud Eagle wishes to thank you for your many years with us. When you emerge from this last test, you will no longer be hive boys. You will be young men.

"As Sheldon Surina liked to say, *May you always move towards perfection.*"

The proctor gave a polite bow to the assembled boys, who were too overwhelmed to do anything but respond in kind. Then he tramped onboard his vehicle and gave a nod to the hoverbird pilot. Within minutes, the ship was noiselessly whizzing southwards, back towards Cape Town.

Sixty-four boys stood at the top of the hill, looking sheepishly at one another and the encampment below. Then, moving as one, they began the hike towards their home for the next twelve months.

• • •

The accommodations were not as primitive as everyone had expected. Four rows of wood cabins lined four dusty streets, watched over by a large metal sign labeled CAMP 11. Of course, these houses didn't behave like the ones they were used to—they couldn't prepare food or obey mental commands or compress themselves to save space—but they were a far cry from the hovels the boys had feared.

The initiates split off into groups of four and chose cabins. Brone and Natch drifted to opposite corners of the camp like enemy kings of chess. Horvil stayed by Natch.

The proctors had provided plenty of clothing, reasonably comfortable beds, and even a rudimentary form of indoor plumbing. Few of the boys had ever seen a real toilet before, and they spent hours flushing them in a symphony of adolescent glee. A scouting party quickly discovered large and well-tended gardens on the east side of the camp, with enough food for all. There were storage rooms stocked with old-fashioned pens and stacks of treepaper, gardening tools, parkas, and pocket knives. It seemed like the only hardship the boys would face out here was boredom.

For the first few weeks, it was all a wonderful adventure. The microscopic OCHREs clinging to their insides stopped working. Hair and pimples sprouted without provocation. Digestive systems resumed their ancient dance with food as if the past two hundred years of gastric engineering had never happened. The boys learned how to clean themselves in the nearby stream, how to groom themselves with knives and scissors, how to use spades to dig tubers from the rock-hard ground.

Everyone experienced at least one morning of disorientation when he groggily tried to summon the morning news or his favorite channel off the Jamm. But all in all, the boys did not have enough time to miss the civilized world. Their days were filled with chores that needed to be done by hand, without the aid of bio/logics or modern machinery. Often, they found themselves without the necessary tools to accomplish a task and had to improvise. All of this took time, and it was not unusual for a boy to look up from the field he had started weeding that morning, only to discover a setting sun.

"It's amazing that our ancestors got anything *done*," Horvil groused to Natch one night. They both lay prostrate on their beds, sweaty and exhausted from a day fending off gophers in the fields. "After gardening, bathing, grooming, shitting, and cleaning, I'm too *tired* to do anything else."

The pressure on the boys was most intense during the first month; they knew that any missteps now would have drastic repercussions come wintertime. The Twin Cities soil was hard and unforgiving, but the hive had provided efficient tools for prying into its skin and tending the crops. Even more useful were the gardening manuals the proctors had left behind. The tips on plowing and crop rotation were nice, but the comments previous initiates had scribbled in the margins proved invaluable. Over the years, tenants of Camp 11 had covered every blank centimeter of treepaper with dirty stories, impenetrable in-jokes, hints about the best places to forage for wild game, what to do in case of rain, and gossip many years gone stale. One book had a list on the inside cover titled

THINGS WE FUCKED UP
(AND YOU SHOULDN'T)

Another contained a treatise on

WHAT THE PROCTORS DIDN'T TELL YOU
ABOUT INITIATION

to which some anonymous wag had added

(THOSE BASTARDS)

During the first few weeks, cooperation ran high among the boys. Even the most odious task was a novelty, and everyone was eager to take his turn pulling weeds and washing clothes. Many of the boys eyed Natch and Brone warily and took bets as to when the fighting would break out between them. But the two retreated to their wary fencers' dance, keeping their distance, looking out for sudden movements.

Spring passed into summer without incident. The boys spent their leisure time improvising rustic versions of soccer and baseball and trying to guess how their favorite teams were performing right now in the civilized world. Horvil slimmed down and lost his irrational fear of the outdoors.

Natch began to take long walks in the woods by himself. He grew fond of the trees, especially the tall ones that stretched up to the edge of his vision. While he walked, Natch mentally played back the conversations with Serr Vigal and Figaro Fi, dissecting them like an occultist looking for clues to the future.

Brone is a vicious person headed for a vacuous career, Vigal had said. *But you, Natch, you're* better *than that. You are* not *ready to run your own company. If you jump into the fiefcorp world too quickly, you will regret it.*

Where is your direction? Figaro Fi had asked him. *You have endless* wants. *But* want *without purpose destroys a person. Those who can't master their* wants *are loose cannons.*

It was all a matter of direction, wasn't it? Natch spent days looking around the spare plains for hints. Which direction should he choose? And how would he know when he arrived at the right one? As far as he could see, the four points on the compass were featureless and drab. It seemed like he could wander the entire Earth following one of those paths and not see a single distinguishing characteristic.

But the trees—the trees pointed majestically upward into the sky. Their leafy arms reached for the sun without shame or compromise. Even the little death of winter could only delay their aims, and it was only a matter of time before they were reaching upward once again.

• • •

Marcus Surina came to visit Natch one night towards the end of autumn. He drifted in the cabin door, tiptoed around a slumbering Horvil, and came to rest barely half a meter from Natch's face. In this ghostly apparition, the great scientist looked just as ruggedly handsome as he did in all the pictures and videos the boy had seen. Except that his eyes, which had been wide and luminescent in life, were now cold and dim and utterly devoid of light.

Watch, said Surina.

Natch huddled into the corner of his bed with chattering teeth as dozens of specters paraded through the room, figures from history and legend frozen in grotesque positions of death: Julius Caesar, Tobi Jae Witt, Abraham Lincoln, Joan d'Arc, Tul Jabbor, his mother. Each figure wafted over to the boy in turn, mouth open as if to speak some horrible truth from beyond the tomb. Yet the ghostly figures remained stubbornly silent. Were they all withholding their secrets from him by tacit agreement? Or had they simply exhausted all their words in life, and now had nothing to say?

The parade continued for an eternity of midnight-time, despite multiple attempts by Natch to cover his eyes and will away his tormentors. He tried screaming, burying himself under the blankets, ignoring them, but the ghosts would not be denied. His efforts only succeeded in summoning more, until the room was thick with their gray, misty effluence.

Finally, after what must have been many hours, the shade of Marcus Surina floated up to Natch and hovered there, centimeters away.

Now, run! said Surina.

Too frightened to disobey, Natch arose and fled for the door. He stumbled outside into the deepening autumn and discovered that the entire camp was enveloped in the same stinging mist. Mist curling over his feet, wrapped around the wooden posts of the cabins, thick and sharp as smoke . . . and full of voices. . . . The voices of his fellow initiates, yelling in confusion. . . .

"Over here!" came a familiar nasal twang. Horvil. Natch felt a fleshy hand grab his shoulder and drag him outside the boundaries of Camp 11 and up a nearby hill. Most of the hivemates had already assembled at a safe spot in the lee of the wind.

"What's happening?" said Natch sleepily. "What's that smell?"

"Smoke," replied Horvil with a groan. "The smell of initiation going up in flames."

• • •

The cabins themselves were not the worst casualty of the fire. Even frightened boys who had never spent a winter outdoors knew that trees could be chopped down and cabins could be rebuilt. Only six of sixteen cabins had burned down completely, while three had suffered minor damage. There was still plenty of room for all to find space indoors.

No, the real calamity was the destruction to their tool sheds and food supply.

One by one, the boys limped out to the fields, where most of their crops now lay under a shroud of ash. Somehow, they had always known there was something unnatural about the variety of nutritious grains and vegetables that sprouted every spring, despite the harsh winters of the midwest and generations of inept teenage farming. Their ancestors had never had such a bounty of genetically engineered supercrops to sustain them. But now, staring at the remains of their harvest—not to mention the twisted ruins of two of the tool sheds and the charred silo containing most of their stored grain—the initiates knew that this game was no longer tilted in their favor.

The origins of the fire were a mystery. Most likely it had been the product of carelessness, someone forgetting to smother the dying embers of a torch. Perhaps back in the civilized world they could have scavenged for evidence and mounted an investigation, but here all they had was vague conjecture. Before long, whispers passed through Brone's side of the camp, laying the blame on Natch's shoulders.

"Why would he do something like *that*?" exclaimed Horvil the first time he heard the rumor. "Do you even have the slightest bit of evidence?"

"The fire started near Brone's side of the camp," one of the boys told him. "Everyone knows those two hate each other. Natch was one of the last ones out, and *his* cabin is fine."

"That's *totally* ridiculous. That's not evidence at all."

The other boy admitted his theory had little in the way of factual support. "But come on, Horv—you're his best friend, right? Doesn't he *scare* you?"

Horvil bristled. "All I know is that Natch's test scores were higher than half the class combined. That means he's *smarter* than you. And *that* means he knows setting fire to the camp would hurt *him* just as much as Brone." The conversation came to an abrupt halt soon after.

There was much to do. The boys went to work right away, picking every edible seed, berry, and root on the horizon, repairing and filling the well, making defensive preparations against unknown enemies. The boys of Camp 11 spent their spare time in an engineering frenzy, attempting to coax the last bit of practicality out of the everyday items around them. A frayed rope strand and several bottles could be converted into a makeshift dumbwaiter. Broken glass could be spread along the roads as an early intruder-alert system. Spare rolls of plastic could be conscripted to channel excess rainwater to the well.

After a week of trying to pick up the pieces and shore up the damaged cabins, it became clear to the initiates that all their preparations might not be sufficient for them to survive the winter. An argument sprang up about how closely the proctors were monitoring their situation here in the wilderness. If the situation grew too precarious, would the proctors come and rescue them? The Proud Eagle wouldn't just let dozens of its pupils starve to death out here, would it?

And then, without warning, winter descended upon them.

The snow marched into Camp 11 under an imperious wind, eager to pound and break any human habitation in its path. Within days of the winter solstice, the boys had abandoned all nonessential duties to concentrate on the snow. But there was much more snow than hands to shovel it. Milky precipitation smothered the plants and killed off the remaining vegetation. The initiates soon discovered that, unlike the geosynchron-regulated snow to which they were accustomed, natural snow could sting and burn. Insulation against the cold became their biggest worry.

A debilitating flu hopped from boy to boy and gave the initiates their first taste of real illness. Back in the civilized world, OCHREs diagnosed all their ailments, and bio/logic programs automatically dealt with them by consulting the Dr. Plugenpatch databases. No more. "I remember reading that you're supposed to *blow your nose* when it gets clogged up like this," Horvil announced earnestly one day. "Does anybody know how to do that?" No one did.

The boys were startled to discover that even without OCHREs and bio/logic programming and Dr. Plugenpatch, the human body had a remarkable ability to heal itself. They came to realize that all the bio/logic technology society relied on for its survival had not been constructed out of whole cloth; it was patterned after cruder motifs passed down through millions of years of genetic heritage. Natch, Horvil, and most of the other boys quickly bounced back from the flu and resumed their duties.

But a few of the boys lingered on in their illnesses, their bodies unable to fully repel the alien microbes wreaking havoc in their systems. The argument about proctor intervention flared up again. If anyone expected the proctors to suddenly swoop down from the clouds and rescue them from their misery, however, they were disappointed.

And so, under a chill wind, the initiates all huddled in the center of the camp one afternoon and tried to hammer out a strategy.

Now, under the pressure of starvation and with the added encouragement of the arson rumors, the much-discussed antagonism between Brone and Natch surfaced with a vengeance. Natch declared that Camp 11 was ruined, and their only chance for survival lay in finding one of the other encampments out in the wilderness. Some of these other camps had to have some stored food available, he argued, as theirs had upon their arrival. But Brone immediately raised objections to this strategy, his opposition all the more intense because Natch had proposed it.

"We can salvage what's left," stated Brone. His voice boomed with the strong and vibrant tones of a born politician. "We can survive here. But if we leave, there's no telling what we're going to find out in the wilderness."

"And what are we going to *live* on?" yelled Natch. His voice was a crow's squawk, the sound of metal grating on metal. "The stores we have are almost gone."

"There are deer running around. We can hunt."

Natch let out a dismissive snort. "You're saying we should start eating *real* meat? Those aren't synthetic deer out there. We'll all get sick again, right when we can't afford to lose any time."

"But we'll survive."

The conflict raged through the afternoon, and gradually the boys began to polarize into two separate groups. Occasionally, someone would manage to insert a fact or an opinion into the discussion, but by and large it remained a conflict between Natch and Brone, the two stubborn boys at the top of their class. When the sun finally slunk down over the horizon, someone suggested the question be put to a vote. Should they abandon their adopted home and search for other encampments, or soldier on here at Camp 11 and hunt for food?

Natch lost.

The boy sat in the center of the ruined camp for several hours, oblivious to the whispers of the rest. All his frustration and humiliation from the Figaro Fi episode rushed over him in a black rage that clouded over his senses. Eventually, the rest of the boys abandoned the convocation and went off to find sleep.

Natch sat and sulked, his mind whirling. The stench of death lay over Brone's plan, as obvious to Natch as the wind or the rain. He couldn't just follow Brone to his grave, could he?

Horvil put a hand on his shoulder. "You know what Sheldon Surina said?" he remarked to Natch quietly. "He said, *The man who doesn't know how to compromise only has himself to blame.*"

"I'd rather think about what Lucco Primo said," rasped Natch in reply.

"What's that?"

"*Never bet on the optimist.*"

● ● ●

The boys had seen little of the local wildlife during their eight months at Camp 11, but that didn't mean the predators weren't out there. Generations of black bears and wolves prowled the woods nearby, living out their own dramas of survival with nary a thought to the humans in their midst. They were not prone to violence, but the Autonomous Revolt had decimated their natural habitats and taught them to be less forgiving. The miserable winter drew them closer and closer to the human encampments in search of food.

Horvil was the first boy to run afoul of the black bears. He was tromping purposefully through the snow gathering firewood when he stumbled on one of the larger specimens. Two hundred fifty kilograms of ursine horror lunged at Horvil with no warning, sending the boy darting back to the camp at a speed he wouldn't have believed himself capable of. Still, the bear would have quickly made a meal out of him if it wasn't nursing a badly injured leg.

"Bear!" yelped Horvil as he stumbled down the hillside, shedding sticks of firewood the whole way. "Bear! Help! Bear!"

The camp instantly descended into chaos. Before anyone could propose a coherent strategy, Brone rounded up a small contingent of boys and armed them with torches. Horvil and a number of others scampered into their cabins and barricaded the doors, assuming the bear would wander off on its own accord. Natch, meanwhile, was out on one of his aimless peregrinations around the woods.

The initiates would debate what happened next for many years afterward.

Brone and his comrades located the beast soon enough. He had headed straight for the storage silo containing their hard-earned stockpile of fruit. But the boys' bravado was quickly snuffed by the sight of a cornered bear rising up on hind legs with claws extended. Brone made a feint with his torch at the injured leg, which only succeeded in frightening the bear into a rage. He charged at one of Brone's companions, sliced him neatly across the chest, then tripped and fell directly onto another boy. A few of the remaining initiates managed to toss their bleeding comrades over their shoulders and make a break for the cabins, while the rest scattered in confusion.

Natch, returning from his walk, observed all this from a distance. *Fools*, he thought. *You can't accomplish anything without a strategy.* He realized that if the camp was going to survive this latest incursion, he would have to take control. It was a strange feeling, to be responsible for others and not just oneself. He tried to pretend that he was not accountable, that he could just run off and let the rest of the initiates fend for themselves. Then the image of poor hapless Horvil came unbidden to his head, Horvil standing and pleading with him, *You'll take care of me, won't you, Natch?* He cursed his friend's name and quickly devised a plan.

Seeing that the bear was now pursuing the firebrands that had taunted him moments earlier, Natch rushed into the fray and ripped a torch from the hand of a campmate. The boy, stunned, put up no resistance. Natch instantly reversed course, waving his torch at the beast and leading him in the opposite direction, away from the camp. Whether he was aware of the bear's infirmity or not, Natch could not have said.

Natch's thoughts were jumbled, incoherent. Primal reflex took over and dispelled any more complex emotion. He could feel the pulse of blood rushing through his legs, the lash and sting of the branches across his face. The bear was constantly a few steps behind, growling, ready to pounce and devour him. Yet he knew these woods like nobody else in the camp did. He knew exactly where he was going.

Until, as chance would have it, he spotted Brone.

Natch whipped around and headed in his direction.

Brone had made his way to a clearing on top of a low hill, hoping to gather his wits there. His torch had snuffed out in the snow somewhere during the frantic escape from the bear, and Brone was now busy scanning the area for a suitable branch to use as a cudgel.

He had only a split second to react when Natch came sprinting by at top speed, and then the black bear was upon him.

• • •

The carnage that followed haunted Natch for many years to come. *You should have listened to me*, he would say to Brone during these midnight pantomimes. *You should have realized we couldn't have made it in that camp. You should have recognized you were wrong.* Then he would turn to the other initiates and uncage his fury on them. *Why didn't you ask better questions? Why did you submit to Brone's leadership and not mine?* He reserved the bulk of his wrath for himself. *If only you had been a better politician. If only you had known how to cultivate friendships among the boys. If only you hadn't been so weak.*

(((12)))

Natch had to stare at him for several hours in the cramped cabin of a Falcon four-seater under the watchful eyes of a fat, irritable pilot and a steely-eyed paramedic. Every few minutes, the paramedic would get up from her seat to examine the gnarled stump that had once been Brone's arm. She would bend down to his chest and listen for the faint wheezing sounds, then she would turn to Natch with a murderous look that seemed quite inappropriate for a healer. Natch was beyond emotion; he simply looked back, expressionless. *Don't they have to take an oath of nonviolence or something?* he wondered.

"Maybe we should just take him straight to a Preparation compound," suggested the pilot. "Cape Town's a long way away, and they got a Preparation compound right near here. I run back and forth to that place all the time."

The paramedic nodded absently. "That won't be necessary."

"You sure? He's suffering, I can see that. They'll take care of him down there, make sure he goes easy—"

"I *know* what happens in those compounds, Clar," the woman said with a tone of finality. "This one doesn't need to join the ranks of the Prepared—not yet, anyway. He's going to pull through."

For the first time, Natch noticed that the pilot and the paramedic both wore dartguns. He gazed at the cartridges of OCHRE-tipped darts hanging low on the guns' underbellies and tried to imagine what kind of code they contained. A paralysis program, maybe, or a routine to cause temporary blindness? He couldn't quite figure out why the two were armed in the first place. Were they looking after his safety, or Brone's?

Eventually, Natch decided it was pointless to search for routine in a trip that was anything but. Nobody had given him a chance to gather his belongings or say good-bye to Horvil; they hadn't even told him whether he would be returning to finish his last few months of initiation. The pilot had simply yanked him out of his cabin and thrown him into the Falcon next to the bloody, twitching Brone without a word of explanation. The whole operation smelled of sweat and desperate improvisation.

As they began their descent into Cape Town, Natch craned his neck to catch a glimpse out the front windows. He could see a small squad of Defense and Wellness Council officers in crisp white robes standing at attention on the runway. Their presence kept a crowd of fifty at bay while the Falcon completed its vertical landing sequence. Natch could see a pack of drudges and Brone's anxious parents among the throng and was suddenly glad the hive had enlisted the Council's protection. The mob might or might not be daunted by the shuttle crew's dartguns, but nobody would dare assault him in plain view of Len Borda's troops. The code in a Council officer's darts could very well be lethal.

Only after Natch had been hustled indoors did he realize that the Council squad was not there to ensure his safety. No, they were still out on the runway waiting for the second Falcon, which had been following close behind.

They were waiting to unload the bodies.

● ● ●

It wasn't the first time Serr Vigal had had to duck out of a fundraising pitch at a moment's notice because of Natch. It wouldn't be the last. When the news arrived this time, he was talking to a consortium of L-PRACGs a hundred million kilometers away on Mars about spinal cord bandwidth. Vigal thought about hopping on the next Earth-bound shuttle, but decided he couldn't afford the delay and headed for the public multi facilities instead. Two days later, he was still waiting for a long-distance multi connection to open up. Finally, he grew impatient and decided to blow his entire Vault account on a teleportation instead.

By the time Serr Vigal arrived at the Cape Town TeleCo station, groggy and ill-tempered from the four-and-a-half-hour transfer process, Natch's name had permeated the Data Sea like a foul odor.

His experience became known to the public as "the Shortest Initiation." The term came from the drudges, whose coverage of the affair showcased their ability to reduce a complex set of human events to the common denominators of Good and Evil. Vigal was saddened to discover that Natch had been assigned the latter role. GREED AND SOLIPSISM: THE LAST LESSONS OF THE HIVE? read one of the story headlines. OUR ANCESTORS MAY NOT HAVE HAD OCHRES, BUT THEY HAD ETHICS, opined another. CIVILITY IS DEAD, claimed a third. The Proud Eagle tried to convince the public that accidental deaths happened every year during initiation, but the people were not placated. Yes, occasionally there were mishaps—brawls and knife fights, flu outbreaks, once even an avalanche—but three boys from one hive mauled by a bear? Unprecedented. Inexcusable. Governmentalists and libertarians alike took to the floors of their L-PRACGs to denounce Natch and the Proud Eagle.

The headmaster and three of the senior proctors met Serr Vigal at the foot of the TeleCo station platform. They bowed before him in a very poor impression of humility.

"So Natch knows I'm on my way to get him?" said the neural programmer.

"I'm afraid we can't permit him to go anywhere yet," replied the headmaster gravely. "Natch is still fighting off the infections he contracted in the wild. I'm sorry, but rules are rules."

Vigal was in no mood for games. "Nonsense," he sighed. "Show me these medical reports that say he's still infected." The proctors exchanged surreptitious looks as the headmaster's charade quickly collapsed. She forwarded the documents to Vigal, who projected them at arm's length for anybody to see. "It's quite obvious the boy doesn't have anything," he said at length, pointing to the array of charts floating in the air between them. "Blood pressure, heart rate, OCHRE functions—all normal. I'm afraid you have no legal right to keep the boy isolated here any longer."

The headmaster slumped visibly. Her eyes darted sidewise at the proctors with a silent accusation: *You said he wouldn't give us any trouble.* "Please understand—we can't let Natch go until the hive finishes its official inquiry. The board of directors might still decide to prosecute him."

"*Prosecute* him?" said Vigal with furrowed brow. "What would they prosecute him for?"

"Believe me, there are things they can do. Most of the boys say that Natch led that bear right towards the other child, that he knew what he was doing the whole time. . . . Now we've got angry parents threatening all kinds of legal action. Natch should count himself lucky that the initiation compound falls under the jurisdiction of *our* L-PRACG and not one of *theirs*." The headmaster combed her stringy gray hair with the fingers on one hand and peered nervously at the pedestrians surging past on the platform. Who knew which of them would turn out to be a disgruntled investor or a muckraking drudge?

"Between you and me," she continued over ConfidentialWhisper, "I think we'll be able to come to some agreement with the parents and make this whole thing go away. We really *are* doing the best we can. But until we can get everything straightened out, Natch is better off at the hive. There are lunatics making death threats against him, drudges sending multi requests at all hours, politicians calling on him to testify . . ."

"But no capitalmen."

"No," the headmaster replied with distaste. "No capitalmen or fief-corp masters or recruiters at all, thankfully."

• • •

Vigal had changed little since Natch had last seen him. He still wore the same impeccable gray goatee and the unostentatious sand-colored robe that signaled a hopeless lack of fashion. Vigal was a monument against time, like the cabins in the initiation compound—something that stood unchanged through the vicissitudes of the seasons.

He had certainly not lost his gift for understatement. "Things are not going so well for you, it seems," said the neural programmer.

Natch sat on his bed and sulked in silence. The hive dorm, which had been unimaginably vast when he was eight, now felt small and constricting.

"Do you want to talk about what happened out there?" prodded Vigal gently.

"No," said Natch. He had spent the past few days staring at the ceiling, trying to recount those panicked few minutes in the woods, trying to decide what had happened. *Had* he purposefully led that bear into Brone's path? Or had it just been a gut instinct, a subconscious split-second decision? Could he have yelled out some warning, waved his arms, something? "I don't want to talk about it. Not while so many things are unsettled."

"What things?"

"Practical things, *now* things." The boy leaned back against the window and traced a finger over the fiefcorp industry pie charts he had put there. "I'm seventeen, Vigal. I should be looking at apartments and shopping for a bio/logic workbench. Picking out L-PRACGs. But instead, I've got no future, no prospects, nothing. I'm the most hated person in the world right now, and all because . . . because . . ." He couldn't find the words to finish his sentence, and bashed his fist against the window.

Serr Vigal pursed his lips into a frown. "Surely it can't be that bad. What about all those recruiters who were hounding you before initiation?"

"Nothing." Natch sighed bitterly. "The capitalmen won't even acknowledge my existence. Oh, a few of the fiefcorp masters will talk to me, but their offers are just laughable. People want me to apprentice for them on spec, not even for room and board. Everyone else just prives me out the instant they find out who I am."

"The whole incident is still in the news, Natch. Maybe you need to give the fiefcorps some time."

"It won't matter."

"You know, you can do so many things other than bio/logics. Maybe—"

"No." Natch pressed his forehead against the window, covering a histogram of fiefcorp share prices. "It has to be bio/logics. There's nothing else out there for me."

The neural programmer cleared his throat and began to say something, then stopped. A statement was slowly coalescing in his mind. At one time, Natch would have lacked the patience to listen to what his guardian had to say, but after nine months in the wilderness surrounded by the impetuosity of teenage boys, Serr Vigal's deliberate manner no longer seemed so irritating. "Do you remember," Vigal stammered, "what I told you before initiation about taking an apprenticeship somewhere close by?"

The boy nodded yes.

"Well, it seems I have some space—I mean, there is an opening—at my memecorp. Brain stem programming. The pay isn't much. But, well, I just thought . . ." He let the sentence waft away.

What a difference nine months can make, Natch thought. Before initiation, his main concern had been finding an appropriate excuse to ignore Vigal's advice on starting his own fiefcorp. Even after the debacle with Figaro Fi, Natch had never seriously considered taking an apprenticeship with the neural programmer. But after all that had happened with Brone and the Shortest Initiation, did he have any choice?

Vigal smiled. "I can see the struggle in your face, Natch. You don't want to apprentice with me because you think the work will be dull and unchallenging. Even worse, you're afraid I'm going to lecture you about what happened at initiation. You think I'll try to *guilt* you into signing up with my memecorp."

Natch's silence indicated his agreement.

"You also know that one day you will be beyond my tutelage," continued Vigal. "Yet you worry that I might try to keep you around by reminding you how I lent a helping hand when nobody else would. Plus—and this may be the most crucial thing—you doubt that you'll be able to find a decent woman in a company like mine to save your life."

The young outcast tried hard not to crack a smile, but he failed.

Vigal chuckled and rose from his chair. He took a seat on the bed next to the boy and put his hand on Natch's shoulder. A rare and yet not unwelcome moment of physical contact between them. "You know that life in the memecorps is much different than life in the fiefcorps, don't you?"

Natch nodded. *"Fiefcorps make money,"* he quoted slyly. *"Memecorps cost money."*

The neural programmer snorted. "Well, that's what those fools at Creed Thassel say. Maybe that was true back when Kordez Thassel and Lucco Primo were alive. But today . . . Today, I think even a hard-core libertarian would be surprised at how much of our funding comes from the marketplace. If you ask me, every bio/logic programmer could use a grounding in the fundamentals of the memecorp world."

The two silently watched the undulations in the Primo's histogram for a few minutes. Vigal's hand communicated an unspoken message of comfort and understanding. Natch could briefly see a widening of vistas, a broadening of horizons.

He tried to picture what life in Vigal's memecorp would be like. Heated debates over brain stem engineering techniques, collaborations with faceless coworkers, long hours fine-tuning bio/logic programs. There were worse ways to spend two years of his life. The money would be a pittance compared to the sums he had been discussing with the capitalmen nine months ago. But all the same, he would be working in bio/logics. And once he had proven his ability in the memecorp world, wouldn't the fiefcorps become that much more attainable?

"So what are your terms?" Natch asked.

Vigal couldn't hold back his delight. He named the terms: Room and board in Omaha. A modest stipend, with the promise of a bonus after two years. Access to the run-of-the-mill bio/logic programming equipment.

"And what about . . . all the bad publicity?" said Natch.

His guardian shrugged his shoulders dismissively. "The publicity will pass. You will discover that one of the benefits of working in the memecorp sector is that we are well protected from that sort of nonsense."

Natch stood back and let the phantom letters of Vigal's contract replace the histogram on the window. He called up Shyster 95.3c to help him negotiate the details. Within minutes, the two were sitting across the small round table in the corner of the room dickering over minor contractual differences. By the end of the hour, they had worked out an agreement. Natch affirmed it without hesitation.

He was now officially Serr Vigal's apprentice.

After a few moments of relaxed celebration, Vigal once again struck a serious note.

"I know you worry about your future, Natch," said the neural programmer in a low voice. "And I am sorry I have always been so preoccupied with all these . . . distractions." He wiggled his fingers up towards the ceiling and let them linger there a moment, as if he could only keep them from drifting into the stratosphere by a colossal act of willpower. "But . . . but when you came to me, I promised myself I would always be there for you. And I intend to keep that promise no matter what the future brings."

Natch ducked his head under the protective helmet of his clasped fingers. Ordinarily, he would have scoffed at Vigal's sentimentality, but he was not in an ordinary frame of mind. "And what if I *have* no future?"

His guardian leaned forward and put his hand on his apprentice's arm. "Of *course* you have a future. And do you know what it is?"

"What?"

"Your future is what you choose to do tomorrow. And the direction you're searching for?"

Natch shook his head.

"Your direction is where you choose to go."

• • •

Natch took a week to get oriented in his new surroundings. There was a lot to do. He needed to find an apartment whose rent fit the narrow boundaries of a memecorp salary; he needed to arrange for a shuttle to carry his belongings out from Cape Town; and most daunting of all, he needed to enroll himself in an L-PRACG.

The apartment was no hassle. Omaha had an abundance of memecorp-friendly housing. Natch picked a modest building about as far away from the Missouri River as you could get and still be inside the city limits. Even in this drab setting, he could not afford exterior walls with real windows and had to settle for a handful of viewscreens instead. There were, of course, no private outgoing multi streams.

Choosing an L-PRACG proved to be a more difficult chore. Legislatures large and small had been bombarding Natch with ads for days now, since the very instant he reconnected to the Data Sea. He found himself in the midst of an ideological battle fought with one-line enticements:

NO TAXES, NO FEES: A Libertarian Paradise

Full Compliance with All Prime Committee Details

The ULTIMATE in PRIVACY PROTECTION

GOVERNMENTALISM at Its Finest

Natch spent a day trying to sort through all the solicitations to pick a government that suited him. But his confusion increased the longer he worked at it; questions nibbled away at the back of his mind like rodents, and only seemed to multiply when he wasn't looking. What basic services did the L-PRACG provide? What kinds of taxes and fees were involved? Did the L-PRACG contract out security or provide its own? How long was the subscription term? How exclusive was the membership?

Finally, Natch threw up his hands and settled on a libertarian-leaning L-PRACG that offered a nice package of bio/logic programs as a membership incentive. If he decided he didn't like his government's policies, he could always let the subscription lapse or supplement it with other complementary L-PRACGs. Natch received a vast dossier of regulations and bylaws, which he promptly filed away and never looked at again.

He awoke the following Monday with a sense of determination he had not felt since before initiation. By 6:40 that morning, Natch was wading through the Omaha traffic towards the tube stations. He was no longer a curious bystander tossing pebbles at multi projections; now he had become part of the flow, a fish swimming upstream with the rest of the workforce. Natch caught a cross-town tube and found himself standing in Serr Vigal's foyer with three minutes to spare.

Vigal emerged from his bedroom fifteen minutes late, ushered Natch inside, and then spent another twenty-two minutes clucking around the kitchen making tea. The young programmer scanned the living room in vain for an extra workbench or a set of bio/logic programming bars. *Where does he expect me to work?* Natch thought.

Finally, he and his guardian sat on opposing couches and got down to business.

"The human brain," said Serr Vigal solemnly. A holograph of the bulbous organ appeared in the air between them. With an unassuming wave of his hand, Vigal enlarged the projection until it nearly filled the room, then set it rotating slowly in place. "And here"—his finger indicated the long trunk that extended out the bottom—"here is the area we specialize in: the brain stem.

"What is the brain stem? The brain stem is the key to understanding humanity. Learn how the brain stem works, and you learn how *people* work."

Vigal stood and began walking slowly around the hologram. His words had the flavor of a carefully scripted lecture.

"The body is a sensory machine," continued Vigal. "A machine that takes careful measurements of what is going on all around us. Sights, smells, sounds, tastes, touches: these are nothing more than dispatches from the outside world. The body transfers this information to the brain through a series of neural networks. And what does the brain receive? Meaningless pulses of electrical activity. Echoes of the world around us. How is the mind to make any sense of it at all? That is where the brain stem comes in.

"The brain stem is the connection between mind and body.

"The brain stem is the mechanism that translates impulse to thought, and then thought to action. It is the body's jumping-off point to higher intelligence. The brain stem passes information to the central processing units of our minds, the cerebrum and cerebellum. It translates this data into a format the higher brain can understand. And when the central processor has determined a course of action, it then routes electrical impulses back into the body through the brain stem.

"What would we be without the brain stem? Without the brain stem, the body would be a useless mass of tissue and bone. Our senses would be reduced to electrical impulses without context—mere random noise. And our minds? Our minds would be isolated from the real world. We would be free to postulate and theorize and deduce, but be forever unable to translate these lofty thoughts into action. We would each be remote stars in the center of a meaningless void.

"All the questions humanity has been asking itself since the dawn of time have their root in the brain stem. Are we creatures of passion, or are we creatures of forethought? How do we balance the needs of the mind with the needs of the body? Should Hamlet follow his heart and avenge the death of his father, or should he follow his head and, through careful reason, devise another course of action?

"These are brain stem questions, Natch. This is what you will be studying here in my memecorp over the next two years."

Natch's eyes began to glaze over halfway through Vigal's speech, and he wondered if this was part of the memecorp's standard fundraising pitch. Natch didn't want to be a philosopher; he wanted to be a *programmer*. He wanted to feel the grooved handle of a bio/logic programming bar in his hand as he stood in MindSpace making logical connections. He wanted to make things *work*.

But over the next few months, Natch obediently buried himself in the lore of the brain stem. He read about the cell composition in the thalamus and hypothalamus, about the mysteries of the medulla oblongata, about the fiber pathways that ran through the limbic system like cranial tube tracks. He studied humanity's slow progress in mastering the brain stem through bio/logics. The early neural programmers had begun with simple programs to monitor the electrical pulses passing through the nervous system, and then later had crafted programs to control them. Soon their successors were using bio/logics to broaden the bandwidth of the spinal cord, to shorten the refractory period a neural cell must wait between transmissions, to intercept and edit and mimic the electrical messages passing through the nervous system. They learned how to plug straight into the message stream and project sensations of their own that were indistinguishable from their "real" counterparts.

During these first few months of his apprenticeship, Natch also learned the ins and outs of the memecorp business. He accompanied his guardian on a round of fundraising and speeches that took them from Omaha to Beijing to Melbourne and even out to the orbital colonies of

Allowell and Nova Ceti. Vigal would begin with the same speech he had given Natch on his first day of apprenticeship, and then segue into lofty promises of future achievements. Accurate recording and playback of mental processes. Clustered brainpower. Group consciousness.

After the speeches, there would be private discussions with the men and women who ran the local programming services departments. Vigal would nod and listen earnestly to their ideas for hours on end, and more often than not end the day receiving a pledge of capital or the offer of a group subscription contract. Natch had always thought most bio/logic programs were sold directly to consumers on the Data Sea; now he discovered three-quarters of the code that ran human systems was "channeled" silently through deals with L-PRACGs and creeds and other organizations.

As Natch learned all this, he also learned about Serr Vigal.

Vigal's professional life had always been an enigma to Natch. He had spent more than thirty years right here at the same memecorp, doing the same work. His products often didn't even have names; instead, they were identified by long, dreary strings of numbers. He had the respect of his colleagues and apprentices, but virtually no social life. If he had ever taken a companion or a lover in the years since Lora's death, he kept it well hidden.

The more Natch learned about Vigal, the more of a mystery the man became. Natch had always dreamed about creating the kinds of programs that inspired raves from Primo's, programs that sparked social revolutions like Sheldon Surina's had. He would have never guessed that his own legal guardian had been doing that for years. In their own quiet way, Vigal's programs had probably influenced the world more than all of Figaro Fi's clientele put together.

But eventually, Natch grew restless. He wanted to stop *analyzing* and start *doing*.

Month after month, he buried himself in his studies. He had barely met his fellow apprentices at the memecorp and never even been given a workbench. While Vigal had him cooped up in his apartment studying the intricacies of the limbic system, Horvil and the rest of the boys returned from initiation. Soon Horvil had set up shop near his family's London manor and started building a reputation as a top-notch ROD coder. Other acquaintances from the hive were savoring their first mentions in Primo's.

"How long until I start *programming?*" Natch snapped to Vigal one day, a little over a year into his apprenticeship. "I haven't set foot into Mind-Space since I got here. If you expect me to learn the whole discipline of neurophysics before I pick up a programming bar, that could take *years*."

Vigal simply smiled that maddening smile of his and shook his head. "I've been studying the brain stem for almost forty years, Natch, and I'm not even *close* to understanding the whole discipline of neurophysics. You are learning no more than the essentials you need to do your job."

"And what *is* my job?"

"You know exactly what your assignment is. You're to update the OCHRE software that monitors oculomotor signals to the third cranial nerve."

"But I *know* the third cranial nerve backwards and forwards!"

The neural programmer let out a heavy sigh and plucked at the white hairs sprouting from his chin. "I'm no fool," he said quietly. "I see that I'm not going to keep you here much longer under these conditions. Perhaps you're right. Let's get started in MindSpace tomorrow. But keep in mind that we are going to proceed *very slowly*."

• • •

Natch had spent plenty of time in the hive tooling around with bio/logic programming bars, but he had never coded anything of importance. One could only do so much testing among a group of upper-class hive children.

The 9971.6a software, by contrast, had a paying subscriber base of thirty million. Its logic fueled one of the molecule-sized OCHREs clinging to the cranial nerves. Natch's work here could conceivably affect the vision of an entire city the size of Omaha. To have such influence, such power . . . He was nearly shivering with anticipation.

Natch stood at his workbench—a hand-me-down that Vigal had finally procured for him from a departing apprentice—and summoned a MindSpace bubble. The bubble was nothing more than a translucent shimmer, a void yearning to be filled. Natch called up 9971.6a. The diagram that appeared was a constellation of purplish blocks held together by thin strands of green.

It was obvious why Serr Vigal had slated this program for revision. Even someone as inexperienced as Natch could see that the code was several years out of date. Many of the green strands were looped around each other in a figure-eight formation that had been officially deprecated by Dr. Plugenpatch, and the program passed off information in a format that was incompatible with newer standards. But more than that, the program, for some indefinable reason, just looked *wrong*. Natch could practically feel it crying out in pain like an animal trapped in a thicket.

Natch reached for the satchel hanging off the side of the workbench and withdrew a plain metal rod from its sheath. Then he extended his arm into MindSpace and got to work.

Bio/logic programming bars looked like plain metal in ordinary space. Hollow tubes of silver labeled with Roman letters, the forearms of some mythical robot. But inside MindSpace, the bars blossomed into their true forms. Some looked like pincers, others pliers, others lariats or hammers or gloves. Each tool represented a specific logical operation that could be applied to a virtual structure.

Bio/logics was a science, but it was also an art form. One had to create the right number of connections in the right places. Too few connections would leave gaping holes in the program that could be exploited by malicious black coders; too many might produce unwanted side effects, or sap the body's computational system of precious resources.

Natch tore into the OCHRE software with the zealotry of the newly initiated. He completed his first round of modifications in three days, but spotted so many imperfections and inefficiencies along the way that he couldn't leave the program alone. Every connection he reassigned contained a logical flaw somewhere if he traced back far enough. And each of those flaws would lead to still other flaws.

For a week, Vigal left his apprentice to his own devices while he attended to other memecorp business. During that week, Natch barely ate or slept.

The neural programmer was completely unprepared for the sight that awaited him when he showed up the next week to inspect Natch's work. He was expecting to see a more polished version of 9971.6a, a purple constellation seen on a clear night. Instead, he saw a formation that might have come from another galaxy altogether. The 9971.7 software was arrayed in MindSpace with an almost military precision, each block tied to its fellows with a tight net of green strands. The offending figure-eights were nowhere to be seen.

"I suppose you *were* ready, after all," mumbled Serr Vigal, flabbergasted. "This is . . . this is . . ."

Natch stood in the opposite corner of the room with a grim smile on his face. *This is extraordinary? This is exceptional? This is awe-inspiring?*

"This is . . . too *much*," said Vigal.

Natch let out an explosive snort. "What do you mean, *too much*?"

The neural programmer turned as if he had just noticed his apprentice in the room. Twitching cheeks bore evidence to the struggle going on in his head between the memecorp master and the parent. "Perhaps you are right," he said slowly, parental instincts in control. "I don't want to be critical, but at the same time—"

"You don't want me getting too far ahead of the other apprentices."

"Don't be a fool!" Vigal snapped with the tone of the memecorp master. "I was going to say, I want you to actually *launch* something while you are here in my apprenticeship."

Natch couldn't think of anything pertinent to say. In Vigal's countenance, the battle of responsibilities began anew, and he quickly found some excuse to sever his multi connection.

The next month was one of the most intense times in Natch's life. Vigal did not repeat his earlier comments; instead, he encouraged Natch to submit 9971.7 to Dr. Plugenpatch at the earliest opportunity.

Plugenpatch approval was an absolute necessity to get the program listed on the bio/logics exchanges, and most OCHRE systems would refuse to obey any program that didn't carry at least a preliminary clearance from the public health agency. But just as importantly, the approval process provided an objective yardstick he could use to measure his progress. Vigal's motivations were transparent: he wanted to both get his point across and avoid confrontation.

Natch worked confidently towards Plugenpatch submission. He stood at his workbench for days on end, and the bio/logic programming bars just seemed to leap into his hands. The pain of the incomplete program was a visceral thing to Natch, a burning sensation that began in the tips of his toes and shot through his calves, sending his legs to pacing and his hands to searching for the cool balm of a bio/logic programming bar. But he was making progress. Little by little, he was liberating this mathematical beast from its confinement.

He finally submitted the program to Dr. Plugenpatch on a dry June afternoon.

The medical programming review system rejected it without comment.

Vigal took a cross-town tube over to Natch's flat that evening. He bore on his face the nervous look that foretold an approaching speech as surely as dark clouds foretold rain. Natch immediately started to lead his mentor towards his workbench, where 9971.7 hung in Mind-Space. But Vigal called him back and had him sit down on the couch facing the living room viewscreen.

"Let us talk a little bit about change in a memecorp," he began slowly, eyes focused on the carpet. "Natch, no bio/logic program is an island. It has complex interdependencies, relationships to other programs." Vigal waved his hand at the viewscreen, causing it to broadcast a holographic blueprint of white, red, and green squares that filled the room. Natch recognized this vast three-dimensional abacus on sight; it was the standard OCHRE engineering map of the human brain. Yet it represented only one small portion of the whole human programming schematic, which might have encompassed two or three square kilometers at this level of detail. "You will notice that these relationships are particularly dense in this area, the area of brain stem software." He pointed to a cluster of beads near the center of the diagram.

"I suppose the one you've highlighted is the cranial nerve software," mumbled Natch, tilting his head towards a blinking circle in the center of the cluster.

"Precisely," replied Vigal. "Now let me show you the programs with a direct relationship to 9971.7—programs that will explicitly rely on the information from your work." The neural programmer pulled back the focus and let a whole new level of the blueprint slide into the room. A disparate group of perhaps twenty beads began to blink. "Now, if we add in the components of the system that rely on information from *those* programs . . ." The focus pulled back even farther. Hundreds of beads were now flashing in perfect synchronization. "And so on and so on," concluded Vigal, waving a jittery hand at the exponential explosion of blinking beads.

Natch could feel the impatience swelling within him. He began drumming his fingers on the side table. "All right, I *get* it. There's a lot riding on this program."

"*Any* neural program."

"Fine. But I don't see what you're worried about. My code meets all the standards. It produces consistent results."

"I have no doubt of that," replied Vigal somberly. "If I ever had any doubts about your programming abilities, Natch, this has certainly dispelled them. It's not you I worry about—it's the companies working on all these *other* programs whose skills I question." He flipped the back of his hand at the pinpricks of light that had replicated throughout the room like a cancer.

"Why should I care?" said Natch through gritted teeth. "That's *their* problem."

"But Natch, you must understand . . . you're not working with skin moisturizers or, or, breath fresheners. This is *neural* software. One major discrepancy between any two of these programs could cause a massive brain hemorrhage. And that is an unacceptable result. That's why we have to work *slowly* and with careful coordination."

"That's why we have Dr. Plugenpatch standards—"

"The standards are only one small part of the procedure," said Vigal with a tinge of sadness in his voice. "For process' preservation, Natch, why do you think I'm always going off to speak at all these conferences? It's so those of us in neural programming can keep on top of what the others are doing. Certainly it's costly and time-consuming, but it's also effective. We have a higher standard to live up to here in the memecorp sector."

Natch crossed his arms in front of his chest and sulked. He tried to look at anything in the room but Serr Vigal. "I don't see how you can make a *profit* doing all that," he said. "I mean, who's going to wait three years for all of you to coordinate an upgrade to some obscure piece of cranial nerve software?"

Vigal shut off the diagram with a snap of his fingers, revealing the cheap carpeting and secondhand furniture of Natch's apartment once more. "You're beginning to understand life in a memecorp," said the neural programmer quietly. "We *can't* make a profit. We *can't* just rely on

Primo's ratings or the whims of the marketplace to test our products for us. Because, as you say, people do not have the time or the inclination to pay attention to most neural software. If we didn't get outside funding, I would have to close up shop and send everybody home."

"Then why do it at all?"

"Because I enjoy it," said Vigal, "and because someone has to."

There was a long pause. Natch could feel 9971.7 laughing derisively at him from its berth in MindSpace. "So what do you want me to *do?* Abandon the whole thing?"

"I want you to do exactly what you're doing," replied Vigal, "but *slow down*. Natch, you've created an excellent long-term plan for the future of 9971.7. Tomorrow, you can begin by rolling back the changes you've put in place, and then we can start to enact that plan one piece at a time."

Natch had no response. He had expected Vigal to point him to some hidden flaw in the program architecture that only a wise and seasoned programmer could see. Instead, his guardian had only confirmed that the problem did not lay with Natch; the problem was the memecorp system itself.

Silently, Natch cursed the day he had ever signed on to an apprenticeship with Serr Vigal, and wondered if he would make it through the rest of his apprenticeship without going completely insane.

(((13)))

A few weeks later, Natch abandoned his grandiose plan for the neural software. He hadn't lost confidence in his abilities; on the contrary, he was more certain than ever that he could bring the program to a higher plain of functionality. But Natch had decided to leave Vigal's employ in eight months, when his contract ended. Until then, he would get much more experience trying his hand at a variety of projects rather than tinkering with just one.

Serr Vigal took the news coolly but with a tinge of disappointment. "Where will you go?" he asked his protégé. "The fiefcorps?"

"That's not the place for me right now," said Natch, leaving the obvious unspoken: he still suffered from the taint of the Shortest Initiation. Hiring someone with Natch's notoriety could provoke a boycott from the creeds and the L-PRACGs, or a backlash from the drudges. "I've decided to set myself up on the Data Sea as a ROD coder," the youth continued. "Like Horvil."

"Are you sure, Natch? ROD coding can be extremely—"

Natch cut the discussion short. "Yes, I'm sure," he said.

Vigal did not begrudge his young apprentice's decision. In fact, he seemed to forget all about it over the next few months. Natch quietly upgraded a number of optic nerve programs to the new Plugenpatch specs, working at the glacial pace his master had requested. When Natch multied to Vigal's office to collect his end-of-contract bonus and say good-bye, the neural programmer responded with a surprised "Oh!" and gave him a feeble hug. Natch could see a host of worries fluttering through his guardian's head, but Vigal had evidently decided to keep them to himself.

Thus ended Natch's brief career in the memecorp sector.

• • •

RODs were Routines On Demand, bio/logic programs that catered to the indulgently rich. There were no contracts, no guarantees, no fringe benefits. ROD coders simply scouted the Data Sea for a spec they could engineer quickly, rushed to build it before someone else did, and then launched it in hopes that their patron would like it enough to pay. The applications for RODs ranged from the frivolous (Fab-u-lous Nails 15, "now with programmable cuticles") to the lascivious (Tit-o-rama 8, "the total breast sensation enhancer") to the purely ridiculous (Disc-Speak 3c, "for the true connoisseur of ancient recorded-sound emulation—now with pop, hiss and warble!").

An expedient programmer could typically launch two or three RODs per week. Horvil had maintained that pace for over a year before moving on to the more specialized field of bio/logic engineering.

"Let's estimate three sales a week," said Natch to his old friend one night as they strode around London discussing career options. He summoned a virtual calculator in the brisk spring air and began plugging in numbers. "So we'll multiply three by the average asking price for a ROD, subtract out equipment and overhead—"

Horvil sliced his hand through Natch's holographic calculator. "Wait a minute, Natch," he said, shaking his head. "It's not that easy."

"What do you mean?"

"I said I *launched* two or three RODs a week. I didn't say anybody *bought* 'em. You *never* sell all the RODs you launch. Sometimes you get beaten to the punch by another programmer. Or your patron changes his mind and pulls the spec from the Data Sea just for the fuck of it. Or you're sabotaged by the competition. There are assholes out there that post fake ROD requests, you know."

Natch frowned and adjusted his numbers downwards. "Well, it's still not that bad—you've just got to factor in recurring revenue. You know, maintenance fees, subscription fees, upgrade fees. That's how the fiefcorps make a profit, right?"

The stocky engineer chuckled, pleased to be in the know for once. "Nope, can't count on any of that either. These are RODs, Natch—you have to build 'em so quickly that they won't withstand any kind of heavy use. The shelf life for a ROD is about twelve to fifteen weeks, and that's only *if* you've done your homework. After that, the buyers just get bored and move on to the next new thing."

Natch began to wonder if he had made a rash choice in leaving Vigal's employ. Memecorp work might be torpid and dull, but at least it provided a sense of stability. But once Natch stepped out on his own, nothing was guaranteed. A year from now, he could be trolling the old cities and living in trashed-up skyscrapers like the diss, like his mother had done.

But certainly Natch could make a decent living in the ROD coding game if Horvil could. He had a tremendous respect for his hive-mate's intellect, but Horvil's business sense was a little skewed. People tended to fall into the ROD world because they couldn't hack it in the real bio/logics market (or because they were rich and bored, like Horvil). But Natch never doubted that he had the skills and the pedigree to make it to the top ranks of the fiefcorps. He was not on his way down; he was on his way up.

All Natch needed to do was persevere, produce quality work, and establish a reputation. Eventually, the ill wind that drifted around him would dissipate, and the brand on his forehead would fade; the Shortest Initiation would be permanently tossed into the dustbin of Yesterday's News. Then the channelers and capitalmen and fiefcorp masters who patrolled the Data Sea for fresh talent would find him, and he would resume his rightful place in the bio/logics world.

• • •

Natch's end-of-contract bonus was enough to keep him afloat for a month or two. Vigal offered to buy his young protégé a set of bio/logic programming bars as a parting gift, but Natch declined and bought the bars himself. He did not want to feel beholden to his guardian for anything. It was not an idle investment; the extended function sets on the new bars would enable him to take coding shortcuts and thus program faster.

Now that Natch had emerged from Vigal's shadow, the city of Omaha held no appeal to him. He hopped around the globe looking for a place to settle, and finally found an apartment in Angelos that suited his tastes. The place made Horvil's spare room look like a palace by comparison. Still, it had everything he would need to start a ROD business. There was a bed to sleep in, space to hold a decent-sized workbench, and proximity to downtown Angelos, where the public multi facilities were abundant and cheap.

The next morning, he got to work.

Natch decided to begin with a field he was familiar with, so he chose optics. He skimmed the Data Sea and found a request for an eye transformation program that looked like it might be a good place to start. Bio/logics had made setting one's eye color as easy as editing a database entry, but the woman who had posted this request wanted something more. Vellux of Beijing wanted her eye color to sync with the colors of nearby flowers. In a room of violets, she wanted violet eyes; in a field of ivy, she wanted green.

It seemed like a simple enough programming task. A morning spent nosing through the Dr. Plugenpatch archives helped him better his understanding of the optical programming interface. Natch fetched the OCHRE specs from Dr. Plugenpatch, projected them onto his workbench in MindSpace, and started planning his strategy.

Natch found plenty of machines floating around the eyeball that he could harness to accomplish his task. Thanks to the OCHREs, he could query the iris and determine the color of its pigment; he could also query the retina and parse the colors in the user's line of sight. But a number of vexing questions remained. How would the program identify flowers in the retinal image? How would it distinguish between petals, stems, and leaves? How would the program funnel the millions of shades of yellows and reds and purples into a narrow palette of sixteen colors? What if Vellux was looking at seven different flowers—how would the program rank the order of importance of these flowers and assign an appropriate eye color?

The longer Natch struggled to unravel these tangled questions, the more questions arose to ensnare him. Normally, it took hours for the body to process color changes through the personal preferences database. Unless this woman Vellux planned to stand still for long periods of time, he would need to find an alternate solution. Luckily, he found a number of subroutines on the Data Sea that would do the job quicker. Natch chose one called Weagel's Eye Wizard, which had received excellent ratings from Primo's a few months back. But the program required access to a batch of proteins for building the pigmentation . . . which could only be done by requesting resources from another OCHRE nearby in the choroid . . . but the OCHRE in the choroid needed to register its supply requirements with the brain stem. . . .

It took Natch most of the day and into the night to come up with a satisfactory blueprint for the project. At six in the morning, he sat back and took stock of his progress. The holographic model floating above his workbench looked like a mutated grasshopper, but Natch knew he could not afford to trifle with aesthetics this time around. As he was examining his handiwork, the building interrupted him to slide a bowl of hot oatmeal onto the kitchen counter. *When was the last time I ate?* Natch asked himself. He could not remember.

But food would have to wait. Natch created a new instance of the MindSpace bubble and placed his model inside it for future reference. Then he grabbed two of the bio/logic programming bars out of his satchel. The new bars were light enough to wave in MindSpace for hours, yet solid enough to withstand thousands of accidental bashes against a workbench. Natch took a deep breath and attacked the empty MindSpace bubble with zest.

Morning became afternoon; afternoon became evening.

The young entrepreneur sculpted his code quickly, using virtual blocks of logic as his marble, and programming bars as his hammer and chisel. Gradually the mass came to resemble the mutated grasshopper of Natch's diagram. He had been working for thirty-six hours straight when he finally laid down the programming bars. The bowl of oatmeal had disappeared, and Natch couldn't remember if he had eaten it or if the building had simply whisked it away untouched.

Natch stepped into the hallway, which was lined on both sides with tulips. He fired up EyeMorph 1.0 in diagnostic mode and was pleased to discover that everything worked as designed. His eyes quickly slid from their natural blue to a mottled shade of purple. Natch retreated to his living room and tested his handiwork against a number of floral images on the viewscreen. So far, so good.

Rest is coming soon, he promised himself. *I just need Plugenpatch approval, so I can launch the program on the Data Sea, and then I'll sleep.*

Natch approached the Plugenpatch process with more than a little trepidation. As he had discovered while apprenticing for Vigal, a successful test was no guarantee of approval. Fiefcorp programmers could not hope to cover all the combinatorial possibilities of a fully functioning OCHRE system. No, only large entities like Dr. Plugenpatch and Primo's had the facilities to do that. Natch swallowed his fear, packaged up his work, and routed the program to Dr. Plugenpatch's automated verification system.

Eight minutes later, as Natch sat on his sofa sucking down a fizzy bottle of ChaiQuoke, EyeMorph returned from the verification system peppered with rejection notices.

Mindful of the time, Natch tore through the Plugenpatch recommendations. He realized to his chagrin that he had left a loophole that might allow excess protein buildup in the choroid. Any decent OCHRE system would be able to deal with such an anomaly as a matter of course, but Dr. Plugenpatch's standards were rigid and uncompromising. The catchphrase from a thousand Creed Conscientious advertisements rose unbidden in his head: *Always preserve your bodily computing resources!* Natch sourly picked up the programming bars again and began reweaving connection strands.

The next rejection took eleven minutes for the system to process.

The rejection after that took sixteen minutes of analysis.

Natch decided to abandon subtlety and just finish the wretched program. He suspected that someone had already beaten him to the Data Sea while he was here fumbling with Dr. Plugenpatch rejections, but he couldn't just abandon the project now. Natch furiously patched up the remaining holes, disabled a few features that seemed problematic, and fed it into the Plugenpatch system.

Twenty minutes later, the verdict was clear: success!

Natch hastily bundled the program together, slapped on the standard fore and aft tables that the Data Sea required for its cataloging agents, and launched. He called up the ROD optics listings on his viewscreen so he could see the results with his own eyes. The evidence on the new releases board glared at him in small black letters:

EYEMORPH
Version: 1.0
Programmer: Natch

Yet he felt no sense of triumph. EyeMorph 1.0 may have slipped past the gates of Dr. Plugenpatch, but Natch knew the program was still riddled with inconsistencies—the kind of inconsistencies that Primo's would certainly notice when they dredged the Data Sea for their bimonthly summation of the ROD coding world. Not only that, but because Natch had used Weagel's Eye Wizard to perform some of the heavy lifting, part of his profits would be swallowed up by licensing fees. He would be lucky to break even on the project.

Natch was shambling towards the bed for a long-overdue slumber when a message arrived.

You gave it your all
I hope you had fun
'Cause you got your ass kicked
By CAPTAIN BOLBUND.

• • •

Horvil was at a loss to explain Natch's failure. He wriggled his head free of the blankets and stared drowsily at the ROD listings scrolling up and down his bedroom viewscreen.

"How does he program so fast?" griped Natch from across the room, where he was wearing tracks into the carpet. "Who is this guy? 'Captain Bolbund'? He beat me by an entire *day* on EyeMorph, Horv! What's he doing that I'm not?"

The engineer flopped around to face the wall. "Maybe it was a fluke," he said. "Maybe he just got lucky. It happens."

"It's not a fluke. This Bolbund has beaten me four times in a row now."

"Four times? How the fuck d'you run into the same guy four times in a row in this business? That's no accident."

Natch shook his head. "Of *course* it isn't an accident. I keep taking him on, and he keeps massacring me. Even worse, he always sends me this awful poetry when he wins." The young entrepreneur forwarded some of Captain Bolbund's doggerel to Horvil.

Horvil read silently for a minute. "This *is* terrible," he mumbled. "Ten thousand spell checking programs out there, and this asshole still spells *slaughter* with a 'w'." He sat up in bed, stretched, and shot Natch a worried look. "Listen, Natch, I don't think you get it. When you're a ROD coder, you gotta keep moving or you'll get in a rut. Didn't your mother ever tell you that *you win some and you lose some, but life goes on?*"

"No," said Natch with a menacing growl.

Horvil winced, causing his pudgy face to shrivel up like a prune. "Oh, fuck, Natch . . . I forgot . . . I didn't mean—"

"Never mind." Natch gazed at the photos lining Horvil's wall, where dozens of fat, happy Horvil look-alikes with inky black hair frolicked in an assortment of lavish London manors. If Horvil were ever to fail, his family would absorb him back into its bosom at a moment's notice. But where would Natch go if his money ran out, especially now that he had spurned Vigal?

"Why don't you hire an analyst, Natch?" offered Horvil. "Business strategy is what these people *do*. They can figure out how to get you through this."

"I don't trust them," Natch muttered under his breath. He didn't want to mention the real reason he wouldn't seek professional advice: his Vault account was running low. In the past two weeks, he had made only one sale, to a doddering old L-PRACG politician whose mistress had been complaining about too much sweat on his upper lip.

But after another few weeks of getting thrashed on the ROD circuit, Natch decided that Horvil was right. He needed professional advice, and he needed it quickly. It pained him to admit he was incapable of defeating Bolbund on his own, but he took solace in a saying by the great Lucco Primo: *There are a thousand roads to success, and nine hundred of them begin with failure.* So Natch swallowed his pride and began hunting around the Data Sea for an analyst he could afford.

One analyst in Natch's price range instantly stood out from the rest. She was a woman named Jara who lived on the other side of London from Horvil. Natch set the InfoGather 77 program loose on the Data Sea and instructed it to follow her scent. What InfoGather discovered surprised him: stellar notices from Primo's, five years' experience with the rising star Lucas Sentinel, a smattering of praise from the drudges. But then the trail abruptly vanished from the Data Sea, only to reemerge six months later with Jara a free agent and her prices far below market level. Natch fired off a message to the woman:

> Why is Lucas Sentinel spreading rumors about you? What did you do to piss him off? And why should I give you any work?

The reply was almost instantaneous:

> I told Lucas he needed to grow a set of testicles. He decided to blacklist me instead. Don't bother hiring me unless you have a pair.

Natch laughed out loud. If there was one thing he valued after his Shortest Initiation experience, it was nonconformity.

Jara arrived at Natch's apartment in multi, a scant five seconds shy of their appointed meeting time. Natch found himself facing a tiny woman with Sephardic features and a massive thicket of curly hair. She was almost twenty years his senior. "You asked for a ninety-minute consultation," said Jara by way of greeting. "You realize that my standard consultation is forty-five minutes."

"*Anything worth doing is worth perfecting*," said Natch, quoting Sheldon Surina.

He could sense this woman Jara sizing him up with one eagle eye. Her piercing look said that she already knew about the Shortest Initiation, that she had already reconstructed his story and needed only the one look to confirm it. Natch stood tall and did not flinch. He had nothing to hide.

"All right," said Jara. "Let's get to it."

Natch brought her over to his workbench and summoned the Eye-Morph program and several others in MindSpace, along with a passel of Captain Bolbund's competing brands. "Tell me why this asshole keeps beating me," he said simply.

As she stepped inside the MindSpace bubble, Jara didn't pause for any social niceties. She eyed the herd of programs like an angry bull. "Give me twenty minutes," she said gruffly, and then reached up and began spinning the logical structures around with her virtual hands. Natch took a seat in a chair, activated the QuasiSuspension program, and let her work. As he drifted off into a light nap, he could sense her making thousands of queries on his files and wondered what kind of analysis routines she had developed to churn through all that data.

Precisely twenty minutes later, Natch awoke from QuasiSuspension and joined Jara at the workbench. "So what is this clown doing that I'm not?" he asked.

"The problem," replied Jara tersely, "is that Bolbund isn't doing *anything* you're not doing."

Natch sat back down in his chair, puzzled. "Huh?"

"His programs don't hold a candle to yours. They're sloppy, they're inadequate, and they'll probably fall apart in a pinch. But he's done a real mind job on you. He's got you convinced that you need to work harder and harder until you drop from exhaustion."

"But for process' preservation, Jara, he launched his eye color program a whole day earlier than me. A *day*! That's life or death in this business."

"You're still not getting it, Natch. What was the spec?"

"She wanted an eye-morphing program to complement the—"

Jara put up her hand. It was as tiny and delicate as a doll's. "That's your first mistake. You thought the customer knew what she wanted. She wanted *an eye-morphing program to complement the colors of the flowers*, right? No, what she wanted was a program to make *her* eyes match *her* flowers."

The agitation flowed down to Natch's feet and made him rise from the chair in a futile attempt to pace it off. "What's the difference?"

"Did you spend any time researching your client before you took on the project? Well, *I* did—just now, while you were dozing—and look what I found." She strode up to the room's lone viewscreen and gave an imperious nod.

A woman materialized on the screen, probably in her mid-eighties but possibly approaching a hundred, decked out in a lavish purple robe that was the hallmark of membership in Creed Élan. VELLUX, read the caption beneath her. The two watched silently for a moment as Vellux puttered around her greenhouse pointing out different specimens of flowers. Five minutes into her nauseating pitch, Natch froze the display. "Okay, she sells flowers. I've already seen this promo. I don't think I'd live through a second viewing."

Jara snorted, but the glimmer in her eyes was not unfriendly. "You may have seen it, but how closely were you watching? Did you notice *this*?" She stretched out her index finger to zoom in on a block of text in the corner of the screen: VISIT US AT THE CREED ÉLAN ANNUAL CONVOCATION JULY 15–27. "Vellux probably didn't mention she was buying this ROD to use at a Creed Élan function, did she? If you were going to traffic flowers to the Élanners, Natch, what flowers would you sell? I'd pick bougainvilleas, lilacs, irises. Red, purple, and lavender, the official colors of the creed." Jara jerked her thumb to the left and focused on the flower vendor's face. "And here's another clue. Did you notice that *her* eyes are hazel?"

Natch stewed quietly in the opposite corner of the room. He could see the gestalt of the situation coming into focus.

"After five minutes, we've narrowed down the task considerably. Instead of creating a program to change *anyone's* eyes to match *any* color flower, we just need to create one that will change *this* woman's eyes to several shades of purple. Not only that, but we know which flowers to scan for in the retinal image. It's much easier to analyze an image for a specific genus of flower than to do the same for *any* flower; I'm willing to bet you can find dozens of subroutines on the Data Sea that will do the trick.

"That's what they call a *tell*. The customer says they want one thing, but their actions *tell* you they want something else. Something simple and easy to deliver. I'm willing to bet this Captain Bolbund character saw that right away, and that's why he jumped on this spec.

"So not only did you take on the wrong task, but you went about it the wrong way. Why actually bother changing the color of her eyes? Why not just change other people's *perceptions* of them? That's a million times easier than all this shit you did with pigments and proteins. Good work, by the way, but who cares? Bolbund's ROD secretes a light pigment onto the surface of the eye through the tear ducts. *Outside* the eye, Natch, not *inside* of it. Clever. It's not a perfect solution, but nobody's going to notice in the middle of a creed convention. Best of all, Bolbund can skip the most intensive OCHRE programming and breeze right past hours of Plugenpatch validation."

Natch looked at his hands, absorbing her analysis and storing it for later use. He could see why Jara's curt manner might have irritated Lucas Sentinel and gotten the other big fiefcorps to boycott her services, why she had suddenly found herself unemployable in the fiefcorp world and desperate enough to advertise cheap consulting services to lowly ROD coders like him. But Natch had no use for flattery. Not in his personal life and certainly not in his business.

"So what if your analysis is wrong?" he said. "What if this Vellux woman isn't using the program at a Creed Élan function at all?"

"Then someone else wins the business and you move on," replied Jara coolly. "All you've lost is a day or two."

"EyeMorph is much better than that shit Bolbund threw together," he snapped.

"No doubt. But what does that matter if nobody buys it?"

"Vellux will figure it out. She'll see she bought a lousy product."

"Maybe she will; maybe she won't. Do you know how hard it is to get your money back from a programmer? She'd have to go to the Cooperative, and that could take weeks. Not worth her time, not for such a trifling amount. Maybe by the time she notices, Bolbund will have fixed all those problems. He offers her a free upgrade, and she goes straight to him the next time she needs something."

The frustration coalesced in his mind like steam, and he was unable to summon any intelligible words through the fog. Natch vented his anger through a brutal kick at the wall.

"I feel like I'm going around in circles," he cried. "I'm just not *getting* anywhere. You ever hear that saying of Lucco Primo's about the three elements of success?"

Jara took a seat in the chair that Natch had recently used for his nap and looked him over with a tough but sympathetic eye. "Ability, energy, and direction," she said. "Yeah, I've heard it."

"So what am I missing?"

"That's easy," replied Jara. "The wisdom to know when to use them."

(((14)))

Sheldon Surina once said, *Progress is persistence.*

Natch was nothing if not persistent. He had chosen the track he would take—from ROD coding, to mastering a fiefcorp, to winning the number one rank on Primo's—and nothing would throw him off course. Soon, Natch was convinced that nothing existed outside of this track. It was only within this context that he could make sense of his humiliating failures to Captain Bolbund. *The track may twist and turn,* he told himself, *but eventually it will lead me to my destination.*

In the meantime, Natch's most pressing problem was cash flow. His Vault account had been drained by weeks of fruitless competition, not to mention the new bio/logic programming bars and Jara's consultation. Even the normally oblivious Horvil took note of Natch's financial plight. The engineer began to discover subtle ways to help. He would pick up the tab for dinner, accidentally leave groceries behind at Natch's place, drastically overpay Natch back for drinks from the night before.

Finally, Natch had to face the fact that ROD coding would not keep him afloat if he insisted on confronting Captain Bolbund again and again. Yet stanzas of Bolbund's wretched poetry kept creeping into his mind late at night, tramplike, refusing all attempts at eviction. Natch refused to give up, but he decided to put ROD coding on the back burner and scour the Data Sea for additional work. Something staid and square and predictable that would pay the bills.

Natch quickly found an open position at a large assembly-line programming shop in southern Texas territory.

"You don't want to go there," Jara advised him. "That's just connecting dots. Customization jobs for L-PRACGs handing out programs to twenty thousand people at once."

"Can't they automate that crap?" Natch asked.

"Too expensive. AIs could have done the grunt work, back before the Autonomous Revolt. But the time and expense to deal with all the contingencies for projects that big . . . it's cheaper to just go assembly-line."

Natch drifted around his apartment that night kicking walls and yelling at ceiling tiles. There had to be *some* other course, someplace else in bio/logics where the opinions of the drudges didn't matter. But Natch could not find any, and his Vault account was nearly empty. He accepted the job. Now his descent to the bottom of the programmer's food chain was complete.

The shop was located in a cavernous warehouse just south of the Sierra Madres. The area had once been the flowering center of New Alamo and the splinter Texan governments, overgrown with gaudy nouveau palaces and indulgent monuments to civic duty. But the Texans' decay had proved a potent fertilizer for programming factories that could make good use of their large open spaces. Natch hopped on a tube every morning to a nondescript building in the warehouse district, where he reported to one of several hundred identical workbenches on the floor. A program materialized before him in Mind-Space, along with color-coded templates put together by some fiefcorp apprentice that instructed him where and how to make connections. There was no room for originality. The system automatically reported any deviations from the template to his supervisor.

Most of Natch's fellow programmers didn't mind the tedium, the endless repetition and constant clanking from a hundred programming bars striking workbenches at once. Their minds were far away. What happened to them in real time mattered little, as long as they could strum and drum and hum along to the orgiastic frenzy of music on the Jamm network. Natch logged on once to see what all the fuss was about. He found a hundred thousand channels of music in every conceivable style, tempo, and mood. Channels would spawn like newts, flourish for days or weeks as musicians jumped on and added their personal touch to the mix, then gradually shrivel up and die. Until then, Natch had thought his coworkers were thumping their workbenches with their programming bars to stave off boredom; now he realized he was listening to the rhythm sections of a thousand different Data Sea symphonies. Natch logged off in disgust and found a good white-noise program to block out the din. He detested music.

Natch earned his assembly-line pittance by day, but he was hardly idle at night. He spent countless hours staring at intricate blocks of programming code in MindSpace, not actually making connections, but simply absorbing the patterns and progressions, waiting for the inevitable blast of inspiration.

• • •

His next vision came to him in the dead hours before dawn.

Natch went to bed early that night and activated QuasiSuspension 109.3, sick of the eternal struggle to find sleep. The program quickly led him there. He used the highest setting, which should have insulated him from the everyday noises of shifting walls and floors.

Yet somehow Natch found himself bolting upright at three in the morning, his face glistening with sweat.

He felt like a lens had snapped into place and brought something wide and terrible into focus. Natch looked for the familiar objects around his bedroom, the cheap bedside shelf protruding from the wall, the pus-green carpet, the viewscreen that had been showing a light snow on Kilimanjaro when he lay down. Now all he could see were bones. The bones of impossible animals with four, five, and six appendages, bones scorched free of flesh and arrayed as furniture.

Natch tore himself out of bed and grabbed a robe from the disembodied index finger on which it hung. He burst out of his apartment, heading for the balcony that stood at the end of the hallway. As Natch rushed out the balcony door, a platform slid from the side of the building with a soft *click*. He feverishly gripped the alabaster railing and watched Angelos go through its typical early-morning routine. Skeletal tube trains stuffed with cargo rushed silently to and fro, anxious to make deliveries before the morning rush. Viewscreens here and there glared seductively at passersby with visions of dead products and ghoulish fashions. A fleet of bleached-white hoverbirds bearing the yellow star of the Council took wing over the Hollywood hills. Haunted tenements performed a graveyard jig with one another, here sidestepping to make room for the neighboring building on the left, there elbowing aside the building on the right to accommodate freshly awoken tenants. Natch could hear no sound but the soft crunch of pencil-thin bones beneath his feet.

As Natch gazed at all this, the bare skeletal structures he saw began to fill out—not with flesh, but with the washed-out hues of MindSpace code. The city was becoming one vast bio/logic program. A compendium of data, numbers, named entities, subroutines, variables. Pieces, no matter how independent, no matter how abstruse, inevitably connected to a larger and more complex whole. Tendrils snaking invisibly between each node, binding everyone together with mathematical formulae.

And the people . . . the people . . . The L-PRACG politicians stumbling from meeting halls after late-night sessions, the businesspeople shuffling mechanically to the tube stations and public multi facilities, the private security guards exchanging curt words with their Defense and Wellness Council counterparts, and yes, there were even a few tourists up and about at this hour. . . . Weren't the people just one more set of objects to be manipulated? Weren't their actions governed by deeply ingrained sets of instructions, and their ideas ultimately predictable? They could be made to obey commands. They, like programming code, could be manipulated.

Natch saw Angelos floating within the giant MindSpace bubble that was the world: *his* MindSpace, *his* world. He could practically hear his bio/logics proctor at the Proud Eagle on his first day at the workbench. *Reach into your satchels, pull out a programming bar. Any one, it doesn't matter! You have twenty-six bars, marked A to Z, each with three to six separate functions. Twelve commonly recognized hand gestures. The grip. The point. The hitch. Unlimited possibilities before you! Unlimited combinations.* This was not strictly true; Natch was wise enough to know that the number of options at his disposal were not infinite. Mathematics dictated that there were limits. But even if his options were not *unlimited*, they were *enough*— enough to accomplish anything he was likely to dream. And if he could find some combination of tools capable of manipulating any structure of data, why not people too? Who was to say that the human nodes within his bubble were immune to the natural laws of cause and effect?

He reached out with enormous hands, each finger a bio/logic programming bar. The city of Angelos responded to his commands. It spun like a globe on an axis. It shifted and shuddered and jittered where he pointed. The world was his. . . .

With the exception of an immense and incomprehensible mass hovering just beyond the horizon . . . a terrible celestial mass that could reshape humanity, if only he could reach it. . . .

Natch rushed back to his apartment with his mind ablaze. He curled up into a fetal position on his chair-and-a-half and sketched an inventory of new tools with fiery holographic letters in the air.

Sex	Stability	Friendship
Power	Greed	Hunger
Money	Guilt	Lust
Love	Desire	Laziness
Vanity	Novelty	Suffering

On through the morning he wrote, brushing aside the urgent wake-up calls he had set for his assembly-line programming job. The work would not be necessary now.

He awoke on the couch in midafternoon, unable to remember how he had gotten there, but confident he was back on track at last.

• • •

Horvil sat upside down on Natch's chair-and-a-half with his feet propped on the chair back and his head hanging near the ground. His face was a jumbled stew of concern and fear topped with a thin crust of nonchalance.

"So you're willing to help me out," said Natch, eyes ablaze. He was practically sprinting from one end of the apartment to the other, teeth chattering and fingertips aquiver.

"It's a little *unorthodox*, I guess," said Horvil, "but heck, I've known you were unorthodox since you were six years old."

"I just don't want you to back out at the last minute."

"I won't. But . . ."

"But what?"

The engineer threw his arms to the ground in exasperation, a move that probably would have sent him tumbling onto his head if he were present in the flesh. "Do you always need to have an evil nemesis, Natch?" he cried. "First Brone, now Captain Bolbund. Can't you succeed on your own without having to *beat* somebody?"

Natch gave a hollow and humorless grin. "You can't win unless somebody else loses."

Horvil flexed his jaw for a moment and watched his friend strut energetically around the room. Natch could see a thousand witty rejoinders crowding into his mind, eager to sharpen their claws on his self-importance. "Okay," the engineer sighed after a minute. "What can I do to help?"

Two days later, Horvil caught up with the flower vendor named Vellux at the annual Creed Élan convocation. The engineer looked quite out of place at this year's event, not because of his size but because he was the only one in the conference hall not draped from head to toe in some shade of purple. Instead, Horvil wore a crisp dun uniform he had borrowed from a friend working in L-PRACG security.

"You are Vellux?" Horvil announced in the authoritative tone of voice Natch had instructed him to use.

The old woman, standing behind a table of lush passionflowers, greeted Horvil with a bland smile. Her eyes shone a soft violet. "And you are?"

"I'm here as part of an investigation into unethical ROD coding practices." *No names, no credentials*, Natch had said. *She won't ask. She'll think you're with the Meme Cooperative, or Primo's, or some special task force from the Defense and Wellness Council.* But Horvil was paranoid about being recognized, despite all of Natch's reassurances, and had insisted on scrubbing his public directory profile for good measure. "Have you recently purchased any bio/logic programming from this man?" Horvil gestured at a viewscreen on the wall, where a gaggle of Creed Élanners were bestowing a garland of flowers upon an addled woman of the diss who was clearly not interested. The engineer erased the display and summoned a particularly unflattering still of Bolbund, caught in midsmirk.

The flower vendor nodded, puzzled. "Yes, as a matter of fact I did."

"I see. Have you purchased any of the following products: NozeGay 59, Aura of the Beach 12c, Flaming Lipps 44d, Floral Eyes 14—"

"Floral Eyes!" cried Vellux excitedly. A wrinkled man in the next stall arched an eyebrow at her in disapproval, and the woman quickly lowered her voice to a conspiratorial whisper. "Yes, Floral Eyes 14. That's the one."

Horvil frowned and tapped his foot for a moment. *Don't tell her what you're doing*, Natch had said. *Make her think you're talking to someone over ConfidentialWhisper. Let her wonder for a minute or two.* Then the engineer abruptly motioned for Vellux to turn around and face the viewscreen. The old woman complied, with a nervous glance towards her table of passionflowers. "This will just take a moment," said

Horvil. He bisected the viewscreen with a gesture, summoning a mirror on the left half and a series of flowers on the right. Daisies, buttercups, baby's breath, sunflowers. He gave an exaggerated stare at the image of Vellux in the mirror, took note of her obviously mismatched eye color, and shook his head sadly. "Bolbund, Bolbund, Bolbund," he muttered with a world-weary sigh for effect.

The confused flower vendor huddled inside her purple robe and frowned. "It's been working perfectly since I bought it," she said. "I don't know what happened. . . . Should I return the program? Should I get a refund, or, or . . . report this to someone?"

Act surprised. Look around quickly. Make her believe that you've said too much and now you're trying to cover up. "Madam," said Horvil, blooming into a nervous smile, "I'm not allowed to make recommendations on bio/logic programs. Please don't make any changes on *my* account. It's nothing. Pretend I was never here. If we get enough evidence to move the investigation forward, we'll be in touch with you."

Vellux smiled wanly and nodded, looking completely unconvinced.

"Towards Perfection," said Horvil, and gave her a formal bow. Then he was gone. The entire encounter took about five minutes.

That afternoon, Natch logged his first sale of the EyeMorph program.

• • •

Natch spent the week tracking down Captain Bolbund's best customers. He did so by personally following the man, who turned out to be as offensive to the eyes as his poetry was to the ear. Bolbund had a body like a misshapen bowling pin, with an uneven beard and a nose like a wedge of putty.

But Natch did not fear his rival now that he had put his finger on Bolbund's mortal flaw: vanity. It was this vanity that led him to conduct his business out in the open, where others could see and post reports on the Data Sea. Where people could observe him personally delivering programs to his customers and reciting lines of his gut-wrenching poetry. Natch had to admit that it was a clever gimmick; customers appreciated the attention, and onlookers remembered his name. During the next few days, Natch and Horvil watched him sell two phallic enhancement programs to old Creed Objectivv devotees and repackage the same eyelash curling program for a handful of debutantes. By the end of the week, they had compiled a sizeable list of clients and the RODs Bolbund had sold them.

The two quickly developed a solid routine. Natch would buy copies of Captain Bolbund's routines (using Horvil's money, of course) and study them in MindSpace for hours on end. Cracking into the programming code was no simple matter, even for such retrograde technology as a ROD. But even without root-level access, Natch could glean a lot of information just by eyeballing a program's surface and running it through a battery of tests. Within a few weeks, he could reverse-engineer Bolbund's code blindfolded and put together improved versions in mere hours. Once a ROD was completed, Natch would pass the customer's name and the script on to Horvil for his unique brand of social engineering.

Horvil was having the time of his life. He pinned bits of ceremonial bric-a-brac to his costume like medals, and constantly pestered his old hivemate with new character improvisations. Horvil had lived his whole life in decadent boredom, every move choreographed by an autocratic family. All Natch had to do was show the engineer a glimpse of spontaneity, and Horvil was dancing to *his* music.

Natch was astonished at how quickly Captain Bolbund's operation folded under pressure. He expected to run into a few snags along the way: programs he could not duplicate, customers he could not sway. But these problems never materialized. Bolbund's customers continued to roll over and switch to Natch's brands. Credits continued to accumulate in Natch's Vault account.

Of course, Bolbund did not accept the ravaging of his client list without a fight. But once again, Natch was shocked by his rival's stupidity.

The whole affair came to a head one morning as Natch was swigging down a cup of nitro and scanning the drudge headlines. The previous night he had relished his first mention in the Primo's investment guide.

Then he received a multi request from a Meme Cooperative official.

Natch activated a serenity program and granted the multi request. Within seconds, he was greeted by a smartly dressed woman flashing the official crest of the Meme Cooperative, the ancient Hebrew character of the *aleph* on a field of azure.

"Towards Perfection," said the woman. She then proceeded to reel off her name, position, division, and supervisor, along with a string of unnecessary provisos and notifications.

"Perfection," replied Natch, his anxiety now well under control. "What can I do for you?"

"You can tell me what your relationship is with this man." The Cooperative official held out her hand and flashed the same obnoxious picture of Bolbund that Horvil had been using in his charades.

Natch rolled his eyes. "Captain Bolbund," he moaned with distaste. "We've been scrapping over ROD customers for months now. He just can't accept that I'm beating him."

"Well, apparently he has gone over the line." The woman nodded towards the nearest viewscreen and began playing back a heated discussion between one of Natch's new customers and an ugly man with large ears. The video had obviously been captured on the sly. Natch couldn't make out the words passing between the two, but they nearly came to blows before the encounter was over. "Do you know this man?" said the Cooperative woman, freezing the display and tapping one of the interrogator's floppy ears.

"No," Natch replied truthfully.

"This man has been passing himself off as a Meme Cooperative official," she said. Natch looked closer at the display and noticed that the imposter's uniform was nearly identical to that of the woman standing in his apartment. "He's been telling people that he's conducting an official investigation into 'unethical ROD coding practices.' When we caught up with him, he told us that this Captain Bolbund has been paying him to put on this charade."

Natch was by now the very model of unconcern. "So what does this have to do with *me?*"

"Apparently, Bolbund specifically requested that his accomplice tell people that *you* were the one under investigation."

Natch masked his laughter by burying his face in his mug of nitro. *You fumbling idiot!* he chided Bolbund in his head. The key to the whole scam was to not mention any specific names or organizations whatsoever. After all, who could accuse Horvil of misrepresenting himself if he never made any representations in the first place?

"I don't know anything about it," Natch said at length to the Cooperative official.

The woman nodded perfunctorily. She had already made the mental leap to the next case. "The Cooperative will be in touch with you if we need any further information." She added another litany of bureaucratic language and was about to cut the multi connection when she had a sudden thought. "This Bolbund—what is he a 'captain' of anyway?"

Natch shrugged. "I have no idea."

And that was that.

Natch never heard another word back from the Meme Cooperative about the investigation, but was pleased to discover via the drudges that Captain Bolbund had received a stiff fine and a ninety-day suspension of his license to sell programming code on the Data Sea. Ninety days was an aeon in this business. Natch breathed a sigh of relief, and not only because he had vanquished his competitor; now Horvil could drop his silly role-playing and Natch could do business in earnest. For months afterward, Natch kept waiting for a reprisal to come his way from the Cooperative or some other legislative body, but none ever appeared.

The final chapter of the Bolbund saga occurred the night of the Meme Cooperative visit, when Horvil took Natch on a whirlwind tour of the London bars to celebrate. Natch was still earning less in a month than the top fiefcorps paid their apprentices as a daily wage. But he had halted his downward slide. He had proven that, by sheer force of will, he could bring the world in line with the visions in his mind's eye. Natch never drank or used alcohol simulation programs, but was content to watch Horvil get pleasantly sauced. At the end of the night, Natch fired off a parting message to Captain Bolbund with Horvil's enthusiastic backing:

> Please don't think I'm rude
> If I tell you YOU GOT SCREWED.
> Guess you finally met your match
> From now on, look out for NATCH.

(((15)))

Natch's challenges did not end there. When Bolbund spread the word about what had happened to him, the ROD coding community took it as a personal affront. ROD coders followed a loose, bohemian ethos where nothing was taken too seriously and thievery was allowed for sport but not for money. Natch's ruse—or at least Bolbund's version of it—violated those principles.

And so Natch had to endure several blatant attempts by third-rate programmers to sabotage his products, steal his customers, and savage his reputation. But this did not faze him. Natch quickly developed a reputation on the Data Sea for his humorless determination and his inability to accept defeat. Beat him once, and he would not stop until he had humiliated you three or four times in return—and fired a few warning shots at your friends and associates to boot.

Captain Bolbund returned to the business after his ninety-day suspension. The Meme Cooperative's penalty had ravaged his client base and sapped his Vault account. But by this point, the ROD coding community had come to the consensus that the best way to deal with Natch was to leave him alone and grease his path up and out of the business altogether. An enterprising young woman in Sudafrica even made a profit out of it by selling a program called NatchWatch that kept other coders abreast of Natch's activities.

Bolbund decided to steer clear of the angry young programmer.

Natch spent another two years honing his skills in the ROD game. By the time Primo's took notice and tagged him as a rising star, Natch's services were in high demand among the elites. He had also acquired a long list of enemies, which was an even greater indicator of success as far as Natch was concerned. *Nobody likes success but the successful*, the ruthless financier Kordez Thassel had once said.

Eventually, Natch decided to move out of his cramped Angelos apartment and settle somewhere else. He chose the city of Shenandoah, whose coffers were overflowing with fiefcorp revenues and whose local L-PRACGs were among the most libertarian in the world. With another financial boost from Horvil, he could even afford a place that included its own private multi stream and a small garden of daisies off the living room.

But the money was still abysmal compared to the sums the capitalmen were tossing into the bio/logic fiefcorp sector every day. The ranks of the diss were thinning, and those of the fiefcorps were inflating. There was talk on the Data Sea of another Great Boom like the one that had preceded Marcus Surina's death.

Natch spent another year freelancing, taking on the occasional ROD but concentrating more on neurological software. As his profile rose, so did his prospects. Natch received multi requests and lunch invitations every week from capitalmen and channelers trying to get a sense of his future plans. They seemed to be competing with one another to see who could slip in the most dismissive reference to the Shortest Initiation. Many of the same fiefcorp masters who had tried to shanghai Natch into worthless apprenticeships a few years ago were now sugaring him with promises of large signing bonuses.

He even heard from a few groups in the bio/logics underground who promised him a fortune writing black code off the grid. The future lay not with fiefcorps and memecorps, they said, but with clandestine teams of programmers sponsored by rich creed organizations and Lunar tycoons, programmers who were being paid to circumvent the restrictive laws of central government and stretch the boundaries of bio/logics.

Natch got into the habit of taking the tube out to the great sequoia forests and zigzagging from station to station for hours while he stared up at the trees and tried on alternative career paths like gloves.

"You've done really well with RODs," said Jara during one of her frequent consultations. "But isn't it time you set your sights a little higher?"

Horvil agreed. "I never thought *I* would be the one telling *you* to get some ambition," he said mockingly. "There's bigger targets out there, and a fuck of a lot more money!"

Contrary to what Jara and Horvil thought, however, Natch had not settled into a rut. He was biding his time, saving up his resources, marshaling his abilities. He wanted to plan his next move carefully so he would not fail again.

One cold winter night at 3 a.m., he sent a Confidential Whisper to Serr Vigal.

The neural programmer didn't mind at all being woken up; in fact, he was overjoyed to hear from his former protégé. Ten minutes later, Natch hopped on an Omaha-bound tube. Within an hour, he was standing in Vigal's foyer. Natch was surprised to find their friendly hug metamorphosing into a real flesh-and-blood embrace.

True to form, Serr Vigal had changed little in the past few years. Memecorp business had risen with the tide of the economy, but this had also caused his fundraising duties to swell to epic proportions. Vigal had just returned from a meeting with some of the minor bodhisattvas at Creed Surina and was due at the sybaritic resort of 49th Heaven in two days to speak about newly proposed OCHRE standards.

"So what causes the prodigal son to visit his old guardian in the middle of the night?" asked Vigal between sips of green tea.

"I need your advice," said Natch.

"Oh?"

"I'm ready to start my own fiefcorp."

• • •

Later that morning, Horvil and Jara agreed to come over to assist in the planning. Following standard etiquette, which said that crucial business decisions should be made in person, the two caught a hover-bird across the Atlantic from London. They met in the flesh for the first time on the runway and gave each other formal bows. By the time they arrived in Omaha, Horvil and Jara were already grumbling at each other like longtime companions.

Natch brought the first meeting of the Natch Personal Programming Fiefcorp to order around Vigal's kitchen table at noon.

From the outset, cash flow was the primary issue. Natch couldn't realistically expect any revenue flowing into the company for at least sixty days, yet there were a number of capital investments that needed to be made in the beginning. Licensing fees to the Meme Cooperative, listing fees to Primo's and the L-PRACGs, bio/logic equipment, administrative programs. Natch's savings would go a long way towards covering these costs, and eventually he would recoup the rest through new-fiefcorp tax breaks. But in the meantime, he was short the credits for apprentices' room and board those first few months.

He turned expectantly towards Horvil, but the engineer surprised him by shaking his head. "Sorry," he said, "but if I'm gonna be your apprentice, Natch, I don't want to complicate things."

Natch's eyebrows creased in confusion. "You want to be my *apprentice?*"

"Sure, why not? You're gonna need a first-rate engineer on the team, aren't you? The way I figure it, the only place I'm safe from that competitive streak of yours is on your payroll."

"But . . . the pay . . ."

"This ain't about the money, Natch," said Horvil jauntily, pleased to catch his friend off guard. "I've got enough of that. I just don't want to miss out on all the fun. And besides—*someone* has to keep you sane."

Serr Vigal beamed at the engineer in approval. "I don't think your credits will be necessary, Horvil," he said. "I can cover the payroll for the first few months."

This outpouring of faith and goodwill began to arouse Natch's suspicions. "And what do you want in return?"

"Do I have to want anything in return?" replied Vigal with a cozy smile.

Natch's face turned a flustered purple. "I'm serious, Vigal," he muttered. "What do you want?"

Vigal sighed and considered the question for a minute. "Okay, then how about a membership on the board, with a stake in the decision-making. A *minority* stake, of course," he added hastily. Natch nodded in mute satisfaction. Young fiefcorps often ended up with a concerned father or generous aunt on the board. "I can't promise I'll be available every day or even every week," continued the neural programmer, "but just remember, I'll always be there when you need help."

Embarrassed, Natch turned towards the last person at the table. He didn't know what to expect from Jara. Unlike his career, hers had not blossomed over the past few years. A gradual détente in her relations with Lucas Sentinel had resulted in the occasional piece of business, but Jara had increasingly come to rely on Natch's consulting fees to make a living.

The fiefcorp master summoned one of his simmering stares, the kind he had learned to use on Jara through trial and error. "I'm going to need a good bio/logic analyst too, Jara," he said.

The small businesswoman shifted uncomfortably in her chair as she tried, and failed, to meet Natch's stare head-on. Eventually, she lost the battle of wills and lowered her eyes to the table. "Count me in," she said finally, gritting her teeth. "But *don't* think you talked me into this, Natch. Everyone knows that fiefcorps are where the real money is these days. I've been waiting a long time for an opportunity like this to come along."

Natch gave his fellow fiefcorpers a predatory grin. *So have I*, he thought.

• • •

Despite all the careful planning and preparation that went into the formation of the Natch Personal Programming Fiefcorp, success did not come easily for the company.

Bio/logic programming was a much different animal than Routine On Demand coding. The work was more labor-intensive, and required the skills of a hard-core nuts-and-bolts engineer like Horvil and the leadership of a generalist like Natch. Because of the difference in scale, the stakes for any one particular piece of code were much higher. Each revision took weeks to complete. You couldn't afford to take the short-cuts commonplace in the ROD coding world. Nor did you have the luxury of wasting time on unnecessary features; you needed an analyst like Jara who had her fingers on the pulse of the market and could pinpoint exactly what revisions would be the most lucrative.

During the first few weeks, Natch worked nearly nonstop. He bounced from Jara's flat to Horvil's flat to Vigal's flat so many times that he was constantly disoriented. But Natch knew he was finally on the right track and moving full steam ahead.

Still, the sales figures in those initial months were abysmal. Natch began each day by examining the upgrades and revisions waiting on the dock for a launch onto the Data Sea. After launch, Jara would sit back in nervous anticipation, senses tuned to the Sea's very molecular hum, waiting for the currents of trade to shift in their direction. And each day she felt the sting of disappointment when traffic failed to come. Besides the occasional sale to a curious browser or the random ping of a cataloging data agent, there was very little activity.

"What are we doing *wrong*?" Jara moaned to Natch one day.

"We're not doing anything wrong," he replied coolly. "We just need the mojo to accumulate. Give it time."

And then one day it happened.

DeMirage 24.5 was a pedestrian routine designed to reduce the effect of optical illusions. Natch had halfheartedly picked up the project hoping to capitalize on all the ocular research he had put over the years into programs like EyeMorph. Jara didn't have much of an opinion one way or the other about the program. Horvil gave it a cursory look and spent a few hours performing delicate surgery on the program's innards in MindSpace. Natch barely paused to write a descriptive fore and aft for the product before launching it on the Data Sea. He assigned a BizWorks administrative agent to watch the traffic and sound a short *ping* for every sale, then went to sleep.

Natch's program hit the Data Sea right in the midst of a major turf war.

The Serly Fiefcorp had been involved in a fierce competition with a fast-rising company known as the Patel Brothers. Each company's partisans were launching a daily barrage of complaints to the Meme Cooperative, to Primo's, and to various L-PRACGs throughout the civilized world. Finally, the battle came to a head when Serly's databases were struck with a malicious piece of black code that temporarily put a small portion of the company catalog out of commission. One of the programs hit was Serly's TrueOptix 88. While Serly's people were assessing the damage to the catalog, they decided to pull TrueOptix from the Data Sea until they could determine if it had been infected. Prosteev Serly immediately brought a complaint before the Meme Cooperative blaming the Patels; but the evidence was thin, and the case quickly vanished like one of the visual phantasms that TrueOptix was designed to prevent.

The Patel Brothers were not known for playing nice.

Prosteev Serly's loss, however, became Natch's gain. Serly had channeling deals in place and packaging agreements to fulfill. Data agents scurried around the Data Sea to find a suitable replacement for the optical program, and located Natch's DeMirage 24.5. Within minutes, Natch's program had become the de facto standard for ocular hallucination management on the Data Sea.

The *pings* began sounding at 8:32 a.m. Shenandoah time and continued throughout the day. Eventually, the noise became so deafening,

Natch had to adjust the program to ping once every hundred sales. As the night wore on, the BizWorks administrative program slowed to pings every thousand sales, then every ten thousand. And still the pings kept coming.

Horvil was ecstatic. "Can I juggle a mean bio/logic programming bar or *what?*" he crowed.

"Beginner's luck," Jara corrected him with a smirk.

Natch shook his head. "Luck," he said, staring intensely at the Shenandoah cityscape, "had nothing to do with it."

3

THE PHOENIX PROJECT

(((16)))

Merri sat on Natch's chair-and-a-half and watched the fiefcorp master make frantic circles through the garden. When he started, he was treading on turf, but as their conversation absorbed more of his attention, he gradually strayed into the patch of daisies. Soon he was carelessly stepping on flower petals and tracking dirt onto the carpet.

"So in another eighteen months, it'll be . . ." Natch stopped and squinted, as if the future were a distant object hovering outside the window.

"May," replied Merri.

"It'll be May," continued Natch. "That's right. So if we extend your contract until then and your shares stay on target, then I expect they'll be worth—*this*. . . ." He waved his hand at the viewscreen, mutating the psychedelic Tope painting into a more prosaic spreadsheet. A sizable boldfaced number sat in the bottom-right corner of the screen. "And that's a conservative estimate. Now that we've hit number one on Primo's, it's only going to go up. So how's this figure suit you?"

Merri gave a slight nod, but Natch could see she had some reservations. Not over money, he was fairly certain; even in this economy, she was not likely to get a better compensation package anywhere else. No, it probably had something to do with the swirled black-and-white logo prominently displayed on her breast pocket, the insignia of a Creed Objectivv truthteller.

Natch gave the woman a long appraising stare while she read over the apprenticeship contract one more time. Merri might have been Jara's diametric opposite. Her large frame dwarfed Jara's, though it did not quite reach Horvil-sized proportions. She had blond features that spoke of Nordic ancestry and a demeanor both easy and reserved. Over the past six months, there had been times when Natch felt like slapping that pious look right off Merri's face—but for process' preservation, one could get only so angry at a woman who possessed such an encyclopedic knowledge of the bio/logics world.

"You're concerned about the workload," said a voice on the opposite side of the room. Merri turned to face Serr Vigal, who had been hovering quietly in the shadows like a spook. Natch hadn't been quite sure whether the neural programmer was even paying attention.

"Well, partly," conceded Merri with a sidelong glance at Natch. "But I'm also not sure how comfortable I feel being a channel manager. I was trained for bio/logic analysis, you know."

Natch faced the window and scowled. He was not about to give up such a precious asset as a channel manager who had taken the Objectivv truthtelling oath. Whatever the reality was, people believed that honest salespeople sold better products. "This is a small fiefcorp, Merri. Everyone gets to do a little bit of everything around here. Shit, you can even grab a pair of programming bars and take on some of Horvil's workload, for all I care."

Merri brightened and gave one of her typical placating smiles. *For a devotee of Creed Objectivv, she fakes her emotions pretty well*, Natch thought. "Would it be all right if I . . . thought about it for a few days?" asked the blond channel manager.

The entrepreneur shrugged. "Fine."

"Okay, then . . ." And with that, Merri cut the multi connection and returned her mind to a red square tile several hundred thousand kilometers away on Luna.

Natch gazed out into the gloom of the Shenandoah dusk. Dark clouds were assembling on the westward horizon and rattling their sabers, threatening a violent thunderstorm. In all probability, the Shenandoah L-PRACGs had already petitioned the Environmental Control Board to steer the worst of the storm clear of downtown using its geosynchron bots. But still, the clouds felt like a heavy-handed omen to Natch. Something was hiding in those clouds, some cruel and brutal creature with Natch's name roiling in its murky consciousness.

He shifted his attention to Serr Vigal. "We've had this discussion before," he said.

The neural programmer had sunk back into the shadows, invisible but for the occasional beard hairs glinting like flecks of silver. "It's common sense, Natch," he replied. "Now that you're constantly neck-and-neck with the Patels, there's a real danger of overworking your apprentices. I think you need to bring more people on board."

"I hired Merri."

"But she's not taking any of the workload off Horvil and Jara."

Natch knew his old mentor was correct, that eventually the two apprentices would snap under the strain of eighteen-hour days in the trenches fighting the Patel Brothers. They would get tired of the sorties in the middle of the night, the maneuvering for field position. The endless exchange of small-arms fire.

But as soon as business started pouring in, Horvil and Jara had forgotten all about their bewilderment and indignation surrounding the black code incident. Natch's interviews with Sen Sivv Sor and John Ridglee had spawned a drudge feeding frenzy, which in turn had produced a tidal wave of sales. Suddenly, important engineers were contacting Horvil for advice and dissecting his recursive functions as if they were ancient Sanskrit texts. And Jara, who was used to shuffling money between fiefcorp accounts to placate some creditors and put off others, was now trying to find places to invest the overflow.

"Horvil and Jara will be fine," mumbled Natch. "Oh, I know you're right, Vigal. I'll need to bring more people aboard at some point. It's just that I don't *trust* anyone else."

"Maybe you need to give those two a holiday," said Serr Vigal. "The fiefcorp is running pretty smoothly. There's no reason you can't slow down for a week or two."

Natch, his arms folded over his chest, turned to glare at the neural programmer. NiteFocus 50c allowed him to peer through the veil of shadow and see the concerned look on his mentor's face. "No," he said, "there *is* a reason."

"Ah, the message."

"Something's coming up, Vigal. I can feel something out there, coming up fast. A tidal wave. *Something*."

Natch nodded towards the viewscreen that was still displaying Merri's apprenticeship contract. He called up a message in its place and enlarged the type so it was readable from across the room.

Natch,

I would like to personally congratulate you on achieving number one in the Primo's bio/logic investment guide. Several members of my administrative staff are devoted users of your programs. Your sleep deprivation utilities, I'm afraid, are particularly popular around here.

As you may have heard, Creed Surina will be holding a cultural festival next week to celebrate what would have been Sheldon Surina's 400th birthday. We are looking for able bio/logic programmers such as yourself to contribute to a presentation on my ancestors' legacy to the world. I would be honored to have you as my guest for dinner at Andra Pradesh this Wednesday, November 23, to discuss the details.

Towards Perfection,

Margaret Surina
Master of the Surina Perfection Memecorp
Bodhisattva of Creed Surina

The letters hung on the screen before him, waiting for some gesture or flicker of the eyeballs to indicate which way Natch wanted to scroll. Finally, the fiefcorp master blinked hard and sent the missive away.

"I'm afraid I don't understand why you're so worried, Natch," said his guardian. "It looks like a perfectly normal invitation to me."

"It just doesn't *feel* right," said Natch. "I can't explain it. It's like . . ." *Like a vast collection of numbers that have some hidden kabbalistic*

*connection to one another. Like a constellation millions of light-years across, and
you're sitting in the middle trying to decipher what it looks like from a distance.*
"Let me ask you this, Vigal. Why invite me to dinner? It means that
Margaret doesn't want to see me in multi—she wants me to trek
halfway around the globe to talk to her in person. That seems awfully
formal for a first meeting. Does she think there's some security risk? Or
maybe she has a business proposition for me. You know the etiquette—
important business deals happen through personal meetings."

The neural programmer frowned. "Maybe you should just take this
at face value."

"*Face value*," Natch scoffed. "I never take *anything* at face value."

Vigal rose from his chair with a creaky sigh, then walked over and
clapped a virtual hand on his protégé's shoulder. "Perhaps you need to
get some rest, Natch." He gave the shoulder a gentle squeeze and then
stepped back, looking the young programmer up and down wistfully.
"Rest—that's advice I think I'm going to follow myself. Make sure you
ConfidentialWhisper me if you need anything."

Minutes later, Natch was alone.

●   ●   ●

The fiefcorp master prived himself to all incoming communication and
darkened the windows. Then he called up the invitation on the
viewscreen once more and crouched on his haunches in front of it.

Could this be some trick by the Patel Brothers? A punishment for
filching the lead on Primo's for those brief forty-seven minutes? He
verified the message's digital signature against the one in the public
directory, and the directory declared it authentic. The message had not
come from the hand of some Surina flunky either, but straight from the
bodhisattva herself. Signatures could be forged, of course, but it was a
fiendishly difficult task. Natch knew all the standard tricks for low-
level signature forgery, and this message used none of them.

He collapsed onto his sofa and instructed InfoGather 96a to find as much up-to-date information about Margaret Surina as possible. The program launched a volley of data agents onto the measureless ocean of information and began bouncing the results off its analysis engines, deducing connections, drawing conclusions, cooking up bite-sized summaries.

Seconds later, the viewscreen lit up with the image of a woman around Serr Vigal's age. The drudges described the heir to the Surina family mantle as a glamorous figure, but Natch could see little glamour in this nondescript woman. Margaret was neither tall nor short, neither heavy nor thin; she could have been one of those composite sketches of women compiled from a hundred different ethnicities. The plain gray pantsuit she wore belied her vaunted sense of fashion, and even her raven-black hair lay unostentatiously on her shoulders. If she did not have the prominent Surina family nose and her father's eyes, preternaturally large and shining with fierce intelligence, Natch would not have believed that this woman was the heiress to the world's largest programming fortune.

MARGARET SURINA (301–)

read the caption that floated next to the woman on the screen.

> The bodhisattva of Creed Surina and master of the Surina Perfection Memecorp, Margaret Surina is heiress to the Surina family fortune and the vast empire left her after the untimely death of her father Marcus. She lives in Andra Pradesh at the residence constructed in honor of her ancestor, Sheldon Surina, the father of bio/logics.

Natch skipped ahead to the section that detailed Margaret's business interests:

> Surina has been the subject of gossip and speculation over the past twenty years since she founded the memecorp that bears her name. To date, the company has released no products and purportedly receives

100% of its funding from Creed Surina. Partisans of the Surinas believe the memecorp is at work on another technological breakthrough on par with such previous family accomplishments as bio/logics and teleportation. Surina supporters have even given this undefined new technology a name: "The Phoenix Project." Detractors, however, suspect that no such project exists and that Margaret Surina is instead using her memecorp to funnel money into libertarian and pro-Islander political causes.

Natch leaned forward and tried to cajole InfoGather into providing him more about this mysterious Phoenix Project, but no tangible details were forthcoming. Pundits on the Data Sea had been scrutinizing Margaret's every move for years now, gossiping about every new visitor to her compound in Andra Pradesh in ancient India, seeking evidence of some übertechnology that might or might not exist. So far, they had come up empty.

The pressure on her must be enormous, Natch reflected. At Margaret's age, Sheldon Surina had already written his seminal paper, "Towards the Science of Bio/Logics and a New Direction for Humanity," the work that jolted the world out of its post-Revolt stupor and signaled the beginning of a new age. Sheldon's grandson Prengal Surina had already put forth the universal law of physics at this stage of his life. Even Margaret's father, the poor doomed Marcus, had become a worldwide icon and pioneer of teleportation by the time he was fifty. The public was growing restless. What would Margaret's contribution to the world of science be?

The entrepreneur remembered his days of infamy following the Shortest Initiation and grimaced. *Why does she need to make any contribution?* he thought. *What if she just wants to be left alone?*

Natch studied the image of Margaret Surina carefully. The photographer appeared to have taken Margaret by surprise; she seemed frozen in the act of turning towards the camera. But there were no surprises written in those unnaturally large blue eyes. Margaret's eyes showed a woman in complete control of her surroundings, a woman capable of swallowing life's surprises whole without the least bit of discomfort. Natch finally had to admit to himself that this woman had him intrigued.

And could this Phoenix Project be that thing just beyond the horizon that he had been waiting for his entire career? Was that why the very words tugged at his soul like a magnet?

He sent a terse reply to Margaret's invitation:

I would be honored to accept your invitation and make your acquaintance.

Towards Perfection,
Natch, Master of the Natch Personal Programming Fiefcorp

(((17)))

The city of Andra Pradesh had few municipal building codes. Tenement high-rises and office buildings hobnobbed with parks and shopping areas and even farmland, all jumbled together without regard to style or function. Andra Pradesh was a city that had rolled down from a mountaintop and sprouted haphazardly out of the wreckage.

On that mountaintop were the Surinas.

Natch saw the massive Surina compound as soon as he stepped off the tube. Even a kilometer away, it dominated the skyline. He could easily make out the austere buildings of the Gandhi University of Andra Pradesh where Sheldon Surina had taught and the absurd towers of the Surina family's private residence. Somewhere below his level of sight were the administrative offices of Creed Surina, the Surina Enterprise Facility, and the Surina Center for Historic Appreciation. Above them all, a lone spire jutted obscenely into the clouds from the middle of the compound. Natch had heard somewhere that this was the tallest structure built since the Reawakening. Down in the city below, dozens of buildings competed for the right to claim second place.

The tube could have deposited Natch right at the gates of the Surina compound, but he wanted the full effect of approaching it from a distance. *I've already wasted several hours on the tube*, he thought. *Why not a few more minutes on foot?*

Natch hustled through the crowded streets and tried to keep his mind blank. The people of Andra Pradesh rushed about at a frenetic pace as if galvanized by the presence of the Surinas in their midst. Conversations were louder, clothing more vivid. People of all colors, classes, and creeds seemed to blend in here, much like the buildings that surrounded them. L-PRACG security guards, street performers, vendors of exotic fruits and vegetables, businesspeople, assembly-line programmers, hoverbird traders and cargo haulers, rambunctious children: here in Andra Pradesh, distinctions blurred.

Finally, he reached the base of the mountain. A dozen guards stood before the gate wearing the green-and-blue uniforms of Creed Surina. Was it just a figment of Natch's imagination, or were they fingering the triggers of their dartguns with a little too much anxiety?

After a few minutes of identity checking, the guards waved Natch through the gate. Two grim-faced women in uniform motioned for him to follow them up the steep mountainside road to a courtyard large enough for a small army procession. They found their way to the Center for Historic Appreciation, a squat pentagonal building in the classic Greek style. It was a scientific museum of sorts, full of haphazardly arranged curio tables and marble statues of the Surina dynasty laid out in solemn, self-important poses. There was even a statue of Margaret as a child sitting rapturously at the feet of her father.

Security guards were everywhere, dartguns drawn and signaling to one another with choppy gestures that Natch could only assume was a form of battle language. The complex appeared to be devoid of visitors, however. Finally, the two guards led Natch down a long hallway and, without a word, deposited him at the door at its end. He opened the door, took a deep breath, and stepped inside.

Natch immediately found himself on a floating platform in a massive library. There was no sign of the exterior hallway; the door he had come through stood by itself with no visible means of support.

SeeNaRee, thought Natch with distaste.

The hexagonal platform was merely one of a thousand identical platforms Natch could see stretching off in every direction, each connected to its neighbors by narrow walkways, like beads on a string. Bookshelves lined four walls of each platform. He counted thirty-two treepaper books of equal size and weight filling each shelf, as if they were just a small part of an unimaginably vast encyclopedia. Natch looked around in vain for some sign of his host, for any human presence at all. After a few minutes, impatient, he reached for one of the leather-bound volumes and flopped it open on the large conference table in the platform's center.

FSLFJ WOPSF O SLJ!
Thwlk po sdl wopi fndvl fdqf poipwytpw, Wtlkd woir z pod. Lsdkf wienhf sdflglsksgd sldkjf? Wogih spapapa slgihd. Qqq! Qqq!

"Never read your Borges, did you?" came a voice behind him. Natch turned and found himself face-to-face with Margaret Surina.

Marcus Surina's daughter had aged quite a bit since that anonymous InfoGather image he had seen the other day. Natch wondered why she had not bothered to use bio/logics to conceal the wrinkles on her forehead, the slight stoop of her shoulders, the tinge of gray that permeated her once coal-black hair. Only Margaret's eyes remained intense and unblemished, as if they would remain brightly lit long after the rest of the flesh had withered away.

"Borges?" said Natch.

"Jorge Luis Borges," replied Margaret. "This library is his creation."

The name meant nothing to Natch, and a quick inquiry to the Meme Cooperative fiefcorp listings came up with no results. "Never heard of him," he said. "Is he a programmer?"

A smile descended onto Margaret's face as if from a great height. "He *was* a writer. From antiquity, from before the Autonomous Revolt. He talked about an infinite library with books that contained every possible combination of words and letters. What you were reading was just one of its countless permutations." She had a grating habit of enunciating every syllable of every word, even those that typically stayed silent or piggybacked on a neighboring phoneme. *Ev-e-ry poss-si-ble com-bin-nay-shun. Count-less per-me-yu-tay-shuns.*

Natch shook his head in annoyance and slammed the book shut. He enjoyed intellectual puzzles, but had little patience for artists. "So why are we here?"

"It's a new innovation that we recently installed in all the Surina conference rooms," said Margaret. "The room automatically gauges your mood and chooses an appropriate bit of SeeNaRee. We have thousands of varieties in our data banks, virtual environments for every occasion. This *is* a museum, after all." *Vir-tu-al en-vi-run-ments for every occ-ay-zhun.*

Natch leaned over the railing and saw only stairs and platforms without end. "*I* wasn't thinking about any library." He sniffed.

Margaret gave a coy smile as if sharing an inside joke. "Ah, this is an ongoing complaint," she said. "People say that the program doesn't always pick the moods and emotions that they expect. The programmer says we are not always aware of what is going on in our subconscious mind. Personally, *I* find that to be a rather charming and unexpected benefit. However, if you prefer something more traditional . . ." With a flick of her wrist, the bodhisattva banished the library to oblivion, to be replaced by a featureless dining room with angular furniture.

Natch felt a surge of irritation rise inside of him, and quickly masked it with a PokerFace 83.4b program. Was Margaret trying to test the limits of his patience, or was this just more paranoia?

"Perhaps you would like a tour of the facilities before we dine," said the bodhisattva.

• • •

When they reached the end of the hallway, Natch realized that he and Margaret were not alone. He took a quick glimpse over his shoulder and discovered that they were being shadowed by an imposing hulk of a man with enormous biceps and a pale blond ponytail slung over one shoulder.

"The atrium of the Surina Center for Historic Appreciation," said Margaret as they walked into a vast domed space. "I don't know whether you got a chance to see it when you came in." The room was littered with bland statues celebrating the great pioneers of science: Aloretus Monk, Tobi Jae Witt, Albert Einstein, Isaac Newton. Sheldon Surina had a prominent place in the canon, of course, as did his protégé and sometime rival Henry Osterman. "We try to ease visitors in to the deeper exhibits with something gentle on the eyes," she said, though there were no visitors around to illustrate her point. She motioned at the hallways behind each scientist, all clearly labeled with his or her respective achievement: Relativity Hall. Subaether Court. Gravity Way.

Natch gave a polite nod. The Surinas' inane tourist attractions did not interest him, not when he had to figure out the mystery of this towering figure with the blond ponytail. The man stayed half a dozen paces behind them like a bodyguard might, and gestured to the sentries lurking at every corner using a hand weighed down with an excessive number of gold rings. But if he were part of the security staff, wouldn't he be wearing the standard green-and-blue Surina livery instead of loose tan breeches and an open-necked shirt?

Then the three of them stepped out of the Center for Historic Appreciation into the central courtyard, and Natch caught sight of a thin copper collar suspended around the man's neck. An Islander!

Natch wondered how he could have missed the other signs: the uneven muscles that sprouted from manual labor instead of OCHRE stimulation, the ruddy complexion from too much time in the sun, the small scars running up and down his arms. Certainly, Margaret couldn't be depending on this man for physical protection. What good were those tree trunk-sized arms without bio/logics?

Who was this man, and why was he staring so intently at Natch?

The tour continued for most of the next hour. They made their way through the halls of the Gandhi University and saw the room where Sheldon Surina had lectured for most of his life. Natch peered through the windows of the Creed Surina auditorium and saw the pulpits where teachers and minor bodhisattvas preached the gospel of scientific innovation. He received cursory introductions to a few distant cousins of Margaret's who appeared to be the only civilians wandering the halls. After twenty more minutes of this, Natch grew increasingly bored. Either Margaret had not inherited her father's fabled magnetism, or she was storing up her energy for more important performances.

The Islander, too, appeared to have lost interest in Margaret's spiel. Every time Natch turned around, he found the big man staring at him with two brawny arms tucked in his pockets like siloed missiles. The stare contained neither malice nor menace. If Natch had to choose a word to describe his attitude, it would be *skeptical*.

A thought occurred to him. Was this whole lap around the Surina compound just an excuse for the Islander to check him out?

As they made their way back to the Center for Historic Appreciation, Natch decided to subject the Islander to a test of his own. He focused all his attention on the Revelation Spire—as the tall protruding spike atop the Surina residence was called—and then pretended to lose his footing. The fiefcorp master would have bet his weight in gold that he would have crashed into Margaret before the Islander could stop him. But in the space of a heartbeat, the Islander lashed out from his rearguard position and gripped Natch firmly at the base of his rib cage. The entrepreneur could feel the rings on the big man's fingers digging into his flesh.

Natch met the Islander's stare, and for a split second he could see straight through the man's defenses. He saw a look of concern for Margaret's safety that went far beyond any expression a bodyguard would have displayed. *This is personal for him*, thought Natch. *This man is no mercenary.*

The husky Islander set Natch back on his feet as he would a toy soldier. For the first time, Natch noticed that the man was about the same age as Margaret. The Islander let a sly grin creep into his countenance. He saw right through Natch's ploy, but instead of being angry, he seemed to appreciate Natch's resourcefulness.

Margaret did not even notice the interruption. The two men exchanged no words as they followed her into the Center for Historic Appreciation and back to the library room, now decorated with a single functional dining table.

Natch made awkward small talk with Margaret as they grazed on authentic Indian cuisine. Curry and cumin danced on the end of his tongue, and he soon found himself settling into a mellow post-vindaloo stupor. Natch was ready to concede to Vigal that his suspicions had been unfounded, that Margaret really just wanted his participation in this upcoming four hundredth birthday celebration for Sheldon Surina. The Islander popped in and out of the room several times, eating nothing. Natch was no closer to figuring out the man's place in Margaret's retinue, but this was a mystery he could solve another time. For now, Natch wanted desperately to draw the dinner to a close and get back to Shenandoah, where his bio/logic programming bars were waiting.

And then, after the dishes quietly slid into a compartment in a back wall, Margaret leaned forward and pressed her fingertips together. "You are probably wondering why I invited you here," she said.

Natch nodded.

"You are here," said Margaret, "because Len Borda is planning to have me killed next week."

• • •

The atmosphere became deathly quiet as Natch tried to think of something pertinent to say. Margaret's eyes suddenly glared at him like spotlights. The Islander stood by the door with the intensity of a coiled snake, looking as if he might pounce at any moment. *That explains why all those guards are roaming around with itchy trigger fingers.*

"So the Defense and Wellness Council is trying to kill you," said Natch, affecting nonchalance. "What does that have to do with *me?*"

Margaret drummed her fingers together. "Sheldon Surina used to say that we are all connected in a fundamental—"

"Don't patronize me," Natch snapped. The bodhisattva gave an exaggerated blink of shock, and couldn't resist a sidelong glance at the equally perplexed Islander standing in the doorway. Natch pressed on. "So Len Borda is going to kill you. That's wonderful. Why should *I* care? If you're so worried, go send a message to Sen Sivv Sor or John Ridglee. I'm sure they'd love to spread the news all over the Data Sea. But me—I've got a business to think about. I don't have *time* for politics."

Margaret's face toyed momentarily with outrage, ventured into amusement, and finally settled on weary fortitude. She laid her palms flat on the table and leaned forward. "They tell me that the only things you care about are money and power," she said. "Well then . . . let me translate this into language you can understand. *I am about to present you with an opportunity for more money and more power than you can possibly imagine.* Number one on Primo's is a child's fantasy by comparison. You can either hear me out, or leave now and go back to fighting for scraps on Primo's. It is *your* choice."

Natch could have chosen to be insulted at the way this woman had casually belittled everything he had fought for since the Shortest Initiation. Sharp retorts hovered on the tip of his tongue. But then Natch remembered how easily he had fallen for the bait that the capitalman Figaro Fi had laid out for him all those years ago. *I won't be manipulated,* he repeated to himself over and over like a mantra. Natch looked at the Islander, who stood, amused, struggling to suppress his laughter. *He* knew, at least, that Natch had proven his point: Margaret's wealth and pedigree would not intimidate him. So instead of shouting, the fiefcorp master activated a relaxation program called OceanBreez 38 and waited a few seconds for the bio/logic code to suffuse his body with calm.

"I'm listening," he said at length.

The bodhisattva spread out her hands in a gesture of peace. "Let us start at the beginning," she began. "I am guessing that you were born sometime in the 320s—"

"Three thirty-one," said Natch.

Margaret nodded. "Three thirty-one, then. You know what kind of position the economy was in at that time. My father's death and the collapse of TeleCo left the bio/logics industry in ruins and millions of programmers in the diss. The Economic Plunge of the 310s, they called it, though it lasted longer than that. People in the orbital colonies were starving for the first time since the Autonomous Revolt. Not a good period for business. Not a good period for *anybody*.

"Of course, by the late 320s, things were already turning around. High Executive Borda had started handing out enormous defense contracts to the fiefcorps, hoping the credits would funnel down to the masses. For ten years, the Council gave subsidies to just about anyone who asked—including me."

Natch's eyes were beginning to glaze over. According to the legends, Sheldon Surina had also been fond of historical digressions. *Did I take the tube halfway across the globe and lose an entire day in MindSpace for a civics lesson?* "So Len Borda gave you money."

"Yes," she continued. "I approached the Council with blueprints for a new set of memory enhancement programs. Programs to drastically extend the potential of the human brain, based on the technology my father left behind at his death. I painted Borda a picture of Council officers with total recall and soldiers who could memorize the tiniest details of a battlefield. He was impressed."

The fiefcorp master frowned. "I don't understand," he interrupted. "Why did *you* of all people need Council credits?"

Margaret gave a wry smile, and her face clouded up momentarily with a far-off look. Then she stood, shook off the gloom, and fetched two tiny cups of Turkish coffee from the access panel in the wall. "Natch, my father might have been a scientific visionary, but he was never a prudent businessman." She deposited one of the cups on the table in front of Natch. "Yes, he made breakthroughs in teleportation technology, but he never figured out a way to pay for them. Let us just say that TeleCo was not the only organization Marcus Surina left on the brink of bankruptcy when he died."

Natch sipped the bittersweet brew from the delftware cup and thought about his mother holed up in the towers of Old Chicago. He felt a brief surge of anger, but batted it away. "So Borda anted up," he said.

"Yes. The Surina Perfection Memecorp received one of the largest appropriations of the entire Economic Plunge. You see, it was a win-win situation. We desperately needed financial stability, and the public desperately needed confidence in the future, in their governments. And who could provide a better hope for tomorrow than the Surinas?"

Natch listened carefully but could find no trace of irony in her voice.

"So everyone got what they wanted," she continued. "We got the funding we needed to turn ourselves around. Borda got a shining example of prosperity to show off. And the economy recovered."

"Which leads us to today."

"We have not been idle all this time. After trying its hand at a variety of projects, the Surina Perfection Memecorp has spent the last sixteen years in research and development. And now Len Borda is about to find out exactly what he paid for all those years ago." The bodhisattva's voice crackled slightly at the end of her sentence. An expression of fear? Of regret?

"The Phoenix Project," Natch said.

Margaret rolled her eyes and gave a knowing look to the Islander, who responded with a smile rich in irony. "I *despise* that name. Some drudge coined the term. It wasn't supposed to be so secretive. We really *did* start out with memory enhancers. We never intended to provoke a twenty-year guessing game on the Data Sea."

"Okay," said Natch, shifting uncomfortably in his seat. "So what's this big invention, then? Not memory enhancers, I take it."

"No. Not really. It's a bio/logic program. But much more than just a bio/logic program."

"You're going to have to be more specific than that."

Margaret remained maddeningly calm. She blew on her coffee and watched the wisps of steam disperse around the room. Her eyes were a lake of measureless depth. "I can't. Not yet."

The mounting tension was too much for Natch. He let out an irritated puff and threw his hands in the air. "So we're back to the original question. What do you want from *me*?"

"I want you to license my technology," said Margaret.

• • •

Nobody spoke for several moments. Natch bounced his gaze back and forth between Margaret and her silent companion, wondering if somehow the Patel Brothers were behind this, if they had conned Margaret into diverting him here while they solidified their number one position on Primo's. The Islander looked Natch up and down as if taking detailed measurements.

"Let me get this straight," said Natch. "You're asking me to license some new product without telling me what it is? And if that's not enough, the Defense and Wellness Council is willing to kill you to keep the whole project quiet? Well, forget it. I don't want anything to do with this. What makes you think I want Len Borda coming after *me*?"

The bodhisattva's demeanor softened, though whether it was an expression of sympathy or merely a change of tactics Natch could not tell. "Let me ask you a question, Natch. What's the quickest way to neutralize a poison?"

Natch thought for a moment. "Dilute it," he said.

"Precisely. Dump any poison into a large enough ocean, and its effects are nullified."

"Okay, I see what you're driving at."

"The Defense and Wellness Council thinks my technology is a poison. *My* technology, Natch—my life's work, which I've spent sixteen years building." Margaret abruptly looped a bony finger through the handle of the coffee cup and raised it into the air. "But pour this poison into the largest ocean of all—the Data Sea—and it becomes part of the ocean itself. It becomes inert. More importantly, *once you release the poison, it cannot be bottled up again.*" She raised the cup to her lips and drank it to the dregs in one angry gulp.

Natch was beginning to get the impression he was not here for a business opportunity so much as an audition. He remembered all the scenes he had set up throughout the years: his confrontations with Brone, his challenges to Captain Bolbund, his ascent to the top of Primo's. Margaret Surina had prepared a script, and she had a part for him to play.

He once again shook off the stifling air, the slowly tightening constriction around his throat. "There's something you're not telling me," he said. "If you want to nullify the poison, go ahead and dump the specs on the Data Sea right now and get it over with. Why bother setting up a licensing agreement with a fiefcorp?"

The bodhisattva nodded pensively. "It's not that simple. This is a complex project. If this program fails to capture the public's imagination, then the Council can just swoop in and take control without a single protest. Besides, the Phoenix code *is* dangerous code, if it's not handled properly. If we just floated the specs out onto the Data Sea, who knows what could happen? I absolutely *refuse* to have blood on my hands." Margaret held her hands in front of her face and stared at them as if they were alien artifacts. "No, this situation has to be handled with the utmost precision. Which is why *you're* here, Natch.

"I need a licensee who can do two things. First, he needs to generate enough ripples on the Data Sea to make the Council stay its hand until I unveil the technology. And then he needs to quickly develop a workable prototype to show the world this technology is real."

"Wait a minute," cried Natch, slicing his hand through the air. "You've spent *sixteen years* building this fucking thing, and you don't even have a workable prototype?"

Margaret was unfazed. "I have many, but none I trust to act flawlessly in front of billions of people. The Council has forced my hand too early."

"All right, fine. So when are you unveiling the Phoenix Project?"

"The end of next week, at the cultural festival honoring Sheldon Surina's four hundredth birthday. Until then, all we need is a little bit of uncertainty. You're an outsider, Natch, and outsiders bring complications. Loose ends. The more Borda fears I have let others in on the Phoenix Project, the more he will hesitate to act."

Natch set his chin on his fist in consternation. He had learned many years ago never to get locked into a situation without an elaborate and many-layered plan for escape. Then he thought of Margaret's words: *More money and more power than you can possibly imagine.* What were money and power? Mere words, vowels and consonants, scrapings of tongue on tooth. But what they represented: open doors. A way out. A way *up*.

"So why me?" he said at length.

"Because you are the best," replied Margaret without hesitation. "Because you are young and hungry. Because you work quickly and demand absolute perfection from your team. Because this enterprise requires someone with a flair for . . . showmanship." She waved her hand and summoned a message in holographic letters on the table. "I need the person who can accomplish *this*."

Natch scanned the letters and promptly switched his PokerFace program back on.

PLEASE PROTECT YOUR HOLDINGS

The Vault has detected a DNA-assisted decryption attack directed at your account. Your holdings have not been compromised, but it is advised that you periodically check the security of your Vault account. This advisory has been automatically routed to the custodian of records for your L-PRACG and, depending on your L-PRACG's policies, may also be forwarded to the Defense and Wellness Council.

Natch could have recited the words from memory, but he pretended to read them over two or three times. Obviously, blackmail was not her objective, or Natch would have been greeted at the compound gates by representatives of the Meme Cooperative. "It's a warning from the Vault," he said simply.

The bodhisattva let it go, banishing the missive into the aether. She seemed to be retreating into her shell. Again, Natch caught the hollow look of fear in Margaret's eyes, and the intimate concern radiating from the Islander standing in the doorway.

"You need to understand something," said Natch abruptly. "Investing in a new technology isn't cheap. I'll need to bring on new employees, conduct research. Buy more equipment. Train my people, find more channelers." He tallied up each item with his fingers while he spoke. "All that takes money. Just because my fiefcorp made number one on Primo's doesn't mean we're number one in *sales*. I don't have that many credits lying around—especially if you expect me to get involved in a new project that isn't going to bring in any money for a long time."

Margaret sighed. "If you are suggesting Surina investment," she said, "I can't funnel money to you through any of our regular channels—not quickly, at any rate. It's too risky, and we can't have anyone suspect that I've put you up to this. For now, you must be a completely independent third party in these negotiations." The bodhisattva glanced over her shoulder at the blond man standing in the doorway, and suddenly Natch wondered if he was there to keep others out or to keep Natch in. "There is an entirely different dance I have to perform here with all the different Surina organizations. Let us just say that some here do not appreciate radical moves."

"So you expect me to hit the ground running with no money, and put together a perfect prototype in a couple of weeks."

"Within *a* week, yes. But I'm not worried, Natch. If I had the slightest doubt you could find the money to do this, you wouldn't be here."

Natch shook his head and snorted in amusement. "I don't understand what you're trying to accomplish."

The descendant of Sheldon Surina leaned forward and touched her lips to her clasped fingers. "Things were not supposed to turn out this way," she said quietly. "You are the contingency plan."

Natch stood up, put his palms flat on the table, and leaned forward with a smoldering stare. "Let's get one thing clear," he rasped. "I am *not* your contingency plan. *If* I get involved in this, it'll be for my *own* reasons. Because you claim I can make a lot of money, and I believe you. If things get too dangerous—for *me*—or if I think the credits aren't worth the risk, then I'll pull out of this whole thing without a second thought and leave you stranded. I'll be a dead man before I get involved in a scheme like this to save *your* hide from the Defense and Wellness Council." He turned to face the burly Islander, as if to say, *That goes for you too.*

Margaret had no reaction. She was beyond affectation right now. "I will forward to you what little information I can at this point," she said in a hoarse monotone.

The entrepreneur nodded and fired another quick glance at the Islander. The big man was smiling openly now. Whatever test he and Margaret had just administered, Natch had passed it with panache.

(((18)))

"Why don't you ask Horvil?" said Serr Vigal.

Natch shook his head. "He's got plenty of credits, but there's no way he can move that kind of money without his Aunt Berilla finding out about it. And she'd rather slice off her own arm than invest in *me*."

"Another fiefcorp, then. Pierre Loget. Or Lucas Sentinel."

"Sentinel?" spat the fiefcorp master, as if the name were a curse word in a foreign tongue. "Are you kidding? He's still furious at Jara. And don't forget that when I pushed the Patel Brothers down to the number two spot on Primo's, Sentinel's company fell to number three. Loget doesn't like me any better."

"What about that financier you met with all those years ago? He said he liked you, didn't he?"

"Figaro Fi? He joined the Prepared a year and a half ago, Vigal. He's probably dead by now."

Serr Vigal pursed his lips and made a noise of dismissal. *Thppt.* He got slowly to his feet and ambled over to the window, which was showing some beachside resort full of bronzed children laughing and throwing sand at one another. A welcome change from the dreary November Omaha rain. "I can help you a little bit, of course," said the neural programmer. "The memecorp has some extra equipment lying around that I can lend you. But I just don't have the kind of money you're talking about."

"Which leaves me back where I started," said Natch with disgust. "The capitalmen." He kicked at a tuft of carpet and scowled at the frolicking children through the window. No self-respecting capitalman would lend him such a large sum of money for a project he couldn't even define. They wouldn't care that he ran the number two company on Primo's, or that he was working on Margaret Surina's fabled

Phoenix Project—they would just ask to see the specs. Natch couldn't blame them. Margaret had no track record to boast of, no prior business successes to point to. All she had was the Surina family reputation. And that reputation hadn't helped anyone recoup their losses from TeleCo, had it?

"This is my worst nightmare, Vigal," Natch moaned. He waved his hand at the screen and changed the display right under Serr Vigal's nose. His guardian blinked in mild surprise as the beach made way for the trading pit of some Melbourne financial exchange. "The biggest opportunity of my life, and I can't make it happen. Nobody will invest until Margaret unveils the technology at the end of next week. But then it'll be too late. I won't have the resources to get this prototype up and running in time."

Serr Vigal rubbed his goatee quietly for a few minutes, deep in thought. "I wonder what this Phoenix Project really is."

"Margaret said she started out with memory enhancers. You know neural programming, Vigal—where could she go from there?"

"In sixteen years? Just about anywhere."

"Well, it has to be a neurological program, doesn't it? She must have looked at my background—she must know I apprenticed with you. She must know the bulk of our catalog is devoted to optics and mental processes. DeMirage 54, EyeMorph 66a, Mento Calc-U-Later 93.9, NiteFocus 50c—I could go on and on. Why else would she come to me?"

"Why indeed?" said Vigal. "There are hundreds of fiefcorps and memecorps out there capable of handling a project like this. And most of them have more experience in this business than you, not to mention greater resources."

"She said she wanted someone with *a flair for showmanship.*"

"And do you believe her?"

"Stop being so . . . so *elliptical.* If you think something's going on here, then just come right out and say it."

Vigal leaned against the viewscreen, screwing up his face with courage. "I don't *think* anything," he muttered. "I simply fear."

"And what do you fear?"

"I fear that Margaret has picked you for this enterprise because she thinks she can manipulate you." The neural programmer took a long, sad look at the traders tussling with one another on the Melbourne exchange floor. Undoubtedly, most of them were only multi projections, but that did not make the scene any less violent or chaotic to behold.

Natch felt the old alienation swooping down on him and constricting his lungs. He snarled angrily, poking a virtual finger into his guardian's chest. "And so what if she thinks she can manipulate me? That doesn't change anything. I've still got to find a way to get into the Phoenix Project, or I'll never get out of this . . . this *horse* race on Primo's."

"And do you know that Margaret's Phoenix Project is a panacea for your problems? I worry that you're throwing everything aside for some vague business venture when you don't even know what it is."

"No. The Phoenix Project is it. This is the answer. This is what I've been searching for. I *know* it; I can feel it with every cell in my body. You don't think I can just ignore an opportunity like this, do you?"

Vigal smiled wanly. "That is a decision only *you* can make, Natch."

• • •

Merri looked as if she had been in her foyer for hours awaiting Natch's arrival. He frowned briefly. There were few things Natch detested more than someone who was too eager to please. *A good employee says no more often than yes*, the great Lucco Primo had once claimed.

"Towards Perfection, Natch," she said softly.

"Perfection," replied Natch. "Ready?"

"Yes, but . . ." Merri flinched, as if raising an objection were the most difficult task in the world. "I was hoping you could shed some light on the role you want me to play today."

Natch checked the Shenandoah central time service. They had almost twenty minutes before the potential investors arrived at the Surina Enterprise Facility. He walked past the channel manager and into her living room, cursing the multi network's insistence on reproducing the wobbly effects of imperfect gravity control. "People don't trust me," Natch said bitterly, taking a seat on a round ottoman covered with a delicate floral pattern. "I've hit number one on Primo's, I've proven myself time and time again, but still nobody worth talking to will do business with me. I need your credibility, Merri."

Merri absorbed all this with an air of mystification. "My credibility?"

"When people look at me, they still see the Shortest Initiation. They look at Horvil and see . . . well, we've been working together so long, they see *me*. And Jara made some powerful enemies when she was on her own. We're all tainted goods, Merri. But you . . . Nobody has said a bad word about you on the Data Sea since you graduated from the hive. You've got an honest reputation."

The blond woman shifted uncomfortably from one foot to the other. "So you're saying you want me there because of *this*." She nodded at the swirled black-and-white pin displayed prominently on her jacket breast pocket.

"Well, of *course* it helps that you're an Objectivv," said Natch. "Come on, Merri, you can put two and two together. We're going to a fundraising pitch. You've taken a pledge not to lie."

Merri wrinkled her nose in disappointment. "It's not quite that simple."

Natch shrugged. He had always disdained the creeds and their arbitrary ethical systems—the Surinas with their slavish devotion to science, the Élanners with their hypocritical advocacy for the poor, the Thasselians with their shallow and pointless worship of business. But he reserved a special irritation for the Objectivvs. Natch could not fathom why the public tolerated, even revered, the creed's disciples. The way they babbled about "the search for objective truth" and dissected every utterance of that cryptic old hermit known as the Bodhisattva made Natch cringe.

"We can discuss philosophy some other time," said the fiefcorp master, rising from the ottoman and nodding pointedly at the red square tile in the hallway. "Right now we've got work to do. Get ready to follow my beacon."

"So," stammered Merri, "what do you want me to *do?*"

"I don't know," said Natch indifferently. "Keep quiet. Act ethical."

He didn't wait for Merri's next disapproving grimace. Instead, Natch closed his eyes, focused on the beaker of concentrated entropy that was Andra Pradesh, and let the cold *frisson* of multivoid envelop him. Seconds later, he stood at the gates of the Surina compound, staring up at the Revelation Spire. Natch stretched his mind out to the multi network and activated a beacon to tag his spatial coordinates for Merri to follow.

She needn't have worried about getting separated from her master. The blue-and-green-clad security officers kept the two visitors waiting at the compound gates for ten minutes. The Surina guards were busy eyeing a group of white-robed Defense and Wellness Council officers across the way who seemed to have nothing better to do than pace at the bottom of the mountain and polish the barrels of their dartguns. Merri shuddered with relief when she and Natch were finally escorted into the safety of the Surina compound.

The Enterprise Facility was an impressive location for a fundraising pitch: twelve stories of blue stretched stone cantilevered off the side of a mountain in defiance of the natural laws of gravity. Merri followed him silently through the throngs of suits up to a room on the ninth floor. A room blissfully free of irritating SeeNaRee. They entered to find eight capitalmen already seated at the semicircular conference table. Natch consulted the time and noted with satisfaction that he was exactly twelve minutes late, which was three minutes earlier than he had planned.

"Towards Perfection," he said brightly, moving to the focal point of the table. The five men and three women returned his greeting with varying degrees of politeness and curiosity. Merri stood respectfully to one side with her hands clasped behind her back, her Creed Objectivv emblem on prominent display, waiting for some signal from her fiefcorp master.

"Let's not waste any time," announced the fiefcorp master, gesturing to the white open space on the wall behind him. An itemized list of business expenses appeared in blocky fixed-width characters. Natch paused to let the capitalmen absorb his list. As expected, their eyes uniformly zeroed in on the big-ticket items at the bottom: ten additional bio/logic programmers and engineers, fifteen channelers, office and meeting space, bio/logic programming equipment, marketing expenses. The total figure spelled out in the bottom right corner was an eyebrow-raising sum. "This is what I need by the end of the week," he declared. "Are there any questions?"

Eight pairs of eyes—nine, counting Merri's—gaped dumbly at the entrepreneur, waiting for some elaboration. But Natch simply stood there and gazed around the room with an intense stare. He looked as if he were preparing to either cut his multi connection or march around the table slicing off heads.

Finally, one of the capitalmen raised her hand timidly. Merri sent an inquiry to the public directory and discovered she was the investment manager for a libertarian L-PRACG and no stranger to fundraising pitches. "Exactly what is all this *for?*" she said with an air of bemusement.

Natch turned his unblinking eyes upon her. "For development of Margaret Surina's Phoenix Project, which I am licensing."

The investors gawked at the entrepreneur as if he had just offered to sell them a set of dragon's teeth. The mythical Phoenix Project, the boondoggle to end all boondoggles. Margaret's Folly. Natch could practically hear his audience's frantic ConfidentialWhisper conversations, their frenzied queries to the Data Sea.

"The Phoenix Project?" continued the capitalman in disbelief. "Are you serious?"

"Dead serious," replied Natch.

"What *is* it?"

"You'll have to wait and see."

A sense of shock crusted over their fury at being lured out to India for such a ludicrous presentation. Merri was surprised to see that Natch had been correct about her ties to Creed Objectivv; the pin on her breast pocket might have been the only thing preventing the capitalmen from vanishing in disgust. But even that would only keep the outrage from boiling over for so long. The capitalmen began hurling questions at him in rapid-fire succession, which Natch answered brusquely and without hesitation.

"What *can* you tell us?"

"I can tell you that if you invest in me, you'll make more money than you've ever dreamed of."

"How much?"

"The sky's the limit."

"What is this Phoenix Project anyway? Is it a bio/logic program? Something you're going to launch on the Data Sea next week?"

"The Phoenix Project is a bio/logic program, but it's much *more* than just a bio/logic program. No launch schedules have been decided on yet."

"Don't you have any specs you can show us? Technical diagrams? Projections? *Anything?*"

"No."

"How do we know we can *trust* you? How do we know you're not just making this all up?"

"If you don't trust me, don't invest."

By the time Natch wrapped up the discussion a scant fifteen minutes after it had begun, Merri's face had turned to stone. She asked no questions and did not react at all when her master said his good-byes and cut his multi connection. Merri cut her own connection and walked out to the foyer of her apartment, expecting Natch to await her arrival there. But the apartment was empty.

She found him in his own flat in Shenandoah. Natch was already at the window fiddling with a series of bio/logic price graphs as if nothing had happened. He seemed unaware of Merri's presence until she cleared her throat two minutes later. "You should catch up on your work while you can," he said gruffly. "We've got another one of these in an hour and a half, and then a third one late tonight."

The channel manager nervously ran her fingers through her milky hair. "Are you really planning to license a bio/logic program from Margaret Surina?"

"I'm definitely *planning* to," replied Natch. "I'd give sixty-forty odds right now that it'll actually happen."

"And do . . . do you really think any of those capitalmen are going to invest in you?"

"No."

Merri blanched. "No?"

The fiefcorp master turned to his apprentice with an impatient mien, like a hoverbird engineer trying to teach a child how to construct a paper airplane. "Listen, Merri—I don't expect any of *those* people to put up a single credit. I'm not going to get any money out of the people we talk to tonight either. That's not what we're doing."

"So . . ."

"So what *are* we doing? We're stirring the pot. We're creating noise. The people I invited to these fundraising meetings aren't the high rollers; they're the ones who like to gossip. By the end of the day, I guarantee you the people I *really* want to hear from will have heard the words *Natch*, *Margaret Surina*, and *Phoenix Project* in the same sentence. Listen, you can't just approach investors and ask them to put up money for this sort of thing. Anyone who's willing to take a risk like this is going to contact me privately and insist on complete secrecy. Not only that, but they have to be convinced that investing in the Phoenix Project is *their* idea."

Merri nodded politely though she understood nothing, and left Natch to his bio/logic price graphs.

• • •

Rumors about Natch's investor meeting quickly percolated through the Data Sea. Most of the comments were laced with the standard pejoratives Natch had seen attached to his name since childhood: *cocky, arrogant, insane.* He didn't mind. People could insult him to their hearts' content, but now that he had the Primo's title under his belt, they could no longer dismiss him so easily.

The second and third investor groups were better prepared and had more penetrating questions, but Natch would not crack. He kept a cloud of mystery over the entire project; if anything, he became even vaguer with his answers. *What could I possibly reveal to these people anyway?* he thought. *I don't know much more than they do.* As for Merri, she seemed to grow more comfortable with her silent performance the longer the night wore on, now that she had convinced herself that Natch was not actively deceiving anyone.

At seven o'clock that evening, word leaked on the Data Sea that Natch was scoping out investors for a new Surina technology that just might be the legendary Phoenix Project. Twenty minutes later, John Ridglee wrangled a terse *no comment* out of the Creed Surina spokesperson.

An admission or a denial from the Surinas would have been news. Refusal to comment was *big* news.

By ten o'clock Shenandoah time, the avalanche of messages had begun. It was mostly the same drivel that had tumbled Natch's way after hitting number one on Primo's a few weeks before. L-PRACG-sanctioned advertisements for financial software. Pleadings for donations to this or that cause. Servile requests from old business associates who had once griped about how Natch had ruined them. Greetings from long-lost hivemates whose names he had never cared to learn in the first place. Buried in the rubbish were a few legitimate queries from anonymous capitalmen, none of which led anywhere.

Horvil and Jara began shotgunning messages, ConfidentialWhispers, and multi requests to Natch by the dozens trying to figure out what was going on. Natch replied calmly that he would explain everything tomorrow night. Then he prived himself to all of their incoming communications and waited.

The Patel Brothers launched a handful of product upgrades just before midnight, further solidifying their number one position on Primo's. Pierre Loget's PulCorp made a surprising leap to second place, bumping Natch down to number three and Sentinel to number four.

And then, at 3:30 in the morning, as Natch was making yet another circuit around the balcony and glaring at the music that wafted up faintly from Shenandoah's entertainment quarters, the message he had been waiting for arrived. Natch had not known what shape or form it would take, but he knew the instant he opened the message that he had found his investor.

> *Time is luxury. Action is currency.*
> —Kordez Thassel

You are cordially invited to breakfast with the bodhisattva of Creed Thassel today, the 25th of November, at 7:45 a.m. Omaha time, in the resplendent Kordez Thassel Complex in the northern reaches of the Twin Cities Megalopolis to discuss mutually beneficial business opportunities.

Natch traced the message signature to a standard administrative account at Creed Thassel. He barely even paused before replying in the affirmative.

Natch lobbed an InfoGather request onto the Data Sea while flipping through his wardrobe for an appropriate suit, then had the results read aloud to him while he dressed.

The creed had been founded almost a hundred years before by Kordez Thassel, a libertarian philosopher and financier whose only qualification to lead a popular movement was that he had failed at everything else. Somehow, his teachings about the virtues of selfishness had earned him a following in the new breed of fiefcorp power brokers. Then he disappeared from view and left public relations in the hands of anonymous creed spin doctors. For years, Creed Thassel worked diligently to protect its mysteries, going so far as to swear its devotees to secrecy and refusing all but the most cursory participation in the Creeds Coalition. Whispers spoke of blood rites, oaths of fealty, and a mythical master program built by renegade coders.

And then the young drudge Sen Sivv Sor published the exposé that made his reputation. Sor's undercover reporting revealed that the blood rites were nothing but parlor tricks, the oaths of fealty were mere confidence schemes, and the mythical master program did not exist. Thasselian membership dwindled, but the core devotees remained. Soon enough, everyone forgot about the scandal, and Creed Thassel abandoned its hokey mystic aura for a more prosaic philosophy of individualism. Membership rolls remained secret, but few cared to pry anymore.

A creed of fools, thought Natch as he walked the early-morning streets of Shenandoah, bound for the hoverbird terminals. *But fools who have no love for Creed Surina or the Council.* Vigal's words from the previous day rang in his ears: *I fear that Margaret has picked you for this enterprise because she thinks she can manipulate you.* Natch's blood curdled at the thought of being someone's pawn, and he felt like throttling his guardian for even suggesting it. Nevertheless, he knew it couldn't hurt to have a third party on his side.

● ● ●

The Thasselians' invitation arrived too late for Natch to take the tube, his preferred mode of travel. So instead, he hopped aboard one of the hundreds of hoverbirds that ferried passengers across the continent every hour. His flight from Shenandoah to the Twin Cities was smooth and without incident.

Natch found the Kordez Thassel Complex to be one of the ugliest human constructions he had ever seen. A series of squat, functional buildings skulking among the lowlands, half hidden in the chill November mist. He followed a narrow bridge from the hoverbird terminal over the complex's surrounding moat and into the Thasselian headquarters. The inside was no better. Hallways stood at odd angles to one another amidst sloping ceilings and crooked doorways; Natch doubted there was a pair of perpendicular lines anywhere in the place. He knew very little about architecture, but he imagined it took a lot of money and patience to construct such deliberate lopsidedness.

Even at this early hour, hundreds of businesspeople rushed through the hallways with stiff, purposeful gaits. Two burly guards pointed Natch through the labyrinth of corridors and conference rooms to his appointed meeting spot. He found himself facing a nondescript door, the old-fashioned kind you needed to physically pull open. He hesitated for a moment and eyed the mahogany slab of door with suspicion. Natch searched his feelings, yet he could find no reason for his unease. He reached for the doorknob.

As soon as the brass tongue slipped free of its sheath, the knob erupted with a jolt of static electricity. Natch squealed in surprise and snatched his hand away. He quickly called up a grounding program to neutralize the charge, but the damage was done. The fingertips of his left hand would be sore for hours.

A hollow laugh echoed inside the room. "You're getting sloppy, Natch!" said a tired voice in a tone reminiscent of an aging diplomat or a patrician. "I could *never* catch you with that trick back in the old days. Horvil was always much easier to fool. But who says we don't learn from our mistakes?"

Natch shivered involuntarily at the sound of the voice that had been mocking his dreams for years. The voice that embodied his worst fears and deepest shames.

Brone.

(((19)))

He sat on a large thronelike chair in the center of a cavernous room. The room itself was a gigantic hollowed-out diamond of exceptional clarity and brilliance. On the table in front of his chair sat a Spartan breakfast of crackers and crusty bleu cheese.

More SeeNaRee, Natch moaned to himself. *Did I miss a trend? Is everyone conducting business in these gaudy fantasy worlds nowadays?*

Brone had changed significantly since Natch had last seen him, bundled in the back of that Falcon four-seater in bloody rags. His aura of youthful entitlement was gone. He had gained a considerable amount of weight, but did not carry it in the dignified manner of a Horvil or a Merri, and the handsome face that had once inspired sighs from female hivemates was mangled beyond repair. Natch traced a long scar from Brone's chin to his forehead, passing straight through the center of his right eye. The eye gleamed with the sickly emerald of a prosthesis.

"You like my face, I take it?" said Brone, his voice devoid of emotion. "I'll bet you didn't even know the bear did that to me. He would have had the whole head for breakfast, but luckily I was able to satisfy him with a light snack." Brone held up his right arm, and Natch gasped in spite of himself. The flesh came to an abrupt end just below the elbow, where it merged with a pale synthetic hand and forearm.

"Oh, don't feel *too* sorry for me, Natch," he said, sneering at the look of discomfort on the fiefcorp master's face. "These imitation limbs work fairly well. Look!" Brone painstakingly unclenched his prosthetic fingers and reached for the cheese slicer. The utensil did a clumsy dance in his hand but finally went clattering to the floor. By instinct, Natch reached down to pick it up, and fell flat on his face when his fingers passed straight through the metal. SeeNaRee. Brone let out a quiet snort and offered his old rival a hand up—the artificial hand. Natch gripped the slick, rubbery limb and pulled himself to his feet. Contrary to the act he had put on seconds ago, Brone actually seemed to be quite nimble with his prosthesis.

All at once, the purpose of Natch's visit rushed back to him: Margaret Surina, the Phoenix Project, investment capital. He needed to keep his focus. "I was invited to breakfast by the bodhisattva of Creed Thassel," said Natch between clenched teeth.

Brone paid Natch no mind; he seemed to be participating in an entirely different conversation. "I suppose you're asking yourself, *What about cosmetic surgery? Organ harvesting? Flesh-repairing OCHREs?*" He leaned back and brought the fingers of his hands together in front of his face, like a spider contemplating its next meal. The glint of reflected diamond was visible in his teeth. "Certainly science has progressed farther than this."

"I came to discuss—"

"Figaro Fi," said Brone in a commanding voice, cutting Natch off in midsentence. "You remember the fat little capitalman Figaro Fi? This whole cripple routine was Figaro's idea. *Show off your scars, my boy,* he said. *Play up your handicaps. Hold out your stump to gain their sympathy, then hold out your good hand to take their money.*" As he spoke, Brone hunched over in a cruelly effective parody of the little man. Long-repressed memories of the night before initiation came flooding back to Natch, and he nearly retched in disgust.

"Perhaps it was a despicable thing to do," continued Brone, "but it worked! Figaro brought me everywhere in those miserable years after the initiation. He would stand me up in these little auditoriums with a group of capitalmen, put a bio/logic programming bar in my hand, and cheer me on like a *monkey* while I performed tricks in MindSpace. Figaro's programming cripple, victim of the Shortest Initiation! Who could withhold money from such a *sad* and *noble* soul?

"And Figaro was right! How amazingly simple it is—all you have to do is admit that the world has defeated you, and the money will come pouring in. It's an intoxicating feeling. And if you make the right connections, if you stroke enough egos, if you convince enough of those shallow, soulless capitalmen that their *gifts* have *soothed your pain*—why, you win the game. The capitalmen begin throwing you private contracts. You can work outside the auspices of the Meme Cooperative, where you don't have to worry about the constraints of Dr. Plugenpatch. You can toss that Primo's bio/logic investment guide in the dungheap where it belongs!"

Brone began rubbing his chin in faraway contemplation, and Natch had to use every ounce of his willpower not to wrap his hands around Brone's throat and begin squeezing as hard as he could. He looked around for something to sit on, and found nothing but diamond outcroppings that were almost certainly illusions.

"I can see you're restless," said Brone, turning to Natch as if noticing him for the first time. He leaned back in the gargantuan chair and laid his arms on the throne, like a withered and haunted king. "You want to sit, you want to stand, you want to move, you want to stay still—it's been like this your whole life, hasn't it?

"Well, let me tell you, Natch, I know where you're heading. I've *been* there. There's a whole economy up in that rarefied air that the drudges know nothing about. And I made riches up there. Riches! You fantasize about living in a Lunar estate someday? I *own* one, Natch, and it's worth every bloody credit. Sunrises over the lip of Tycho while you watch and sip chai in a gravity-controlled dome . . . servants at your beck and call . . . pretty young gardeners pruning all those twisted moon plants. There's nothing like it.

"But the Lunar estate grows tiresome after a while. So do the sycophants and the bootlickers. It sounds like a cliché, but it's true. I bought myself the gaudiest estate I could, and the private hoverbird service, and the baubles and jewels and gadgets. And then I asked myself: *Now* what?

"So I went searching again.

"First, I went to the medical specialists. *Hack the body, and the mind will follow*—isn't that what Sheldon Surina said? But can you believe what a superstitious world we live in, Natch? The Autonomous Revolt was hundreds of years ago—and yet the Prime Committee *still* won't allow a simple tank-grown limb! *The only place for human flesh is on the human body*, they say." His voice rumbled up to a dangerous level, as if he were playing to the rafters in some imaginary amphitheater.

"So they gave me the next best thing." And then, as Natch looked on in horror, Brone unsnapped his fake arm and thrust it onto the table, where it landed on the bleu cheese with a sickening *thwup*. A circle of plastic prongs shone wetly on the end of Brone's stump, like octopus teeth. "Completely self-contained, no nerves or blood required: a miracle of engineering. You would be surprised to know how quickly one can tweak it to work in MindSpace like a bio/logic programming bar. And, of course, having an artificial limb gives one certain . . . *advantages*." When the fingers of the disembodied hand began twitching of their own accord, Natch leapt back and nearly sprawled on his face again. The fingers tore through the rind of the cheese and performed a gooey dance, spackling the floor with bits of white.

Natch felt sick. He recognized his own ruthless utilitarian tactics at work. What was it that old Kordez Thassel had said? *Do not let taboos and social restrictions stop you from gaining advantage over your enemy.* OCHREs rushed to defuse the acid in his stomach, and Natch would have supplemented their soothing effects with a bio/logic program if he thought it would help. "I—I came here today," he stuttered, "to—"

Brone completely ignored him. "So the replacement arm and the replacement eye were dead ends," he said with a shrug. "I knew as soon as they were installed that I had been using my handicap as an *escape*. It was an easy way to distract me from what I *really* wanted to do, from the one thing that would make me happy.

"And that was killing *you*."

Natch edged back, flailing his arm behind him in search of the door. He realized with dismay that it had vanished. He didn't want to know anymore why Brone had invited him here this morning, or what his interest in the Phoenix Project was; Natch just wanted *out*. But the diamond walls completely surrounded him now. He was trapped.

Brone leaned back in his throne and regarded Natch with sepulchral eyes, like someone watching from a separate plane of existence. The disembodied forearm began tapping out a mad rhythm on the cheese plate. "I spent months planning the whole scenario. I followed you around, Natch, did you know that? I scouted out a thousand locations for the perfect ambush. Should I follow you to Cisco and shoot you down in the forest? Or plug you full of black code on a side street in London? Or just push you off your own balcony in Shenandoah and be done with it?"

Natch rubbed his back against the diamond wall and did not breathe. The door had to be there *somewhere* . . . if he could just pierce the veil of this confounded SeeNaRee. . . .

"But don't worry, Natch," said Brone, his voice one big sneer. "You're not in any danger here today." He spread his hand and stump wide in a conciliatory gesture. His smile was the smile of a ghoul. "You see, I have found religion."

The fiefcorp master stared at his old enemy, not comprehending. "The bodhisattva of Creed Thassel," Natch croaked under his breath. "Where is he? What did you do with him?"

Brone gave a long and uncomfortable pause, like a robot in suspended animation. "I *am* the bodhisattva of Creed Thassel," he said at last.

• • •

It took a minute for the words to penetrate Natch's defenses. He turned them around in his head, breaking them down into small digestible pieces to try and make sense of them. *Brone* the head of the Thasselians?

Before he could get a grip on the situation, the SeeNaRee changed.

Suddenly, they were hurtling through black space in a small star-craft not much bigger than the Falcon that had transported them home from initiation all those years ago. Rocks and chunks of ice whizzed by at breakneck speed. Natch looked out the starboard window just in time to see an asteroid the size of a tube train hurtle past them, missing the ship by half a meter.

"I could turn you in to the Prime Committee," Natch gasped. "You can't hide exits like that. It's against the law. And you can't just switch environments on the fly without giving me fair warning."

Brone sat back in his padded captain's chair, toying idly with the steering panel that rose before him from the floor like a metallic mushroom. He did not react at all to the first asteroid collision, which made the rickety craft shudder as if it were a few bolts away from completely collapsing. "How ironic," Brone croaked. "*Natch* threatening to turn me over to the law? Here at Creed Thassel, we take a more laissez-faire approach to laws. As old Kordez used to say, *Rules are for those who follow rules.*"

"But—" The rusted hull of a dead spaceship slammed into the side of their craft, sending Natch sprawling onto the floor once again with his teeth chattering. He bit the inside of his cheek with an audible *chomp*. Brone remained comfortably seated, and Natch noted that the disembodied arm sat motionless on the table. *Yet another infraction,* thought the fiefcorp master bitterly. *Inconsistent laws of physics.*

"Creed Thassel was really in abysmal shape when I found it," continued Brone, studying the fingernails of his good hand intently. "You'd be surprised how many people think Creed Thassel ceased to exist twenty years ago. There was that exposé by Sen Sivv Sor. Financial scandals. A real *paucity* of leadership. The imbeciles running the organization were even on the brink of losing control of the Kordez Thassel Complex. So when I got religion, Natch, I got it for a real bargain-basement price. They needed my money. They needed my vision and my initiative."

Cosmic debris continued to slam into the ship, leaving Natch huddled on the floor with his hands over his head. OCHREs had already stanched the bleeding in his mouth, but he couldn't help probing the scar with his tongue. He knew he cut quite a ridiculous figure to his old rival, but survival was all he cared about at this point.

"Forgive me," sighed the bodhisattva, his voice devoid of supplication. "I suppose I've gotten carried away." He waved his hand in the air—the hand of flesh and bone—and the cluttered field of debris outside the ship vanished. The virtual gravity stabilized. "So let us discuss business, you and I."

Natch warily got to his feet and brushed himself off. It seemed strange that an hour ago, the only thing occupying his mind was his dire need for capital. Now suddenly, he was treading water in a sea of old landmines. "Do I have any choice?" he muttered.

"Game playing!" shouted Brone abruptly, his eyes ablaze. He arose from the chair and stood at the port window, his stump resting wearily against the glass. "All these games we've played throughout the years, you and I. And this whole setup—the invitation, the SeeNaRee, throwing the arm on the table—just another move in the game. A way to put you off guard. But believe it or not, after all the hurt and pain and suffering you have caused me, Natch, I am capable of forgiving you."

Natch gritted his teeth. *Forgiving me for what?* he thought.

"Soon, we will all be moving beyond games," continued Brone. "All of us . . . you, me, the drudges, Horvil, the idiots at the Defense and Wellness Council, all those narrow-minded bean counters at Primo's. Soon, it will make no difference who the winners and losers are."

"I have no idea what you're talking about."

"I'm talking about Margaret Surina, of course. I'm talking about 'the Phoenix Project.'" Natch could practically hear the belittling quotation marks.

"I don't know—"

"Oh, please!" snapped the bodhisattva in a sudden fit of pique.

"Don't waste your breath. The Phoenix Project is the whole reason you held those little fundraising charades of yours, isn't it? It's the whole reason you're here. But even if you hadn't held those meetings, Natch, I would have come looking for you. I know all about your visit to Andra Pradesh. Thasselian agents were watching when you walked in and out of those gates at the Surina compound, and they attended your little performances yesterday too. That's the advantage of having an organization with a secret membership.

"Let me be forthcoming. You're a step behind in this game, Natch, just as you've always been a step behind me in everything else. The struggle for the Phoenix Project was well under way before you butted your nose into it. I have no problem with your pathetic attempts to grab a little portion of the pot, but don't think you can walk away with the whole thing. There are too many people who know too much."

Natch gave a haughty sniff in Brone's direction. "And what do you know that I don't?"

"I know what you have been trying to find out—I know what this technology of Margaret's is." Natch could practically feel Brone's grim smile, even though he was facing the other direction. "Let me tell you, it is everything you suspect it is, and more. Perhaps even more than Margaret imagines."

The fiefcorp master hesitated and felt Serr Vigal's suspicions rushing in to fill the hole in the pit of his stomach. Could Brone be telling the truth? The Thasselians continued to pledge their devotees in secret, after all, and there were no Creeds Coalition bylaws preventing people from pledging to more than one creed. "So what are you wasting time with me for?" said Natch with affected nonchalance. "If you're so far ahead of me, go talk to Margaret yourself."

"I have tried, many times. The Surina woman does not listen."

"Perhaps she's put off by your winning way with people."

Natch's wisecrack did not succeed in penetrating Brone, now standing at the window rubbing his chin with his handless stump.

Natch couldn't help but shiver. "Obviously, you cannot see the forest for the trees, Natch. I wish I could say this surprises me, but it does not. So let me tell you the truth of the situation that has so far eluded you." Brone spread the fingers of his good hand out against the window, as if straining to reach something beyond the black void. "I have seen the future, Natch. And the future is you and I, in business together, selling the Phoenix Project."

The thought made Natch nauseous. "Bullshit."

"I understand your dilemma, Natch," said Brone, his voice barely a whisper now. "You want to walk out the door right now and never see me again." He nodded towards the rear of the spacecraft, where a plain metal door suddenly materialized out of nowhere. "But Margaret Surina has dangled the carrot just beyond your reach, like everything has always been just beyond your reach. You *need* my help. Nobody is buying your fundraising pitch, and you're running out of time. You need the money that I can provide—money that's just sitting in the coffers of Creed Thassel waiting for a worthwhile investment. I can transfer the credits to your Vault account before the hour is up."

The entrepreneur snorted. "And what do you get in return?"

"Nothing at all. This is simply a cash loan. Repayment over five years with Vault standard interest rates."

Natch stared uncomfortably at the plastic teeth of Brone's stump. He could feel the wheels of his mind spinning and spinning but gaining no traction. "Why would you do that?"

"Because," replied Brone with maddening calm, "you need money and I need a foot in the door. If I attached strings to the offer, you wouldn't take it."

"Let me see the contract," Natch said with a grunt.

Brone stepped away from the fiefcorp master's side and gave a sweeping bow towards the window. The twinkling stars of space were replaced with the dull black-and-white text of a legal document. Natch scanned the length of the contract in less than a minute, then read it over twice more to make sure he wasn't missing anything. The contract was conspicuously short and completely free of legal double-talk or hidden provisos. Try as he might, Natch couldn't think of any possible way Brone could trip him up with such an agreement.

"I don't get it," Natch rasped.

"That is because you have a limited intellect," said Brone. "This is an act of *trust*, Natch. It is a concept beyond your understanding."

The fiefcorp master looked back and forth between his wraithlike nemesis, the grubby hand on the table, and the blocky letters on the viewscreen. *If I had the slightest doubt you could find the money to do this,* Margaret had said, *you wouldn't be here.* He checked his internal calendar and looked once more at the menacingly small block of days remaining until Margaret's planned unveiling of the Phoenix Project.

Suddenly, with his mind's eye, he saw a raging bear in the wilderness. A battered and bleeding boy lying in the backseat of a Falcon hoverbird. *An act of trust?*

Natch quelled the inner voice screaming dire words of doom. He blocked out the chortling of Figaro Fi and Captain Bolbund and the Patel Brothers that echoed through his head. Then he reached out with his mind and affirmed the contract.

Brone smiled. His detached hand dragged itself painstakingly to the edge of the table and then threw itself to the ground, where it wriggled like a fish out of water.

(((20)))

Horvil studied the viewscreen with as much concentration as he gave his bio/logic programs. "If you ask me—"

"Which I'm *not*," muttered Jara.

"If you ask me, daisies would work much better in here than violets." The engineer put his nose up to the viewscreen as if trying to give individual attention to every pixel. Then, in feng shui mode, he glanced around Jara's apartment with eyes narrowed. "A garden of violets is going to stick out in here like a sore thumb," said Horvil. "But daisies, they're so . . . light and . . . airy. They'd look terrific with this blank wall effect you have going on here." He made an expansive gesture at the unadorned white plaster running the length and breadth of the room.

Jara snorted loudly. Was this clod actually *serious* for once, or was he just being sarcastic? She couldn't tell which option was worse. The fact that Horvil had absolutely no taste or personal style whatsoever only compounded the problem. *Then again*, Jara thought bitterly, *why would you need to* have *fashion sense if you've got enough money to* buy *it instead?* She remembered the rare ceramic sculpture Horvil had hanging on *his* wall with a stray glob of peanut butter encrusted on its bottom edge, and she cringed.

The analyst forced herself to stop this dreadful internal monologue. She couldn't blame Horvil for *her* failure to carve a home out of this tiny apartment. She could only blame herself. And that was why Jara had decided she was going to order a new garden and wall hangings today. Who cared if she could ill afford them with her meager savings. She had to draw the line *somewhere*. "I'm going with violets," she said between tense grinding teeth, and gave the viewscreen a silent command.

In the blink of an eye, the living room wall shifted back a meter to make room for a row of holographic violets that slid up from the floor.

Horvil yelped and quickly scooted out of the way. As Jara searched for a suitable layout, he took a seat at the kitchen table and watched the shifting kaleidoscopic patterns on the floor. "Maybe you could try layout fifty-seven, with a few daisies sprinkled in to match th—"

"Horvil, *please.*"

He shut up. Jara settled on a slight arc that spanned the length of the room, and confirmed the order. *Delivery tomorrow at 3:25 pm*, the system told her. Somewhere on the Data Sea, computational agents for the tenement building cut a thick slice out of Jara's Vault account.

This was all a diversion anyway, a way to pass the time until they could squeeze some information from Natch about what was going on. He had promised to explain everything in a fiefcorp meeting at seven o'clock. But by the time eight-thirty rolled around with no sign of Natch, the three apprentices decided their fiefcorp master wasn't coming. The same thing had been going on for a week. Horvil tried to get in touch with Serr Vigal, but the neural programmer had predictably prived himself to incoming communication, probably off fundraising. So Horvil and Jara spent the next few hours in Jara's apartment listening to Merri explain what little she knew about the Phoenix Project. The three tossed improbable theories back and forth, and got nowhere. Eventually, Merri decided to cut her connection so she could spend some time tending to her companion Bonneth, who was bedridden with another one of her crippling fevers.

Jara was ready to kick Horvil out and get some sleep when she felt an incoming multi request.

Natch appeared in the room, looking as bothered and beautiful as always. He was already pacing the length of the room before he had completely emerged from the haze of multivoid. "Horv, I'm going to need you to interview some new engineers and programmers," he said, as if they had been discussing the topic for hours.

"Are we expanding?" asked Horvil.

"What does it *look* like?"

Horvil shot a glib look at Jara. "How many do we need?"

"I don't know," replied Natch without missing a beat. "Two. Five. Ten if they're stupid."

The engineer stood with arms akimbo and sucked in his stomach as if girding for battle. "I hear and obey, brave commander," he said, and vanished.

Natch swiveled on the ball of his left foot and stopped directly in front of Jara. The analyst felt the familiar hollow sensation in the pit of her stomach as the entrepreneur locked eyes with her. *Sapphires*, she thought. "And you," said Natch in a feathery voice. "Why don't you tag along with Merri for the next couple days. She's meeting with Robby Robby tomorrow to get him up to speed on how we do things around here."

Jara gulped. "Who's Robby Robby?"

"Our new channeling partner. He's a bit of a character, but he's got a staff that could sell you the clothes on your back while you're still wearing them."

The analyst nodded. Her own clothes seemed uncomfortably tight and constricting at the moment. "All right, I'll do that." Then, seeing that Natch was about to cut his multi connection, asked, "So what do you think—violets or daisies?" She tilted her head towards the holographic arch that the fiefcorp master had plowed straight through several times now.

Natch turned and studied the flower arrangement for a moment. "I'd say daisies," he announced, and then severed his multi projection without another word.

Jara cancelled the violets and ordered daisies instead.

• • •

Natch's thought processes had always been a mystery to Jara, but she soon began to wonder if he was losing his grip on reality. That night, he went on a titanic shopping spree. Natch bought everyone in the fiefcorp a new workbench with expanded MindSpace capabilities and the fanciest set of bio/logic programming bars on the market. He let Horvil loose on the Data Sea to pick out the best code optimization routines and analysis algorithms. He set up a permanent account at the Surina Enterprise Facility so he could commandeer an office or a conference room at a moment's notice.

Where he got the money for all this, nobody knew. Jara was intimately familiar with the fiefcorp's Vault accounts, and she knew they couldn't withstand this kind of pummeling. True, the jump to number one on Primo's had provided them a good financial cushion. But Natch's reckless spending would soon put them into bankruptcy.

Somehow this prospect cheered Jara up.

So instead of protesting, Jara did as she was told. Over the next few days, she accompanied Merri to several meetings with the channeler Robby Robby. If anything, the man was even more insipid than Natch's description. He dressed in whatever ludicrous fashion the high-society brats were wearing at the time—this week it was kimono pants and open-collared silk shirts—and went through programmable accents like other people went through socks. The cost of these silly peccadilloes went on the tab of the Natch Personal Programming Fiefcorp, of course.

Jara soon discovered what made Robby Robby so valuable, however: he was completely unperturbed by the idea of selling a mystery product. "What do you think my channelers do every day?" he said, walking them through a room of baby-faced salespeople holding ConfidentialWhisper conversations from their desks. There were perhaps twenty in all, each impeccably dressed and relentlessly cheerful. "Selling isn't about the product you're *offering*, Lady Merri. It's about what the customer *wants*." Every time Robby Robby called her *Lady Merri*, Jara wanted to give him a swift kick in the knees. But even though she was a Creed Objectivv devotee, Merri seemed to get along with the slick salesman just fine.

Meanwhile, Horvil worked feverishly through the weekend to find capable engineering candidates who would fit Natch's high standards. He managed to round up a dozen applicants. All had the credentials to work in the top fiefcorps, and all were eager to sign on, which was no small accomplishment in such a tight labor market. But Natch found fault with every one of them. He even managed to send a top-flight engineer from the Deuteron Fiefcorp fleeing an interview in tears.

Finally, an exasperated Horvil brought in his nineteen-year-old cousin Benyamin for an interview. Horvil meant it as something of a joke. Ben's only real-world experience was an apprenticeship managing a floor of assembly-line coders, and he was the youngest son of Horvil's dreaded Aunt Berilla to boot. But to everyone's surprise, Natch made the boy an apprenticeship offer on the spot. Benyamin readily accepted.

"I don't get it," Jara told Horvil after he had relayed the story to her. "No offense, Horv, but Natch has been turning away *everyone*. How did Benyamin convince that bastard to hire a nineteen-year-old kid with no experience?"

Horvil shrugged. "I dunno."

"So how many hours was Natch grilling him?"

"Less than one. Ben says that Natch listened to his pitch without saying a word, and then asked him just one question. *You're not going to go crying to your mother the first time I keep you up three days in a row, are you?*"

The outside world did not come to a standstill while the fiefcorp beefed up its operations. In the midst of all the commotion, Pierre Loget released a bevy of upgrades on the Data Sea that sent his Pul-Corp rocketing to the top of Primo's. Billy Sterno and Lucas Sentinel quickly followed suit. For a couple of hours, the Patel Brothers sank as low as number four before they managed to pump a few more bio/logic programs into the system and reclaim the top spot.

Natch mysteriously shrugged the whole thing off and seemed content to sit in fourth place for the time being. He spent all his time reading the latest news about the Prime Committee and the Defense and Wellness Council. Jara would multi over to his apartment to find him meditating to the libertarian ravings of politician Khann Frejohr. The craggy face of High Executive Borda stared back at her from every window. When the story broke about a battalion of Council officers bivouacking in China, Natch was glued to a map of the Orient for hours.

Jara felt like a spectator in a game she didn't understand, played by titans on a board she could not see. At least the days were passing quickly now, bringing the elusive end of her apprenticeship contract closer all the time.

On Monday morning, Jara awoke and slipped into her comfortable routine like an old shirt. She had barely fired up Doze-B-Gone 91c when she was assaulted by a screaming headline from Sen Sivv Sor:

THE PHOENIX PROJECT UNVEILED
*Is This the Long-Awaited New Surina Technology,
or Just a Publicity Stunt?*

John Ridglee's morning commentary quickly morphed to keep pace, sending his fawning profile of Pierre Loget to an out-of-the-way side column. Before long, the two drudges were engaged in a frenzied competition to see who could quote more unnamed industry sources offering the wildest speculation about the Phoenix Project.

Within an hour, the entire world had shifted its focus to the upcoming four hundredth birthday celebration of Sheldon Surina. Curious onlookers from Earth to Luna to the farthest orbital colonies began tracking the comings and goings at the Surina compound, hoping to find clues to what Margaret had been up to for the past twenty years. Even those with little interest in bio/logics began streaming into Andra Pradesh to soak up the electric vibe in the air.

Horvil and Jara camped on opposite sofas in the engineer's apartment and watched Surina mania overtake the Data Sea. L-PRACG politicians stood up in open sessions to spout platitudes about the impact of another breakthrough Surina technology. One after another, the creeds released statements spelling out their positions on scientific innovation. The Islanders raised their obligatory protest about technology being thrust upon them against their will; the orbital colonies raised *their* obligatory protest about technology not reaching them quickly enough. The bio/logics markets careened up and down as investors decided the end was near or the best was yet to come. Even the revered bodhisattva of Creed Objectivv emerged from seclusion to make some inscrutable pronouncement about the state of universal truth in the wake of the Surinas' accomplishments.

"I don't get it," Jara said, throwing her hands up in confusion.

"You've been saying that a lot lately."

"Yes, but *think* about it for a minute, Horv. People have been talking about this stupid Phoenix Project for years now. Natch was just throwing around rumors about it a few days ago. Why is everybody so interested *now?* What's changed?"

Horvil bounced his arm off a stack of dirty laundry on the couch, trampoline-like. "It's called public relations. The Surinas are masters at it."

"You think all this hubbub comes from a few leaks to the drudges?"

"That's exactly what I think."

"But—"

"Come on, Jara. Don't you remember what happened a month ago? We've seen firsthand how this shit spreads."

The analyst twirled a few stray locks of curly hair, trying to mask her sudden embarrassment. Horvil was right. They had personal experience with the capriciousness of the public imagination, and with the ways a few, choice power brokers could channel the energies of sixty billion people to their cause.

Horvil fixed her with a narrow-eyed stare. "What's wrong?" he said.

"If what Merri says about us licensing the Phoenix Project is true, then all this publicity is going to be really good for business."

"But?"

"But once Natch gets in the spotlight, who's to say someone's not going to hijack all this attention and turn it against him?"

• • •

Serr Vigal settled back into his chaise longue, mumbling something about how creaky his joints got in erratic gravity and how glad he was to be back from his latest visit to Patronell for memecorp funding. But Natch was distracted, not listening. "Tomorrow will be a momentous day," said the neural programmer, in an effort to catch his protégé's attention.

"Tomorrow, I finally get to find out what this Phoenix Project *is*," said Natch. "It had better be worth all the trouble."

"Margaret still won't tell you?"

"No. I haven't heard a word from her in days. She's totally prived herself to the world. I can't even get her to sit down with me to iron out the details of this contract addendum." Natch shook his head glumly. "I just hope Len Borda gives her the chance to explain herself."

"Why, has he been making more threats?"

The entrepreneur swiveled around and gave his mentor a puzzled expression. "Threats? Haven't you been paying attention to the news? Borda's got several legions of Council troops heading for Andra Pradesh right now. That's not a threat. It's a bloody declaration of war."

(((21)))

A cloud of hoverbirds darkened the sky over Andra Pradesh late Tuesday afternoon. The troops disembarked in the fields west of the city instead of at the commercial hoverbird facility, and before long an army of white was marching towards the Surina compound. Several thousand Defense and Wellness Council officers moved with perfect synchronization through the streets of Andra Pradesh. A few curious vendors hung around to gawk, but most quickly packed up their wares and fled before the advancing army. The soldiers in white trudged on. There would be no looting on High Executive Borda's watch.

The Surina security forces stood their ground at the base of the mountain, looking scared, outgunned, and hopelessly outnumbered. The chief of security positioned himself directly in front of the compound gates, trying to present a model of dignity to the green-and-blue troops behind him. The Council had not made such a display of force in several years, at least not in a connectible city. One would have to look back to the Melbourne riots during the Economic Plunge to find an incident of actual large-scale combat.

The Defense and Wellness Council troops reached the base of the mountain and came to a halt. Their ranks were neatly bisected by the shadow of the Revelation Spire. *Is there any force in the solar system capable of opposing them?* the security chief asked himself.

The legion's commanding officer stepped out from her formation and strode calmly up to the chief of Surina security. The chief took stock of the woman's white robe and yellow star, the smock she wore over her shoulders as a mark of office, the gray boots that seemed impervious to the monsoon season's mud. Holstered at her right side was a two-handed dartgun. The Surina security chief wondered what bio/logic code sat on the tips of those darts, waiting for a fresh bloodstream to infiltrate.

The chief's own darts were programmed to kill. With Margaret Surina's explicit authorization.

"Towards Perfection," announced the Defense and Wellness Council officer as she flashed a quick hologram of her public profile. *Commander Tanis*, it read, *242nd Brigade.* Volunteering directory profiles was one of the few meaningless gestures Borda had made to public relations over the years. "I have been ordered by High Executive Len Borda to secure the Surina compound and the city of Andra Pradesh." Her tone of voice indicated that the occupation was a foregone conclusion.

The security chief stayed put. "Please convey our thanks to the high executive, but Her Eminence the bodhisattva of Creed Surina needs no additional protection."

"Nevertheless," replied Tanis icily, "the Council has been charged by the Creeds Coalition to protect its interests here, and protect them we will."

This was a new development. The Surina official scratched his bald pate in puzzlement. "You're here to protect the *Creeds Coalition's* interests? From what? We *are* a creed."

Commander Tanis did not hesitate a heartbeat. "Large public gatherings bring a high risk of damage and destruction." Tanis held out her hand, palm up, and displayed a holographic message in the air. "Bodhisattvas of several major creeds have asked the high executive to protect the common cultural heritage of the creeds here at the Surina compound." The security chief examined the letter, confirmed that it stated precisely what the Council woman had said, and noted dejectedly that it did indeed bear an authentic signature from the secretary of the Creeds Coalition. But he nearly erupted with laughter when he saw what "common cultural heritage" Borda presumed to be protecting.

A representation of Isaac Newton, on permanent loan from Creed Élan . . . A bronzed effigy of Tobi Jae Witt, owned jointly by Creeds Bushido and Dao . . . A sculpture of Albert Einstein that Creed Conscientious had lent to the Surinas while their new administrative facility was under construction.

The scientist statues in the Surina Center for Historic Appreciation.

This couldn't really be happening, could it? Len Borda couldn't be so brazen as to march into the Surina compound with such a minuscule fig leaf of an excuse, could he? The security chief gazed past Tanis at the row upon row of motionless Council officers, and saw not a single smile or good-natured smirk. *Politics*, thought the security chief bitterly. *How many times have I complained to Margaret that she isn't keeping up good relations with the other creeds? And what did the Council offer those other bodhisattvas to make them roll over so easily?*

The security chief cast a sidelong glance at the inadequate forces under his command. The teeth of the green-and-blue soldier beside him were chattering uncontrollably.

"Stand down," said the commander of the Surina security forces with a sigh.

Tanis nodded and signaled her officers to enter the gates. The security chief watched gloomily as the white armada sailed through the gates and up the path towards the courtyard. None of them, he noticed, were headed for the Center for Historic Appreciation.

• • •

Natch thought he was still enveloped in the haze of multivoid when his field of vision turned white. Then he realized that his transmission to Andra Pradesh had gone through after all, and the white glare was the sun's reflection off a Council officer's steely dartgun.

The main courtyard was crawling with figures in white robes where Natch had expected blue and green. The few Surina employees in view were milling about aimlessly, trying to maintain the façade that they were still in charge. Yet the Council troops showed no sign of interfering. Their only agenda at this point, it appeared, was to stand with dart-rifles drawn and act menacing. If they intended to stop people from watching Margaret's presentation, they could do little from the courtyard; even the thickest Council thug had to know that standard crowd control procedures for an event like this would confine all multi projections to inside the auditorium.

Natch scooted quickly along the fence, hoping to make it unnoticed to the Center for Historic Appreciation. But he was not destined for such luck. Two officers immediately zeroed in and corralled him into a corner. As they scrutinized him, Natch waited for the officers to say something—didn't the Council troops in the dramas always say *your identification, please* or *state your name and business?*—but they kept eerily silent. He supposed they could gather all the information they needed by feeding his image through the jaws of their vast intelligence databases. Speech was superfluous.

"*There* you are," growled a voice. "Leave this one alone. He's with me."

Two arms brusquely made a path between the Council officers, into which stepped Margaret's mysterious Islander. His scruffy tunic and wild ponytail stood out like a scar in a courtyard full of crisp white uniforms. Natch didn't know whether to feel scared or comforted when the man put an arm across Natch's chest, like a parent claiming a wayward child.

The larger of the two Council officers eyed the Islander's copper collar with disdain. "So *this* is Margaret's Islander," he said, elbowing his cohort in the side. "Remember the one with the ponytail that came at us down in Manila? Looked just like this one."

His fellow officer let out a malicious chuckle. "I remember," she said. "Shot him full of darts. Bastard just kept coming."

"Finally had to crack his skull, right?"

The Islander maintained his composure and did not take the bait. "I'll bet you found a stack of Council officers' corpses lying there when you finally took him down, too."

"Better watch your manners, *unconnectible*," sneered the Council man, clearly irritated at the Islander's demeanor. "You're not in the Pacific anymore. Without *this*, we could have you begging for mercy in two minutes." Then he fearlessly reached one hand up and flicked his finger against the collar.

Before the *ping* of the vibrating metal had faded away, the Islander was in motion.

Natch had never seen anyone move so fast. One second, the Islander was standing at rest; the next, he had zipped around and placed the offending officer in a chokehold. The second guard reached for her dartgun in a panic, but it was too late. The Islander had already lifted her comrade's weapon from its sheath and aimed it squarely at her forehead. "Yes," he hissed savagely, "but which one of you is going to take it away from me?"

Within seconds, officers all over the courtyard were scrambling towards them with weapons drawn. Natch had never actually faced the barrel of a Defense and Wellness Council dartgun before; now he found himself facing at least thirty of them. The fact that he was present only as a multi projection was slight comfort. It became less comforting still when Natch realized that several of the dartguns pointed at him were actually multi disruptors. If the libertarian drudges were to be believed, Council disruptors were just as capable of passing black code as dartguns.

The Islander shook off the tension with a dismissive snort. He released the officer from the crook of his arm and shoved him roughly towards his companions, tossing the dartgun on the ground as an afterthought. Then he flipped his ponytail over one shoulder and parted another path in the crowd as if nothing had happened. "Well?" he called to Natch. "Are you coming or not?" The entrepreneur forced his knocking knees to follow. Scores of Council eyeballs watched in silence as the two walked briskly through the courtyard and into the Center for Historic Appreciation. Natch let out a loud breath of relief as soon as the doors closed behind them.

The atrium was empty of visitors, except for two Council guards standing idly against the wall discussing baseball. Neither gave Natch or the Islander so much as a glance as they threaded their way between the scientist statues and headed down one of the corridors.

"Bloody tracking devices," muttered the Islander. "Do they think we actually *want* to wear these fucking things?" He reached up with one hand and tugged at the collar as if about to fling it boomerang-style down the hallway. Natch noticed for the first time that the collar was not actually suspended in air, but balanced on the man's neck over a fine latticework of metallic thread. The contraption looked hideously uncomfortable.

"Did you say that thing is a tracking device?" asked Natch, struggling to keep up with the Islander's giant strides.

"Of *course* it's a tracking device. Why else would they make them so fucking conspicuous? You can see an Islander with a collar from a kilometer away. Keeps us segregated."

Natch was usually not interested in cross-border politics. But he had to keep this strange man talking, if only so he might figure out his relation to Margaret and the Phoenix Project. "But you need those outside the Islands," he said. "How else you going to survive out here without OCHREs?"

Halfway up a flight of stairs, the Islander stopped dead in his tracks. "You've got a lot to learn about your governments, boy." He reached into his pocket with a scowl and dug out a small disc the size of an ancient coin. "See this little device? You can pin it to your collar, or wear it on a string around your neck. Made from spare parts, and you can see multi projections with it, interact with bio/logic code. Explain *that* to me."

Natch eyed the circle with embarrassment. "So why aren't you wearing that thing instead?"

Margaret's Islander gazed at Natch with an unspoken accusation of gullibility hovering just behind his eyes. "Because wearing these collars is *the law* if you're an Islander," he sneered. "And if you don't obey *the law*, you get visits from the Defense and Wellness Council and the

Prime Committee and fuck knows who else." Then he slipped the disc back into his tunic and kept climbing the stairs.

Natch trotted alongside the big man as they crossed a covered walkway over the courtyard and into the Surina Enterprise Facility. A hoverbird bearing the Council insignia zoomed across the skyline directly in front of them. "Where are we going?" said Natch. "That message I got this morning . . . Are you taking me to Margaret?"

"No. Margaret's locked herself in the residence, preparing for the speech. You'll see her afterwards—if there's anything left to see."

"So what's this 'performance' you need me to do? Or was that it down there in the courtyard?"

The Islander shook his head. He had led them to the end of a wide corridor and an imposing set of double doors. "The performance is in here," he said grimly. "Just be yourself. Stick by me and make sure everyone sees it. Speak if you have to, but don't say anything memorable." The doors slid open of their own accord, but not before the man thrust one hand forward and slammed it against the metal with a *bang*. "And one more thing you'll need to know: my name is Quell."

Beyond the doors was a large bowl-shaped meeting room. A lavish bouquet stood in the center of the room, underneath a revolving banner that flashed HAPPY 400TH BIRTHDAY, SHELDON SURINA over and over in ten-second intervals. About four or five dozen guests congregated in small clusters around the room, all of whom had turned their attention to the sudden and noisy arrival of Natch and Quell.

It's the whole bio/logics industry, Natch thought with a quickly stifled gasp.

If it wasn't quite the entire industry, the guest list for this little reception certainly encompassed its top tier. Natch saw hated rivals and fierce competitors in every corner. Jara's old boss Lucas Sentinel was camped near the bouquet with a group of well-known channelers and capitalmen. A pasty man with a mop of black hair, Sentinel did not tower over his companions so much as sway awkwardly in their midst like a tree. The drudges Sen Sivv Sor and John Ridglee were holding court on opposite sides of the room. Libertarian rabble-rouser Khann Frejohr sipped chai alongside the shrewish programmer Bolliwar Tuban. Natch felt a hand clap him on his shoulder, and turned around to face Billy Sterno. "Nice entrance, pal!" chirped the fiefcorper before scuttling off, his Chinese eyes glinting with mischief.

I need a licensee who can generate enough ripples on the Data Sea to make the Council stay its hand until I unveil the technology, Margaret had said.

I guess that's what we're doing, thought Natch. *Generating ripples.*

Natch and Quell began a slow stroll around the periphery of the room. The fiefcorp master put on a haughty look and did his best to forestall any conversation. For the most part, it worked. The members of the bio/logics elite seemed content to stay in their balkanized clusters and throw scandalized looks at the fiefcorp master and the Islander from afar. After ten minutes of this, however, Natch started to get restless. Everyone in the room had noticed them already, and the crowd would soon be gathering in the auditorium to await Margaret's speech.

"Okay, have we made enough of a show?" he muttered in a low voice, unsure whether an Islander could respond to a Confidential-Whisper.

"Not yet," replied Quell calmly. "I want to catch one of the stragglers."

Natch frowned. "Stragglers?" Then he heard a violent cough behind him, and turned to see the bulldog face of Frederic Patel.

Natch did not bother with formal greetings, because he knew he would receive none from Frederic. The short, barrel-chested programmer had not inherited the slick mannerisms and sharp fashion sense that made his older brother Petrucio so popular among the drudges. If they did not share the same olive complexion and lithe moustache, one would be hard-pressed to identify the two Patels as brothers. But even during the worst days of their vitriolic competition, Natch had to admit that Frederic was one of the few engineers in the business whose skills stood up to Horvil's.

"Well, if it isn't the thief," snarled Patel.

The fiefcorp master laughed scornfully. "Watch who you're calling a thief. Looks like you've stolen your number one slot back, for a little while at least."

"Primo's." Frederic gave a dismissive flip of the hand, leaving Natch to wonder what else he had stolen from the Patels recently. "A little while. What's *that* mean?"

"That means, sometimes history repeats itself."

Frederic made a whistling sound with his nose that, after a moment, Natch realized was laughter. He swept his gaze to the Islander, who stared back with an impenetrable glare. Natch suddenly remembered Quell's instructions to say as little as possible, but the big man no longer seemed to care. "You heard your boss's speech yet?" Patel said, addressing Quell.

"No," replied the Islander.

"We're not gonna be bored to death, are we?"

"The world might be a better place if you were," Quell said, deadpan.

Again the whistling sound. "So that's the game you two are playing, eh?" Patel rasped. "Well, fine with me. But now it's *our* move."

The level of conversation in the room had dipped noticeably since Frederic's approach. Lucas Sentinel had wandered close and kept taking discreet peeks at the confrontation like a nervous hyena. John Ridglee was not even trying to disguise his blatant attempts to read lips.

Natch was trying to decipher Frederic's comments and formulate a response when a loud neutral tone sounded throughout the room. The marquee displaying birthday wishes to the dead Sheldon Surina was now announcing the imminent arrival of his descendant Margaret onstage. Within seconds, industry mavens were cutting their multi connections to the party and preparing to reconnect inside the nearby auditorium.

Frederic Patel vanished without so much as a glance back in their direction. Natch breathed a sigh of relief, following Quell out the same doors they had entered through. The show was about to begin.

(((2 2)))

"I'm telling you, this can't go on forever. One of these days, the Data Sea is just going to collapse."

"They've been saying that for a century."

"But come on, look at how much more bandwidth we're using these days. Multi, the Jamm, the Sigh. Even quantum computing has its limits."

"One point three billion multi projections at Marcus Surina's funeral, and not a single glitch. That's all I have to say."

"Yeah, but—"

Jara stood and listened to the jabber of the couple beside her as she waited for Margaret Surina to take the stage. Personally, she sided with the doomsayer who feared the imminent collapse of the computational system. She looked around at the thirty-five thousand visible spectators filling the arena and tried to imagine the seraphic order of number needed to describe the bandwidth requirements for so many people.

But the vertigo did not end there. The Surina auditorium statistics told her there were actually *413 million* multi projections here waiting for Margaret to reveal the mystery behind the Phoenix Project. Four hundred thirteen million people whose brains were trying to maintain the illusion that they were real bodies inhabiting real Cartesian space, when that was clearly impossible.

The analyst summoned a calculator and wide-eyed her way through the math. Four hundred thirteen million people wedged into a space designed to fit thirty-five thousand real bodies. Which meant that right now almost *twelve thousand* people from every corner of the solar system believed they were standing in the *exact same spot* as Jara. . . .

Then she noticed that the attendance had skyrocketed another 150 million spectators. Jara shook her head violently. Human minds could not comprehend such vastness. Better to swallow the sweet lotus of multi and be done with it.

Especially when she had so many more urgent questions to contend with. Like where was the rest of the fiefcorp? What was this "Phoenix Project" that had so entranced the public's imagination and completely absorbed the world's richest woman for years? How did Natch fit into this whole puzzle? And how would this new technology affect her job?

Just then, a young woman in a green-and-blue Surina security uniform passed mere centimeters away from Jara's right side. The woman—no, the *girl*—had her dartgun drawn and was clearly petrified. *I'd be petrified too*, thought Jara, *if I had a few thousand Defense and Wellness Council troops on my heels.*

Which brought up the most perplexing question of all: What was the Council waiting for?

Moments later, Margaret Surina took the stage. Jara hadn't seen her arrive, so she couldn't say for sure whether Sheldon Surina's heir had multied onto the stage. Margaret had chosen a formless robe that draped across the floor like a tent and slowly changed colors from blue to green and back again. Her frosted black hair lay across her shoulders. She seemed completely calm, like the commander who had already greenlighted a battle plan and now waited for its outcome to slowly unfold.

And just as the bodhisattva opened her mouth to speak, a hundred doors slammed open at once, and the Council made its entrance.

With dartguns crossed over their chests and eyes fixed forward, they came marching into the auditorium single file, like zombies. The crowd parted anxiously to make way for the soldiers. Some cut their multi connections on the spot, but most quickly recognized that the officers were carrying few disruptors. No, whatever High Executive Borda's intentions were, sowing panic in the crowd was not one of them. The lead Council officers stopped meters away from the stage.

If Margaret feared an imminent death, she did not show it. She regarded the intruders with an icy stare that said, *Whatever you have planned for me, you're going to have to do it in front of 700 million people.* Jara did not know much about Margaret Surina aside from the standard drudgic platitudes and generalities, but at that moment she felt a great surge of admiration for the woman.

The Council troops stood at attention, their rifles before them, and did nothing.

A hush fell over the crowd as the bodhisattva began to speak.

● ● ●

"Once upon a time," said Margaret, "we believed in technology.

"Our ancestors were the original engineers. They discovered the laws that govern the universe and learned how to master them. They paved the Earth with rock and sent wheeled machines to rumble across it. They spread to the four corners of the Earth and, not satisfied, flew to the heavens. *Still* not satisfied, they flew to the stars.

"And somewhere along the way, they got lost.

"Somewhere between the first man to build stone tools and the first woman to create an artificial intelligence, our ancestors became separated from their innovations. They stopped seeing their creations as *extensions* of themselves, and started seeing them as *external* to themselves. Other. Distant. Remote.

"Science became an impersonal god, a grim idol beyond reproach or appeal.

"And once technology was no longer a part of them, it became an enemy to conquer.

"The god that had been embedded within them all became a force to be chained and made to do their bidding. Instead of seeking communion with the god, instead of striving to understand the kernel of truth that is within us all, they sacrificed their own skills to feed him. *Our machines will do more so we may do less,* they said.

"And so, in the apogee of their folly, our ancestors created the Autonomous Minds."

A rustle of disapproval from the audience. A hateful murmuring.

"The Autonomous Minds: eight machines committed to managing the world economy, eight machines entrusted to safeguarding the environment, eight machines consigned to solving the problems of human diplomacy. Eight intelligences so vastly *other* that our ancestors feared to 'taint' them with human morals and ideals. Imagine having more faith in a lifeless machine than in a human being!

"Our ancestors abandoned their independence to the Autonomous Minds. They delivered the reins of the earth into the hands of the Minds. They trusted in the order of the Keepers to convey their will, using the arcane machine tongues that only the Keepers could speak.

"It was to prove humanity's greatest mistake."

A monolithic structure floating in the midst of the auditorium, a holographic representation of the world's first orbital colony, Yu. Circular platforms within platforms performing an intricate dance to the symphony of g-force. Gardens of unparalleled lushness and beauty like that mythical garden lost in the deeps of time. Citizens basking in the warm spring of eternal Progress under controlled atmospheric domes.

"Yu," Margaret continued. "Humanity's greatest hope. An experiment to bring us out of Earth's cradle and into the stars. A self-contained community of ten thousand, constructed in orbit above the Earth, stocked with a cross-section of humanity's best and brightest. Yu was the culmination of thousands of years of Chinese art, science, and culture—and its controls were placed in the hands of the Autonomous Minds and their Keepers.

"But this arrangement was not destined to last."

Shrieks, sighs, tears of anguish from the crowd at the first detonation. And the second.

Daisy-chain explosions rocking the orbital structure, domes bursting and debris spinning off into the void of merciless space. The spinning discs suddenly still. Pandemonium. Colonists scrambling like mad for their primitive spacecraft. Companions reaching to hold their loved ones in a last embrace. And then the death spiral—the shuddering descent into the Earth's atmosphere—the shrieking burning hellfire plunge through the clouds, in an unstoppable trajectory towards the lofty towers of New York City . . .

Bracing for impact—

The simulation vanished. Margaret was once again alone onstage.

"We may never know what caused the Minds and their Keepers to strike the first blow in the Autonomous Revolt," she said. "Were the Minds acting in collusion to exterminate the human race, as some have suggested? Or was the sabotage of Yu a power grab by the Ecumenical Council of New Alamo? Did the cloned soldiers of the Allahu Akbar Emirates have an agenda of their own?

"The ultimate truth lay buried beneath the rubble of eight continuous years of war, along with the empty burned-out husks of the Autonomous Minds.

"Humanity's cult of the god had ended.

"The consequences of our ancestors' folly? Nearly two billion dead and the great nation-states of antiquity left in ruins.

"During the Big Divide which followed, the elaborate technologies of our ancestors were gradually forgotten—forgotten, or sabotaged by Luddite mobs intent on destroying all that the Minds had touched. The triumphant engineering works of our ancestors gradually fell into disrepair. New Alamo descended into murderous fundamentalism, the Allahu Akbar Emirates disintegrated, the Chinese Territories and the Democratic American Collective vanished into irrelevance."

A panoply of still pictures now floating about the auditorium, portraits of an age. Skeletal cities. Haggard mobs with makeshift uniforms marching through city streets. Smoke rising from pyres fueled by the gnarled carcasses of inventors and scientists. Demagoguery, fanaticism, starvation. The corpse of a child.

Margaret continued: "And so the surviving nations bowed down before the whims of the mob. Strict antitechnology laws appeared around the globe. The innovators of the age had to present their discoveries on bended knee to the moralists and functionaries and politicians who used the fears of the masses to cling to power. Works of the ancient programmers and physicists moldered in decaying books and unreadable discs written on dead machines.

"Science was on the cusp of extinction. Humanity had fallen into its own death spiral.

"My ancestor Sheldon Surina changed all that."

• • •

As Margaret paused for breath, Jara surveyed the crowd. The attendance had settled at 738 million multi projections, if the auditorium figures were to be believed, and who knew how many billions more were watching or listening remotely. Whatever the number, Jara had never seen such a mass of people so mesmerized before. The only sound to be heard throughout the arena was the quiet susurration of shifting fabric and shuffling feet.

Jara looked around and noticed that the Defense and Wellness Council troops remained aloof. No hint of purpose crossed their placid brows.

"Sheldon Surina," intoned Margaret. "The man whom we honor here tonight. The man who would have been four hundred years old today." The father of bio/logics himself floated over her head, a scrawny man with a big nose standing in midspeech with his arm extended. "My ancestor stood before the proctors at the Gandhi University here in Andra Pradesh—just across the courtyard, in fact—and declared, *There is no problem that we cannot solve through scientific innovation.* Moments later, he turned this statement into a mission for humanity: *There is no problem that we* should not *solve through scientific innovation.*

"Think of the courage that required! Think of telling a world decimated by technology and hobbled by superstition—a world ruled by the draconian edicts of the Ecumenical Council and the crazed prophecies of the Three Jesuses—think of telling *that* world that science could solve all its problems!

"Sheldon Surina did.

"Had he stopped there, the man we have come to know as the father of bio/logics might have ended up just another martyr to the ideals of science. But Sheldon Surina did not just *say* we should look to science—he came down into the real world and *showed us how*. He invented the discipline of bio/logics. He designed the first programs to automate the care of the human body. He *created* the industry that conquered the virus, the industry that tamed the brain, the industry that prolonged life and reengineered birth. All without MindSpace, without bio/logic programming bars, without the Data Sea as we know it today.

"Most of all, Sheldon Surina renewed our faith in the powers of *humanity*. He taught us that scientific enlightenment does not descend to us from *without*, but grows from *within*. He showed us we did not have to forfeit our intellects to Autonomous Minds or suffer from the ignorance of Luddism—instead, we could use technology to empower ourselves. Sheldon Surina's words and ideals were the beginning of the Reawakening, that great age of progress and prosperity which continues to this day.

"Of course, progress did not come without peril. The founder of this house spent many years of his life in hiding from the Texan governments that had sworn to destroy him. He watched his friend and colleague Henry Osterman, founder of the OCHRE Corporation, slowly succumb to bitterness and paranoia. He spent his own latter days combating the forces of tyranny which sought to dominate the world with their ruthless and narrow-minded oppression. A fight that continues to this day."

Margaret's allusion to the Defense and Wellness Council did not go over the audience's head. A low murmur snaked through the crowd. Jara saw one of the white-robed men near her break into a wry grin.

"All things come to an end, and Sheldon Surina's life was no exception. But after Sheldon's death, the Surinas did not shirk their duty to humanity. Through the Center for Historic Appreciation here in Andra Pradesh, through Creed Surina and through the Surina family investments in bio/logics, we have continued to serve humanity's quest for progress and enlightenment.

"And Sheldon Surina was not the last visionary to emerge from Andra Pradesh.

"Six years after his death, Prengal Surina proposed the universal law of physics, which unlocked the potential of every rock, tree, and blade of grass to serve as a quantum energy source. His work freed us from the dictates of our surroundings, the limitations of our resources, the oppression of ancient Einsteinian physics. Without Prengal Surina and his universal law, an event like this one today would not be possible. Multi projections would be a pipe dream, and subaether communication would be an arcane tool of academics.

"In recent years, my father Marcus took up the family's mantle of service. Marcus Surina had spent many years denying his heritage. But when he finally took his rightful place as the heir to the Surina family, he pioneered bold new approaches to teleportation technology. Many believe that, had he not suffered a tragic death in the orbital colonies—had he been given the opportunity to fulfill his mission—Marcus would have brought cheap and efficient teleportation to the world, and we would live in a better place."

Above Margaret's head, the stern visage of Prengal Surina shifted to that of Marcus in all his Adonic beauty. Jara stared at the dead man and felt the same tangled knot of emotions his face always stirred up. Few had inspired so much hope. Few had left so much devastation.

"And so, what have we, the Surinas, contributed to the world?" Margaret continued.

"I believe Sheldon Surina and his descendants have remained true to the highest ideals of humanity. We have used scientific advancement to improve the human condition. We have provided choices and expanded opportunities. We have enlightened the mind instead of constricting it. And it is in that spirit that I stand before you today."

Margaret paused and took a few dramatic steps forward. "Citizens of Earth, Luna, Mars, and the colonies—Islanders and Pharisees—I stand here on the occasion of Sheldon Surina's four hundredth birthday to announce the ultimate fulfillment of his ambitions."

All at once, several hundred million spectators took a sharp intake of breath. Inside herself, Jara could feel a gathering hurricane of emotion, wrath and hope that threatened to sweep out of control. She could feel the clouds gathering throughout the arena, and for a moment it seemed as if the hopes and dreams of humanity had suddenly coalesced around one blue-eyed woman in Andra Pradesh.

The Council officers began to shift nervously on their feet. Dozens of dartguns and disruptors surreptitiously crept off the floor and into the soldiers' hands.

Margaret Surina continued, her face devoid of emotion.

"The Surina Perfection Memecorp is preparing to unveil one of the most important scientific breakthroughs since the dawn of the Reawakening—possibly *the* most important advance in the history of humanity.

"It is the ultimate freedom.

"It is the ultimate empowerment.

"It is the path to complete control over our destinies.

"The Surina Perfection Memecorp has discovered a technology to create multiple realities, and we call this technology MultiReal."

And with that, the storm broke.

• • •

It began with a low rumbling of information, a mental thunder the likes of which Jara had never experienced. She could actually *sense*, somewhere off in the distance, a disturbance in the Data Sea's flow. Data agents converging on some faraway point in the informational topography.

Then there was a sudden eruption.

Jara could hear random soundbites echoing through her head, echoes of Margaret's words spoken in a thousand different voices: *Ultimate freedom. Complete control over our destinies. Fulfillment of the Surinas' ambitions. MultiReal.* This split second of chaos was nearly enough to make her lose her balance. The analyst quickly fired up UnDizzify 93 and, by instinct, reached for something to steady herself against—only to discover that the entire crowd was swaying with vertigo. Everywhere Jara looked, spectators were blinking in confusion at the sudden blast of cerebral white noise.

Black code, she thought.

Jara instantly shot off a request to check the security of her possessions. Her Vault accounts, her dismal apartment, the databanks holding all her programming and personal information. Everything seemed fine, but with the deluge of incoming messages and ConfidentialWhispers washing in from every side, it was hard to tell. The Vault was spouting off warnings and informational bulletins by the dozens, followed in close succession by scores of redundant updates from the Meme Cooperative, the Prime Committee, her L-PRACG. Horvil, Merri, Vigal, and her sister sent her two messages apiece asking if she was okay.

Jara closed her eyes and tried to screen out the chaos. She could only imagine the computational mayhem caused by half a billion multi projections spraying billions of simultaneous requests at the Data Sea.

Things were no better when she opened her eyes.

The Council officers were on the move. Men and women in white robes advanced on the stage with grim looks on their faces, dart-rifles drawn. A handful of disruptor blasts sent multi projections flickering out into nothingness, clearing a path to the front of the arena. The rest of the crowd began scattering this way and that in confusion. Meanwhile, the Surina security forces had drawn their rifles as well and had formed a rapidly tightening circle around the stage. Several dozen guards on both sides lay twitching on the ground with black code darts jutting from their torsos.

Unbelievably, Margaret was still speaking. Either none of the darts was flying in her direction, or none of them had managed to hit her yet. Her face was ghosted over with panic, yet she stood firm and tried to make herself heard over the tumult.

"The creation of multiple realities," she said. "It sounds like a tale we tell children in the hive. But soon we will consider multiple realities as common as OCHREs, as practical as bio/logic programs, and as necessary as oxygen.

"What would our lives be like if we had made different choices? In the Age of MultiReal, we will wonder no more—because we will be able to make *many* choices. We will be able to look back at checkpoints in our lives and take alternate paths. We will wander between alternate realities as our desires lead us.

"The ever-changing flux of MultiReal will become reality.

"Just as bio/logics freed us from the tyranny of the body . . . just as the universal law of physics freed us from the tyranny of nature . . . just as teleportation freed us from the tyranny of distance . . . so MultiReal will free us from the tyranny of cause and effect itself.

"Throughout human history, we have been striving towards greater freedom. Freedom is our destiny and our birthright. And in the age to come—in the Age of MultiReal—we will all be empowered to pursue our individual freedoms however we choose.

"And I say this:

"Only when we can truly choose our own destinies will we be completely free."

Jara could not say for certain whether or not Margaret had finished her speech. Because at that moment the Surina security guards elbowed their way onstage, a mere two steps ahead of the Defense and Wellness Council troops. Jara watched with mouth agape as a white-robed officer raised her dartgun at Margaret Surina and prepared to fire.

But then an enormous man with a blond ponytail swooped out of nowhere and wrapped his arms around the bodhisattva, shielding her from harm. *My goodness,* thought Jara, *is that an Islander?* The Council officer aimed her weapon high and let off a warning shot. Within seconds, the man had whisked Margaret through the stage door. A number of Surina functionaries quickly scrambled after her.

Among those hustling backstage, Jara noted with slack-jawed amazement, was a certain lean fiefcorp master whose wolfish grin she would have recognized anywhere.

4

THE SURINA/NATCH MULTIREAL FIEFCORP

(((2 3)))

Dozens of kilometers above the Earth's surface, a cluster of hydrogen atoms danced in a copper tube. After several billion oscillations, the hydrogen maser clock declared that a second had passed.

It was midnight.

The news passed via subaether to a processing station run by the Meme Cooperative. The station—itself a small metallic box also floating in geostationary orbit—consulted its internal tables and determined that the time had come to spawn a data newt for the Pierre Loget Fiefcorp. The newt was born mere picoseconds after midnight.

A data newt did not need sixteen years of hive education to fathom its purpose. The mother station had stamped a destination into the newt's very atomic structure, a destiny to fulfill. But it was impossible to know what paths the data structure would need to take or what obstacles it would face along the way. And so the newt was endowed with a level of autonomy and given all the logical tools it would need to carry out its duties. Internal schedules, communication routines, self-replication instructions, maps of the quantum universe. Then the mother station ushered the newt out into the world.

The newt accessed its internal schedule and noted that its first stop was a set of spatial coordinates in a nearby processing station. Upon its arrival, the station challenged the newt to state its credentials and destination. The newt consulted its fore table and found the answers to these perplexing questions: *Pierre Ulyanich Loget Fiefcorp, BizWorks 139.5f, Natch Personal Programming Fiefcorp.* Satisfied with the newt's response, the station directed its microscopic visitor towards a collection of static information belonging to the Natch Personal Programming Fiefcorp.

A rote conversation ensued. Was BizWorks 139.5f listed as an acceptable expense in the Natch Fiefcorp data stores? Yes, it was. Did the unique identifying code stored in the newt's memory correspond to the one expected by the Natch Personal Programming Fiefcorp? Yes, it did. Was the price quoted by PulCorp agreeable to its customer? Yes, it was.

The answer triggered an innate response in the data newt. The newt replicated itself, stamped its clone with a subset of the required tools, and waited patiently as the newcomer sped off to the Vault. Billions of newts had already queued up at the nearby Vault processing center to retrieve and deposit payments large and small, but there was no disagreement or jockeying for position in a world of indelible, unalterable rules. The data representative of the Pierre Loget Fiefcorp slid into line in its prescribed position. After a few nanoseconds, the newt reached the front of the queue and presented the Vault agent with its transaction: *Natch Personal Programming Fiefcorp, Pierre Ulyanich Loget Fiefcorp, 0.03 credits*. The Vault agent made all the appropriate inquiries and finally responded with a credit authorization. What happened to the credit authorization after that was of no concern to the cloned newt; it reported a transaction summary back to its master and returned to the mother station.

With a credit authorization in its databanks, the data newt at the Natch Fiefcorp data stores determined it was ready to proceed. It consulted the fore table to look for its Defense and Wellness Council–sanctioned processing precedence, and lined up behind OCHRE transmissions, geosynchrons, Prime Committee statistical algorithms, and agents of L-PRACG taxation. Finally, the newt arrived at the front of the line and completed the task for which it had been born: the recording of an order by the Natch Personal Programming Fiefcorp for a replacement part on one of Horvil's bio/logic programming bars.

All that remained was housecleaning. The newt spawned another clone to relay the order back to the mother station. Meanwhile, the newt consulted its own aft table for special instructions on completing a business transaction. The L-PRACG with jurisdiction over the Natch Personal Programming Fiefcorp dictated that all programs must log a record of their activities in the fiefcorp's data stores. This task done, the newt performed a quick self-examination to see if it had lost data integrity or left any stray bits of information in the fiefcorp's holdings or needed to do any unusual acts of maintenance. All indications were that the newt had conducted a clean transaction.

And so the data structure left the Natch Personal Programming Fiefcorp holdings to perform a sweep of the remaining 4,293 fiefcorps on Pierre Loget's subscription list.

Several thousand nanoseconds later, the newt returned to the mother processing station—the prodigal son back home at last. The data structure reported a summary of its activities for the statistical programs to compile and then reported back to the Meme Cooperative energy stores. There the newt uncomplainingly self-destructed, having successfully fulfilled its mission of existence.

A few billion oscillations of hydrogen later, another second passed.

(((24)))

More than twenty-four hours had gone by since Margaret's speech, and Jara had slept for none of them. Had she not been propping herself awake with Doze-B-Gone 91c and AntiSleepStim 124.7 and two cups of nitro, the analyst might have taken more notice of her surroundings. Instead, Jara sleepwalked past the guards at Andra Pradesh and up three stories of the blue Surina Enterprise Facility with hardly a glance in any direction.

She opened the conference room door and found herself standing in a corporate boardroom from antiquity.

Jara blinked hard, twice, wondering if the opulent surroundings were the hallucinations of a sleep-deprived mind. The oval-shaped room sported a faux mahogany table that could have seated twenty, glass windows that overlooked a panoply of phallic skyscrapers, and a wet bar complete with Waterford crystal and Kentucky bourbon. But Jara was in no mood to start tapping things to figure out whether they were real or SeeNaRee. She approached the table and slumped onto a chair, which automatically scooted in and adjusted to the contours of her body. This one, at least, was virtual.

The analyst, consulting the time, realized she had arrived fifteen minutes early for their fiefcorp meeting. Jara scowled an order to the building for another cup of nitro, and then called up the morning drudge reports on a nearby window.

Nobody could quite recall who had coined the term *infoquake*, but within hours it had become common currency throughout the civilized world. Infoquake: a mysterious computational disturbance of unknown origin and awesome destructive power. Even the handful of residents living at remote experimental colonies beyond Jupiter were now bandying the word around like they had been speaking it for years.

Unfortunately, the terminology was just about the only thing the pundits could agree upon.

"Once again, the Data Sea has exhibited its juvenile tendency to turn everything into a conspiracy," wrote the drudge Mah Lo Vertiginous.

> According to the preliminary analysis from Creed Conscientious, the infoquake was a simple bottleneck of information; nothing more, nothing less. An unheard-of concentration of multi projections in a single space, vying for access to the same facts and figures on the Data Sea. Is it so hard to imagine that a series of overloaded data agents could cause OCHREs to fail?

But Vertiginous' opinion was by no means the majority along the drudge circuit. Sen Sivv Sor had a considerably darker view of the previous night's events:

> Some governmentalist cretins would have you believe we suffered from *a simple bottleneck of information* last night. Unfortunately, dear readers, nothing could be further from the truth.

> Since when does *a simple bottleneck of information* stop several hundred weak hearts from beating? Since when does *a simple bottleneck of information* cause a generator malfunction on Furtoid and send two hundred people to an icy death? Since when does *a simple bottleneck of information* wreak havoc with the gravity control on 49th Heaven and fling three dozen people into freefall?

> Mark my words: Disasters like the infoquake are not natural occurrences. Wherever you find such poisonous medicine, there's a human hand nearby administering the dose.

"Let me guess," said a voice. "Tokyo circa the Second American Revolution."

Jara whipped her head around to find Horvil surveying the room. The elaborate SeeNaRee only seemed to heighten the engineer's already high spirits. As soon as he spotted the wet bar, Horvil bounded across the room on some undefined errand of mischief. His movement revealed a nervous-looking youth who had been standing in the engineer's shadow.

"It's not Tokyo," said Jara. "It's New York City, before the orbital colony hit. See, that's the Hudson River over there." She regarded the young man with a cynical eye, noticed his inky black hair and five o'clock shadow, and decided he must be a relative of Horvil's. His face had the same air of bonhomie, but Jara could also see an undercurrent of piety that could only have been a genetic gift from the infamous Aunt Berilla. "You must be Benyamin."

The youth nodded and gave a polite bow in Jara's direction. "Towards Perfection," he said. "I guess you're Jara. Horvil's told me a lot about you."

Jara shot a suspicious glance at the engineer, who had begun to juggle the Waterford crystal. Over his head, patterns of reflected sunlight danced crazily on the ceiling. "Oh, *has* he?"

"Don't worry," said Horvil. "I really only told him a tiny bit. Just the good things."

Benyamin sensed the tension and immediately assumed the role of diplomat. "Ah, the drudges," he said, nodding at the chaotic display of fully justified type on the window. "You know, Khann Frejohr thinks High Executive Borda caused it."

"Caused *what?*"

"Well, the infoquake."

Horvil had moved from three pieces of stemware to four, and their arcs of flight were growing longer by the second. "Yeah, I saw that speech he gave last night," he said. *"The evil work of the Defense and Wellness Council. Len Borda's last-ditch effort to muzzle the Surinas once and for all.* You gotta love that Khann Frejohr."

"What a load of shit," said Jara with a grimace. "Come on, Horvil. Borda pulled his troops out of Andra Pradesh almost as soon as the infoquake was over. If he wanted Margaret dead, she'd be dead by now." She waved her hand, banishing the news coverage from the window screen. "So how did Borda react to Khann's speech? He must have gone completely offline."

Benyamin nodded. "That's putting it mildly. He shut down the Sigh and the Jamm and all other 'resource-intensive pleasure networks' until further notice."

"He *shut down*—?"

"Len Borda isn't our problem right now." The three fiefcorp apprentices swiveled around to find Natch standing in the doorway. Jara saw that he had come with wolf's grin and invisible audience in tow, not to mention an impeccable pinstriped suit that would have been at home in ancient New York. "So let's get down to business already."

Horvil caught three pieces of stemware but accidentally let the fourth slip through his fingers. The virtual Waterford landed on the marble floor with a *clang* but did not break. "What about Vigal? And Merri?" asked Horvil.

"Vigal's off to another one of his seminars in Beijing," said Natch. "*Effects of Orbital Colony Gravitational Fields on Neural Pathways*, or something like that."

"Nothing stops a scientific conference," muttered Jara.

"And *I'm* right here," said Merri. The blond channel manager had apparently snuck in while nobody was paying attention. Merri had taken a seat near Natch's side of the table and projected a set of notes visible on the dark wood in front of her. Her penmanship was crisp and perfect, something that gave Jara an inexplicable pang of jealousy.

"So what's everyone waiting for?" cried Natch in a sudden fit of pique. "Sit the fuck *down*."

• • •

Natch planted himself in the cushioned leather chair at the head of the table and surveyed his four apprentices with a barely suppressed smirk. A snapshot of the Council troops tromping through the Surina courtyard loomed large on the window behind him; Jara realized she must have accidentally left open one of her morning news stories. The four apprentices gazed expectantly back and forth between the photo and their fiefcorp master. Margaret Surina, the Defense and Wellness Council, investor meetings, infoquakes, MultiReal—hadn't the time finally come for Natch to let them know what was going on?

The entrepreneur turned to Jara with pronounced matter-of-factness, his face a riddle. "Why don't you start us off with an analysis of the latest sales figures," he said.

Jara shrugged. *Sales figures? Who can think of sales at a time like this?* But she knew Natch, and had prepared a brief analysis this morning anyway. She snapped her fingers briskly, causing a three-dimensional chart to hover over the surface of the conference table. Lines in primary colors raced one another to see which could climb to the top right corner the quickest.

The analyst indicated an uncharacteristic dip at the end of a green line labeled MENTAL INDEXX 39. "Looks like one of our programs took a hit yesterday," she said. "An eighteen percent drop in the last twenty-four hours. It must have suffered a few glitches during the infoquake." She gave Horvil the evil eye. "Billy Sterno's DataReorg 55c had a forty-three percent jump in sales during the same period."

Horvil sat back confidently, measuring the table as a possible resting spot for his feet. "Glitches happen. Mental Indexx 40'll bring 'em back into the fold."

As she crunched the numbers, Merri plucked at the chart lines like guitar strings. "I see there's a silver lining here as well."

Jara smiled. "Yeah, I see it too. . . . It looks like the Patel Brothers had a few glitches of their own, and Primo's took note." The chart shifted from sales figures to Primo's scores. If anything, the incline of the race became even steeper. "So even though we lost market share to Billy Sterno, we gained ground against the Patels on Primo's. Looks like we're back up to number three!"

Horvil broke out in a spirited cheer, which Merri and Benyamin echoed with a pair of quiet grins. Natch seemed oddly oblivious, a mystery that Jara did not feel like pursuing. *Maybe this infoquake was the end of the whole thing*, she thought. *Maybe all this hassle will just go away, and my last ten months will be business as usual.*

"Okay, so if we look at the big picture, what've we got?" said Horvil.

"An eighty-two point four percent gross increase in revenues so far this year," stated Jara, "most of that *after* we hit number one on Primo's. And only a seventeen percent increase in expenditures." She banished the bar chart to data-limbo with a wave of her hand. "I'd say we're doing pretty well."

A look of concern slowly rippled across Merri's face. "Only a seventeen percent increase in spending—how is that possible?" The soft-spoken channel manager began counting on her fingers. "In the last week alone, we've bought new bio/logic programming bars . . . analysis algorithms . . . these conference rooms . . . not to mention hiring a new apprentice. . . ." She nodded her head towards Benyamin, who merely sat with a bland smile on his face. Merri took a deep breath. "I was hoping, Natch, that *you* might be able to explain some of this."

Natch raised one eyebrow. A private in-joke with his invisible audience. "What do you want me to explain?"

"Well, for one thing, I don't see any of this showing up on the books. . . ."

"Jara does the books, not you."

"Yes, I know, but still—"

Jara had had enough. Her longed-for ten months of peace and quiet suddenly imploded. She lodged her left elbow firmly on the table and used it as a base to launch an accusing finger at the fiefcorp master. "Come on, Natch! First you start fundraising for a product we don't make, and then out of the blue you start spending money we don't have. You totally ignore the Primo's ratings. And now you've gotten us involved in this whole mess with Margaret and the infoquake. You've put us off long enough, Natch! What the fuck is going *on?*"

She had unleashed enough verbal thunder to send any of the other apprentices scampering for cover, but Natch remained unmoved. He gave a sidelong glance to Horvil, but the engineer was gazing at Jara with dumb awe.

"All right then." Natch's eyes glittered. He leaned back in his chair and clasped his hands behind his head, as if he needed a cradle for all that excess brainpower. "In a little over twelve hours, I will officially dissolve the Natch Personal Programming Fiefcorp. We are getting out of the regular bio/logic programming business. Tomorrow, you will all be apprentices in a new fiefcorp devoted exclusively to MultiReal."

His announcement was greeted by a stunned silence. Jara had a protest half formed in her mouth but strangled it when she remembered the portability clause in their contracts, a clause that essentially gave Natch the right to pass off their apprenticeships to whomever he chose. She looked at Merri and Horvil and saw their faces meld into bland expressions of unconcern, a telltale sign that they had both flipped on PokerFace 83.4b. Benyamin closed his eyes and ducked his head as if he had just been punched in the gut.

"When did you decide all this?" said Jara weakly.

"Yesterday."

The silence remained. A pigeon fluttered by the window with a loud *broo.*

"Now, I know you're all getting impatient with just room and board," Natch continued, touching his fingertips in front of his face. "Your shares all mature this year, and some of you are thinking of cashing out. So I'm prepared to sweeten the deal. Yes, that includes you, Ben. Cash out your shares *today* and I'll release you from your apprenticeship with no penalty . . . or sign on to a two-year contract with the new fiefcorp for *ten times* the compensation, plus bonuses. The offer stands until midnight tonight, Shenandoah time."

Jara felt a wave of emotion crash over her. A week ago, she had wanted nothing more than to be set free from Natch's shackles, to run as far as possible and not look back. She remembered that carefree Meme Cooperative official in Melbourne, sitting at his desk all day, his mind adrift in some SeeNaRee fantasyland. *For process' preservation, I could use a job like that*, she thought. *A nice, dull desk job of looking at data maps and bar charts sounds perfect right about now.*

But then suddenly Jara thought of her old proctor from the hive, the one who had stimulated the governmentalist ideals of her youth and negotiated the surrender of her virginity while he was at it. Had he been somewhere in that crowd last night, as spellbound by Margaret's lilting voice as the rest of them? Would the bodhisattva's words have filled him with hope, or would he have had some cynical counterpoint to make?

And what would he think of Jara now, almost twenty-five years down the road, ready to throw aside the remainder of her ambitions and slip into a SeeNaRee stupor?

Horvil interrupted her reverie with a loud clearing of the throat. "So what's gonna happen to all those programs we've been slaving over?" he said. "NiteFocus and EyeMorph and Mental Indexx and the rest of them?"

The engineer might as well have asked about the fate of an obsolete set of bio/logic programming bars. "They'll be sold off," Natch replied with a shrug. "You didn't think we were going to upgrade them forever, did you? We won't have time to maintain those old programs, and the money they generate is nothing compared to what MultiReal is going to pull in."

Across the table, Jara could see a little piece of Horvil die at Natch's pronouncement. The programs he had weaned and nurtured from RODs and hive projects into Primo's powerhouses would soon belong to the graveyard of history. Qubits of information stranded on some forgotten atoll on the backwaters of the Data Sea.

"Natch, let me be honest here," said Horvil, his voice clouded with anger. "I really had *no idea* what Margaret was talking about yesterday."

"It *was* a vague speech," agreed Benyamin with a sigh.

"I mean, what *is* this MultiReal? What does it look like? What does it do? Did Margaret ever sit down and do a—a needs analysis or a survey or something to figure out if anybody *wants* multiple realities? I've tackled a lot of tough problems in my life, but I can't remember a single time I said to myself, *You could fix this if you just had a few alternate realities.*"

Jara found herself nodding her head vigorously in agreement. "Listen, Natch, even if Margaret is on the right track, what makes you think this, this, *daydream* of hers will work? We have no idea how good an engineer this woman is. That licensing agreement you made with her might be totally worthless."

"The licensing agreement is dead," said Natch. "I'm a co-owner now."

"*What?*"

"Hold on, everybody. Act confident. Pretend you know what's going on. . . . Towards Perfection, Margaret. How are you?"

Jara whipped her head around, only to see Margaret Surina herself watching from the doorway. Part of the SeeNaRee? No, this woman was *real*. *Of course she's real, you idiot*, Jara chided herself. *She lives right across the courtyard.* The analyst slammed on PokerFace 83.4b as quickly as she could, and the rest of the staff followed suit.

"Perfection, Natch," said Margaret, with a slight bow. "What a great environment." She rapped her knuckles on the illusory table, and gave a wan smile at the SeeNaRee-generated knocking sound.

"We're just wrapping up a few details here," said Natch, his voice laced with SmoothTalker 142. "Why don't you go ahead and take a seat? I'm sure a few of these chairs are real."

Margaret shook her head quietly. On closer inspection, Jara realized that this was not the same serene woman who had confidently faced down legions of Defense and Wellness Council troops last night in front of 700 million people. The bodhisattva looked as if she had been eviscerated. She had not changed clothes since the speech, and from the diminished sparkle of her eyes, it looked as if she had not slept either. "I'm afraid I can't," she sighed, making a noticeable effort at nonchalance. "There's so much going on. All that trouble out in the orbital colonies . . ." Margaret's voice cracked, and for a minute Jara could have sworn she was fighting back tears. "Len Borda is furious."

Natch chuckled. "He'd be even more furious if he knew you were here with *me*."

"That's a chance I'll have to take. I . . . just came to tell you that, if you're ready, my people will be sending out a release to the drudges."

"Ready as I'll ever be."

"Outstanding." Margaret exhaled loudly. She looked as if she might melt into the ground right then and there. "We can iron out the details over the next few weeks."

"So you've spoken to Quell, then?"

"Yes. He has decided to stay with the MultiReal project. He's busy getting everything prepared; he'll be here Saturday at noon."

"With access to the program, I assume."

"Naturally."

Jara was growing irritated at this light exchange. So many pleasantries, so little content. Natch and Margaret Surina could very well be reciting memorized lines.

"Then Perfection to you, Margaret," said Natch, rising and giving a deep bow. "It's a pleasure doing business with you, as always."

"And you, Natch. Sheldon Surina once said, *There are no ends, only means*. So here's to a long and fruitful partnership."

And with that, she turned and walked away.

● ● ●

"A partnership," said Merri, as her PokerFace morphed into a look of concerned perplexity.

Natch nodded and made a motion like someone stifling a yawn. He had replaced his inscrutable mask as soon as Margaret had turned her back. "The Surina/Natch MultiReal Fiefcorp," he said. "Surina/Natch with a slash. But don't worry, it's mostly a silent partnership. Margaret's handing over all the day-to-day operations to me."

"*Surina/Natch!*" Horvil bellowed with glee, then pounded out a drum fill on the table. "Surina/Natch! I can't wait to hear what Aunt Berilla thinks about *that*."

"So Margaret provides the product and the capital—," began Merri.

Natch cut her off. "Not the capital. Not all of it, anyway."

"Then where did *that* come from?" asked Jara, leaning forward to project her venom as close to Natch as possible.

"A third party."

"*What* third party? One of those loopy capitalmen you and Merri reeled in at your fundraising pitches last week?"

"It doesn't matter," snapped Natch, suddenly annoyed. Jara congratulated herself on derailing his train of thought, if only for an instant.

"So Margaret provides the product, and an apprentice, and meeting space," continued Merri, shrugging off the interruptions. "Not to mention a name with four hundred years of history. I don't mean to be presumptuous, Natch . . . but what do *we* bring to the table?"

The fiefcorp master sat back with fingers intertwined and raised one eyebrow. Jara could practically hear the ominous trumpets blaring out notes of suspense inside Natch's head. "Me."

Jara threw up her hands. "You?" she spat out.

But Natch would not be thrown off track again; like a mutating virus, he had already adapted to her caustic attacks. "You're missing the point," he said calmly. "Margaret is *scared*. You all saw her standing there a few minutes ago. She looked like a fucking ghost. She needs to get MultiReal out to the public, and she needs to do it *quickly*, before she becomes a victim of another assassination attempt."

Horvil's eyes went wide and his jaw plummeted. "Assassination attempt?"

"Why do you think those Council troops were there last night? And for process' preservation, what do you think the infoquake was? It was a distraction. It was Len Borda's attempt to create pandemonium so he could do his dirty work while no one was looking. Except he made a few miscalculations, and Margaret managed to slip away. Come on, you didn't really believe that bullshit about *a simple bottleneck of information*, did you?"

"*I* did," muttered Benyamin, blushing furiously. Jara remembered Sen Sivv Sor's words in that morning's editorial: *Wherever you find such poisonous medicine, there's a human hand nearby administering the dose.*

"Well, it's nonsense. Borda wants MultiReal to disappear. He wants Margaret dead. And the only way to prevent that is to spread MultiReal far and wide before Borda gets a chance to strike. Because once everyone from here to Furtoid is swimming in multiple realities, the Council won't be able to stop it.

"So Margaret needs a good product, and she needs it quickly. People around her are dying. The Council has already proven they'll march right into her compound without a second thought. She's never had to work under pressure before, and she just doesn't know how to take a product to market on a tight deadline. What does Margaret need? She needs the best programmers in the world to put together something marketable *now*.

"That's where *we* come in.

"You want quality? The Natch Personal Programming Fiefcorp is the best in the business. We've got the best analyst and the best engineer and the best channel manager around. You want fast? We climbed to number one on Primo's faster than anyone in history. We know how to work under pressure, and we won't be intimidated by *anyone*."

As Natch's words pricked Jara's skin and sizzled her hormones to a white-hot intensity, she felt a sudden charge of electricity in the room.

He actually called me the best analyst in the business, she thought. An hour ago, she'd been ready to submit to the doldrums of a government desk job. Jara looked around and noticed that Benyamin and Merri both had an excited gleam in their eyes, and Horvil was actually fidgeting in his chair like an eight-year-old boy. *How in the world does he take control of a room like that?*

"So how long do we have?" said Jara.

"Ten days," replied Natch. "We make our first presentation at 7:00 p.m. on December eleventh, Andra Pradesh time. MultiReal goes on sale the next day."

Silence descended upon the bio/logic apprentices and snatched the breath from their lungs. It was already late evening here in Andra Pradesh. Assuming that Margaret's apprentice arrived with the Multi-Real program by Saturday at noon, that would leave them approximately eight days. Eight days to learn a brand-new technology that promised to revolutionize the world; to adjust to the parameters of a new company structure; to go through the entire product conceptualization and development cycle; and to perfect that product for release to billions of voracious consumers. Jara felt like crying. For such a huge project, eight weeks or even eight *months* would have seemed too short a time.

"And what about the Council?" piped in Benyamin.

"What about them?" replied Merri.

"Well, if Len Borda was prepared to murder the richest woman in the world to get his hands on MultiReal . . . what makes you think he'll hesitate to come after *us*?"

Jara quietly tallied up in her head all the Council officers she had seen wandering around this week, prowling the narrow side streets of Andra Pradesh, the avenues of Shenandoah, the cobblestone paths in front of her London apartment. She usually paid them little heed, the soldiers in white robes. Keepers of the peace, minions of High Executive Borda and his Javertian obsession with public safety. To be on the run from such a ubiquitous enemy—it was simply *unthinkable*.

Natch was grinning that feral grin of his. His eyes had focused on an invisible spot in the middle of the room, a place where nobody else was looking. "You still have a choice," he said. "Until midnight tonight Shenandoah time, you are all still apprentices of the Natch Personal Programming Fiefcorp. You can either jump on board the new company with both feet or bail out while you have the chance."

Horvil let out a squeak. Natch swiveled his way. "Borda?" whimpered the engineer.

"Len Borda," said Natch contemptuously, grinding his teeth as if chewing his words. "The high executive might have scared Margaret out of her wits, but he's never dealt with *me*."

$(((25)))$

The two men in the tube car were trying very hard to be nonchalant. *Too* hard. The taller one with the mole on his cheek completely avoided looking in Natch's direction, while the short, dark one swept his attention past the fiefcorp master at precise metronomic intervals. Neither of them took more than a token sip from his mug of nitro.

Natch expected better surveillance tactics from the Defense and Wellness Council.

The entrepreneur spent the dark hours bouncing between Cisco and Seattle staring at redwoods. He expected Jara's notice of resignation at any minute. But midnight Shenandoah time arrived with no message traffic of consequence, just the usual jumble of political propaganda and L-PRACG–sanctioned advertising. He gave one last glance at the Council spooks and allowed himself to fall into a light sleep.

Natch awoke at three in the morning to find the strange men gone. He wondered how long it had been since he had actually slept horizontally in a bed rather than vertically on a contoured tube seat. No matter. He still had plenty of time to make his way back east and prepare the fiefcorp's catalog of bio/logic programs for sale before Quell arrived with the MultiReal databases. Once the sale of their catalog hit the market, Natch would have boldly marched across the Rubicon; there would be no turning back. Had a general ever led his troops into battle with such nebulous weapons?

Then he stepped off the tube at Cisco station, only to be confronted by an image of his own face.

On the viewscreen, Natch recognized the three-meter-high photo from the media blitz following his ascent to number one on Primo's. He stood and watched his doppelganger tick off a few important points on his fingers to an unseen interviewer. His face showed that stern look of concentration he got while pacing and talking business.

Superimposed over the image:

SOLD TO THE LOWEST BIDDER!
*Margaret Surina Enters into Partnership
with Unscrupulous Fiefcorp Master;
Future of Groundbreaking MultiReal Technology in Doubt*
(Read about it in this morning's John Ridglee Update)

Natch hustled through the tube station, an act he could have performed blindfolded by now. Five minutes later, he left the local line behind and boarded a larger express train that would take him across the continent to Shenandoah station. A young man with a purple-striped goatee elbowed his friend in the side at Natch's approach. The two gave him mute looks of disgust and vacated the cabin as soon as the fiefcorp master sat down.

Must be quite an article, he thought.

Natch projected the story onto the faux leather chair in front of him. Compared to Sen Sivv Sor's curmudgeonly countenance, Ridglee's was young and foppish, with left eyebrow so far aslant that it was almost in orbit. His commentary was similarly skewed. The article contained little news beyond that contained in the Surinas' press release, relying instead on a grab bag of fictional anecdotes and unattributed rumors. Yet the drudge had certainly done a thorough job of digging up the details of Natch's past. Everything was there: the Shortest Initiation, the confrontations with Captain Bolbund, the citations from the Meme Cooperative, the hardball tactics he had used over the years against the Patel Brothers.

The tube hurtled underground for the nearly two-hour trip across the continent. As daylight gave way to the tunnel's artificial glow, Natch watched his name take over the Data Sea.

Within twenty minutes, the delegates at the Congress of
L-PRACGs were already quarreling over his partnership with Margaret. *The Surinas are a public treasure!* cried the Speaker on a viewscreen
half a meter from Natch's head. *Are we just going to sit back and let this
man peddle their works all over the Data Sea like a common ROD?* Dozens
of glum representatives nodded in agreement.

The dour voice of Khann Frejohr broke in from the libertarian side
of the chamber. *It's just like the governmentalists to suggest it's our duty to
interfere in the workings of a free marketplace. . . .*

Primo's began advertising a special supplement that promised to
analyze Natch's professional career in depth.

At the first opportunity, Sen Sivv Sor weighed in on the crisis,
denouncing the young fiefcorp master in ways Ridglee had only hinted
at. *All of the other major players in the bio/logic industry are devotees of the
creeds, even the despicable self-serving ones like Creed Thassel,* wrote Sor. *But
I have looked Natch directly in the eye, dear readers, and saw no evidence that
he possesses any morals or ethics at all.*

On the viewscreen, the hook-nosed Speaker was crazily waving her
index finger around in the air. *We have plenty of precedents for government
intervention in the markets, Khann. Didn't the Prime Committee break up the
OCHRE Corporation?*

The libertarian snorted. *That was two hundred fifty years ago,
Madame Speaker. Besides which, the Committee was acting to disband a
monopoly. Sounds like democratization to me.*

Then how do you explain Dr. Plugenpatch's success? A quasi-governmental
entity with open standards that has gloriously extended life expectancy . . .

Natch leaned his head back and let out a deep belly laugh. The
fools, the fools! He was climbing the peaks of tall mountains, and
down below the Powers That Be could do nothing but scramble
around and bicker over the pebbles. He could see the paradise that
awaited him at the top now: Lunar estates, immutable wealth, the
stewardship of an entire industry.

And what an industry it would be! Natch didn't know precisely the shape a MultiReal business would take—an egalitarian product sold to the masses? A technology channeled to the L-PRACGs? Military licenses to the Council and the Prime Committee? No matter what path the business took, it would inevitably lead him to the same glorious future.

Natch laughed again. Three more riders in the tube gave him peculiar looks and rose to find other seats.

• • •

Natch's good mood lasted through the morning, until Horvil began flinging panicked multi requests in his direction. Natch knew his old hivemate was in a panic; that was the only logical explanation for Horvil being awake and alert before noon.

"Drop everything," said the engineer, materializing in Natch's foyer and lumbering his way towards the office. "Drop everything, everything, *everything*."

Natch was in MindSpace, stacking chunks of recursive code on a ledge of NiteFocus 50 like a boy lining up dominos. After fifty iterations, he would have expected the program to be perfect, but the more mindpower he devoted to NiteFocus, the more problematic it seemed to become. "What is it, Horv?"

Horvil emitted a *harrumph* and sliced his left hand through the line of dominos to catch his boss's attention. "You're going to want to turn off the bubble for this, Natch," he said. "*Trust* me." The fiefcorp master looked on skeptically as Horvil waved his hand at a viewscreen on the opposite wall.

A holographic projection of Petrucio Patel appeared in front of the screen. He was by far the handsomer of the two Patel brothers, and actually cut quite a dashing figure in his triple-buttoned suit and wispy black mustache. The projection was a recording, of course;

Natch knew from experience that his hated rival was much taller in real life.

"Towards Perfection," said Petrucio Patel in a rich baritone. "We say that all the time to one another, for hello, for good-bye, for peace, for health. 'Towards Perfection.' But do we really know what it *means?* Well, Sheldon Surina knew. The father of bio/logics said that *Perfection is a safe shore in the tempest.*"

"Slick bastard," Horvil mumbled under his breath.

"Shhh."

"Isn't a safe shore what we're all looking for?" continued Petrucio Patel. "But as the events of last night have clearly shown us, we live in a time without charted waters or safe shores . . . unless you're using one of the Patel Brothers' new MultiReal programs, under direct license from Margaret Surina herself."

Natch could feel a hole open up in the small of his back, out of which slithered a host of hidden anxieties. The *Patels* with a license to sell MultiReal? How was that possible? He turned off the MindSpace bubble and sank onto a stool.

Petrucio waved his brown-skinned hand and summoned forth a typical programming floor. Behind him in the shadows, half a dozen apprentices toiled away in their MindSpace bubbles, while the portly silhouette of Frederic Patel waddled from one workbench to the next. "PatelReal 1.0 will bring you a whole set of practical applications for multiple realities that are *safe* enough to use in your own home," said Petrucio. As soon as the word *safe* passed from his lips, a second Petrucio materialized on his left. Same triple-buttoned suit, same debonair smile.

"PatelReal *easily* keeps track of the confusion and complexity of multiple realities," said the second Petrucio. And with a nod, he brought forth a third clone. "PatelReal can help you navigate the troughs and waves of multiple realities . . . and bring you to a safe shore!"

Finally, the third Petrucio Patel snapped his fingers, causing the rest of the display to vanish. "The Patel Brothers: a safe shore in the tempest," said the lone remaining Patel. "Now, we know you have questions—and we have answers! Come attend the world's *first* demonstration of MultiReal technology next Tuesday, at the Kordez Thassel Complex near the Twin Cities. See PatelReal 1.0 in person! Until then, Towards Perfection—and a safe shore!"

The slick programmer took a bow, and vanished.

• • •

Questions buzzed like hornets inside Natch's head, too many and too fast to handle. He sat paralyzed on his stool, feeling like he himself had wandered into some kind of alternate reality. Horvil collapsed in a quivering heap on the visitor's chair in the corner.

Just when Natch thought he had everything figured out, just when he knew who all the players were in this game, the rules had suddenly changed. How could he have agreed to form a new company with Margaret when his greatest enemies had already struck a licensing deal with her? Was this entire MultiReal project a trap? Who *else* had a piece of MultiReal?

Natch's mind flashed back to the bio/logics industry gathering before Margaret's speech and his confrontation with Frederic Patel. *So that's the game you two are playing, eh?* the engineer had said, and Natch had naïvely assumed that Frederic had been speaking to him.

Natch's legs began to ache; he climbed slowly to his feet and began marching back and forth across the office. He needed to explore the practical dimensions of this latest news, not to mention the legal and financial dimensions. It wouldn't be long now before word of this debacle reached the drudges. Merri, Jara, and Benyamin would have questions. Vigal would be sending him an awkward message of condolence any minute now.

Two minutes later, a multi request did indeed click inside his head. But it was not from a fiefcorp employee. Natch grabbed a bio/logic programming bar off his workbench and clutched it like a samurai warrior as he accepted the request.

Brone.

"Gaaah!" shouted a distressed Horvil as the Thasselian strode into the room. If the engineer had been present in the flesh, his recoil would have sent him tumbling backwards and probably smashed the chair to bits.

"Still the same after all these years, I see, Horvil," Natch's old hivemate said with a minuscule trace of amusement.

"But—but you're—"

"What? Dead?" said the bodhisattva with a dismissive snort. "No, not yet, I'm afraid, despite your friend's best efforts."

Natch eyed his old enemy frostily. The prosthetic arm, false eye, and scars were still evident, but now Brone wore them as comfortably as he wore his expensive cream-colored suit. Horvil did not seem to have even noticed his handicaps yet.

Then Natch caught sight of the three vertical stripes pinned to Brone's chest, the emblem for Creed Thassel, and the tumblers in his mind began to turn. The Thasselians . . . Brone . . . the Kordez Thassel Complex . . . Petrucio Patel's demo next week . . .

"Did *you* have anything to do with this?" he snapped.

A puzzled Brone blinked several times in quick succession. "Did I have anything to do with *what*?" he replied calmly.

Natch looked his old hivemate in the eye and tried to penetrate that thick gauze of death. Could he actually be telling the truth? "Play it back, Horv," he said with a shrug. "I'm sure that promo's all over the Data Sea anyway."

Horvil had caught sight of Brone's rubbery right hand, and now couldn't stop staring at it. "Ffft," he said, tilting his head slightly in the direction of the viewscreen.

The bodhisattva of Creed Thassel looked around for somewhere to sit, but his search only turned up the chair that Horvil had planted himself in and the stool Natch was zealously guarding. He turned towards the viewscreen, then stood in a dead-on imitation of politeness while the holographic Petrucio went through his spiel. A small smile gathered on Brone's face as he watched the performance.

"Quite clever," said Brone after Patel faded into nothingness. "The whole world's in an uproar over this 'infoquake' nonsense . . . and now the *Patel Brothers* of all people are going to show us the way to safety. How disingenuous."

"You didn't answer my question," said Natch through gritted teeth.

"Creed Thassel might be a small organization, Natch, and yes, I am the bodhisattva of Creed Thassel. But there are still a few hundred thousand devotees on the rolls. Even if I knew whether Frederic and Petrucio have embraced our philosophy—which I *don't*—you certainly can't expect me to know what they're up to twenty-four hours a day."

"They're holding a demo at the Kordez Thassel Complex."

"Creed Élan and the Vault directors and the Meme Cooperative hold meetings there all the time," Brone shrugged. "You don't suspect *them* of being Thasselian spies, do you?"

Natch growled vehemently and raised the programming bar in his hands as if preparing to strike. Why did Brone always have to show up when his head was so full of cobwebs? "So what the fuck are you doing here?" he said.

"Business." Brone drifted over to the workbench and began studying the bio/logic programming bars with his virtual fingers.

Horvil, his jowls flapping, whipped his head back and forth between the two old rivals. Comprehension dawned on his face in a sudden rush. "*He's* the 'third party' that's financing us?"

"'Third party'?" said Brone mockingly, his gaze suddenly focused on the engineer. "Your master and I are business partners now, Horvil. Surely you know that already. Natch needs some quick cash to get in on Margaret Surina's game. He goes looking for all those business associates who *like* him and *trust* him enough to make this kind of investment—and he can't come up with a single name. Certainly a mathematician like you can see the inevitable approach of consequence."

The engineer gave his master a wounded look. "You could have come to *me*."

Brone walked over and regarded Horvil with an otherworldly stare. The engineer flinched out of reflex. "Be realistic, Horvil. What would your Aunt Berilla think? She'd start moralizing. Or worse, she'd start asking for *shares*. No, Natch would rather go to a faceless organization like Creed Thassel, where he can work strictly on a cash basis." Brone knelt slowly on the floor and leaned forward until he was close enough to kiss Horvil's nose. "And do you know *why*?"

The engineer was trembling. "Why?"

"Because he wants MultiReal all for himself," he rasped. "And he doesn't want *anybody* to get a piece of it—*especially* his old friend Horvil, who will understand how it works much better than he does."

Natch had had enough. He stalked around the workbench and stood toe to toe with his old rival, causing Horvil to scurry across the room for cover. Brone was at least ten centimeters taller than the fiefcorp master, but the ferocity in Natch's eyes lent him a presence that dominated the room. "All right, this little business arrangement ends right here," he hissed.

The bodhisattva arched an eyebrow. "What do you mean?"

"I mean I'm ready to pay off your loan in full, right here, right now. And then you can get the fuck out of my apartment and never set foot in here again."

Brone pursed his lips like a proctor considering the request of a dim-witted pupil, then sidestepped Natch's glare and took a seat in the chair that Horvil had so recently vacated. Within seconds, he had retreated back into his detached emotional fortress. "Margaret Surina's money."

"Of course."

"I predicted you would do this," said Brone, crossing one leg over the other. "But I will admit I did not expect you to hit Margaret up for money to pay me off so soon. I thought you would be *smart* enough to let bygones be bygones and recognize a potential alliance when you saw one."

"You really think I'm going to stay in debt to you one *minute* longer than I have to?"

Brone shook his head in that maddeningly supercilious way of his. Natch suddenly wished the man were here in the flesh so he could muscle him outside and toss him over the balcony. "Where is the mind I used to respect so? Where is the *killer intellect* Figaro Fi used to speak of? Natch, that pittance of a loan I gave you was an act of *trust*. It was a foundation on which to *build*.

"Think, Natch! You know how much trouble you had finding investors. The drudges despise you across the board, and you can certainly imagine what the Defense and Wellness Council thinks of you right now. What happens when Margaret Surina grows tired of you, as she surely will? Who will you turn to *then*? Or are you naïve enough to think you can do all this alone?"

Natch had retreated back to the safe fortification of his workbench, where he stood silently and wondered how much of this he could take before he severed Brone's multi connection. Why hadn't he done so already? Horvil stood in the corner and watched their tête-à-tête with a miserable look on his face.

"Natch, when are you going to realize that you're in over your head?" continued Brone in a completely even tone of voice. "You must know by now that Margaret isn't dealing with you in good faith. I can see it in your eyes. You don't know what she's up to, do you? What makes you think you're not being made a fool of?

"And *here* sits Brone, the man whom you wronged all those years ago. He is angry. Yes. He hates you and would love to see you dead.

Yes. Indisputable facts. But when you get into a tight spot, Brone shows up with Creed Thassel money to bail you out, and offers you a loan at Vault standard rates. He may insult you, but at least he puts all his cards on the table.

"I cannot be any more forthcoming, Natch. I want to throw the past aside and start a new business. You should be asking yourself one question now: Why trust your fate to a woman whose motivations you *don't* know, instead of trusting your fate to an old enemy whose intentions are written all over his face?"

Natch tightened his grip on the metal bar and slowly advanced towards his old enemy. A miasma of fury was radiating from his every pore, clouding his vision and blocking out the sound of Horvil's whimpers from the corner. "I don't trust my fate to *anyone* but *me*," he said.

He reached the chair and took a crushing swing at it with his bio/logic programming bar. But it was too late; Brone had already cut his multi connection and vanished.

● ● ●

"You lied to me," Natch growled like a hunted tiger.

"I was planning to tell you about it when things calmed down," replied Margaret.

The words Brone had spoken a little over an hour ago still burned in the pit of his stomach. *What makes you think you're not being made a fool of?* "Don't split hairs with me, Margaret. You should have told me everything from the start."

The bodhisattva merely yawned and continued sorting through her notes for the presentation she was about to give to Creed Surina. The presentation had nothing to do with MultiReal or business mergers or bio/logics; it bore the aggressively mundane title *Revised Fourth-Quarter Budget for Diss Technology Distribution Program.* Even a fleeting glance over Margaret's shoulder at the formation of integers lining the spreadsheet columns was enough to make Natch drowsy. He looked out into the audience of the small auditorium, where a few sluggish creed bureaucrats had begun to take up residence. In the fifth row sat an old woman who had dozed through the ending of the last meeting and looked like she might snore through this one too. Margaret was handing control of MultiReal over to Natch so she could conduct tedious seminars like *this*?

"I'm waiting for an answer," said Natch.

Margaret frowned. "An answer to what? Would it have made the least bit of difference if I had told you all about the Patel Brothers' license in the first place? No, it would not have. If you hadn't reacted so strongly to Len Borda's involvement, I might have told you at the beginning." She tapped on a header in the spreadsheet and then craned her neck as a video clip of a lethargic diss child filled the viewscreen behind her.

"The least you could do," he said under his breath, "is tell me the details of your agreement."

"Frederic and Petrucio have a limited license. They can release MultiReal products, but they will be subordinate to yours."

"Subordinate how?"

"The Patel products will have a limited number of choice cycles, whereas yours will be infinite."

"And exactly what is a 'choice cycle'?"

Margaret sputtered out a sigh and rubbed her forehead. "It's complicated. Quell will explain everything to you."

Natch crossed his arms petulantly over his chest. He paced to the edge of the stage from which Margaret would be delivering her soporific report in half an hour. Everyone from here to 49th Heaven was discussing this mighty new technology and speculating about the kinds of secrets Margaret and Natch were exchanging; in reality, however, Natch could barely catch her attention.

"So you didn't tell me because you thought I would back off," he said with a grunt.

"It occurred to me, yes."

"That means you basically lured me into this deal on false pretenses, knowing I wouldn't say no, that I would *have* to jump at this kind of opportunity. And now that the word is out, you know I won't back down."

Margaret turned towards the fiefcorp master with haunted eyes. "You find yourself capable of strange things when you run out of choices," she said, as if she had been condemned to watch a gruesome execution over and over again.

"Tell me why," Natch demanded. "You owe me that. Why Frederic and Petrucio Patel, of all people? You had to know they hate me with a passion."

The descendant of Sheldon Surina leaned her elbows on the podium and delicately parked her chin on her palms. "I went to Pierre Loget first. But he was evasive and I didn't trust him. So then, almost nine months ago, I approached the Patel Brothers. They sat down with me and swore up and down that they wanted to bring MultiReal to the public, that they could see a glorious new age of opportunity arising."

"So what happened?"

"The Council bought them off."

Natch inhaled sharply. Everywhere he turned, he saw a place someone else had long since scouted out and claimed for his own. "How do you know?"

"I suppose I don't really *know* at all," said Margaret with a weary, far-off look. "The Patels deny that they're in collusion with anybody. But sometimes we can just sense these things, can't we? Too many coincidences, too many nosey questions, too little fear of the consequences. The entire Patel Brothers Fiefcorp got onboard a hoverbird a few weeks ago and disappeared for two days, I don't know where. They've clearly been bought by *someone*."

"So why don't you just break the license? Cancel the agreement."

"Believe me, I've tried." She pulled one hand out from under her chin and extended a bony finger off to the east. "Dozens of legal experts have been working around the clock in the Enterprise Facility trying to find loopholes in the contract. We've got lobbyists rubbing elbows with the Prime Committee, and delegates in the Congress of L-PRACGs pushing legislation. That contract is ironclad."

Natch shook his head in disbelief at the morass Margaret had made out of the whole affair. Did this woman completely lack an imagination? "Listen, Margaret," he said, "it's just a contract. They're just words. Cut the Patel Brothers off from the MultiReal databases and put the burden of proof on *them*. They'll have to file something with the Meme Cooperative or the L-PRACG courts. Getting a final decision could take years."

The bodhisattva sighed and turned back to her presentation. "And give Len Borda the perfect excuse to send another legion of Council troops here? I don't think so."

Natch threw his hands up in the air, a despondent plea to the half-empty auditorium. Down in the fifth row, the old woman flopped over with a loud snort while Natch looked on in contempt. Margaret had foisted her problems off on him, but he had no such luxury. If someone needed to take action to keep the Phoenix Project out of the Council's hands, that someone would have to be Natch.

You find yourself capable of strange things when you run out of choices.

(((26)))

On Saturday morning, Natch was the first to arrive at the Surina Enterprise Facility, and so his mood dominated the conference room SeeNaRee. The fiefcorp apprentices found themselves sitting at a table in the middle of the African veldt. But this wasn't the modern veldt any of them knew, that bustling metropolis crammed full of autonomous business clusters, tube tracks, and Sudafrican suburbs; it was the veldt of some mythical African past. Giraffes chomped at lofty tree limbs. Lions roared their displeasure through a thin tissue of mist. Ghosts and spirits floated past in ethereal majesty.

By a quarter past noon, there was still no sign of Quell or the Multi-Real programming code. Horvil and Ben would have been content to gossip about family business all day, but Natch had no use for idle time. "Let's just get started," the fiefcorp master snapped. "We can't afford to wait for Quell anymore. Has everyone seen the Patel Brothers' promo?"

His question was met with an uncomfortable silence. All the apprentices had seen it, but their critical faculties were so dulled by weeks of constant surprises that nobody knew what to make of it.

"I don't understand, Natch," began Jara. "Margaret just unveiled this MultiReal technology three days ago. And now the Patel Brothers are already selling it?"

"They had a nine-month head start," put in Merri.

Jara let out a guttural curse. "Nine months—that's when everyone started catching up with them on Primo's," she said. "I just *knew* there had to be a reason why their programs were such easy targets."

"*I* don't understand this whole fucking *thing!*" cried a frustrated Horvil, banging his fist on the table hard enough to send a flock of marabous scurrying. "'Multiple realities' . . . 'safe shores' . . . It sounds like *voodoo* to me! Does anybody understand this MultiReal stuff?

What the heck would you need an alternate reality for? Has the whole world gone entirely *offline?*"

"Well, apparently Frederic and Petrucio understand it," muttered Benyamin.

Natch had been listening to his apprentices' jabber with eyes closed, as if participating in an internal dialogue with an unseen consultant. "How do you know?" he said.

Jara felt her mental gears grind to a halt. The rest of the apprentices sported dumb looks as well.

"Petrucio didn't say they were going to *launch* a MultiReal product on Tuesday," Natch continued. "All they're doing is holding a demo. As far as we know, the Patel Brothers are *months* away from launching anything that'll float on the Data Sea."

"Which means—"

"Maybe Frederic and Petrucio don't understand this technology any better than we do. Maybe they never got much cooperation from Margaret, and now they're frantically trying to put together something that will look halfway decent for their demo. A good channeler can make lots of deals before there's anything to sell. The Patels could be trying to shut out the competition before anyone else realizes there's something to compete over."

Horvil snorted. "What about *us?*"

"Us?" said Jara, starting to comprehend the vector of Natch's thoughts. "Horv, Margaret never said anything about *products* in that speech of hers. She called MultiReal a *scientific breakthrough*. As far as the public knows, we could be planning to hold on to the core technology and collect licensing fees. Or we could be some kind of charitable technology bank."

"So you think the Patels are bluffing," said Merri. "Putting up a . . . a smokescreen to scare everyone else out of the MultiReal business." As a devotee of Creed Objectivv, she seemed to find the entire possibility distasteful.

"More or less," said Natch. "If they really *are* working for Len Borda like Margaret suspects, then I'm sure that would suit him just fine."

Silence briefly engulfed the room. Natch's eyes remained closed. Jara could hear the cawing of vultures overhead, the rustling of amorphous beasts out in the brush. *Nobody ever said that SeeNaRee had to be subtle*, she thought.

"Well," said Benyamin faintly, "why can't we do the same thing?"

Natch's eyelids snapped open, and the blue orbs beneath emitted a ghoulish glow. The virtual sun dipped below the treeline as if on cue and cast them all in shadow. "That's *exactly* what we're going to do," he said through a fierce grin. "The Patel Brothers made the first strike by releasing this promo and scheduling a demo so quickly. But on Tuesday, we're going to beat them at their own game—*because we're going to demo our products first.*"

Jara groaned. "And how do you expect us to do that?" she cried, her hands balled into miniature fists. "It was bad enough when you wanted us to create an entire industry in eight days. Now you want us to do it in *three*?"

The fiefcorp master did not even pause. "Yes."

"Natch, who knows how long the Patels have been preparing for this demo? Days, weeks, months! Horvil's right—we barely even know what this program *is*. None of us had even *heard* of MultiReal this time last week. How are we supposed to get started? We don't have the code; we don't have the expertise; we don't have anything to work with."

"Not true," Natch replied tersely. "We have all the bio/logic code we need."

Merri ran her fingers through her blond hair quizzically. "Natch, I thought you started liquidating all our bio/logic programs this morning."

"All the *released* programs, yes. But not the old ones we've taken off the market. Not the Routines On Demand."

"RODs?" yelped Horvil, springing up from his chair. "I don't believe this. You're pitting us against the Patel Brothers with some of your shitty old ROD programming?"

Natch smiled cruelly. "Not *my* old programming, Horvil. Yours."

All the color drained from the engineer's face. He sat down gingerly, not even bothering to put on a PokerFace to mask his dismay. "Oh no, Natch. You're not talking about Probabilities 4.9, are you? Man, that program is in sorry shape. It's nowhere *near* ready for production."

The fiefcorp master nodded. "That's the one."

Horvil whimpered incoherently.

Jara cut in. "Natch, I don't see any record of Probabilities 4.9 on the Data Sea." She narrowed her eyes, casting her mind out in a wider net. Primo's ratings, fiefcorp launch schedules, Meme Cooperative filings, drudge reviews, InfoGathers—all came up empty. "As far as I can tell, this program was never released. It doesn't even look like it's been run through Dr. Plugenpatch."

"Well, of *course*," said Natch, irony oozing from his pores. "Do you think we'd put the code to our top-secret weapon out on the Data Sea, where anybody could see it?"

"You wouldn't *let* me release it," whined Horvil. "You said it was shit."

Merri interposed a hand into the middle of the table, attempting a peacemaking gesture. "Horvil, if our MultiReal demo is riding on this program—"

"And all our contracts too," snarled Jara.

"—then maybe you'd better tell us what it is."

Horvil gathered his breath and sucked in his voluminous gut. He started reciting a sales pitch that had long since calcified in memory. "'Probabilities 4.9 is designed to take chaotic real-world events and quantify their random elements into a meaningful array suitable for prediction. Its intended audience is any person looking for an array of random elements on which to place a wager. For instance, Probabilities 4.9 might track the number of dust motes in a particular square meter and determine the odds of any one dust mote hitting the ground first. . . .'"

"It's a gambling calculator," said Jara, shaking her head. "We've quit the bio/logics business to sell a gambling calculator?"

"Actually, it's more like a statistical distribution engine that—"

"Probabilities 4.9 is absolutely *not* a gambling calculator!" said Natch, rising from his chair and waving his fist like a tin-pot dictator. "It's the turbine that powers Possibilities 1.0, the first in a revolutionary line of MultiReal products based on the principles of Margaret Surina! It will quantify and order multiple realities! It will find the patterns within the chaos!"

Jara's temples were beginning to throb. She could feel panic lapping up against the seawalls of her mind, threatening to spill over and flood her synapses. *All our contracts and our shares are riding on some tossed-off contraption of Horvil's. . . .* "So what's the plan then, Natch? Are we just going to go out there and pretend this Probabilities thing is MultiReal?"

"No, I'm afraid Horvil's right. It's a piece of shit."

"Hey!"

"Probabilities 4.9 is really just going to be the front end for Margaret's MultiReal code. When Quell gets here, we'll hook the two programs together in MindSpace. They operate in the same general field. There ought to be some similarities we can work with. Enough to get us through the demonstration, at least."

Merri had been watching the back-and-forth between Natch and Jara like a spectator at a duel. "I think I'm beginning to understand," she said. "Horvil knows the Probabilities code inside and out. . . . Presumably, this apprentice of Margaret's knows the MultiReal code inside and out. . . . So, if we can just build a bridge between the two, we can make this demo work."

"Precisely."

Horvil had already pushed aside the injury to his pride for the more pressing issue of an intellectual challenge. Using the tip of his finger, he was busy sketching lengthy equations on a virtual slate. The engineer ended up with a very large and unwieldy number at the bottom. "Totally impossible," he said.

"What?" asked Natch.

"This is going to take a lot of grunt work, Natch. A *lot*. If this MultiReal program is as complex as Margaret says it is, it's bound to have thousands of nodes we'll need to hook up. Tens of thousands, maybe. Even if you and me and Quell and Ben work on this nonstop, we couldn't get it done until"—Horvil scribbled his way through a maze of algebra—"December nineteenth."

"You see?" cried Jara. "There's no way we can do all this by Tuesday. No *way*."

The fiefcorp master flashed her the barest hint of a suggestive look, which Jara could feel right between the shoulder blades. Natch extended his finger towards Benyamin. "You've managed assembly-line coders," he said. "Do you know a shop that can pull this off at the last minute?" The young man looked wide-eyed at his cousin, inhaled deeply, then nodded. "Good, then it's settled."

Jara felt the tingling between her shoulder blades diffuse down her back and into her spine. She remembered getting this feeling while playing chess against her grandfather, a professional who had jousted with the masters in the 49th Heaven tournaments. Inevitably, halfway through every game, she would discover that her grandfather had accounted for all of her two-dimensional feints, that the moves she had taken at face value were but the smallest strokes of an overarching blueprint that had been in place since the first tentative pawnstep forward. Natch possessed this same talent. Had he known where Benyamin would fit in the grand scheme when he hired him? Had he known all those years ago that Horvil's Probabilities code would one day prove useful? Did he have some hidden purpose reserved for *her*?

"So that still leaves Jara and me," said Merri quietly. "What should we be doing?"

"Yeah, I suppose we get to stay behind and keep the home fires burning," Jara snapped with a swagger she didn't feel.

Natch focused the full force of his sapphire orbs on Jara. "You have the most difficult job of all. You write the script."

"That's not difficult. I *bleed* marketing copy, Natch."

"But this isn't like any marketing copy you've ever written before, Jara. Those people out there—they *hate* me." He made a sweeping arc with one hand that encompassed nearly the entire veldt. "By the time I step out on that stage on Tuesday, the drudges will have convinced everyone I'm a public menace. You need to counter their propaganda *and* explain a completely foreign technology *and* get the audience revved up—all in fifteen minutes or less."

"*Fifteen minutes?*" the analyst yelped.

"Margaret's speech was too long. *Much* too long. Ours needs to be different. We need to get the audience keyed up in an *emotional* way. I don't want anybody *thinking* too much about this technology. I just want one simple demonstration that cuts to the chase. How simple? A four-year-old should understand MultiReal after I'm done speaking; that's how simple it's got to be."

Merri cleared her throat politely. "And me?"

"Work with Robby Robby and his channelers. Start warming up the leads. And then, the instant the presentation's over, *bang!* I want a fucking sales *blitzkrieg* out there. Take no prisoners."

Jara looked around and saw nothing but eager faces spiked with adrenaline. All the apprentices had feared this new fiefcorp was flailing around in the dark, aimlessly searching for direction. *But Natch has a plan*, Jara thought. *We should have known. He always has a plan.*

"There's one more topic we need to cover," Natch said with an abrupt change of tone. Either he was suddenly being sincere, or he had made new strides in his mask of personableness. "The Defense and Wellness Council is out there, and they don't want this demonstration to go forward. Maybe the Patels are on their payroll and maybe not.

But you all saw what happened at Margaret Surina's speech. When this meeting is over and I send out the announcement of our demo, we've got seventy-two hours till showtime—and once Len Borda knows that, he might resort to something desperate."

"What about the Patels?" said Jara. "Are they going to come after us too?"

Natch scratched his elbow thoughtfully. "I don't know. I can't see the angle in them resorting to violence. And Frederic and Petrucio never do *anything* without an angle."

Horvil eyed a pack of hyenas in the distance as if they might be Council informants. "So what do you want us to *do?* Lock our doors? Hire bodyguards?"

"Maybe we should just lie low until Tuesday," suggested Ben. "Find somewhere the Council can't get to us."

Merri gave the young apprentice a dark look. "Like where?"

There was a long pause. Somewhere in the distance, a cluster of African bats shrieked. The Defense and Wellness Council had a presence in every city on the globe, every chartered settlement on Luna and Mars, every jerry-built outpost orbiting the sun from Earth to the asteroid belt. Was there anyplace in the whole of human civilization where Borda couldn't find them?

Natch leaned forward, balancing his chin on the tips of his two index fingers. "All right, then," he said. "Everyone's going to come out here to Andra Pradesh as soon as possible. We can't wait for Quell anymore. The Surina compound's got plenty of accommodations and the best programming facilities in the world—not to mention armed security."

"What good is that going to do us?" said Jara with a grimace. "The Council marched right inside the gates the other day while Surina security just sat there and watched. What makes you think they'll stop Borda this time?"

The entrepreneur closed his eyes once more, and Jara realized he had explored this situation a thousand times already in his head.

"Where else can we go? Any place that's primitive enough to escape the Council's notice is too backwards for us to put together a demo in. And I've looked everywhere—the Islands, the Pharisee Territories, OrbiCo space freighters. It's the same wherever you look. At least in Andra Pradesh we'll see them coming."

"What—what about Serr Vigal?" stuttered Horvil.

"Vigal will be all right. He's got his own private security team at the conference, and everyone knows he doesn't have much to do with our day-to-day operations. He promised he'd show up for the demo."

"Natch, what about *me*?" Merri's tone of voice was distraught, almost tearful. "I don't think there's any shuttle that can get from Luna to Terra that fast. The presentation will be over while I'm still in transit."

"I haven't forgotten about you. I've made you a reservation at TeleCo later this afternoon."

Jara's eyes went wide with disbelief. "Teleport—from the *moon*? Are you kidding? Do you know how expensive that is? That's like our entire third-quarter budget right there."

"Not as expensive as replacing a dead channel manager at the last minute," said Natch.

Nobody could argue with that.

• • •

Ten minutes later, Natch cut his multi connection. He stood on the red square tile in his hallway and took stock of preparations for Tuesday's performance. All the pieces were set on the board: the auditorium space had been reserved; the proper documentation had been filed with the Meme Cooperative; the press release had been blasted to every corner of the Data Sea. He gave the drudges another fifteen minutes before they started a blitzkrieg of their own.

He consulted the time and shook his head. Precious seconds were ticking away, time disappearing forever into the void. He would need to drive his staff *hard* in order to complete this massive undertaking. He would need to thrash a little sloppiness out of Horvil; to wink and cajole a little extra effort out of Jara; to give Merri that zone of comfort that allowed her to produce consistently excellent work. Benyamin's motivations were still a mystery to him, as were those of the Islander Quell. But Natch felt confident he would find their hooks before this crunch was through.

The fiefcorp master made a quick list of things he would need at the Surina complex. His satchel of bio/logic programming bars. A few shirts. An extra pair of pants. The gabardine suit he had purchased for important events. Natch tucked the hermetically sealed packets of clothing into his satchel, wolfed down a sandwich, and was on his way. As he left the building, he imagined he could hear his apartment breaking down and compressing into its component pieces.

November afternoons in Shenandoah were dreary affairs. It would not be unusual to expect a dusting of early snow, but Natch's L-PRACG weather service was predicting rain. Indeed, a group of ominous dark clouds had assembled on the city's western edge, trying to decide whether to advance downtown or move on to riper targets. The threat of rain was enough to empty the streets. Why slog through the rain when you could multi to some sunny locale halfway around the globe instead?

The large viewscreen down the road from Natch's building had long since moved on from its ChaiQuoke advertisement. Now it showcased a bosomy woman with a lustful gaze that followed everyone who passed by. Above her shoulder were the words:

I'LL BE WAITING FOR YOU IN 49TH HEAVEN.
Vacation packages for all ages and income brackets.

But Natch paid as little heed to the sign as he did to the mounting rain. His head was already inside MindSpace at the Surina Enterprise

Facility, toying with the intricate code stored in the MultiReal databases. By the time he made it halfway to the TubeCo station, his hair had drooped mop-style onto his forehead, bogged down by the afternoon drizzle.

He leaned forward to shake off the watery accumulation, causing the first dart to whizz past his right ear.

Natch snapped his head up and saw a small needle embedded in the side of the building he had been walking past. Undoubtedly, the dart's payload of OCHREs was discharging harmlessly into the concrete.

Darts . . . OCHREs laden with . . . black code!

Natch's animal instincts took over as he sprinted for cover. He caught a glimpse of a figure in a black robe flecked with crimson, shouldering a dart-rifle. Firing.

Thwip! Thwip! Two more projectiles slammed into the wall mere centimeters away, sending miniature starbursts of rainwater into the air.

Natch dove around the corner into an alleyway of sorts, a temporary opening between buildings that did not need the space. An avenue of shadows that would be gone long before anyone got around to naming it. Natch dimly realized that his ending up here was no accident; this assault had been well planned.

He risked a glance back across the street, where he had seen the figure in the black robe. If the man was a Council officer, he was not wearing any of the standard-issue uniforms. The robe draped him from head to toe, and the red formed some kind of pattern—Chinese characters, perhaps. Illegible at this distance, in any event.

The man was making brusque hand signals in several directions. He was not alone.

Two figures went tearing past the alleyway in an attempt to establish a flanking position on the other side. In one fluid motion, Natch drew a bio/logic programming bar from his satchel and hurled it like a discus.

The bar hit home, and one of the black-robed figures went down with a grunt. Definitely human, definitely male, and definitely *not* a multi projection. He doubted he had used enough force to cause major damage, but a solid metal bar in the gut was enough to bring anyone to the floor for at least a few minutes.

Natch could see more scrambling motions in the shadows, and more figures in identical black robes. He swung his head around wildly, looking for someone on the street to yell to, some method of escape. But the street was empty, and the only way out of the alley lay some fifty meters ahead of him. Natch bolted down the corridor, frantically trying to think of a bio/logic program he could use for self-defense. Forty meters to the end of the alley . . . thirty meters . . . almost halfway there . . .

And then Natch felt the pinprick of a needle in his back, near the base of his spine, and the black code slammed into him.

He flopped around and saw one of his mysterious pursuers standing at the end of the alleyway, dartgun mounted on his shoulder. Before Natch could react, he was hit twice more in the side and the right forearm.

As the malevolent dart tip OCHREs flowed into his bloodstream, he felt surprisingly little pain. All the same, he knew it wouldn't be long before the insidious machines had nullified his defenses and reprogrammed his internal systems. The rules of the Meme Cooperative, the strictures of Dr. Plugenpatch, the protective matrix of OCHREs, and the red blood cells in his body—all could be circumvented, given time and expertise and direct access to the major arteries carrying cellular traffic.

Natch tried one desperate ConfidentialWhisper request to Horvil, but it was too late. He collapsed face-first into a puddle of rainwater and continued down below street level into darkness.

$(((27)))$

The apprentices, conscious of the press of time, cut their multi connections and made arrangements to cart their bodies to Andra Pradesh. Only Jara stayed behind at the Enterprise Facility to await Quell's arrival.

Horvil's tube ride to Andra Pradesh was uneventful. No Council officers in white robes lurking around, no strange looks from fellow tube passengers other than the ones Horvil was used to getting. The engineer had ascended halfway up the steep hill inside the Surina compound gates before it occurred to him that a three-day stay at Andra Pradesh might require more than his bio/logic programming bars and a thermos of nitro.

He was the first one back at the safari SeeNaRee. Quell had still not arrived. While Jara tried to wrap up the first draft of a speech outline before she fetched her body from London, Horvil made camp at the antiseptic conference table. He conjured up a diagram of Probabilities 4.9 and began poring over the details, trying to familiarize himself with a program he had unceremoniously discarded five years ago. It was like reading old hive poetry; the coding was sloppy, the connections strained and amateurish. Probabilities 4.9 would not even have passed muster at Dr. Plugenpatch five years ago, and the bio/logic standards had evolved so much since then. He couldn't wait to find a workbench and tear into this program in MindSpace.

Suddenly, a shadow fell across the table, obscuring the holograph. Horvil looked up in irritation. *Not another one of those SeeNaRee elephants . . .*

It was no elephant. An immense man stood before him, possibly fifty years old but with the physique of someone half that age. A pale blond ponytail slunk down one shoulder and splayed out over his great barrel chest. The man could have cracked Horvil's head like a walnut between his biceps and forearm, but his demeanor was calm, almost sardonic. "I presume you're Horvil," he said.

Horvil balked, his mind a blank. "And you are?"

"I'm your new apprentice," replied the man. "Quell." He extended a hand in Horvil's direction at precisely the same time Horvil arose and started to bow. The plump engineer stared at the calloused and many-ringed hand in confusion.

"You're supposed to shake it, you idiot." Jara walked up and placed her tiny palm in Quell's. She had to tilt her head back just to look him in the eye. "Towards Perfection. I'm Jara, Natch's bio/logic analyst. Don't mind Horvil—not *everybody* here is that clueless about your customs." The big man enclosed her virtual hand in his flesh fist, and they went through the awkward mechanics of a handshake. Finally, she pulled her hand away in frustration. "Maybe you can see why we bow instead."

Quell did not miss a beat. "And maybe *you* can see why I insist on shaking anyway."

All at once, comprehension came flooding into Horvil's head. He caught sight of the plain tan breeches and the thin copper collar suspended from the man's neck. The breeches were cinched tightly around his waist with a snakeskin belt that looked like it was actually made out of snakeskin. "Y-you're an unconnectible!" the engineer exclaimed in surprise.

"Yeah," replied Quell, "although I think the term you're looking for is *Islander*."

Horvil was so fascinated with the man's collar that he completely missed the faux pas. He had seen plenty of Islanders at a distance, of course—they did sometimes venture beyond the borders of their little demesne in the South Pacific—but actually *meeting* one in person was a different matter altogether. Horvil tried to picture what this room would look like to Quell if he removed that collar. No SeeNaRee, no Jara, no multi projections of any kind.

"I thought you were a bio/logic engineer," he said, thoroughly baffled. "Weren't you supposed to bring us the MultiReal code?" Horvil peeked around the Islander as if he expected to see a string of Mind-Space blueprints bobbing behind him on a string.

"I *am* an engineer," said Quell with scarcely masked impatience. "And don't worry, I have access to the code."

Horvil peered up and down the big man doubtfully. "If you're an engineer, where's your bio/logic programming bars?" He patted his own neatly folded knapsack and felt the reassuring heft of the metal inside.

The Islander let out a breath. He had obviously dealt with such skepticism many times before. "Let's just get this over with," he groused in a dangerous tone of voice. "We don't have time to fuck around. Follow me." He pivoted on one heel and stomped towards the metal doorframe standing incongruously in the middle of the veldt. Horvil and Jara looked at one another, shrugged, and set off in pursuit. All at once, the African SeeNaRee was replaced by the blue stretched-stone walls of the Surina Enterprise Facility.

Quell strode through the halls as if the facility had been constructed solely for his benefit. None of the Surina security guards seemed eager to contradict this impression. They parted dutifully for the Islander with deep, respectful bows, while casting suspicious glances at Jara and Horvil. Throngs of businesspeople hustling to and from meetings stepped aside because of the Islander's intimidating presence. Finally, Quell led them to a door surrounded by Surina security people and walked into the most gorgeous workspace Horvil had ever seen.

The room's four walls bore no SeeNaRee or decorations of any kind, not even one of those extendable programming bar holsters that Horvil had seen in so many offices lately. Quell's workbench, however, was anything but shabby: a four-sided metal monstrosity with a sliding panel that allowed access to its center. The Islander snapped his fingers and conjured up a gigantic MindSpace bubble, large enough to hold three or four of Horvil's programs simultaneously. A serpentine block of bio/logic code wended partway around the bubble in hues of gray, brown, and violet.

"Watch this," commanded Quell. And then he plunged his bare hands straight into the middle of the holograph.

Horvil gasped as connection strands rose like snakes charmed from a basket and wiggled their way to the Islander's fingers. Soon, Quell had amassed a bundle of data fibers in each hand, which he proceeded to weave in and out of the code blocks with astonishing alacrity. The connections looked just as well seated as if they had been stuck there with a pricey set of programming bars.

"I didn't even know you could *do* it that way," said Horvil. He thought of the clunky silver slabs roosted against his side and felt a rush of inferiority.

"How do you think people made code before bio/logic programming bars?" replied Quell. His noodling did not seem to have any purpose other than demonstration; he was tying and untying the same collection of strands over and over again. "With their bare hands, that's how. On the Islands, we remember such things."

"But . . . the connection strands . . . they're *floating* to your fingertips . . ."

The big man's eyes twinkled with a craftsman's pride. Suddenly, he clenched his hands into fists, and the snakes drooped limply back to the desk. "The rings," he said, twitching his fingers in the air. "They each broadcast a unique signature, just like a programming bar."

Jara had been watching Quell's display with characteristic skepticism. "So what *is* this thing?" she said, gesturing at the roller coaster structure of the program. "That was a nice demonstration, but how do we know it even works?"

"This *thing* is EnviroSelect 14," retorted the Islander. "And you know it works because it's been choosing the SeeNaRee for you every time you've stepped into a Surina conference room."

Jara pursed her lips, embarrassed. "Oh."

• • •

When they arrived back at the conference room, Benyamin was waiting for them. He didn't show the least bit of surprise at Quell's traditional Islander handshake, causing Horvil to wonder how his younger cousin could be so much more worldly than he. There was no sign of Merri yet, but that was to be expected; teleportation was challenging enough without the additional complications caused by 380,000 kilometers of space. She would not be here for a few more hours yet. Jara took one last look at her notes, muttered something unintelligible but definitely not pleasant, and then cut her multi connection.

Horvil and Ben dutifully followed Quell back through the hallways to the workroom where the engineering would begin. The Islander seemed inclined to walk several meters ahead of the two cousins, but Horvil managed to hustle to the big man's side.

"I was hoping you could explain something," said the engineer. "Obviously, you can make bio/logic programs with those funky rings there, but how do you *test* 'em?"

Quell eyed his counterpart with scarcely concealed suspicion. "What do you mean?"

"I thought Islanders didn't run bio/logic programs because bio/logics is unholy, or something like that."

"You're thinking of the Pharisees. That's not us at all. We run bio/logic programs in the Islands; people there install most of the basic OCHREs. Our Technology Board just discriminates a lot more carefully than your connectible governments."

"*We* discriminate pretty carefully," said Horvil in a wounded tone of voice.

Quell shook his head, and for a second the engineer thought he was going to burst out laughing. "How much code do you have floating around your system right now, Horvil?" he said.

Horvil thought carefully, trying to account for all the programs he activated willy-nilly every minute, the background code created by his L-PRACG and the Prime Committee, the constant hum of molecular activity instigated by his OCHREs. Processes whose names he didn't know, routines that had been installed by hive technicians before birth and running constantly since then. "I don't know," he said. "Thousands, probably."

"And do you know who wrote them all? How do you know they're all going to work together flawlessly?"

"That's why we have governments. That's why there's Primo's and the Council."

"Governments. Primo's. The Defense and Wellness Council." The Islander spat out the words as if they were the names of particularly odious criminals. "Do you trust *them*?"

"Not entirely. But I'm not gonna sit around all day and weed through bio/logic programs either."

Benyamin, who had been listening a few paces behind, now came trotting up on Quell's right side. "But we have a system for opting out of bio/logic programs," he said. "The Islander Tolerance Act of 146. High Executive Toradicus signed it."

"Spoken like a true governmentalist," said Quell, though his tone of voice was not unkind. "Create an opt-out provision, and put the onus on *our* taxpayers, on *our* governments. The Technology Board has a huge team that does nothing but register these 'Dogmatic Oppositions' twenty-four hours a day to keep your bots and data agents out of the South Pacific. And who do you think pays their salaries? Do you think your Prime Committee has ever sent a bloody credit our way to fund their Tolerance Act?"

Horvil blushed furiously. He had heard of Dogmatic Oppositions, of course, but to him the term had just been verbal dressing tossed around in Khann Frejohr's speeches. He had never met anyone to whom these things actually *mattered*. "Politics," muttered Horvil. "I hate politics."

At that, the Islander let out a Titan-sized laugh of such gusto that all the security guards in the hallway instantly felt for their dart-rifles. "If you hate politics," said Quell, "you're in the wrong fiefcorp."

"So how many programs do *you* have running in *your* system?" snapped Horvil.

The Islander looked at Horvil with an expression that hinted at fondness or amusement. "Twelve. And seven of them are for my asthma."

• • •

Horvil had started to drift into an interior monologue about the evils of politics when he was jarred back to reality by their arrival at Quell's workroom. The Islander made an obscure hand signal to a unit of blue-and-green Surina security officers, and a dozen of them instantly marched up to the workroom door and formed a protective ring around it. This was no loose formation like the one Horvil had seen here half an hour ago; these troops had their fingers on the triggers of their guns and were clearly ready to use them. "Thank you," said Horvil inanely as he stepped into the room with Ben and Quell and closed the door behind him.

Two dozen guards at the gates to the Surina complex, thought Horvil. *And then more guards blocking the way into the Surina Enterprise Facility . . . and now even more right outside the door . . . You'd need an army to get past all those dartguns.*

Then he remembered that Len Borda *did* have an army. Several armies, in fact. He shivered.

Quell was obviously used to the pressure. He marched into the center of the workbench and waved his hand around the table. Ben and Horvil jumped back in awe as a dozen interlocking modules of pink and blue appeared in the MindSpace bubble. Horvil now understood the need for the large workspace; the program took up every square centimeter and extended halfway to the ceiling like a Gothic castle. Connection strands stretched from module to module in startling and intricate patterns, some circumnavigating the whole mass several times. Even an observer who knew nothing about bio/logic coding could lose himself for hours studying the beautiful detail, the interplay of colors, the endless number of aesthetic themes that replicated across the surface of the program. Horvil had seen entire nervous system simulators that were less complex.

"So this is MultiReal." He gulped. Next to the Byzantine topography of the MultiReal program, Probabilities 4.9 would look like a pastel-colored pimple.

"That—that's *amazing*," stuttered Ben.

Quell's face showed a mixture of pride and sadness, the palimpsest of some epic experience that Horvil could hardly begin to imagine. "After sixteen years of work," he said, "it ought to be."

"Sixteen *years?*" said Horvil, his jaw hanging low. He couldn't imagine working on the same program for sixteen *months*.

"And that's just Margaret's part of it. Half of this code was passed down by her father when he died—and she contracted out a lot of bits and pieces."

Horvil nodded as if Quell's statement were self-evident.

"*Now* are we ready to start coding?" Quell asked.

The two cousins nodded in sync, and they got to work.

Probabilities 4.9 did indeed look quite puny beside the gargantuan MultiReal engine. Its double-helix shape was a child's trick in comparison, a second-rate sleight of hand. Horvil found the sight of the two programs side by side a big metaphor for the entire situation Natch had gotten them into. *The Surina/Natch MultiReal Fiefcorp?* thought the engineer, wishing he could just erase the Probabilities ROD and pretend it had never existed. *This is the Margaret Surina MultiReal Fiefcorp, plain and simple. We don't belong here. We're completely out of our league.*

Quell spent the first half hour pointing out the MultiReal program's basic hooks to his fellow apprentices. There wasn't enough time for a more in-depth explanation. When the Islander wrapped up his brief overview, Horvil still had no idea what an alternate reality was or why you would want to create one. But now he felt confident he could at least steer this MultiReal vessel, even if the workings of its engine room remained a mystery.

Horvil was gratified to see that his original estimate of the work involved was accurate. Clearly, it would be madness for Quell, Horvil, and Benyamin to attempt to make all those thousands of connections in less than seventy-two hours; even Natch would have to admit that. So the two senior engineers spent the next few hours making detailed blueprints for the assembly-line shop and marking up their code on templates even the greenest programmer could follow. There wasn't enough room inside the workbench for Ben to squeeze in, not alongside two men of such bulk. So he kept to the corner of the room, where he took notes on a holographic tablet and stared intently at Quell's finger-weaving technique. Horvil felt like an ancient relic swinging around his clunky bars of metal, but there was nothing he could do about it.

As the day ebbed away and night fell, Benyamin began to grow impatient. He kept sidling up to Horvil and slipping him urgent ConfidentialWhispers about the time. "I *told* the assembly-line manager I'd get this to her by midnight," he said.

"What do you want me to do?" 'Whispered Horvil in return. "It's just not done."

"If the shop doesn't get it by midnight, they can't guarantee they'll finish by Tuesday."

"And if we rush to get it to them by midnight, *I* can't guarantee it will *work* on Tuesday."

Benyamin quieted down.

Midnight passed, but Quell and Horvil labored on. Ben began popping in and out of the room to make use of the multi facility down the hall.

Once the basic blueprint had been constructed and Probabilities sat loosely tethered to the MultiReal engine, another job awaited the fiefcorpers: security. Sending an assembly-line coding shop the full Possibilities program in all its manifold glory would be an invitation to disaster. Horvil wouldn't take such a risk with even an ordinary bio/logic program; there were too many thieves, cutthroat competitors, and black coders who would love to get their hands on commercial source code. So Quell and Horvil spent the early-morning hours fastidiously cordoning off enormous chunks of programming, locking out sensitive areas and encrypting the sections that would have to remain open. By the time they finished, the program would look like any other large-scale project that passed through an assembly-line floor. An economic modeling program, perhaps, or the basic subsystem for an internal organ. No one would be able to tell they were really working on Margaret Surina's famous MultiReal engine.

Quell turned out to be an ideal coworker. He didn't clog up the grinding gears of Horvil's concentration with a lot of chatter, and what he did say was always concise and to the point. After a few hours, the two dropped nouns and verbs altogether and stuck to the lingua franca of mathematics. The engineer had to admit he was starting to like this Islander. And he could swear the feeling was mutual.

Horvil finally tossed aside the bio/logic programming bars a few minutes shy of six in the morning. They had worked through the night without a single break. He gazed at their handiwork, and then exchanged a silent glance with the Islander. The look was unambiguous. *MultiReal isn't ready. It's not going to work.* But now they were bumping up against the unstretchable limitations of time, and Benyamin was positively apoplectic. The two engineers sighed and nodded as one; it would have to do. "You ready to take the baton, Ben?" said Horvil, stretching his sore arms above his head.

Benyamin's raven-black hair was in complete disarray from the action of nervous fingers. "I've been keeping the shop up-to-date on our progress," he said. "They're all ready to go. Just give me the word, and I'll get them started."

"Do you think they can do all that barwork in time? That's a big mound of coding, and Natch'll be *onstage* in less than forty-eight hours."

"I don't know. I've never had to put them on such a tight deadline."

The engineer's eyes narrowed. "*No*, Ben, don't tell me you're taking it . . . *there*. You can't! Are you insane?"

Benyamin cast his eyes to the floor and stuck his hands in his pockets, mirroring one of Horvil's standard poses. "We don't have a choice anymore. I had a couple of assembly-line shops willing to take on the job last night, but now this is the only one. And I had to call in a few favors even to get *them* on board."

Quell watched the cousins' conversation from the opposite corner of the room, where he had stretched out on the floor. "What's going on?"

Horvil let out a *tsk*. "He's going to bring MultiReal to my Aunt Berilla's shop—his mother's company."

"*One* of her companies," corrected Ben. "One of her *many* companies."

"They do good work, I'll give them that—but it's not like they actually have to *compete* against anybody. Creed Élan throws them all kinds of softball projects without even soliciting bids. Which isn't any real surprise because Berilla is like *this* with all the Élan bodhisattvas." He held two chunky fingers together like Siamese twins attached at the hip.

"Don't you get it, Horvil?" Ben replied defensively. "Nobody else'll take on the project this late. We *have* to use them now."

The Islander shook his head in confusion. "So what's the problem?"

"The problem is that Aunt Berilla absolutely *hates* Natch with a passion. Don't ask me why. She doesn't want anything to do with him.

She doesn't want *us* to have anything to do with him. If she realizes this is Natch's coding job—if she thinks it'll *help* Natch in any way—she'll yank it right off the floor. No, even worse, she might actually *sabotage* the fucking thing."

"She won't find out," Ben insisted. "Really, Horv, this is all under control."

Horvil sighed. "Let's hope so."

• • •

They returned to the conference room to find Jara and Merri in the midst of a heated debate. Jara had been up all night weeding through marketing theories for a model to use in the presentation until, desperate, she had asked Merri for help. Since the moment she'd stepped off the teleportation platform, the channel manager had been slingshotting around the globe to sales meetings with Robby Robby. She hadn't even found the opportunity to change out of the horribly unfashionable gray robe TeleCo made its customers wear during the transfer process. Yet she had readily agreed to help, a decision she now appeared to regret.

A pack of SeeNaRee hyenas studiously watched the back-and-forth from a safe distance in the brush.

"*Tell* her we need something simple," said Jara, turning to Horvil as if looking for an ally.

Merri frowned. In a futile effort to stop the trembling, a common side effect of teleportation, she was gripping her thighs hard enough to draw blood. "The Four Phases of Technological Evolution *are* simple. They're not—"

"Creed propaganda."

"They're *not* creed propaganda. Just because they're part of Objectivv doctrine doesn't mean they're not universal. Everyone knows the Four Phases—it's a part of the culture now."

"I've heard people talk about them at Creed Élan," said Benyamin.

"You see? It's really very simple. Observation: humanity distinguishes itself from nature. Exploitation: humanity establishes its dominance over nature. Synergy: humanity learns to become one with nature. Transcendence: humanity surmounts the rules of nature altogether. Take the example of teleportation—"

Jara threw her hands up in the air. "Natch wants *simple*. Fifteen minutes or less. Petrucio Patel kept crowing about 'safe shores' in his promo. *We've* got to be excitement and adventure on the high seas. I'm sorry, Merri, but the Four Phases will just put everybody to sleep. We need a sales pitch, not a sermon."

Quell, who had been standing quietly, now poked his sizeable nose between the two bickering apprentices. "Maybe a demonstration would help," he said. Merri looked up in shock at the giant Islander, apparently noticing him for the first time. "I can't show you the latest version until it's back from the shop, but I can show you one of the prototypes Margaret and I put together."

Merri and Jara looked at one another and nodded simultaneously.

"Good," said Quell. "Horvil, help me change the SeeNaRee. Can't do a thing with this miserable collar."

The Islander whispered in his ear as Horvil cast his mind out to the facility databases. A succession of three-dimensional pictures flashed in his head. He chose one, and the African veldt disappeared with a flash.

The air around the apprentices suddenly filled with bass-thumping music, the kind of xpression board monotony that instinctively caused teenaged girls' hips to gyrate. Then came the smell of freshly cut grass. The apprentices found themselves standing at the nexus of two interlocking diamonds in the dirt. A smattering of white hexagonal bags lay at the corners.

A baseball stadium.

"No, no, Horvil. I want a *classic* field," said Quell. Horvil nodded and switched to the more traditional playing field endorsed by the classic leagues. Soon, the fiefcorpers were standing in a stadium set up like those the ancients had played: a single diamond, four bases, an enormous outfield. Without prompting, Horvil called up a catalog of baseball bats containing everything from laser-polished aluminum to synthetic ash. He selected a squat Kyushu Clubfoot, summoned a cart of classic league baseballs, and then handed the equipment to Quell. "Smoke and fucking mirrors," muttered the Islander as he fumbled with the virtual bat, trying to get a grip on it. Not an easy task without a sense of touch, Horvil realized.

"See that target?" Quell pointed to a bull's-eye painted on the outfield wall captioned with the words BETCHA A BOTTLE OF CHAIQUOKE YOU CAN'T HIT ME. Then he flexed a muscular set of pectorals, tossed a ball up in the air, and knocked it towards right field. The ball hurtled into the wall at the precise center of the target.

"So you can hit a baseball into a bull's-eye," sneered Jara. "What does that have to do with multiple realities?"

The Islander said nothing. Instead, he reached into the cart of baseballs, threw them into the air one by one, and smacked them towards the ChaiQuoke promo. *Bang bang bang bang.* All twenty-four baseballs plunked the bull's-eye in the same exact spot. Quell threw his ponytail over his shoulder and made a low purring noise of satisfaction.

Jara gaped at the collection of virtual balls lying under the bull's-eye. Words escaped her.

A light went on in Horvil's head. He trotted around the infield, his jaw swaying this way and that with excitement. "Don't you get it, Jara? The whole thing's just mathematics. The swing of the bat, the grip, the angle you're holding it, all those neurochemical reactions in your brain—you can describe it all with math. Possibilities just lets you try out different variables and choose the outcome you want."

Quell nodded. "An oversimplification—but yes."

Horvil flopped down onto the grass and stretched out, snow angel style. "So *that's* why we modified those dendrite modules . . ."

Ben paced slowly towards the ChaiQuoke advertisement and rubbed the paint, as if he expected to feel some kind of magnetic generator in the wall. Meanwhile, Merri retreated into the visitors' dugout and watched the proceedings with hollow eyes as she tried to get a handle on her teleportation-induced trembling.

"Let me get this straight," said Jara, seating herself delicately on the grass next to Horvil. "MultiReal—Possibilities—creates alternate realities inside your head?"

Quell strode onto the pitcher's mound. His voice took on the tone of a drill instructor. "Let's start from the beginning.

"Forget about MultiReal for a minute. What happens when you throw a ball in the air and swing a bat? The mind takes in sensory input—the sight of the ball, the weight of the bat, the feel of the wind—and processes it. You decide on a course of action. Then the brain sends instructions down the spinal cord into your muscles, right? Electrical pulses tell your body what to do. You swing the bat. It all happens in a fraction of a second.

"But we can *track* all those electrical pulses, right? We can reduce them to mathematical equations. Isn't that how multi works? OCHREs in the brain stem intercept these pulses and transmit them onto the multi network instead of into your own body.

"So what happens if you take these electrical commands from the brain and plot out the results? You get a simulation of what's going to happen. You can see if the swing of the bat is going to turn out the way you want.

"Now, let's go a step further. Once you have a mathematical model in place, what's to stop you from trying out different scenarios? If I had twitched my right arm like *this* instead of like *that*, what would have happened? What if I had gripped the bat a little harder, swung a little faster? You make thousands of tiny unconscious decisions like that every instant. Why not just loop the whole process in your mind and compute it over and over again with different variables until you find a result you're satisfied with? Keep swinging until you hit one out of the park.

"Then—and only then—you choose the reality you want to happen, the *predetermined reality*. Your mind now has an optimized set of instructions to send into the nervous system. The brain outputs those electrical pulses to your body—what we call *closing the choice cycle*—and it happens."

Horvil was making incoherent burbling sounds of delight. But Jara was not convinced. "That's all well and good if you're just trying to hit an inanimate object," she said, hands planted belligerently on her hips. "But what if you've got an outfielder out there trying to catch it first? People aren't mathematical models. You can't just use algebra to *predict* what they're going to do. What *then*?"

Quell was unruffled. "Ben," he called out across the field. "Go ahead. Try to catch it." The young apprentice nodded, summoned a SeeNaRee baseball glove, and assumed the crouch of a seasoned right fielder in front of the ChaiQuoke target.

Thwak! The Islander knocked the first ball over Benyamin's shoulder, a perfect hit.

Thwak! The second ball flew inches past his face.

Thwak! Another hit.

The charade went on for another dozen swings, with Ben failing to catch the ball each time. Even seemingly easy pop flies slipped through his fingers and smacked unerringly into the wall. The irritation was beginning to show on the young apprentice's face when Quell raised his hand and signaled that the demonstration was through.

"That program has to be pretty good," said Horvil, eyebrows aloft. "Ben's no Angel Palmero, but he's caught a few fly balls in his day."

"It wouldn't have mattered," replied Quell dismissively. "Angel Palmero wouldn't have done any better." He stood the Kyushu Clubfoot on its end like a mercenary displaying his weapon. "MultiReal is a collaborative process."

Horvil's cousin came trotting over from the outfield, clearly perturbed at his poor defensive performance. "Wait a minute—I didn't *collaborate* with anything."

"You don't think you did. But for every missed catch, there were dozens of alternative reality scenarios played out *inside our minds* before they ever actually 'happened.' The whole sequence looped over and over again—dozens of my possible swings mapped out against dozens of your possible catches—dozens of choice cycles—until I found a result I liked."

"But I don't remember any of that happening."

"No. You wouldn't. Not without MultiReal."

Benyamin and Jara sank down into the grass with Horvil, overcome by the dizzying spiral of probabilities and possibilities. Horvil wasn't doing much better. Questions were clambering to the forefront of the engineer's head, but no answers accompanied them. No bio/logic program could conceivably turn the concept of cause-and-effect on its head like that—and yet, somehow, MultiReal just had.

Horvil heard the echo of Margaret Surina's words, spoken three and a half days ago, an incomprehensible lifetime in the past: *The ever-changing flux of MultiReal will become reality. MultiReal will free us from the tyranny of cause and effect itself.*

He thought of the crack team of security guards standing guard just outside, and the multitudes of armed troops patrolling the premises. It seemed like a pitifully small amount of protection. Who knew what MultiReal was really capable of? Who knew what lengths the Defense and Wellness Council would go to in order to possess it? Horvil tried to imagine working under this pressure every day: furtive looks over your shoulder, armed backup whenever you flipped on your workbench. He felt claustrophobic from working in Andra Pradesh for a single evening. Quell and Margaret Surina had been doing this for *sixteen years.*

Merri's tired voice echoed from the dugout. "I think we've found our demonstration." Jara whipped her head around hawklike towards the channel manager, thought for a moment, and then nodded with mute agreement.

Suddenly, Benyamin perked up. "Wait a minute!" he cried. "If we already have the demonstration we're going to use on Tuesday, then we don't have to worry about the assembly-line shop, do we?"

Quell shook his head, causing the young apprentice's demeanor to cloud over once again. "It's a collaborative process, remember? The MultiReal engine Margaret and I put together won't work in front of a big crowd—at least not yet. We need a good predictive engine like Horvil's Probabilities ROD to sort through all the permutations."

Ben shifted uncomfortably. "A collaborative process running among hundreds of millions of people—that's gonna take a heck of a lot of computing power, isn't it?"

"Oh fuck," moaned Jara, burying her head in her hands. "Info-quakes."

Rivers of fear coursed through Horvil's skull. He thought back to the disturbance at Margaret Surina's speech, those sickening few minutes of paralysis and vertigo. Computational vortexes, communication breakdowns.

The Islander's countenance turned predatory. "That's exactly what Len Borda wants you to think," he said.

"And what . . . what if he's right?" said Merri quietly from her alcove in the dugout. The trembling had started up in her arms again, but Horvil wasn't sure if it was a lingering effect of the teleportation or a new surge of fear.

"Margaret Surina is not an *imbecile*. In all the time she worked on MultiReal, don't you think this problem occurred to her?" Quell's face had turned bloodred with rage, and Horvil could see his fists clenching on the bat until it vanished. "People have been talking about computational resource limitations for years now, long before anybody ever heard of infoquakes. This is not new. Are there risks with MultiReal?

Of course. But give us a few more years to optimize the code, and we can limit the risks. In a *rational* and *responsible* society, there's no reason why this program shouldn't see the light of day."

A cold wind blew through the bleachers and made a whistling sound off the metal railings. Suddenly, his tirade over, the Islander seemed to have aged a dozen years. "You think you see all the possibilities now?" said Quell. "Think again. There are possibilities that will scare the living wits out of you. Possibilities you haven't even *dreamed* of."

(((28)))

Robby Robby's grin began just below one ear and undertook an impossibly long journey down his chin to reach the other. Merri could find no evidence a single granule of stubble had ever blemished that slick face.

"You're looking particularly good this morning, Merri," said the channeler, his voice lightly greased.

The fiefcorp apprentice held back a smirk. She didn't take Robby's Casanova act seriously; she had seen enough of the man's tactics to know it was just part of his sales patter. Robby Robby never walked down any path unless he was convinced a pile of credits awaited him at the end. Still, Merri wondered if her fiercely protective companion would regard his charade quite so casually. "So we're here to discuss the market survey," she said in a no-nonsense tone.

"The market survey, yes." Robby bobbed his head, which Barb-ur-Shop 125k had coifed with a perfect cube of hair. Behind him sat his entire troupe of two dozen channelers, fresh young faces either untouched by experience or polished smooth by it. All had adapted the same ridiculous cube-haired do as Robby. "The folks we're contacting are confused, Merri. They've all heard of the Surina/Natch MultiReal Fiefcorp—we've got *huge* amounts of name recognition. And of course, after that mess with the infoquake, who hasn't heard about MultiReal by now?" Robby's channelers gave sanctimonious nods of agreement up and down the conference table.

Merri smiled. "So is there a problem?" she asked. Of *course* there was a problem.

"Well, when our pollsters started asking folks if they were interested in MultiReal, almost ninety-five percent said yes. Great numbers across the spectrum! But when we asked people whether they thought MultiReal was something they might actually *buy* . . . What was that number again, Friz?"

"Seventeen point three percent," replied Frizitz Quo, a perky Asian channeler sitting to Robby's right.

The grin on Robby's face narrowed a few microns. "Seventeen point three percent interested in buying MultiReal. I don't need to tell ya, Merri—that's not an encouraging number! Nobody knows what this MultiReal stuff is *for*."

Merri gave a rueful sigh and placed her hands palm up on the table in a gesture of sincerity. During the past few months, she had learned that body language was crucial in the channeling business. "This is a brand-new industry, Robby," she said. "The sky's the limit. We've barely even started counting the possibilities." She thought back to Quell's demonstration yesterday and tried to use deductive reasoning to figure out more practical uses for MultiReal. But as usual, her mind came up blank. "Baseball, for one."

"Yes, baseball." Robby nodded slowly in an unconvincing imitation of agreement. To a pathological yes-man like Robby, the only way to express a differing opinion was to agree less vehemently. "So that leads us to your script. This baseball thing—is Natch going to be able to *do* that at the demonstration? Is it *possible?*"

"It is," said Merri firmly. "I've *seen* it."

Robby scratched his head as he pored over the latest draft of Jara's speech, which he had projected onto a viewscreen at one end of the table. Even with the font size bumped up to drudge-headline proportions, the entire script still fit easily within two screenlengths. Robby made a show of flipping through the presentation again, pretending to read it carefully when Merri knew he was really holding a Confidential-Whisper conversation with his staff—and it was a heated conversation, if the worried grooves on the channelers' foreheads were any indication.

"You know, Merri, I've been working with Natch for a few years now," said Robby. "I *know* this guy pretty well. I've heard what he has to say about the Surinas and their creed babble, and it ain't pretty."

Creed babble? Merri bristled at the slick channeler's characterization, and immediately began rallying a passionate defense of creedism inside her head. Then she imagined how the bodhisattva of Creed Objectivv would respond—*we often call a thing babble that we cannot ourselves understand*, he would say with a good-natured shrug—and she simmered down.

"The point is," Robby was saying, "our man Natch is cynical to the core. Are you *sure* he's okay with this?"

"I've given you access to a whole library of detailed analysis, Robby. You've got an entire history of the Surina name, a list of the Surina clan's accomplishments and inventions, and all those stellar Primo's ratings Natch has been accumulating over the past few years. Robby, this is going to be one of the biggest technological advances the world has ever seen, and Natch wants *you* with us on the ground floor! Trust me, he can *definitely* do everything in that script." Merri paused to take a deep breath. She couldn't remember the last time she had been so agitated.

"I'm curious, though," Robby mused with a sly look. "If Natch is so committed to this Surina stuff, how come he didn't show up for the meeting today?" He gestured ever so slightly towards the empty chair at the opposite end of the table.

Merri had been wondering precisely the same thing, but she was not about to tell Robby that. She felt the keen temptation to lie, to slip free from the bonds of her Objectivv oath, if only just this once. *Natch had some last-minute coding to finish up. He's doing an interview with Mah Lo Vertiginous right now. He's meeting with Margaret across the courtyard in the Surina residence.* Who would be the wiser?

The depths of this game had suddenly become unfathomable to Merri. Even with company allies in a private meeting, messages were being broadcast, challenges made, gauntlets thrown down. What place did absolute truth have in this cesspool?

Instead of lying, Merri found herself plastering a WinningGrin 44 on her face. "Robby, *you* know what a perfectionist Natch is," she said.

"How he wants everything done *his* way, down to the last detail. You know he's going to insist that every last connection strand is absolutely perfect before he goes out on that stage."

Again the placating smile, the fake burst of comprehension. "No doubt!" Robby exclaimed. "So that just leaves us with one more topic."

"Yes?"

"The Council." Merri quickly tossed a PokerFace 83.4b atop the WinningGrin. "They've been—heck, Merri, they've been harassing my boys and girls here." He tilted his head in the direction of his "boys and girls," who all murmured their assent.

Suddenly, Merri felt very tired. "What do you mean by 'harassing'?"

"It's just your typical Defense and Wellness Council aggravation," said Robby, sweeping his concerns over one shoulder with a long, bony hand. "Requests to see our permits, people following us around, that kind of thing. Friz here got cited for 'walking too close to a tube track' the other day." Friz, the junior channeler, jutted his bottom lip forward and gave his best hangdog look. "Nothing we can't handle, of course. But you know, if we have another one of those infoquakes . . ."

Robby Robby let the sentence drift off, but Merri was all too ready to complete it. *If we have another one of those infoquakes, the Council might swoop down and take MultiReal from us by force. The public might get frightened away from the product altogether. The drudges might start calling for Natch's head. Any way you look at it, it's entirely possible none of us will make a single credit off this crazy enterprise.*

Again, Merri found herself stretching the bonds of her oath, reaching for the sweet opiate of prevarication. She adopted her most confident tone of voice and enhanced it with bio/logics. "Robby, nobody knows what's really going to happen out there tomorrow— much less next week or next month! Your team is going to be put on the spot, and you might have to do a lot of improvising. You'll probably have to endure a few more of those bogus citations from the Council. But Natch is utterly committed to this product. He hasn't just staked *our* careers on it; he's staked his own. And in the years you've known him, has Natch ever steered you wrong?"

The channeler seemed to be weighing his options for a few excruciating seconds. His eyes flickered on the black-and-white swirl of the Objectivv pin riding her left breast. Finally, Robby dispensed one of his Cheshire cat smiles. The same smile quickly rippled down the table until all two dozen channelers were wearing it. "I gotcha, Merri," said Robby. "You're absolutely right. If this is what Natch wants, this is what Natch gets. We trust in Natch."

I wish I did, Merri said to herself glumly.

• • •

Benyamin was experiencing déjà vu, but it had nothing to do with any of Natch's bio/logic programs.

He was standing on the balcony overlooking his mother's assembly-line floor where he had stood for most of the past year. Two hundred workbenches lay in a grid below him. He was younger than many of the programmers, and had less coding experience than almost all of them. It felt like nothing had changed in the past few months, like he had never decided to step out from under Berilla's oppressive wing and seek a job in the fiefcorp sector.

As always, Ben listened for some undercurrent of resentment running through the staff. Were they jealous of this kid who had leapfrogged to the management office straight out of initiation? Did they resent the fact that the monthly interest on his trust fund exceeded half their salaries combined? The answer to these questions, it seemed, was still no. If there was any embittered muttering going on here, it was drowned out by the rumble caused by hundreds of clanking bio/logic programming bars. The assembly-line coders were oblivious. Too busy concentrating on tunes from the Jamm and holding ConfidentialWhisper conversations with distant companions.

"Thirty-one percent done," came a smoky female voice, late forties or early fifties.

Benyamin turned to find Greth Tar Griveth, the woman who had replaced him as floor manager, walking onto the balcony from his old office. *Her* office now. Ben sensed that the job, which had been a whistle stop on the track to success for him, was more like a post of permanent exile for Greth. She had only been here for six weeks, but she had already adapted the vacant stare, the careless flip of the hand, the bored midsentence yawn that had been hallmarks of Ben's seventh and eighth months.

"Only thirty-one percent?" said Ben with a groan. "But we need this done in less than twenty-four hours!"

Greth stood next to him at the railing and let out a weary *ffff*. "We'll get it done. I think."

"You *think*?"

"The second shift is coming on now, and they're much quicker than the first. Plus, we just finished up a gig for the Élanners, so we'll have some more coders to put on the job. Look, over there."

Greth Tar Griveth pointed at the rightmost row of programmers, where Ben could see the Surina/Natch templates slipping silently into the production line. One by one, the workers in that quadrant of the floor completed their current projects and watched blue and pink chunks of code pop up in their MindSpace bubbles. Small bricks in the Gothic castle that was the MultiReal engine. Other coders were gazing numbly at pieces of the Probabilities ROD. If any of them suspected they were plugging away at the world's most notorious compendium of bio/logic code, they showed no sign.

Nor did the salty assembly-line floor manager have a clue what program her crew was laboring away on. Ben had made sure that the words *Natch*, *MultiReal*, and *Surina* did not escape his lips, and he praised the Fates that his apprenticeship to the Surina/Natch Fiefcorp was not yet common knowledge in Creed Élan circles. Still, he took no chances, and made sure a fat sheaf of credits was sitting in Greth's Vault account to dissuade her from asking questions.

"Here's the real test," said Greth, pointing to a gangly kid in the epicenter of the floor whose workbench could have rivaled Horvil's in sloppiness. "They call that kid the Robot. Arrived just after you left, and already he's leading the floor in output. Never complains, never says much of anything."

Ben fastened his gaze on the Robot, who was wrapping up work on someone else's tangled web of a program. Indeed, the young man was tearing through the template with astounding speed. Ben watched as the Robot whirled the mass around with one hand, grabbed the programming bar he needed with the other, and then caught the template backhanded, just in time to make the appropriate connection. "So why's this guy a good test?" said Ben.

"Because he's got absolutely no imagination," replied Greth. She stretched, nearly poking Benyamin in the eye with a stray elbow. "Give him your ordinary coding job and he'll sweep through it in record time. But make the slightest flaw in your template, and he just folds. Look."

True to her words, as soon as the kid moved on to his next job—a golden program that looked like a bowl of fruit—he froze up. The bio/logic programming bars in his hands hovered in place, vibrating like stuck gears. Ben could practically hear the ConfidentialWhisper conversation from his supervisor guiding him through the obstruction. After a ten-minute pause, the Robot hesitantly got back to work. Soon, he was a blur of motion once again.

"If *he* can handle the templates your cousin put together," said Greth Tar Griveth drily, "we'll be okay."

Ben held his breath as the Robot finished up his current assignment and made the swirling-hand motion signaling his readiness to accept a new template. A pink blob, one small corner of the MultiReal engine, appeared in front of him.

The Robot whipped through the template in twenty-two minutes.

Greth loosened her grip on the railing and let out a deep breath. "It'll be close, but I think we'll get your job done on time. Maybe even twenty or thirty minutes early."

Ben inhaled a draught of cool air, expelling a warm puff in return. The billow of air failed to accomplish the calming effect he had intended. "That's cutting it a little too close."

"Yes," replied Greth, not bothering to contradict her predecessor. "It is."

• • •

Horvil had almost forgiven the Surina guest lodge for the lumps in its mattress and found a route to sleep when an urgent ConfidentialWhisper reached his mental inbox. The engineer accepted it. He found himself flailing against the wall under the gale-wind force of an angry Jara.

"Emergency meeting!" she cried. "Emergency meeting *now!* Everyone report to the Enterprise Facility!"

Horvil groggily threw on yesterday's clothes and made his way across the Surina compound, discovering along the way that he had put on only one sock. The central courtyard was aflurry with security officers going about their midnight routine, questioning passersby, relentlessly patrolling, checking their weapons and loading dart canisters from their belts. Horvil was not surprised to find the Islander Quell in their midst. He told the newest fiefcorp apprentice about the meeting, and the two quickly followed Jara's beacon to a conference room on the fifth floor of the Enterprise Facility.

They wandered into a piece of SeeNaRee titled Seurat's *Sunday Afternoon on the Island of La Grande Jatte*. Jara stood beside a cool river rendered in tiny pinpricks of color, while Parisian matrons in ridiculous hooped petticoats sauntered on the opposite bank. Her fiery mood made a sharp contrast with the calm pointillist trees. Horvil was about to chide Quell for his SeeNaRee program's poor selection when he caught sight of Merri in the river a few meters down, wading barefoot and watching the ducks. Obviously, the channel manager had arrived here first.

Benyamin showed up moments later, and the five apprentices sat at a plain conference table overlooking the river. "So what's the emergency?" said Ben jauntily.

Jara gestured to the empty chair at the head of the table. "Natch."

"What's wrong with him *this* time?"

"He's disappeared."

Four blank faces gazed back at her.

"You mean he hasn't been in touch with you at all?" cried Horvil. "I thought he was supposed to be at that meeting with Robby Robby this afternoon."

Merri shook her head. "He didn't show up."

"Well, where the fuck *is* he? Hasn't anybody talked to him since the last fiefcorp meeting?"

Nobody answered. A cloud of black and gray dots descended on them from the east, threatening to dump pixels of rain on the congregating Parisians.

"I've tried requesting a multi connection," said Jara, rubbing the pulsing vein on her temple. "I've sent him at least twenty ConfidentialWhispers. Nothing. I even tried Margaret, but her secretary says she's been holed up with those diss L-PRACG people for three days straight now. Natch isn't there."

"Did you try Serr Vigal?" asked Merri.

Jara nodded grimly. "*He's* not answering me either, although that's not a big surprise. I checked the schedule of that conference in Beijing. He's probably delivering the keynote address right about now."

"Maybe Natch is . . . *testing* us or something," said Ben to nobody in particular. "Maybe he's just trying to make sure we're on our toes. I know he has some pretty unconventional management tactics."

"Unconventional, yes," replied Horvil. "Totally fucking insane, no."

"Doesn't the man have any private security?" asked Quell.

Jara glared at the Islander as if he had grown a horn from his forehead. "Are you *kidding*?"

Quell let out an animalistic grunt. "I can't believe this," he snarled. "No common sense, just like Margaret. Natch knows he has enemies, doesn't he? The Patel Brothers, the Defense and Wellness Council, the Pharisees, all those programmers and ROD coders and drudges he's pissed off over the years. The list is practically endless."

"Don't forget Lucas Sentinel," put in Horvil, counting on his fingers. "And the Meme Cooperative. Brone. Creed Thassel. Creed Élan. My Aunt Berilla—"

Ben groaned out loud.

"All right, that's enough!" shrieked Jara, slapping one open hand against the table and sending a loud *thwak* echoing through the SeeNaRee. The Parisians snapped their heads up in surprise, as did the rest of the fiefcorp. "It doesn't matter right now. We could sit here for a week naming people who hold a grudge against Natch. What we need to do is *stay focused*. We've got a presentation tomorrow at four o'clock, and I intend for us to *be ready for it*."

Horvil felt a smile slowly creep onto his face. There was no officially designated Number Two in the fiefcorp hierarchy, but Quell, Merri, and Benyamin seemed ready to follow Jara to the heart of a simmering volcano. At that moment, Horvil was too. "So what do you want us to do?" ventured the engineer.

"I want *you* to go looking for Natch," said Jara. "You've known him longer than any of us, Horvil. See if you can get into his apartment and look for clues. Go everywhere he might possibly be hiding. Quell, I want you to comb every centimeter of the Surina compound and make absolutely *sure* he's not holed up here somewhere. As for you two, Ben and Merri—just keep working. If those assembly-line programmers don't finish in time—or if the channelers aren't ready—this is all going to be a moot point anyway."

"I've got a friend with the Élanners who runs a private detective agency," said Ben. "Maybe I could—"

Jara cut him off. "No. We don't want word of this to leak out to anybody outside the fiefcorp. *Anybody*, do you hear me? Not even Margaret or Robby. The last thing we need is for the drudges to start spreading rumors. As far as the rest of the world is concerned, Natch is cooped up here with *us*, working on Possibilities."

"And what are you going to be doing, Jara?" asked Merri.

Jara clawed briefly at the vein in her temple, which had begun to throb once more. "I'm going to stay here and come up with a plan."

"A plan for what?" said Ben.

"A plan for what to do if Natch doesn't show up tomorrow."

The panic that had been bubbling beneath the surface now struck the fiefcorp like a miniature infoquake. Merri looked like she might pass out at any minute, while Quell gripped his connectible collar as if preparing to snap it in two. Horvil could feel his OCHREs working to slow a madly racing heart, and he would have bet anything his cousin was using his faraway look as cover while he reviewed his apprenticeship contract. Even the painted denizens of the SeeNaRee were milling around, opening and closing their parasols in confusion.

Only Jara appeared to have mastered her emotions. She stood up and placed her hands flat on the table. "Listen," she said through gritted teeth, "there's only so much time we can spend looking for Natch. You all know him as well as I do. If he doesn't want to be found, he won't be found."

"Why wouldn't he want to be found?" Merri asked.

Glum silence shrouded the table.

"If any of us had the slightest inkling of how Natch thinks, we wouldn't have signed on to this bloody fiefcorp in the first place," said Jara. "Let's get moving. It's one-thirty now. Everybody report back here at nine a.m. sharp."

(((29)))

Natch stood alone on the beach.

Civilization had not reached this place yet, or maybe it had left long ago and taken all of culture's detritus with it. The billboard advertisements, the black code darts, the tube tracks, the hoverbird clouds, the political manifestos, the buildings both large and small, the silly trappings of fashion—all of them gone.

The world reduced to sand, sky, and sun.

The world a million years after humanity had breathed its last gasp.

The sun had risen to its midday perch and looked as if it might stay there for a while. Beneath his feet, the sand had begun to absorb the heat. As the temperature rose and the sand began to sizzle, tiny creatures burrowed their way to the surface of the beach. Sand mites by the millions scrambled around, wildly looking for some relief from the burning, but there was none to be found.

Natch closed his eyes and cast his mind out to the Data Sea to find a bio/logic program that would protect his tender soles, but he could find none. No bio/logic programs, no chatter from the drudges, no Data Sea. Was the vast corpus of human knowledge extinct too? Had it ever existed at all in this place? He opened his eyes again and scanned the horizon, looking for something, anything. A tree to shelter under, a rock with a cool face to it. But the world was completely flat and featureless.

He had begun to hop up and down to ease the burning when he felt an icy drop of water tickle his feet.

The tide was rising. The water carved rivulets in the sand dunes as it spilled onto the beach. Natch leapt down towards the sea and dunked his feet in the spray. He heaved a tremendous sigh of relief and allowed the anxiety to slip from his mind.

Minutes passed before Natch noticed the vast panicked retreat going on in the sand. Millions of tiny creatures—sand mites, miniature crabs, black segmented insects—all dashing pell-mell for higher ground. The saltwater was licking his ankles before he came to a sudden realization: the insects weren't fleeing the heat; they were fleeing the tide.

He turned and headed back up the beach. But the tide was rising faster than he could run. By the time he overtook his own footprints running in the opposite direction, they were submerged beneath half a meter of water. Natch began running as fast as he could, lifting his legs in the air, storklike, to stay above the tide.

The ocean had risen up above his knees when he realized he was not going to make it. The angle of the beach was too shallow, the progress of the tide too rapid. The strip of land he had been aiming for receded farther and farther away with each second. Natch stopped for a minute and turned around to see if there was another place he could head for, someplace safe from the rising tide. But there was nothing in any direction now but endless sea.

He began scrambling madly for higher ground. His splashes were the only noise that could be heard anywhere; the ocean itself did not crash or break or even ripple. Its surface was unbroken and lifeless. Eternal.

The water rose up to his chest, and Natch abandoned all hope of wading. He tried to leap up into a swimming position, but a remarkably strong force pulled on his legs, keeping him down. A deep underwater vortex into which the entire world would eventually sink.

Natch struggled wildly, clinging to his ambitions and desires. MultiReal was out there somewhere. So were number one on Primo's, a Lunar estate, riches, glory. But one by one, he could feel all his cares draining out of him and sliding deep into the watery void. There were no fiefcorps down in that demesne of the drowned, no fiefcorps or memecorps or bio/logic programs or Primo's ratings.

He desperately tried to keep his head above water, but the current was too strong. The tide of nothingness, the Null Current, pulled him under.

Natch could see the light of the sun receding. He could feel the tug of the nothingness below, which was his final destination. His struggles and his worries seemed so petty once the Null Current had pulled him in. Down here, desire was irrelevant, because the undifferentiated mass of nothingness that was his destination allowed no changes, accepted no arguments, admitted no standards by which to measure and compare. In the deeps, there was nothing to want because there was nothing to gain, nothing to fix because there was nothing to break.

He stopped struggling as the darkness closed in, as the surface became a distant memory, as he was sucked down by the vortex that had no end, the vortex that spiraled down infinitely until it was no longer a vortex, until he and it and everything else melted together and merged into one endless eternal line, a vector pointing nowhere, a vector whose beginnings were irrelevant and improbable, and whose end was forever unreachable.

(((30)))

The apartment building was not much to look at by West London standards, but for Shenandoah, it had style in abundance. One might have said the building *jutted out* from the side of a hill, if not for its sine-wave shape that architects often used to camouflage the constant structural flux. A more appropriate description would have been that the building *rippled* or *undulated* from the hillside. Not the kind of thing you found crammed amidst the pointed abbeys at Bishopsgate.

Horvil had been inside the building a thousand times, of course, at all hours of the day and night. But he usually skipped the exterior view and multied straight to the network gateway in Natch's foyer. Funny how you could spend so much time embedded in a place that you didn't really know what it looked like from the outside.

From the ground, the engineer looked up the side of the tenement and saw several balconies like the one where he, Natch, and Jara had stood and tested NiteFocus 48. It seemed like a million years ago, during a vanished era of innocence. Now all the building's balconies were occupied by strangers.

Horvil walked inside the front doors, nosed around the atrium for a few minutes, then ascended the lift to Natch's flat. He hesitated at the fiefcorp master's door for a few seconds. If Natch wasn't here, the apartment security program would probably let a trusted presence like Horvil invoke emergency protocols and enter. But that would trigger warning messages to Natch and possibly the building management as well. He didn't mind Natch receiving such a message—the entrepreneur might actually *respond* and put an end to this madness—but how much could you really trust a landlord these days? A series of gloating drudge headlines flashed in Horvil's brain: BREAK-IN LEADS TO MASSIVE MANHUNT FOR MISSING FIEFCORP MASTER. . . . NATCH LEAVES APPREN-

TICES HIGH AND DRY. . . . MISSING ENTREPRENEUR 'A WORTHLESS HUMAN BEING,' SAYS LANDLORD.

Horvil entered, stood in the foyer, and counted to twenty. Nothing happened.

It took Horvil only a few minutes to determine there was no bloody corpse stinking up the premises. No scattered debris on the counters, no body standing on the red tile, no sign of a struggle. But he could see no evidence the place had been inhabited the past few days either. Not that Natch's messes could compare to the colossal disasters Horvil usually left for his cleaning bots, but a few half-drunk cups of chai or nitro could usually be found on his table at any given time. Today, however, nothing.

Horvil knew the real test was not in the common areas, but in the office. That was where Natch spent most of his time anyway. The engineer poked his nose into the room and made a major discovery: Natch's bio/logic programming bars were gone. Of course, they could be lying in one of the drawers under the workbench, drawers that a multi projection could not physically open. But in all the years Horvil had known him, Natch had never set his programming bars anywhere but the top of the bench or on a side table within easy reach.

Wherever Natch went, he took his bio/logic programming tools with him, thought Horvil. *So what does that mean?*

The fiefcorp apprentice wandered to the window and tuned it transparent. Natch would have headed northeast past the billboard (BANDWIDTH CONSERVATION IS PEOPLE PRESERVATION: *A message from Creed Conscientious*), towards the main city, towards the TubeCo station.

Towards the small cluster of officers in white robes now pointing in Horvil's direction.

Horvil instantly flipped on the window's sunblock and ducked out of the officers' line of sight. *Don't be so paranoid, Horv,* the engineer scolded himself. *Just Council officers doing a routine patrol. They weren't pointing at* you.

But was it really so implausible to think Len Borda's goons might be scoping out Natch's apartment? Especially now, when he was mere hours away from demonstrating MultiReal to an audience of billions?

Horvil scurried out of the apartment and down the lift, whether to hide from the officers or to follow them, he could not say. He stood in the atrium and looked out the window, still vacillating between courses of action, when his eye caught a glint of metal on the ground reflected from the just-risen moon, past the billboard in the gutter on the side of the road. Horvil launched NiteFocus 50c and fine-tuned his vision with Bolliwar Tuban's TeleScopics 88 to make sure. Yep, definitely a bio/logic programming bar.

Eventually, the coven of Council troops moved westwards toward the hoverbird facilities. The engineer thrust his head outside the front door and scanned the horizon, left to right and back again. None of the officers carried bulky disruptors, but who knew which of the surrounding buildings contained one the Council could summon at a moment's notice? When the coast was clear, he darted northwest as fast as his feet could carry him.

Horvil kneeled to the ground and examined the object closely, wishing his multi projection could solidify long enough for him to pick it up. A thin rod of burnished metal, nondescript but for the Roman letter S embossed near one end and a small dent in one corner. The kind of dent a tightly wound programmer might make by repeatedly whacking the bar against a hard workbench.

If this was indeed Natch's bio/logic programming bar, then what were the odds of Horvil finding it here? The fact that the municipal L-PRACG had not swept it up by now was a pretty astronomical coincidence in itself.

And if it was Natch's—how did it get here? And what did its presence mean?

• • •

Jara had the same questions.

"I'm not saying it means *nothing*," said the analyst, looking drawn and haggard from lack of sleep. "I'm not saying the bar *doesn't* belong to Natch. But there have to be hundreds of people who walk by that spot every day carrying programming tools. Anybody could have dropped that bar."

"But the dent," protested Horvil. "The fact that the bars weren't in his apartment—"

"Circumstantial evidence. And besides, what if you're right? What if that *was* Natch's stuff lying on the street? It's useless information. Unless Natch left a trail of metal bars leading across town like bread crumbs, it won't help us."

Benyamin rocked back and forth in his seat impatiently. "The *least* we can do is send someone to go *get* it."

"No," said Jara. "Multi projecting to Shenandoah is one thing, but sending someone there in the flesh is another. What if someone's trying to use that bar to lure us away from the Surina compound? We came here to Andra Pradesh to keep safe. We need to stay here."

The young apprentice muttered something under his breath and arose from his chair with a look of defiance. "*I'll* go," he said.

"No, you *won't*," snapped Jara. "You need to ride herd on those assembly-line programmers and make sure we've got a product ready to show this afternoon. Now *sit down*." Blood rushed to Benyamin's face. He looked to Horvil, Merri, and Quell for support, but found only awkward silence. Horvil gave an almost imperceptible gesture downwards towards the chair, and his cousin crumpled to his seat.

"I think we need to try contacting Serr Vigal again," said Quell.

Jara shook her head. "What's the matter with you people? We've been through this, Quell. We keep going round in circles, the same arguments *over* and *over* again for hours." The analyst scoped out the conference table for a suitable object to use as a projectile, found none, and pressed her fingertips to the mahogany all the harder. "Even if

Vigal was returning my messages, we can't have *him* deliver the speech. He's just not a good enough huckster. Have you ever sat through one of his neural programming speeches? They're excruciatingly boring."

"I'm afraid to say it, but I agree with Jara," offered Merri.

"But Vigal's got a reputation in the programming community," said Quell. "He's got a following. He *knows* what he's talking about."

"And after the tenth time he stops midsentence to scratch his bald head, people are going to wonder where Natch is. They're going to think something has gone terribly wrong in the Surina/Natch Multi-Real Fiefcorp, and consumer confidence in us is going to plummet before we can even get a product to market. Blowing your first major company presentation is worse than not doing one at all."

"So why don't we cancel already?" mumbled Horvil, his head bowed to the table under the confining archway of his clasped hands, as if waiting for a guillotine to drop.

"Because we have an alternative," said Jara.

The Islander let out a brutish noise halfway between a grunt and a laugh. "Now *you're* the one who's going around in circles. How many times do I have to say this? Margaret won't do it. She's handed the project off to Natch—she's not going to jump back into this whole business again."

Jara frowned, brushing one finger slowly over her bottom lip. "I realize you've known Margaret longer than any of us—for process' preservation, I've never even *met* her except for that two-minute appearance she put in at the fiefcorp meeting the other day. But I'm just not convinced. We've got a first-rate demonstration. Merri's been working with Robby Robby to get the crowd fired up. The entire thing is laid out. All Margaret has to do is stand up and deliver it. How can she refuse?"

"The infoquake," said Quell. "She keeps saying the whole thing was her fault. She thinks those people died because of *her*."

"Delusions of grandeur," muttered Ben.

Quell glared sharp slashing daggers at the young apprentice. "When you're the daughter of the Surinas," he snarled, "there's no such *thing* as a delusion of grandeur."

"That notwithstanding," said Jara, "I have to try to convince her. For process' preservation, Quell—this woman is a scientist. She'll listen to reason, won't she?"

(((31)))

Jara marched through the Surina Center for Historic Appreciation with her miniature fists clenched. Security guards haloed her like massive blue-green planets orbiting a small but furious star. She approached the atrium through an archway labeled SUBAETHER COURT. A score of disgruntled visitors glared at Jara when she passed, as if she were responsible for their being muscled out of the atrium.

But the fault lay with the nondescript woman in the center of the domed room gazing up at the statue of a skinny man with a large nose. He was not the largest of the scientific titans adorning the dome, but his stone effigy had an almost mythical presence. The man stood calmly with one hand extended, not offering a welcoming gesture so much as making a commanding sweep. At his feet were carved the words:

> ANYTHING WORTH DOING IS WORTH PERFECTING.
> —Sheldon Surina

Next to the father of bio/logics, Margaret Surina was a half-presence at best. She looked like she might disintegrate inside her bodhisattva's robes at any moment. Her face was solemn, even apologetic. An internal monologue flashed behind her eyes like distant lightning.

Jara could spare no time for pity. She shook herself loose from the Surina guards and stalked to the bodhisattva's side. The guards established a perimeter around the room and kept their distance. "I've been trying to find you for almost *two hours*," said Jara.

Margaret did not even acknowledge Jara's presence. "The Texan governments tried to assassinate him," said the bodhisattva, her gaze never leaving that of her ancestor. Even carved in stone, Sheldon Surina bore a look of self-importance. "The public hated him for a long time too. People always forget about that. The Three Jesuses called him a devil, and the Pharisees slaughtered thousands of his supporters for sport. He came up with the idea for MindSpace sitting in a cave in the Himalayas."

"Natch has disappeared," said Jara.

"I know."

The bio/logic analyst took a step back in surprise. Margaret *knew?* Then why hadn't she answered all the messages and ConfidentialWhispers Jara had been flinging her way? As one of the firm's senior partners, why hadn't she immediately called a meeting to discuss alternative plans for the presentation? Jara felt like crying at the unfairness of it all. *Why does it feel like I'm the only one willing to fight for this fiefcorp? Why is it that when push comes to shove, Natch disappears, Serr Vigal prives himself to all communication, and Horvil just falls apart? And yet I'm the one who's trying to get out of this whole nightmare. I'm the one who wants to put this MultiReal shit behind me and get on with my life.*

"If you want to honor Sheldon Surina's memory," Jara said in a slow and deliberate tone of voice, "then you'll stop feeling sorry for yourself and help us figure out an alternate course of action."

Margaret recoiled as if she had just been slapped. "I have no idea where Natch is. I didn't do anything to him."

"I'm not suggesting you did. But *you're* the one who set this whole thing in motion."

"Indeed?"

"Come on, Margaret! You created this fucking program; you dragged Natch and the rest of us into this business. You stood up there in front of billions of people and announced a bold new era of multiple realities. It's too late to back out now. You have a responsibility—no, an *obligation*—to see it through."

"An obligation to whom? To *you?*" The descendant of Sheldon Surina snorted haughtily. "I don't *know* you."

"You know Natch," said Jara. "You know Quell."

Margaret firmed up her jaw, looking again at the cool stone representation of her ancestor. Natch's name had produced barely a ripple on the bodhisattva's face, but mention of the Islander had obviously shaken her. "My obligation," she replied, "is to him." By *him*, clearly, Margaret meant the big-nosed stone statue and not anyone this side of the grave.

Jara stomped her foot and, only by sheer force of will, restrained herself from yelling at the venerable bodhisattva. Hadn't she been through this same scenario with Natch just a few weeks ago, when he all but announced his intention to frame his apprentices for that little black code scheme? Was there something inherent in the bio/logics trade that caused fiefcorp masters to lose their moral bearings? "So after sixteen years of working on this thing, you're just going to give up."

"Now who's playing the victim? You're not an invalid, Jara." Until that moment, Jara had not been sure the bodhisattva even knew her name. "I'm quite certain Natch didn't hold a dartgun to your chest and force you to sign an apprenticeship contract. When you start a new business, there always are risks. You didn't think Natch and I were going to take all those risks while you sat back and watched millions of credits pour into your Vault account, did you?"

Blistering words clawed at Jara's windpipe, struggling for release. But at that moment, a Surina security guard trotted up to Margaret with a fist raised chin-level in salute. The bodhisattva gave the man a sidelong glance. Then the color drained from her face in response to some word she heard over ConfidentialWhisper.

"Go ahead," rasped Margaret, stumbling towards the window with a hand clutching her stomach. "You might as well tell *her*."

The officer turned to Jara and saluted smartly. "The Defense and Wellness Council is coming."

"*What?*"

"Several hundred hoverbirds have been spotted on the outskirts of

Andra Pradesh. Three or four legions of Council officers are heading this way."

Jara felt her knees buckle, and before she knew it, she was sitting on the ground, woozy, her back leaning against Sheldon Surina's toes. Was it going to happen this easily? Just like Margaret's speech last week, Len Borda's troops were going to surge into the Surina compound and disrupt the proceedings—maybe even seize MultiReal by force—in front of the entire world.

Margaret pressed her forehead against the glass. A look of doom washed over her face. "You see?" she cried. "He's never going to stop, not until I'm dead and MultiReal is under his control. And what can anybody do about it? *What* can anybody *do* about it?"

Jara said nothing. Words seemed quite beside the point.

"Nothing to say? I thought so." The bodhisattva cast a hateful glance back at Jara, reached into a gap in her robes, and drew a sleek silver dart-pistol. "Well, don't worry. The high executive is about to find out that confiscating MultiReal won't be as easy as it looks.

"The Spire!" she roared to her security detail, then stormed out the front door into the courtyard. Her cordon of guards followed close behind.

• • •

Millions of spectators had already poured into the Surina auditorium to await the first public demonstration of MultiReal. Despite Creed Conscientious' pleas, nobody seemed deterred by the prospect of another infoquake. They wanted to catch a glimpse of the infamous Natch, to see if he really deserved his reputation among the drudges. They wanted to measure Margaret Surina's accomplishments against those of her ancestors. More than anything, they just wanted to bask in the glow of history.

A carnival atmosphere swirled through the arena. Drudges and politicians of every ideological stripe wandered around broadcasting their analysis of the spectacle to their constituencies. Fiefcorp apprentices flaunted product slogans on their shirts and foreheads in vivid glow-in-the-dark colors. Creed devotees multied into the arena dressed in full creed regalia, while bodhisattvas from fringe groups stood on chairs and preached to anyone who would listen. Groups of children clustered together under the aegis of their hives, accompanied by stern-faced proctors of business, programming, politics, and ethics. A few dozen L-PRACG activists multied into the auditorium stark naked and began chanting a tepid protest of Vault lending practices. One by one, they were caught in the beam of the Surina security disruptors and their multi connections cut. Council officers were nowhere to be seen.

Merri had been standing at the foot of the stage since the first thirty-five thousand spectators arrived and the auditorium began overlapping multi projections. She felt a strange sense of privilege to be here as a real body; it was quite literally a one-in-a-million opportunity. Fiefcorp apprentices living on the moon usually did not receive this kind of privilege.

Her reverie was interrupted by a reedy voice Merri had heard all too often over the past few days. "Say you run an assembly-line programming floor, and you're on a tight deadline. You don't have time to make mistakes." Merri zeroed in on the source of the voice, and saw Frizitz Quo not three meters away, holding court before an audience of Meme Cooperative officials. "Every time one of your workers fumbles a connection, that's a few precious minutes you've wasted. A few credits MultiReal could have saved you. Now multiply that by a few hundred workers, and that's *real* money. . . ."

Merri tuned out the sprightly Asian and called up the grid that would show her the location of Robby Robby's entire team of cube-headed channelers. A diagram of the arena appeared in the air before her, speckled with purple dots to indicate the coordinates of each team member. A legend in the corner of the diagram silently tallied up audience demographics.

Robby Robby himself had roped together an ad hoc group of nearly six thousand orbital colony residents, and was busy preaching the gospel of . . . something. Merri tuned in a video feed. "We know what you're going through out there," exclaimed Robby, his idiotic grin wobbling sympathetically. "The last to know. The last to hear. The last to be *noticed*. Right?"

A lukewarm cheer from the crowd.

"Who suffered during the infoquake last week? Was it the Terrans? Was it the Lunars? No, of course not—it was *you*. Am I right? You citizens of Allowell, of Patronell, of Furtoid, of 49th Heaven, of Nova Ceti, and all the rest—it was *you* who bore the brunt of that terrible catastrophe, wasn't it?"

A righteous buzz of discontent. A few raised fists.

"Well, keep those multi connections right here in Andra Pradesh, ladies and gentlemen, because tonight the Surina/Natch MultiReal Fiefcorp is gonna show you a whole new dawn for orbital colonists—"

Merri cut off the feed and shook her head. Robby and his channelers had been wandering all over the map during the past few hours, voicing new sales motifs at every exchange. Her instincts told her she should rein Robby in, insist he stay on message. But did it really matter what the channelers said at this point? They were pitching a technology nobody understood to crowds that had no idea whether they should care. Merri couldn't really ask any more of Robby's staff than to keep the audience interested and upbeat.

She was about to head backstage for a much-needed break when she felt a tug at her elbow. "There you are!" cried a worried Benyamin. "I've got to show you this. You won't believe—"

Merri put a calming hand over Ben's. "Slow down," she said. "Take a deep breath. How's the assembly line going?"

"Almost done. They're putting the final touches on right now. But *this* is more important."

The channel manager let him drag her across the stage and up into the mezzanine. She was feeling the first twinges of impatience when the word *Petrucio* caught her ear.

"Yes, yes, yes, of *course* it's true that the Patels are licensing Multi-Real from Surina/Natch," stated a rail-thin woman of Polynesian descent who stood on a makeshift podium fielding questions from several thousand fiefcorp masters. "Why bother to deny it? The MultiReal you're going to see here today is the same MultiReal Frederic and Petrucio will be demonstrating later tonight. Same product, different brand."

Merri fed the woman's face into the public directory and soon verified her suspicions. She had never actually seen Xi Xong outside a viewscreen, where her emaciated frame often sat alongside Robby Robby, Phrancoliape, and the Felwidge Group in drudge roundups of the top channeling firms. But given the amount of work Xong did for the Patel Brothers, Merri should have expected her appearance here tonight.

"There have to be some kind of Meme Cooperative regulations against this," 'Whispered Benyamin. "That woman can't just come here into *our* audience and start stealing customers, can she?"

"I'm afraid she can," replied Merri with a sigh. "There's not really much we can do about it. If we kick her out, she'll only draw more attention."

As it was, Xong did not seem to have any trouble attracting attention. With her opal-bedecked kimono and her glittering nail polish, she presented quite an elegant contrast to Robby's slick hucksterism. "The Patels look forward to a long and prosperous relationship with Margaret and Natch," continued Xi Xong, responding to a muffled question from the crowd. "Competitors? Why, certainly the Patels have had a little friendly competition with Natch over the years. What of it?"

"Friendly?" protested one of the onlookers. "They've done everything but try to kill each other."

A frothy laugh bubbled from Xong's china doll lips. "Don't believe everything you hear from the drudges!" she said with a dark twinkle in her eye. "So there's no love lost between Natch and my clients.

What does that matter? MultiReal is a wide-open market, and there will be more than enough room for two fiefcorps here. Besides, don't they say that a rising tide lifts all boats? As long as that tide pushes a few boats towards our safe shores, then everyone wins."

Merri couldn't help but admire the woman's poise, even if her wardrobe was too gaudy for the channel manager's taste. She caught sight of one of Robby's boyish cube-heads bounding up the aisles, and for a split second wished she could exchange sales teams.

"Do you want to know what the worst part is?" said Benyamin. "She's not the only one here trying to poison Natch's reputation."

Merri frowned. "Who else?"

"You might as well ask who *isn't* here. Lucas Sentinel has a whole group here spreading lies. PulCorp, Billy Sterno, Bolliwar Tuban, the Serlys, the Deuterons, Studio Fitzgerald—they've all got their own people mouthing off in the wings."

"Jara was right."

"About what?"

"It's too late to cancel. With all these fiefcorps looking for blood, we've got to pull this demonstration off, or we're *finished* in this business."

• • •

Jara tried on several courses of action in her head, but none of them fit. She could run, but there really wasn't anywhere to run to. She could hide, but that would be utterly futile given the surveillance technology at the Council's disposal. Jara thought about what the protagonists of the dramas did in these kinds of situations. They relied on glib words and cool detachment, of course, two things that Jara did not possess. What would Natch do?

A low crescendo of thunder swept across the courtyard and set the window panes vibrating. Rhythmic thumps. *Boom boom, boom boom.* It took her a few minutes to decipher the sound as that of a thousand boots marching on travertine in perfect synchronization. She listened intently for signs of battle—the high-pitched whine of continuous dartgun fire, the muffled boom of disruptors, all the war noises the dramas had trained her to recognize over the years. But if there was indeed a skirmish going on outside, none of it was reaching Jara's ears.

The tourists who had been kicked out of the atrium half an hour earlier came scurrying by. Over her mother's shoulder, a toddler gave Jara a curious look as they fled past Albert Einstein into Relativity Hall. They were followed shortly by a phalanx of panicked green-and-blue Surina guards, fumbling with their dartguns as they scrambled to reach some defensive checkpoint. Jara dissolved as much as possible into Sheldon Surina's open-toed sandals, but nobody paid her any attention. Obviously, Len Borda had not even bothered repeating his fiction about protecting the scientist statues this time.

Outside, the first row of Defense and Wellness Council officers strode past the window. Their white robes looked positively spectral in the cloudy afternoon light, an affront to the notion of camouflage. Their faces bore the kind of stonelike neutrality that only bio/logics could produce. They were aiming squarely for the Revelation Spire, where Margaret was presumably holed up in a high story awaiting some kind of apocalyptic showdown. Jara peered out another window that gave her a view closer to the Spire. She had seen a squadron of Surina security forces there earlier, but now they had vanished.

What would Natch do under these circumstances? Jara knew exactly what he would do: he would go ahead and give the presentation anyway, until someone physically dragged him off the stage or blew him into a million pieces.

An idea popped into Jara's head, an idea that had been percolating for hours even though she had refused to acknowledge it.

Why couldn't *she* deliver the presentation?

Casting her mind out to the Surina facilities, Jara discovered that the spectators were indeed staying put in spite of Len Borda's little incursion. The Surina/Natch MultiReal Fiefcorp was scheduled to hit the stage in little more than an hour, and the auditorium already held almost 400 million multi projections. If these numbers kept up, this would be an even *larger* crowd than the one Margaret had garnered last week—maybe even large enough to rival the 1.3 billion who had attended Marcus Surina's funeral forty-six years ago.

When the tromp of the troops became deafening, Jara put her hands over her ears and slithered even farther into the shadows. Still feeling exposed and vulnerable, she reached into her bio/logic bag of tricks and turned on Cocoon 32, a Lucas Sentinel program that had helped calm her down many times in the past.

Jara could instantly feel the tumult from the outside world fading away as her OCHREs filtered out the sounds around her and dimmed her sight until everything had faded to a dull gray. No Confidential-Whispers, no incoming messages. No background chatter from the Data Sea.

Could she really stand up in front of a billion people and demonstrate a technology she barely understood herself? And not just any technology—perhaps the most radical invention in the history of humanity, and one that was almost completely untested.

There were a million reasons why she couldn't deliver the presentation. Jara had no experience speaking in front of large crowds. She had a bad reputation in the bio/logics industry. She hadn't swung a baseball bat in nearly twenty years.

But what other options did she have at this point? Slink off to a tube station and go home? Wait for the hubbub to die down and then drop a groveling ConfidentialWhisper to Lucas Sentinel asking for her old job back?

Face it, Jara, she told herself. *You want to fail.*

The thought surprised and angered her. She wanted to fail. She wanted Natch's latest business venture to go down in flames. The analyst conjured a mental picture of herself: a small, fluttering, frightened thing, cowering at the feet of marble goliaths, men and women with minds and hearts and wills of stone.

And suddenly something inside of her rebelled. *That's not me*, she thought. *I can't be like that. To settle for failure—that's like accepting death. If I just sit back and let things happen, I might as well have never lived in the first place.*

Jara took a deep breath, counted to twenty, and flipped off the Cocoon. She had made her decision.

At just that moment, a familiar figure came barreling around the corner. He screeched to a halt in the middle of the room as soon as he saw the analyst, but the tub of jelly around his gut obeyed the laws of inertia and kept going. The statue of Isaac Newton looked on with amusement as Horvil toppled to the ground in accordance with the good scientist's theories.

"Oh, thank goodness!" bellowed the engineer, crawling his way across the floor to Jara's side. "I've been looking all over for you."

Jara gave her fellow apprentice a look of steely determination. "Horv, I'm going to deliver the presentation."

Horvil's mouth gaped open. "No luck with Margaret?"

She shook her head. "Quell was right. Margaret's gone totally offline. She ran to the Revelation Spire with a dartgun. I think she's going to make some kind of last stand up there. So with Natch gone and Margaret out of the picture, I guess it's up to me."

The engineer's face turned white. "Jara, there are *Council officers* out there. Thousands of 'em."

"I don't care. I'm not just going to *sit* here and do nothing."

"They'll stick you with black code darts like a pincushion before they let you set foot on that stage."

"Then they'll have to do it in front of a billion people."

Horvil's face took on a look of panic. His eyes tilted upwards as if beseeching the father of bio/logics for an infusion of sanity. "Listen to me," he said, grabbing Jara's tiny hands and clutching them tightly within his own. "We can delay the presentation. Nothing says we have to do ours before the Patel Brothers do theirs. We can just lie low and do the whole show some other time."

"Are you completely deranged? If we put this off, the Patel Brothers will eat us for lunch. They'll pounce on us, and we'll have to spend the next month digging ourselves out."

"So what? Is it really worth it, Jara? Maybe Margaret's right. Just let it go."

"Horvil, these are our *lives* we're talking about here. This is our *business*. Don't you care about the fiefcorp and MultiReal and—and everything we've worked for in the past five years?"

"No."

Jara blanched, momentarily struck dumb. "No?"

The engineer's face blossomed into a shy smile completely devoid of irony. "All I care about is not losing you."

Jara sat stunned, unsure what to say. Was he trying to put her off her guard? Or maybe this had something to do with their unspoken rivalry for Natch's favor? Certainly the big lummox couldn't be sincere. In the three years she had known him, Horvil had barely uttered a single word that wasn't laced with sarcasm. Jara sighed. Why was it that as soon as she found her own moment of mental clarity, everything else had to slide out of focus?

"Horvil," she said gently, bundling her hands inside the warm nest of the engineer's palms. "I hope you can understand this. But I have to make that presentation. I just *have* to. This isn't about the fiefcorp or Natch, or—or product release schedules. It's about *me*. It's about . . . not backing down. Not *failing*."

The engineer considered this for a moment. Jara couldn't imagine what thoughts were running through his head. Could a rich boy from the other side of London who had never had a moment of financial instability in his entire life still understand a crisis of conscience? "You have to promise me you'll be all right," he said.

Jara smiled sadly. "I'm afraid that's not up to me."

There was no burst of comprehension, no sudden epiphany behind Horvil's eyes. But finally he nodded and clenched the analyst's hands tightly. "Okay," he said. "So how can I help?"

"You can help me navigate. Do you know if there's a back entrance to the arena?" She gestured through the window at the now-familiar sight of Council officers roaming freely around the Surina courtyard. Their ranks ringed the Revelation Spire like a white crown, and lined the boulevard to the arena's front doors as well. The Surina security guards were nowhere to be found. "Obviously, we can't go that way."

Horvil jutted his chin out with determination, and the two of them rose to their feet. "As a matter of fact," he said, "there's a side entrance, through the museum here. Quell took me past it yesterday."

Jara brushed off her trousers and gave the Surina statue a respectful nod. "Let's go, then."

The fiefcorp apprentices zipped past the statue of Tobi Jae Witt and down the hall. They dodged their way through a warren of curio tables and around a variety of large metal contraptions that had once housed Witt's experiments in artificial intelligence. The halls were now mostly empty of people. The few stragglers they did see were either terrified tourists looking for an escape route or Surina security forces hustling back towards the square.

Something about the conversation in the atrium had completely changed Horvil's demeanor. Minutes ago, he had been fearful for Jara's safety. But now he was taking the lead, lumbering into corridor intersections as if preparing to use his belly to shield her from a barrage of darts. Jara looked at the engineer with a broad smile on her face. She wondered whether Horvil planned on taking the stage with her, and whether she would try to stop him if he did.

Horvil and Jara crossed over a walkway that bridged the Center for Historic Appreciation with the auditorium. They tried to keep low to avoid attention, but most of the soldiers below were fixated on the Revelation Spire anyway. Hundreds of dart-rifle barrels poked from the notches in the Spire walls, daring the Council troops to come any closer.

"The arena's just past that door," said Horvil. "The stage entrance is down the stairs."

Jara opened the door to the arena and found herself confronted with a sea of white robes.

The gathering crowd still stood at half a billion strong, but their ranks now included a large number of Defense and Wellness Council troops. The officers surrounded the stage and lined every aisle in the place. Just like last time, they silently shouldered their dartguns, their faces sculpted of stone.

Horvil gulped. "You ready?"

"As I'll ever be."

They galloped down the stairs, opting now for speed rather than stealth. The two reached the bottom and rounded the last corner. Sure enough, the corridor angled upwards and ended in a single metal door that would lead them directly onto the arena stage. Jara had not expected this last approach to the stage to be unguarded. But when she saw the three people standing in front of the door, she gasped and snapped on a PokerFace 83.4b.

Serr Vigal, the preeminent neural programmer.

Len Borda, high executive of the Defense and Wellness Council.

And Natch, master of the Surina/Natch MultiReal Fiefcorp.

(((32)))

Jara took an awkward step backwards, tripped, and fell neatly into Horvil's arms.

She hadn't realized that Len Borda was so *tall*. He towered over the rest of them like a thin rock pillar, his bald head its capstone. She would have recognized his dour face instantly anywhere in the world, whether or not he wore the Council's white robe and yellow star.

Jara tried but could not shake her head clear of historical vertigo. Standing before her was the high executive of the Defense and Wellness Council himself. The man who had led the world's most feared military and intelligence organization for fifty-seven years and counting. The man who had personally sparred with giants like Lucco Primo, Kordez Thassel, and Marcus Surina. The man who had single-handedly defeated the Economic Plunge of the 310s. The man who had mastered the intricacies of his post long before Jara was born.

She thought of all the wild and unverifiable rumors she had heard about Len Borda over the years. The secret interrogations . . . the hidden fortresses . . . the pitiless military strikes . . . the all-pervasive network of spies and snooping programs. And now that face was directly in front of her. Were the firm grooves on the man's brow a manifestation of evil intent, as the libertarian drudges contended, or merely the chiseled remnants of nature's implacable forces?

The high executive barely noticed her presence. "I will speak to the crowd," he said to Natch in a gravelly basso profundo. "You have ten minutes."

Jara glanced at the fiefcorp master. At first glimpse, Natch appeared calm and collected, dressed in a sharp navy-blue pinstripe suit. Only someone who had studied his every pore and wrinkle ten thousand times could tell he was tottering on the brink of collapse. She detected traces of the stimulant program QuickPrep on his face. "I need twenty," Natch said firmly.

"Twenty then." Borda's tone of voice left the impression that twenty minutes was what he had been after all along. He waved a hand, and the door to the arena stage slid open, bathing him in the spotlight.

Jara mustered all of her courage and spoke to the retreating high executive. "What about all those troops out there?" she cried.

Borda paused and gave her an unyielding look. The look of a man who could pinpoint her precise location, down to the minutest degree, in the orgchart of the universe.

The analyst felt a hand on her shoulder, and turned to find Serr Vigal. "Jara, the Council is here for our protection," he said gently. "It was Natch's idea."

She gaped at the neural programmer, uncomprehending. "And . . . Margaret?"

"She'll be fine," replied Borda. "Unfortunately." The high executive continued through the doorway and disappeared onto the stage. The door closed behind him.

Natch was already huddled with Horvil, listening intently to the engineer's instructions on how to operate the MultiReal program. There was no time to break down all that complexity into bite-sized pieces; Horvil was speaking pure calculus at this point. Natch gave no sign he understood the formulas his old friend was reeling off.

Jara turned to Serr Vigal. The neural programmer looked exhausted, and his eyes were full to the brim with concern for his protégé.

"Natch was hit with black code," said the neural programmer in response to her unspoken question. "He just woke up a few hours ago."

"The Patels?"

"Maybe, maybe not. He doesn't remember very much."

The fiefcorp master and the engineer were now dashing around trying to find a conference room with SeeNaRee capabilities. Quell happened to show up at that precise moment, and he quickly led them to an out-of-the-way door under the stage. Natch, Horvil, Jara, Quell, and Serr Vigal rushed in and found themselves standing at home plate on the baseball diamond again. Horvil conjured up a ball and a Kyushu Clubfoot, then tossed them to the fiefcorp master. Natch took a deep breath, threw the ball skywards, and swung.

He missed.

He picked up the ball, chucked it in the air, and missed again.

On the fifth attempt, Natch finally connected. But the bottom edge of the bat barely nicked the ball, causing it to limp towards first base and roll to a stop in the infield.

"I can't get this fucking thing to work, Horvil!" cried Natch, flush with rage. "Didn't Ben's people hook those programs together? What the fuck have you all been *doing* these past few days?"

"Benyamin's team got the job done," said Quell, doing his best to ignore the fiefcorp master's slight. "I tested the program myself."

The engineer patted his boss's virtual shoulder. "Just as you begin the swing, you've got to reach out with your mind towards the Possibilities interface and make sure you don't—"

"Never mind," Natch said gruffly. "There's no *time*. I'll figure it out. Jara, show me the script."

She did. *Let me do the presentation instead*, she almost said. *I'm ready, I've had a chance to experiment with Possibilities 1.0 in the past few days.* But Jara could see the iron resolve in Natch's eyes, the single-minded insanity that kicked in whenever he was backed into a corner. Her little catharsis at the museum withered, wormlike, into the dust. It was inevitable. Natch would never turn down a chance to perform in front of an audience of this size. As she had predicted, he would either deliver a perfect presentation, or die trying. Jara wondered fleetingly how the living, breathing audience upstairs compared to the invisible audience Natch had been playing to in his head all these years.

"Jara, tell me whether the auditorium can handle all these calculations," said Natch suddenly. His eyes were yellow and coyote hungry. "Tell me we're not going to cause a hundred more of those infoquakes."

"Well, the Surina people think that—"

"I don't want to hear it! Tell me *yes* or *no*."

The bio/logic analyst pursed her lips for a full three seconds in thought. She had never hated Natch more. She had never found him so irresistibly sexy. "Yes."

"Good! Now go find Ben and Merri. The three of you comb the crowd and find the most sickeningly sweet little girl on the face of the Earth. I'm talking five years old, pigtails, the whole thing."

"They don't allow anyone younger than eight on the multi network, remember?"

"Fine, eight years old then. But not a *day* over eight. Tag her spatial coordinates with a beacon so I can find her. Horvil!" The engineer saluted briskly, looking as if he were ready to give his life for the cause. "Go find a workbench. I need you to do the quickest programming job you've ever done in your life. We've got a couple of alterations to make."

"What did you have in mind?"

Natch spouted off a few polynomials. Horvil turned to the Islander, who nodded. "It can be done," muttered Quell. "Maybe." Seconds later, the three of them bolted out the door and down another hallway.

"I've never seen him so frightened, Jara," said Serr Vigal as the two of them walked back towards the stairs and a door that would take them into the audience. "I don't think I've ever been so frightened *for* him either."

Jara wrapped a comradely arm around the neural programmer's waist. Nobody would have mistaken Vigal for a young man, but he seemed to have aged twenty years in the past few weeks. "I'd be frightened too if I got shot full of black code," said Jara. "But don't worry, Vigal. He's already survived one attack, and with all those Council officers swarming through the arena, I doubt anyone would be stupid enough to try another."

Vigal gave her a curious look. "I don't think you understand. Natch isn't afraid of another black code attack. He's still worried about the first one."

"You mean . . . ?"

"Natch is still infected. The program didn't self-destruct after it knocked him unconscious. In fact, we think it was the code that woke him up."

"Well, what does the code *do?* What's it waiting for?"

"We don't know. *That's* what we're afraid of."

• • •

Anyone who might have suggested two weeks ago that half a billion people would be standing in the Surina auditorium awaiting a product demonstration from Natch—Natch the scoundrel, Natch the upstart, Natch the arriviste—would have been roundly denounced by the bio/logic pundits on the Data Sea who Clearly Knew Better. Now the drudges were asking themselves, If an unknown businessman could jump to the top of the hierarchy with such stunning swiftness, if one man could leapfrog generations of accepted practice and standard operating procedure, then was anything safe anymore?

High Executive Len Borda emerged from the stage door, and the crowd went silent. The audience, which had just watched a second incursion of Council troops with good humor, suddenly clouded over with gloom.

The high executive marched to center stage and swept the auditorium with his piercing gaze. Half a billion onlookers waited expectantly without uttering a single word. A minute passed.

Finally, the Council chief spoke in a voice like rolling thunder. Borda's words were unhurried, untouched by focus groups, and spoken with a formality that might have been labeled *pompous* if the labelers did not fear having their Vault transactions scrutinized to the last decimal point by men in white robes. "My word is the will of the Defense and Wellness Council, which was established by the Prime Committee two hundred and fifty-two years ago to ensure the security of all persons throughout the system. The word of the Council *is* the word of the people."

A shudder whipped through the crowd like electricity. Those words had rarely been known to precede a happy occasion.

"Last week, thousands of lives were lost in the orbital colonies due to a new computational disturbance on the Data Sea known as an *infoquake*," continued Borda gravely. "The Council and the Prime Committee have been studying this phenomenon but have yet to draw any conclusions as to its root cause.

"The epistemological implications of this phenomenon may be uncertain, but the duty of the government remains unchanged.

"It is the solemn obligation of the Defense and Wellness Council to prevent any such disturbance from happening again. Towards that end, the Council has proposed to the Prime Committee a number of temporary measures designed to curb the risks of computational disorder. I have just been informed that the Committee has unanimously approved those measures."

The crowd's silence was broken by a low murmur from contingents of hard-core libertarians. Even though the high executive still followed parliamentary procedure, everyone knew that the final word belonged to Borda and Borda alone. Who could recall the last time the Prime Committee rejected one of the Council's military "recommendations"? *Remember the statues in the Center for Historic Appreciation*, whispered the dissidents in the crowd. *Remember that flimsy excuse they conjured up last time to advance their agenda.*

"These are the strictures that the Prime Committee has enacted into law as of eight p.m. Melbourne time," said Borda.

"Until further notice, multi attendance will be capped at five hundred million persons in any one location.

"All persons assembled at tonight's event will have their access to the Data Sea severely limited.

"And in the case of an infoquake or another eruption of black code, the Council will enforce its right to shut down programs on the Data Sea *at its sole discretion.*"

The murmurings of unrest from the libertarians flared into full-out yells of protest. High executives had always had the ability to shut down certain programs deemed harmful to the public welfare—as long as they ran their decisions through the Prime Committee and the Congress of L-PRACGs first. But now, had the infoquake given Borda license to act unilaterally, without consultation?

A vocal element of the crowd began stomping its feet. Dire headlines appeared in drudge columns throughout the Data Sea. Chants of *Borda must go* echoed in one corner of the arena, until a rash of Council officers stormed in that direction and began conspicuously fingering the triggers of their multi disruptors.

Borda was unmoved. He stood and waited for the commotion to simmer down before proceeding. "The mandate of the Defense and Wellness Council—the entire reason for its *existence*—is to preserve the safety of every citizen in the civilized domains, from the four corners of Earth to Luna, Mars, and the farthest orbital colonies," said the high executive dispassionately. "Should the infoquake be deemed a natural occurrence, then the Council will continue to take measures necessary to prevent it from happening in the future.

"But if it should be determined that the infoquake was an act of war by rogue elements of society . . ."

Borda's words hung in the air for a moment.

". . . then let it be known that the Defense and Wellness Council will not stand idle. Our armies are poised, on high alert, around the globe and throughout the human territories. The Council is ready to take action against any group—*any* group—that tries to take advantage of a sudden lapse in Data Sea integrity.

"We are prepared to *act*, immediately and irreversibly, without appeal or exemption.

"Whether the Council acts or not is up to *you*."

Borda extended one long, bony talon from his fist and aimed it into the midst of the crowd. The audience grumbling instantly came to a halt, as 500 million people held their breath. And then, without any more formalities, the high executive cut his multi connection and vanished.

● ● ●

Natch had woken up from his mysterious slumber four hours earlier—woken up alone and in one piece, lying mummylike on his own bed with no recollection of how he had gotten there. Vague and incomprehensible images hovered in his head, just beyond the reach of his irises. He could not say whether they were dreams or memories or something in between.

For advice, he had turned first to Serr Vigal, reaching his old mentor on an emergency message protocol the two had used for urgent communications since Natch's days in the hive. It had taken them less than half an hour to conclude that the black code was still active in Natch's system, and that only one man had the clout to scare off any potential attack. By the time Natch and Serr Vigal materialized in the Defense and Wellness Council's administrative offices barely three hours before the presentation, the fiefcorp master was ready to agree to almost anything that would buy some time.

So Natch had promised Len Borda access. Access to MultiReal in exchange for protection from the black code.

But what exactly did *access* mean? The term had come from the high executive's mouth, not Natch's, and so he really had no way of knowing what subtle shades of meaning Borda applied to the word. How did *access* differ from *cooperation*? And did it also imply *control*?

Did it at least fall short of the wholesale thievery that Margaret had been trying to prevent?

Or had Natch just given Len Borda the very thing Margaret Surina had been trying to keep from him for all those years?

If he had not been so pressed for time, perhaps Natch could have dickered with the Council over subtle interpretations. Once again, Margaret's words arose from the graveyard of the mind to haunt him: *You find yourself capable of strange things when you run out of choices.* Hadn't Natch indeed run out of choices? Anyone who would go to the trouble of assembling a strike force like the one that had ambushed him in Shenandoah certainly had the power to put together a lethal piece of black code.

Lethal black code. The implications made Natch's bones tremble. A program that could tear through his bodily defenses like rice paper and cause his OCHREs to run amok. Who could predict what would happen? A jolt of electricity into the brain? Blockage of the main arteries leading to his heart? Or perhaps something slower, more insidious, more painful?

But it wasn't cowardice that had driven him into Borda's office. *I'm not a coward*, Natch had insisted to himself, over and over again like a mantra. *I'm not a coward. There's a lot more at stake here than my own life.* The high executive had provided all kinds of rationalizations for Natch's actions. After all, who could say what his black-robed assailants were after? Perhaps they wanted Natch to go onstage in front of 500 million people and unleash a ferocious black code attack. Perhaps they wanted to gain control of him so they could unlock access to MultiReal or kill one of his colleagues.

Or maybe these people in black robes wanted Natch to kill you, Vigal had mused out loud in Borda's direction, oblivious to the seven or eight Council disruptors that suddenly spun towards his sparsely carpeted head.

Borda himself had not expressed the slightest inkling of fear at the neural programmer's suggestion. *I'd like to see them try it*, he had said, his amusement registering on some subconscious level of the conversation.

And now, as Natch stood at the stage door watching Borda wrap up his impromptu speech, another possibility came streaking to the forefront of Natch's mind. What if the thugs who had assaulted him in that Shenandoah alleyway were working for the Defense and Wellness Council?

He thought about the offhanded way in which Len Borda had tossed him twenty minutes of speech prep time while pretending that all he could spare was ten. The high executive was a man accustomed to getting what he wanted. What if this entire episode was some kind of trap? What if the assailants in the black robes had been sent to push him straight into Borda's clutches—and Natch had unwittingly done their bidding?

After the high executive cut his multi connection and vanished, Natch looked at the millions in the crowd and tried to will himself to take those last few steps to center stage. But doubts weighed at his heels like shackled cannonballs. What if he had made the wrong decision to enlist the Council's help? What if he couldn't get MultiReal to work? What if his demonstration caused another infoquake?

The anxiety crescendoed to a mind-splitting intensity—and then suddenly switched off.

The presentation did not matter. None of this really mattered.

Natch was already doomed.

Black code prowled his system like a merciless reaper, relentless, insatiable, and ready to mow him down at any time. Even if the Council was dealing honestly with him—even if they had no involvement with the shadowy figures in the black robes and sincerely wanted to protect him—Natch doubted that Borda could act swiftly enough to stop the rogue program from taking his life. The black code had become a part of him. An internal attack could happen at any moment, between one breath and the next. It could happen *now*.

He took the first tentative step up the narrow ramp towards center stage. It was a straight path, without detours or alternate routes. Natch could either walk away, or he could soldier on and trust that he would get through the presentation in one piece. He would have to trust that Borda would abide by his promise; he would have to trust that Jara's script would wow the crowd; he would have to trust that Horvil and Quell's engineering had done the job, that Benyamin's assembly-line shop had performed as advertised, and that Merri and Robby had wedged open enough minds in the audience to give him a chance.

Natch reached center stage an empty husk.

Millions upon millions of people stood arrayed before him—people of all shapes and sizes and colors and creeds swirled together. Chattering insects. The temporary organic effluence of the Null Current, dredged from the water for a brief flickering instant between tides, an aspect of the endless sea of nothingness that surrounded them all.

Jara's words floated to the front of his mind.

"Towards Perfection," said Natch. The auditorium amplified his words to every corner of the arena. He was surprised to find his voice rich and melodic and unstressed.

Natch paused for a moment to scan the crowd, then did a double take, exactly as Jara's script dictated. Five hundred million pairs of eyes were scanning him back. The entrepreneur made an incredulous gesture towards the stage door, where a fictitious staff stood egging him on. "That's funny," he said. "I expected to be talking to you about what's real and what's MultiReal—but I didn't expect this whole setting to be so *surreal*." The joke was not really funny at all, and yet millions of people were laughing anyway. Of course, the presence of several thousand grim Council officers standing at attention with dart-rifles drawn did lend a certain absurdity to the whole scene.

The fiefcorp master smiled and continued. "MultiReal is the creation of new realities," Natch announced. "Alternate realities. *Separate* realities. The ability to visualize many things at once in order to do *one* thing exactly as you want.

"And what will we do with these realities?

"We'll do the same things we've always done, of course—eat, work, strive, struggle, make love—only better. Smarter. With more control.

"Now, my engineers wanted me to stand up here and blather on about the architecture of our program. All those MindSpace connections, all those complex mathematical formulas Margaret Surina has worked so hard on for the last decade and a half. And my analysts, they wanted me to talk about budgets and cost/benefit ratios and a lot of nonsense I didn't understand.

"But I said—why don't we just show them a simple demonstration?"

The fiefcorp master blinked and summoned from the arena a Kyushu Clubfoot bat and classic league baseball, just as he had done twenty minutes earlier. He shifted his grip ever so slightly, trying to find the perfect spot on the bat, the spot that his fingers melted into like an extension of his own multi projected fingers. There would be no opportunity for mistakes.

"There's an ancient legend about a player who could hit a baseball wherever he pointed. He would point to a seat in the stands, wait for the pitch, and then—*wham!* Knock the ball right there. They say he was the greatest baseball player who ever lived. Well, today I'm going to try to channel some of that magic for you."

Natch broke into a grin, stretched out his arm, and then whirled around in a 360-degree arc. His pointing finger encompassed the whole crowd.

He tossed the ball high into the air and swung the bat.

He activated Possibilities 1.0.

A resounding *crack* echoed through the arena.

• • •

Jara had found a comfortable position in the middle of the crowd where she could get an objective reading of the audience. So far, the speech she had written was performing as planned. Natch's folksy tone of voice was soothing nerves and smoothing wrinkles, providing an antidote to the poisonous invective the drudges had been spewing over the past few days.

Her apprehension began when Natch did his spinning-and-pointing routine. The script had been clear, hadn't it? Natch was supposed to point at an audience member—a *single* audience member—and start popping fly balls his way, one after another in quick succession, then repeat as necessary. What kind of fool stunt was the fiefcorp master trying to pull?

Jara nearly collapsed in shock and horror when Natch swung the bat.

There was just *one* ball flying through the air—and Natch was making no motion to hit another.

Already Jara had begun a mental search for scapegoats. Was Natch unable to activate the Possibilities program? Had Horvil and Quell bungled the coding somehow and caused the MultiReal engine to sputter? Had Benyamin's assembly-line shop missed a few connections? Was this another of the Patel Brothers' perfidious acts of sabotage, or the work of the black code flowing in Natch's veins?

And of all the hundreds of millions of people to choose from, why had Natch decided to hit the ball directly to *her*?

Jara stretched out her hand and winced as the ball landed squarely in her palm with a soft *thud*. She felt the light sting of horsehide on flesh. The analyst turned the ball over in her hand and brought it closer to read the letters printed around the stitching.

OF COURSE IT'S NOT REAL—IT'S MULTIREAL

The fiefcorp apprentice blinked, shook her head, and looked at her empty palm. *You're daydreaming, Jara,* she told herself. *There's no base-ball in your hand.*

But this was no daydream. The baseball had been there—and now it wasn't.

A few seconds later, gasps of astonishment simultaneously burst out of 500 million spectators as comprehension slowly filtered through their brains. Five hundred million stinging palms, 500 million empty hands. *A collaborative process.*

Jara smiled in spite of herself.

"You have just experienced the awesome power of Possibilities," said Natch after the initial shock had worn off.

"Five hundred million swings of the bat. Five hundred million possible catches. Five hundred million possible separate realities, all created *up here*"—the fiefcorp master tapped his forehead—"and experienced *out there.*" He gestured broadly to the audience.

"But we don't live in a world of multiple realities. MultiReal may give you hundreds of millions of possibilities, but we still have to make a choice. A single choice. And so the path I have chosen is—*this* one."

Natch snapped his fingers, causing a spotlight to spear a tiny figure far away in the crowd. A wave of applause came crashing towards Jara, rippling out from the center of the spotlight until it enveloped the entire audience. In the center of the spotlight stood a girl not more than eight years old holding her father's hand, grinning adorably and brandishing a MultiReal baseball in her elfin little fingers.

"Let the word *impossible* be permanently eliminated from our vocabulary!" cried Natch. "There are no more impossibilities! We have entered a new Age of Possibilities—a new Age of MultiReal—and from now on, the choices are *yours.*

"Towards Perfection, and I thank you for choosing to attend."

• • •

Robby Robby stuck to Horvil's side like a bad odor.

"They're going absolutely *offline* out there, Horv-o!" the channeler squealed, his cube of hair bobbing enthusiastically to some triumphant march playing inside his head. "My team is getting mobbed—it's like being in the middle of a fucking *orgy*! Everyone wants to hear more about MultiReal!"

"Yeah," said Horvil, his own face sporting a lopsided grin. "Including me." Robby let out a laugh that continued much too long to have any correlation to the wit of Horvil's comment. If Merri hadn't shown up and ushered him out to join the sales blitzkrieg, he might have kept going until his spleen ruptured.

The chaos continued for over an hour after Natch had vanished from the stage. Horvil's cousins and uncles and cousins-of-cousins and third-cousins-twice-removed-by-companionship multied in from every crevice of the known universe to pat him on the back. Every member of the extended family except for Aunt Berilla, whose hatred for Natch apparently outranked her pride in Horvil and Benyamin. Once the family had dissipated, friends and business acquaintances that Horvil didn't even recognize began pressing in from all sides asking for more details about MultiReal. The engineer did his best to provide vague answers, especially when some of his "old hive buddies" revealed that they had taken up the drudging profession.

Horvil shook off his pursuers and scanned the foot of the stage for the rest of the Surina/Natch apprentices. They all seemed to be in the same pickle. Jara was being mobbed by a horde of L-PRACG representatives trying to negotiate a bulk rate on the spot. Ben was happily enfilading an entire squadron of creed devotees with upbeat chatter about MultiReal. Quell was engaged in a vigorous argument with a small pocket of Islanders, all tugging uncomfortably at their connectible collars. Merri was presumably still off crowd surfing with Robby Robby. Only Natch and Serr Vigal had made a clean getaway.

Somewhere in the middle of the confusion, Horvil noticed a line of white-robed Defense and Wellness Council officers moving silently out the door, their guns safely holstered.

"Did you hear?" he said in a rush as Jara walked up to him. "Sen Sivv Sor tracked down the little girl who caught the baseball. Apparently, the kid lives in a hive that just got its budget slashed by a bunch of L-PRACG bureaucrats. Can you believe that luck? I wonder who Natch wants as our next spokesperson. A stray kitten? A monk? Or maybe a prostitute with a heart of gold who—"

Why am I laying it on so thick? thought Horvil.

Jara waited patiently for the engineer's shtick to ramble to a close. "Good publicity is good publicity," she said softly, distantly.

Horvil smiled and nodded, then began inching away from the analyst towards an exit. He could ponder the mysteries of womanhood another time. Right now, too many loose ends needed tying up. Like who had ambushed Natch and shot him full of black code? What kinds of surprises did the Patel Brothers have waiting for them later tonight? And how in the world had Len Borda gotten mixed up in all of this?

5

DEMONS OF
THE AETHER

(((33)))

"I swear to you, Natch," said the man, "I had nothing to do with this. I didn't hire anybody to ambush you in the street. I don't know any group that runs around in the shadows wearing black robes attacking people, and I wouldn't have anything to do with them if I did."

Natch's eyes blazed with doubt as he looked at Petrucio Patel.

He could only guess why Petrucio had agreed to come talk with him here in the Surina Enterprise Facility, mere hours before the Patel Brothers were due to take the stage at the Thassel Complex. Natch's cold rage would have been evident from the instant Petrucio stepped into the conference room and found himself enveloped in the windswept Arctic tundra, a forbidden land with Lovecraftian menace lurking over every hillside. If he didn't already know that his rival was beyond such emotions, Natch might have guessed that Petrucio was experiencing shame or guilt.

"I don't believe you," said Natch.

Petrucio burst into laughter. "You don't believe me! You think Frederic and I hustled the fiefcorp off to Shenandoah and started handing out robes and dartguns? Wait—you didn't see a short, fat one in the group, did you? Maybe that was Frederic. He's quite the marksman, you know."

Natch's face remained deadly serious, and Petrucio muzzled his glee with great effort. He peered back over his shoulder at the thirty-five-meter dropoff just behind his heels. A long way to plunge just to see if the SeeNaRee's automatic pain cutoff was operational. Petrucio straightened his tie and brushed ice crystals off his jacket, gestures to signal his command of the situation. "Natch, what would we gain by hiring some goons to hit you with black code? It just doesn't make any *sense*. How do I know you're not just making the whole thing up?"

"Don't be a fool, 'Trucio," snapped Natch irritably. "You've got the whole MultiReal market to gain. Billions of customers and no competition."

"That's absolutely ludicrous. We're not just your competitors anymore, Natch—we're your *licensees*. If I hired someone to kill you, who knows where control of MultiReal would end up?"

"It would stay with Margaret, who's scared for her life—"

"—and wants nothing to do with us anymore. Follow the logic, Natch! She'd just find someone else to partner with. Haven't you ever heard the old adage about preferring the enemy you *know* to the enemy you *don't*?"

"How pithy. You're the second person to tell me that this week."

"Obviously, you have a lot of enemies, then. Listen, Natch, I'm not going to sit here and pretend that the Patel Brothers are your friends. I don't like you. I never have. But just because we're not your comrades doesn't mean we don't know how to compete honorably."

Now it was Natch's turn to let out a hearty laugh. "What about MemoryMiner 98c? Do you call that *honorable*?"

Patel sighed and stroked his elegantly waxed moustache in consternation. "I don't know if there's anything I could possibly say to convince you that I had nothing to do with this so-called black code incident. Okay, I'll admit, MemoryMiner 98c—that was a shitty thing to do. But that was a long time ago, Natch. And what about all of those dirty tricks you've played on *us* in the past couple years? Remember DeMirage 24.5? NiteFocus 13, 34, *and* 48? Your reputation in this business isn't exactly unblemished. Shall we count citations from the Meme Cooperative and see which company is the cleanest?"

"Fine, let's."

Petrucio rolled his eyes. "I've already *told* you, Natch. We don't do business like that anymore. I've gone through a lot in the past year. This whole MultiReal opportunity has turned the company upside down. I've been far too busy preparing for *our* presentation—which, in case you've forgotten, starts in two hours—to worry about *you*. My companion died—"

"*Please*, Petrucio, spare me the sad stories. You slept with half the channelers in the eastern hemisphere behind that woman's back. Don't tell me you've had some kind of eleventh-hour conversion."

The elder Patel's nostrils flared, and his moustache twitched in rage. Natch thought Petrucio would definitely cut his multi connection now, but instead the man stayed and slowly mastered his anger. "After my companion died, I made some *changes* in my life," Patel said in a low voice, whipping aside the lapel of his jacket to reveal a small pin in the shape of a black-and-white swirl.

Natch blinked hard and took a step back in surprise. Petrucio Patel a truthteller? "Anyone can wear a pin." Natch gulped.

"Check the membership rolls—it's public information. I took the oath a few weeks after she was gone. The bodhisattva of Creed Objectivv administered it to me himself. You know what that means, don't you? It means I would be honor-bound to tell you if I knew anything about any black code."

"How come this is the first time *I've* heard anything about it?"

"The creed has several hundred million members. Not all of us who pledge are crass enough to advertise it on our chests, like your friend Merri."

Natch paced back and forth on the icy plain, his eyes tracing the patterns their footsteps made in the snow. It was not outside the realm of possibility that Petrucio was making the whole thing up, although the details of his story were easily verifiable. More likely he simply planned not to get caught telling lies. According to the drudges, Creed Objectivv's enforcement of the truthtelling oath was only slightly more effective than the Meme Cooperative's enforcement of fiefcorp business ethics.

"So let's say I take you at your word," said Natch frostily. "*You* had nothing to do with this black code attack. *You're* a devotee of Creed Objectivv now. *You're* an honorable businessman. What about Frederic?"

A look of stupefaction dashed across Petrucio Patel's face until his features abruptly morphed into a perfect PokerFace. "And exactly what are you suggesting?" he said.

Natch narrowed his eyes to slits as he strode up to his rival's face, close enough to take a bite out of his hawkish nose. "I know all about those Objectivv tricks," said Natch. "You pledge to always tell the truth, so you play subtle word games. '*I* had nothing to do with this. *I* didn't hire anybody to ambush you in the street. *I've* been far too busy preparing for our presentation.' But listen carefully, Petrucio. Until you can prove to me that both you *and* Frederic are playing on the level, the Patel Brothers are number one on my hit list. And you haven't *seen* how I do business when I'm really pissed off. I'll tear you to pieces. I'll use every fucking trick outlawed by the Meme Cooperative. I'll throw that MultiReal license to the dogs without thinking twice about it, and *fuck* the consequences."

Petrucio nodded almost imperceptibly, the look on his face a hybrid of amusement and respect. Then he was gone.

• • •

Shortly after the conclusion of the Patel Brothers' presentation, the Surina/Natch MultiReal Fiefcorp held a meeting. The apprentices all arrived at the conference room with their belongings in tow, since they were planning to head home immediately afterwards.

Natch was surprised to discover that Margaret Surina had not come down from her perch in the Revelation Spire after the Council's departure, although most of the guards had already been redeployed around the compound. The scuttlebutt among the security staff was that Margaret was busy right now moving her office to an alcove in the Spire's peak. But whatever the reason, the bodhisattva had not responded to any of Natch's ConfidentialWhispers. Instead, she sent a token message of congratulations to the entire team, the same kind of pro forma civility they had received from Lucas Sentinel, Prosteev Serly, and Billy Sterno, among others.

As for Frederic and Petrucio Patel, their product demo did not go well.

Their misfortune was partly the result of a breaking news story that quickly occluded any other topic on the Data Sea. The Speaker of the Congress of L-PRACGs had been caught in a major embezzlement sting involving a group of highly placed TubeCo lobbyists. That, along with Borda's heavy-handed and highly unpopular speech, had caused a groundswell of support for the libertarians. Opponents were clamoring for a vote of no confidence in the governmentalist Speaker. The drudges were now predicting that, within the next twenty-four hours, control of the Congress would fall to rabid libertarian Khann Frejohr.

But the Patel Brothers could not completely blame their failure on bad timing. They had compounded their misfortune with a number of poor choices of their own. They had no hands-on demonstration to show the crowd. The PatelReal 1.0 program schematics floated, unused, in an enormous MindSpace bubble above the stage, while Petrucio prattled on about *raging waters* and *safe shores*. Frederic wore a hideous chocolate-brown suit that offended the sensibilities of even the most fashion-challenged members of the audience. Afterwards, the drudges spent hours comparing notes on the rampant headaches caused by the thumping bass drum of the Patels' soundtrack. Even those commentators who had been overtly hostile to Natch a day earlier had to admit that the Surina/Natch MultiReal Fiefcorp had clearly beaten its rival to the punch.

Thus, Natch and his apprentices were in a celebratory mood.

Horvil arranged for a platter full of margaritas to be delivered to the conference room and made a big production of turning off his alcohol-metabolizing OCHREs. He clinked glasses loudly with Jara, Merri, Benyamin, and Quell in a show of solidarity. Even the multi-projected Vigal sipped an illusory drink from a virtual glass. Natch had never

cared for the unsatisfying sensation of multi food; all taste and no substance. Yet he too had a confident smile on his face, and his tranquil
mood inspired the room to summon a cozy New England SeeNaRee.
The conference table sat on a bearskin rug in the midst of an old-fashioned ski lodge, while a fire crackled on the hearth behind them.

"Anybody been scouting around the Data Sea for reactions from
the drudges?" said Horvil.

"Of course," replied Jara. "Everyone is totally polarized over your
demonstration, Natch. Some people are wondering if you released
some hallucinogenic black code on the audience. And there's an
amusing debate going on about whether or not you actually swung the
bat five hundred million times."

"Did you?" asked Ben, a little uncertainly.

Natch laughed. "Not even close! Five hundred million *possible*
swings, but only one *actual* one. You want to take a stab at explaining,
Horv?"

"It's simple, really," began Horvil. "Once MultiReal has reduced the
swing of the bat into a formula, you just plug in parameters and create
a mathematical progression of realities. So, you swing the bat at ninety
degrees and then ninety-one degrees and then ninety-two degrees and on
and on . . . and then you don't actually have to *do* them all."

"Then you'd have an *infinite* number of baseballs," Benyamin
pointed out in confusion.

"No no no." Horvil conjured up a virtual calculator on the conference table and began drunkenly plugging in numbers. "See, if you con-
vert the field of vision into a grid of Cartesian space and calculate the
coordinates of each audience member, then you can plug x, y, and z
values into the MultiReal program and work backwards to generate a
baseball hit to that point. Then, of course, you have to factor in wind
resistance and gravitational pull—"

"Enough, Horv!" interjected Jara. "We get the point. What *I* want
to know is why everybody *remembered* those discarded realities. Quell,

you told us nobody would remember them unless they were using MultiReal themselves."

"Right," said Quell. "That was the alteration Horvil made at the last minute."

"I wasn't even sure it was going to work," mumbled the engineer. "Just lucky it did, I guess."

"The important thing is that few people seem to doubt that the demonstration was genuine," said Serr Vigal. "Billions of people watched the whole thing over a video feed, and most of them accept what they saw as the true and actual version of events."

Quell stretched his beefy arms out behind his head and leaned back in his chair, looking well pleased. "I can't imagine a better way to introduce MultiReal to the world," he said. "A little girl holding a baseball. You don't get much better PR than that."

"Natch, who is Magan Kai Lee?" blurted Merri out of nowhere.

The fiefcorp master's visage darkened. A sudden gust of wind caused the cabin door to slam open, and a SeeNaRee coyote started baying off in the distance. "Why?"

"Someone by that name keeps sending me urgent messages," responded the channel manager sheepishly. "Four times in three days. He even showed up at my apartment the other day and scared Bonneth out of her wits. He won't say what it's about, but I assume it has something to do with MultiReal."

Serr Vigal planted his chin on his fist with a look of exhaustion. He exchanged a dark glance with Natch, who passed him some silent signal to proceed. "Magan Kai Lee is one of Len Borda's lieutenant executives at the Defense and Wellness Council," said the neural programmer. "He was there with the high executive during our meeting this morning. We think Borda has put him in charge of dealing with MultiReal."

"Lee . . . is he the guy who's been speaking at the Council news conferences lately?" said Horvil, scratching his head. "He's real short. Chinese, I think."

Natch gave a weary nod. "That's him."

"I don't understand," said Jara. "What do they *want* from us? If Borda's so worried about infoquakes, why are they terrorizing Merri? We didn't have anything to do with that disturbance during Margaret's speech. Shouldn't they be talking with the Data Sea architects?"

"Haven't you figured it out yet?" said Natch. "These *infoquakes*— if they even exist—are the least of Borda's concerns. MultiReal is dangerous, Jara. Think of an assassin who can fire a black code dart that hits its target every time. That's scary enough. But imagine what an *army* of people running MultiReal could do."

Nobody said anything for a good two minutes.

"So yes, Merri, we're going to be hearing a lot more from Len Borda and Magan Kai Lee," said Natch. "You can count on it. They're going to be our biggest hurdle from here on out."

All trace of levity had vanished from Benyamin's face. "Our *biggest* hurdle? What other hurdles are there?"

"Don't be naïve, Ben! It's a big world. All kinds of fanatics are going to decide MultiReal is the solution to their problems. Do you think *everyone's* going to sit patiently and wait for us to go through the product development process?"

"Someone has already decided not to wait," interjected Merri in a hoarse whisper.

Silence shrouded the room once again.

"Have we made any headway on the black code problem?" said Jara. "Do we know what it does?"

Vigal shook his head. "I've taken a few cursory scans of Natch's system, but I haven't been able to come up with much. It's capable of putting him to sleep. That much is clear. All I can say is, be patient. There are thousands of OCHRE machines in the human body. It may take some time to examine them all."

"How do you know the code is still there?" asked the bio/logic analyst.

"Programs have signatures, Jara," explained Horvil. "They leave traces." His alcohol-inhibiting OCHREs were back on in full force; the engineer was now stone-cold sober. "Your typical piece of black code self-destructs after it's done all its dirty work. No incriminating evidence, right? But there's so many safeguards against erasing OCHRE programming that you usually know it if a piece of black code self-destructs inside of you."

"That is often the only way people know they've been infected at all," added Vigal. "They don't notice the insertion, but the self-destruct they can feel."

"So who are the prime suspects?" asked Jara.

Natch muttered something noncommittal.

Jara tugged at a few stray curls of hair in frustration. "Well, who do you *think* did it? The Patel Brothers? Lucas Sentinel? This other bodhisattva you've been working with? Who?"

The fiefcorp master's face suddenly twisted into a rictus of fear, anger, and pain. His right fist flew out and slammed into the conference table with a reverberating *thump* that caused everyone to gasp in astonishment. "*I don't know!*" he cried out. "I just don't know, Jara! But it's *my* problem—not *yours*! Leave me the fuck alone!"

Nobody spoke for a few moments as Natch wrestled with his emotions. The fiefcorp master seemed to be on the verge of losing complete control. Vigal raised a hand and started towards Natch's left shoulder, then thought better of it and returned the hand to his lap.

The SeeNaRee picked up on the foul mood and hurled a blistering wind off the mountain outside. There were so many possibilities, so many potential enemies. Everyone had heard stories about the shadowy organizations that existed outside the dominion of the Prime Committee and the Defense and Wellness Council. The violent factions of the Pharisees who yearned to bring humanity back to God's Natural Order . . . the unpredictable masses of the diss who escaped, eluded, or just plain ignored the edicts of the law . . . creed bodhisattvas on the fringes who preached destruction while spurning the normalizing umbrella of the Creeds Coalition . . . radical libertarians who denied the legitimacy of the central governments and actively worked for their destruction. And this list didn't even include the disruptive forces arrayed against them *inside* the bounds of civilized society. L-PRACGs desperate to get their hands on any ultimate weapon that could put an end to ancient ethnic rivalries . . . unscrupulous fiefcorps that would leap headlong into thievery and murder if it would help them make a profit . . . drudges and demagogues with narrow personal agendas who could whip the public into a revolutionary frenzy . . . conservative politicians who could quarantine MultiReal behind a wall of rules and regulations to ensure that the program never saw the light of day.

Soon, Natch had muscled the panic into a temporary chokehold, and his face showed nothing but the normal intensity, the normal restlessness, the normal insanity. "I don't think we need to worry too much about the black code for the moment," he said. "Len Borda's people are sniffing around looking for the ambushers. I think his show of force this afternoon scared them off. If these people in the black robes wanted me dead—or wanted *you* all dead—it would have happened by now."

"But if you're looking for a way out . . ."

Without warning, the wolf inside took over and Natch burst into that predatory grin. The grin of the savage beast, the grin that put fear inside his friends and enemies alike.

"If you want a way out, I'll *give* you one. You all have twenty-four hours to liquefy your shares and cash out your contracts at no penalty. Anyone who doesn't have the stomach for this, anyone who doesn't want to keep looking over their shoulder wondering where the next surprise is coming from, now's your chance to get out."

(((34)))

Night came to London. For Jara, it was not a falling but a terrible rising, a mute upsurge of blackness that seeped from every pore of the apartment walls and puddled along the floors until it soaked her to the chest, constricting her breath.

Jara sat on her bedroom floor, Indian style, with her head cradled in her arms. She found a comfortable rocking motion between her haunches and the side of her knees, and tried to concentrate on that for a while. Every few minutes, she would open her eyes to peer at the window on the far wall, which was showing an exterior view of her building. But that was too depressing. With every glance, corporate office towers and tenements shrank more and more as their inhabitants left work or went to sleep. A succumbing to the blackness, visceral proof that the forces of Being were tottering on the brink of extinction.

Her old hive proctor had once told her that the universe was almost entirely comprised of empty space. He brought Jara and her hivemates into a green field SeeNaRee and used peppercorns and chestnuts to approximate the position of the planets in the solar system, with the sun represented by a rubber ball. The students were astounded to discover themselves standing hundreds of meters apart near their chosen planet. *So what's in the rest of the field? What fills up all that space?* Jara had asked. *Nothing,* the proctor had replied. Jara had been young and foolish enough to look upon that lacuna as a void to be filled by good deeds and great works. And the proctor had encouraged that passion. He had fanned those flames and then sent her off to initiation believing she had been the aggressor in their relationship, that she could set the empty heavens ablaze.

She wondered what her proctor would have thought of Natch.

She wondered what advice her proctor would give her now.

A scant three weeks ago, Jara had been bemoaning her fate and counting the days until she could free herself of the Natch Personal Programming Fiefcorp's fetters. And now, as if responding to her silent command, events had conspired to spring her from her prison ten months early. Natch had given the apprentices twenty-four hours to liquidate shares and part ways, or continue their contracts with the new Surina/Natch MultiReal Fiefcorp.

So why was she hesitating? Why was she huddled here on the floor of her apartment, rocking back and forth and staring at inanimate objects, instead of liquidating her shares? If she cashed out, she need never see Natch again. She could just dissolve her apprenticeship and walk away right now, ink the final period in this chapter of her life and close the book on it.

She would have money. Jara fired a data agent at her Vault account and studied the number that returned. When she added the liquidated shares at current market value, she saw a nice round number with a small army of zeros marching off the end. Jara began to dream up things that these newfound credits could buy. A bigger apartment closer to Horvil's end of London, one with real windows and a garden that would put her meager daisy patch to shame. Stylish furniture to spruce up that apartment. Lavish dinners, expensive champagne, cosmetic bio/logic programs, weeks and weeks of decadent fun on the Sigh network. A trip to the never-ending bacchanalia that was 49th Heaven. She could polish off her sister's tuition payment for that useless degree in metal sculpture she was pursuing in Sudafrica. Or she could simply stay put for a while, do nothing and decompress.

Then what?

Then she would have to look for work again. Perhaps a wise capitalman could stretch the money for five or six or even seven years, but her investment skills were moderate at best. No matter how prudently she acted, sooner or later she would find herself sitting across from some arrogant fiefcorp master answering questions about bio/logic analysis and trying to explain the gap in her curriculum vitae.

Jara could hear her mother's accusation across thousands of kilometers: *Why do you have to stick with bio/logics? Why not become a politician or a civil servant? Or maybe an artist like your sister?*

No, Jara retorted silently. Bio/logics was all she knew, all she had ever cared about, and she was simply too old to start fresh somewhere else, to stumble through all the virginal mistakes you had to endure in any new industry.

If only she had gotten a chance to deliver that presentation. If only she had not been yanked away from her trial by fire before she had tasted the flame.

Suddenly, Jara felt the full force of Natch's insidious offer bear down upon her. Now she understood the feral smile that had taken possession of the fiefcorp master's face last night. If she left the fiefcorp now, she would have enough to be *comfortable*. Not rich, not poor, but comfortable. Natch was asking her a question.

Do you want to settle for *comfortable*?

Jara pounded her open palm against the floor until the cool tile stung her flesh. How could she not have seen? She should have known that Natch's apparent act of generosity would eventually turn out to be a referendum on *him*. He had offered her the choice of giving up, of resigning herself to mediocrity and *comfort*; or of staying with the fiefcorp, of driving ahead, of tilting against self-loathing and dissatisfaction until they yielded or she died trying. There was no third path. To continue in the fiefcorp world under a different corporate umbrella was to become Natch's competitor, and Natch had ably demonstrated he could vanquish any competition. But to quit was to admit she had failed.

Why don't you reframe the question? asked an interior voice she recognized as Horvil. Poor, sweet Horvil, so untouched by the world's misery. *Don't accept the question on* his *terms. Ask your own question.*

But Natch had cannily eliminated all other questions during their years in business together. One touch at a time, he had broken down her defenses and seduced her into his ethos. Jara had become a slave to

Natch's worldview—and what was worse, she had willingly held out her wrists for the cuffs.

I'm sorry, Horv, she thought, *but I don't know how to reframe the question anymore.*

Jara got up and straightened out her robe, as if wrinkles in the fabric were a sign of poor character. She slunk into the breakfast nook and ordered herself a pigeon's dinner: snap peas and steamed rice, raw cauliflower, and water, cold and sharp as the edge of a knife. And as the twenty-fourth hour approached, Jara sat and forked food into her mouth, desperately trying to convince herself she was hungry.

(((35)))

Natch took the tube out to Cisco again to see the redwoods. He sat for hours mesmerized by their beauty, until they merged together in his mind, until all he could see were different aspects of one universal Tree.

Of course, the challenges had just begun. They had *always* just begun. Natch had connived and bargained and bluffed his way through the bio/logics game, only to find himself playing in a much more complex game. The stakes were higher here. You could lose your business. You could lose your possessions. You could lose your *life*, and the lives of those around you.

But had anything really changed? He remembered being five years old and feeling the oppressive weight of that bureau pressing down upon him. He remembered a very real fear that the blocks he had used to prop it up would slip away and leave him dead on the floor.

He stopped in Omaha on the way home.

"I think she's going to quit," Natch said to Serr Vigal, sitting on a velvet chaise in the neural programmer's study.

Vigal was in his kitchen, preparing tea the traditional way, by steeping fragrant leaves in near-boiling water. Natch found it a peculiar time-wasting habit. But then again, he had trekked across the continent enough times for a glimpse at the redwoods to look past a petty vice like caffeine. The older man carefully drew the antique china cup and saucer to his lips, blew softly, and took a tentative sip. Relaxation immediately rippled across his face. "Which one?" he said. "Merri or Jara?"

"Jara, of course. Mark my words, she'll be taking orders from that peon Lucas Sentinel before the end of the week. As for Merri—I think she'll stay aboard."

"Are you certain?"

"I know what you're afraid of, Vigal. You're thinking that sooner or later, Magan Kai Lee is going to get to her and start playing the morality card. *Would the bodhisattva of Creed Objectivv want you to stand up for a man like Natch? He hasn't been asking you to lie and violate your vows, has he?* But I think she's stronger than she looks. Merri won't turn on us."

The neural programmer came into the study and took a seat across from his protégé. Natch watched his mentor squint at something out the window. He knew from long experience that Vigal wasn't preoccupied with the view of downtown Omaha two hours before sunup; he was preparing to make an emotional statement. "So who *do* you think was responsible for the black code, Natch?" he asked finally. "The Patels?"

"Petrucio says he doesn't know about any black code," replied Natch. "And even though I've never trusted him before, there's something different about him lately. He really *did* pledge to Creed Objectivv. He was telling the truth about that much at least. Maybe Frederic ordered the black code attack—although if it was Frederic, he did it behind Petrucio's back."

"So if not the Patels, who then? One of your other competitors?"

"Like who? Bolliwar Tuban, or the Serlys, or Billy Sterno? They don't have that kind of imagination. Pierre Loget has the expertise to put together a piece of black code that powerful, but it would never occur to him. And Lucas Sentinel is afraid of his own shadow. The Meme Cooperative scares him silly, let alone the Council."

"What about your old hivemate? Have you considered whether he might have been involved?"

"Brone." The word came out like a sneer. "Well, he certainly has the motive. And he has all those Creed Thassel resources at his disposal. But I stood in the same room with him for an hour, Vigal, and I came out in one piece. If Brone wanted me dead, Len Borda wouldn't have scared him off—he would've pulled the trigger and gotten his revenge on me regardless."

"Borda, then."

Natch rose impatiently from the chaise and began to tread around the room, doing his best to avoid the Oriental knickknacks stacked in every corner. "That's my worst fear. Hasn't everything turned out his way? After sixteen years of failed negotiations with Margaret, he's finally gotten his foot in the door. But if shooting me full of black code was Borda's way of getting me under his thumb, he went to some pretty extraordinary lengths to pull off the bluff. If Borda knew I wasn't in any danger, why did he order a legion of Council troops to swarm all over the Surina compound and make all those threats? It just doesn't make sense."

"Perhaps his henchman Lee ordered the attack without Borda's knowledge."

"Maybe. Magan Kai Lee is a weasel. Who knows what that man is capable of."

Vigal caressed his goatee thoughtfully. Natch could see a grand topic of conversation sequestered behind that furrowed brow, waiting for the right moment to spring. "I know this might sound absurd," said the neural programmer, "but have you considered the possibility that Margaret Surina was behind this?"

Natch halted midpace and gave Vigal a look as if the caffeine had addled his brain. "*Margaret?* Why? She brought me into this whole mess in the first place."

"I don't know." The neural programmer finished his tea down to the dregs and set the empty cup on a side table. "I really can't think of a motive. But she certainly has the ability to create that kind of black code—and plenty of people at her disposal to marshal a strike team. And let us not forget that you've been conducting all these fiefcorp meetings at the Enterprise Facility. She could very easily have put you under surveillance."

Natch shook his head. "Margaret can't be too happy about my making a deal with Len Borda so quickly, but I'm not sure she even knows about it yet." Brone's words echoed in his mind: *Certainly you must know by now that Margaret isn't dealing with you in good faith. What happens when Margaret Surina grows tired of you, as she surely will?* Natch thought back to that conversation and barely stopped himself from kicking over Vigal's ceramic tea service in anger. "I wonder what Margaret's going to do. I can't believe she's just going to sit up in that tower and forget about MultiReal."

"Yet that appears to be what she is doing."

The two remained silent for a few minutes, lost in thought. Natch moved to the window to watch the predawn lights from Omaha's gambling quarter. Behind him, he could hear the neural programmer delicately crack his knuckles in preparation for a strenuous lecture.

"Natch, do you remember what that capitalman once told you about the natural *wants* of the universe?" the neural programmer burst out suddenly.

"Figaro Fi," Natch replied. "Everything that asshole said is permanently stuck in my head. *The universe just won't stay still. It* wants *to move; even its smallest particles* want *to be in motion.*"

"Have you ever thought," said Vigal hesitantly, "about whether the universe *wants* you to succeed?"

The laughter came bubbling out of Natch like a hot spring. "What a silly thing to say! Do you think the Demons of the Aether are out to get me?"

"Demons of the Aether?"

"You know, those old stories about bio/logic programs that *come alive* . . . and *turn* on their *masters*!" The fiefcorp master raised his hands in mock horror as he pantomimed the old dramas, the trite serials that used to exploit people's fears of the Autonomous Revolt. "So you think I was attacked by ghosts in Shenandoah. Is that it, Vigal?"

His old mentor smiled good-naturedly and rolled his eyes. "No, no, no, I didn't mean it that way. The Data Sea isn't conjuring up evil robots to interfere with your sales demos. There's a depressingly human explanation behind that black code incident, even if we haven't been able to figure out what it is."

"So what *do* you mean?"

Vigal ducked his head shyly and plowed on, his eyes glued to the carpet. "I mean that the world runs by natural laws, Natch. Just as there are laws of physics and thermodynamics and gravity, there are laws of social dynamics too. Laws of humanity. Figaro Fi was right: the universe does push and pull you in certain directions, but that doesn't mean it *wants* you to succeed. For thousands of years, we've been telling tales about the dangers that befall people who accomplish too much. Why? Because those tales have an underlying truth: power unbalances the natural energy of the world.

"Stop chuckling! I'm quite serious. You follow the bio/logic markets, don't you? You see this happen every day. A business triumphs over its rivals and gets stronger. Others become jealous and resentful. Eventually, the company's enemies conspire together to bring it down, or it rots from within. It's the same thing that happens with animals . . . plants . . . trees. Why? Because there's some mystical force guiding our actions? No, because too much power concentrated in one place creates stasis. And stasis is anathema to a universe that desires constant motion and change."

Natch grimaced and tugged at his hair, but there was more annoyance than anger in his voice. "Vigal, you can be *so* frustrating sometimes!" he protested. "All this nonsense about what the universe wants—you're worse than all the creed bodhisattvas put together! Why do you have to make some kind of—of *fairy tale* out of this whole thing? I'm just a businessman trying to sell some programs. That's all."

The neural programmer gave a self-deprecating shake of the head. "All right, you want more down-to-earth advice? Sheldon Surina once said, *Practice should not precede theory.* Savor your moment of triumph and don't do anything rash."

"If I never did anything rash, I'd still be coding RODs."

"All I'm saying is that Margaret worked on MultiReal for sixteen years without bringing it to market. She must have had her reasons.

You've had control of the program for less than a week and you're ready to sell it to everyone from here to Furtoid."

"That's called *capitalism*, Vigal. What do you want me to do? If I don't keep moving, someone else will just snap up MultiReal and do the same thing."

All at once, Serr Vigal looked weary and old. He shrank deeper into his chair, as if trying to will himself into the seams of the fabric. "I think you're too young to understand this. The natural *wants* of the universe do not work in our favor, Natch. Autumn always follows summer. Everything dies. You may be on top of the world now, but you cannot stay there forever. The world is not kind to conquerors."

The fiefcorp master stood at the window, facing the sunrise with a gladiator's belligerent stare. He could feel faint echoes of death emanating from the black code inside him. But during the past twenty-four hours, he had found a new confidence flowering beside the dread, a confidence fertilized by desire and sprouted from fear. He had seriously expected to be dead by now, and the fact that he was still living and breathing and staring out Vigal's window gave him hope.

"Don't worry about me, Vigal," he said. "I can handle everything the world throws at me. Just watch."

● ● ●

APPENDIXES

APPENDIX A
GLOSSARY OF TERMS

For more comprehensive definitions and background articles on some terms, consult the Web site at http://www.infoquake.net.

TERM / DEFINITION

49th Heaven
A decadent orbital colony known for its loose morality; originally founded by one of the Three Jesuses as a religious retreat.

aft
One of the descriptive components of a program that helps the Data Sea sort and catalog information. See also *fore*.

Allahu Akbar Emirates
A nation-state that once existed in what is now mostly Pharisee territory. "Allahu Akbar" means "God is great."

Allowell
An orbital colony saved from extinction by High Executive Tul Jabbor.

analyst
One of the standard positions in a fiefcorp. Fiefcorp analysts typically focus on areas such as marketing, channeling, finance, and product development.

Andra Pradesh
A center of culture on the Indian subcontinent. Home to Creed Surina and the Gandhi University.

Angelos
A major population center, known in ancient times as Los Angeles.

apprentice — An employee of a fiefcorp, under contract to a master. In the traditional fiefcorp structure, apprentices sign a contract for a specific number of years. During their apprenticeship, apprentices receive only room and board as compensation; but at the conclusion of the contract, their shares mature and they receive a large stake in the company and a share of the accumulated profits.

Autonomous Minds — The sentient supercomputers that rebelled against humanity during the Autonomous Revolt.

Autonomous Revolt — The rebellion of the Autonomous Minds, which caused worldwide destruction and hastened the collapse of the nation-states.

beacon — A tracking signal that allows one to be located in the multi network.

Big Divide — The era of worldwide depression and chaos following the Autonomous Revolt.

bio/logic program — A set of logical instructions designed to enhance the human body or mind. Most bio/logic programs act on the body through microscopic machines called OCHREs placed throughout the body at (or before) birth.

bio/logic programming bars — The set of tools bio/logic programmers use to create and modify bio/logic code. Programming bars are categorized with the letters of the Roman alphabet (A to Z), and are largely indistinguishable to the naked eye. They interact with virtual code through holographic extensions that are only visible in MindSpace.

bio/logics — The science of using programming code to extend the capabilities of the human body and mind.

black code	Malicious or harmful programs, usually designed and launched by seditious organizations.
bodhisattva	The spiritual leader of a creed. Most creed organizations are spearheaded by one individual bodhisattva. Some creeds are run by an elected body of major and minor bodhisattvas.
Bodhisattva, the	When capitalized, usually refers to the first leader of Creed Objectivv, who originated the title; or his successors, who abandon their names upon confirmation.
capitalman	Individual who raises start-up money for fiefcorps. Following long tradition, the term is gender-neutral.
carbonization economics	A colloquial term for a type of economy where fiefcorps form quickly to serve a specific purpose, and then dissipate to make room for new ideas.
ChaiQuoke	A popular tea-flavored beverage.
channel	The process of marketing and selling products, usually to groups rather than individuals.
channeler	A businessperson responsible for driving sales to specific markets.
Cisco	A major population center, known in ancient times as San Francisco.
Confidential-Whisper	One of the most popular bio/logic programs on the Data Sea, ConfidentialWhisper provides a silent, completely internal communication venue for two or more people.
Congress of L-PRACGs	A representative body composed of most of the L-PRACGs in the solar system. The Speaker of the Congress is one of the most powerful elected officials in government.

connectible	Able to link to the Data Sea. Cultures who shun modern technology (like the Islanders and the Pharisees) are said to be "unconnectible," and refer to the remainder of society as "connectibles." See also *unconnectible*.
connectible collar	The thin copper collar that Islanders and other unconnectibles wear to allow them to see and communicate with multi projections.
credit	The standard unit of monetary exchange in civilized society.
creed	An organization that promotes a particular ethical belief system. Creeds promulgate many of the same types of moral teachings as the ancient religions, but are generally bereft of religious mythology and iconography.
Creed Bushido	A militaristic creed that was formed around the time of the Autonomous Revolt and based on the ancient Japanese warrior code. Since the Reawakening, the creed has become more focused on asceticism and rigorous discipline.
Creed Conscientious	An environmentally conscious order pledged to preserve the integrity of the Data Sea.
Creed Dao	An order that stresses Daoist principles of harmony with the universe instead of conformance to the dictates of society. A strong repository of Chinese cultural history and tradition.
Creed Élan	One of the more prominent creeds, Creed Élan teaches the value of philanthropy. Its members tend to be wealthy socialites. The creed's colors are purple and red.

Creed Objectivv — A creed dedicated to the search for and promotion of absolute epistemological truth. Members take an oath to always tell the truth. Its logo is a black-and-white swirl.

Creed Surina — The creed founded in honor of Sheldon Surina after his death. Creed Surina promotes the agenda of "spiritual discovery and mutual enlightenment through technology." The official colors of the creed are blue and green.

Creed Thassel — A once-common creed of the business class, dedicated to the "virtue of selfishness." Its symbol is three vertical stripes.

Creeds Coalition — The blanket organization that promotes inter-creed understanding and cooperation.

Data Sea — The sum total of all the communication networks running in the civilized world. Includes such networks as the Jamm and the Sigh.

Defense and Wellness Council — The governmental entity responsible for military, security, and intelligence operations throughout the system. The Council is headed by a single high executive, who is appointed by the Prime Committee. Many fear and resent the Council for its secrecy and the fact that it is unaccountable to the public for its actions.

Democratic American Collective (DAC) — An ancient nation-state formed after the disso lution of the United States of America. See also *New Alamo*.

disruptor — Weapon that allows attacks on multi projections by disrupting or altering their signals. Often used by the Defense and Wellness Council in conjunction with dartguns.

diss	The urban poor. The term is alternately thought to be derived from "disenfranchised," "disaffected," and "dis-associated."
dock	An area fiefcorps use to keep pending projects that are being prepared for launch on the Data Sea.
Dogmatic Opposition	A legal appeal to the Prime Committee to block or nullify a specific technology. Used primarily by the Islanders to maintain a nontechnological society.
Dr. Plugenpatch	The network of medical databases and programs that maintains the health of nearly all connectible citizens.
drudge	An independent reporter or journalist who writes regular opinion columns to a list of subscribers. Drudges are considered one of the public's main resources for government accountability.
East Texas	One of two former splinter states of New Alamo. See also *West Texas*.
Economic Plunge of the 310s	Period of worldwide collapse and unemployment following the death of Marcus Surina. Widely thought to have been eradicated by massive Defense and Wellness Council spending.
Ecumenical Council	The religious governmental body in New Alamo that was responsible for much of the violence and bloodshed of the Big Divide.
engineer	One of the standard positions in a fiefcorp. Engineers are traditionally responsible for the "nuts and bolts" bio/logic programming for a fiefcorp's products.
Environmental Control Board	The governmental body that controls and regulates the planetary environment, from species preservation and protection to weather control.

ex utero	The state of an embryo that has been removed from its mother's uterus in preparation for hive growing and birth.
fiefcorp	A business entity that typically consists of one master and several apprentices. Fiefcorps are usually short-lived, lasting less than a decade. The economics of the fiefcorp business are such that it usually makes better sense to dissolve a fiefcorp and sell its assets every few years. See also *memecorp*.
flexible glass	A strong, glasslike building material that can be very easily stretched and molded, even at room temperature.
fore	One of the descriptive components of a program that helps the Data Sea sort and catalog information. See also *aft*.
"for process' preservation"	A common phrase roughly translatable as "for Pete's sake."
Furtoid	A distant and troubled orbital colony in constant danger of collapse from poor engineering and economics.
Gandhi University, the	The institution of higher learning in Andra Pradesh where Sheldon Surina taught. Each of his descendants has held an honorary chair at the university.
gateway zone	Designated entry point for a multi projection into real space.
geosynchrons	Programs that regulate the geophysical and meteorological activity of the Earth. Geosynchrons are categorized as Levels I through V, I being the lowest level (regulation of atomic activity) and V being the highest level (regulation of complex environmental activity).

governmentalism | The political movement that espouses a belief in strong centralized government (though not necessarily the current centralized government). See also *libertarianism*.

GravCo | A semigovernmental memecorp that regulates gravity control among orbital colonies and other outworlders.

high executive | The official that heads the Defense and Wellness Council, appointed by the Prime Committee.

hive | A communal birthing and child-rearing facility for middle- and upper-class children.

hoverbird | Flying vehicle that can travel in air and low orbit. Primarily used for travel over long distances, hauling cargo, and defense.

infoquake | A dangerous burst of energy in the computational system, thought to be caused by a disproportionate amount of activity at one time or concentrated in one particular area.

initiation | A twelve-month rite of passage that many youths from middle- and upper-class backgrounds go through before being considered adults. The initiation consists primarily of depriving children of modern technology.

Islander | A resident of the Pacific Islands, where the governments shun most modern technology.

Islander Tolerance Act | The law that created the Dogmatic Opposition in an attempt to ease relations between connectible and unconnectible cultures.

Jabbor, Tul | The first high executive of the Defense and Wellness Council.

Jamm   A network that allows never-ending musical "jam ses-
                    sions" between musicians all over the world.

Keepers   The order that was assigned to program and operate
                    the Autonomous Minds. Often blamed for starting the
                    Autonomous Revolt, although the extent of their com-
                    plicity in the revolt will never fully be known.

launch   To officially release a product onto the Data Sea for
                    public consumption.

libertarianism   A political philosophy that believes in decentralized
                    government run principally by the L-PRACGs. See
                    also *governmentalism*.

L-PRACG   Local Political Representative Association of Civic
                    Groups, the basic unit of government throughout the
                    civilized world. Pronounced "ELL prag."

master   One of the positions in a fiefcorp. The master is the
                    person who forms the fiefcorp, and has full authority in
                    all business decisions. Masters take on apprentices who
                    then work to earn full shares in the fiefcorp after a spe-
                    cific contractual period.

Meme Cooperative   The governmental entity that regulates business
                    between fiefcorps. Largely perceived as an ineffectual
                    watchdog organization.

memecorp   A business entity whose membership subscribes to a
                    particular set of ideas ("memes"). Frequently relies on
                    public or private funding, as opposed to the fiefcorp,
                    which relies solely on the free market. See also *fiefcorp*.

MindSpace   The virtual programming "desktop" provided by a
                    workbench for programming. It is only in MindSpace
                    that the extensions to bio/logic programming bars can
                    be used to manipulate bio/logic code.

Monk, Aloretus	Physicist and discoverer of subaether transmission, a method of instantaneous communication made possible by quantum entanglement.
multi	To project a virtual body onto the multi network. Can be used as a verb or an adjective.
multi connection	The state of existing virtually on the multi network. When the user returns to his or her physical body, they have "cut their multi connection."
multi network	The system of bots and programs that allows people to virtually interact with one another almost anywhere in the world and on most orbital colonies.
multi projection	A virtual body that exists only through neural manipulation by the multi network. Real bodies can interact with virtual bodies in ways that are almost identical to actual physical interaction.
MultiReal	A revolutionary new technology being promoted by Margaret Surina.
multivoid	The few seconds of mental "blankness" that occurs when switching (or cutting) multi connections.
nation-state	An ancient political entity, bounded by geography and ruled over by a centralized government or governments. Superseded by the rise of L-PRACGs.
neural programmer	A bio/logics specialist who concentrates on the programming of the human brain.
New Alamo	An ancient nation-state formed after the dissolution of the United States of America. Included many of the USA's southwestern states and portions of Mexico as well. Became a dominant and terrorizing world power during the Big Divide. See also *Democratic American Collective*.

newt	A digital servant that can be programmed to obey orders.
nitro	A popular beverage full of concentrated natural stimulants, usually served hot.
Nova Ceti	An orbital colony.
Null Current	Poetic term for death. The term is of uncertain vintage but is thought by many to have been coined by Sheldon Surina.
OCHRE (1)	A generic term for any of a number of nanotechnological devices implanted in the human body to maintain health. After the OCHRE Corporation, which pioneered the technology.
OCHRE (2)	The Osterman Company for Human Re-Engineering. Founded by Henry Osterman to pioneer nanotechnology. Dissolved almost 110 years later after a protracted legal battle with the Defense and Wellness Council. Often (redundantly) called "the OCHRE Corporation" to distinguish it from the nanotechnological machines that bear its name.
offline	Slang term for "crazy."
OrbiCo	The quasi-governmental agency that controls the space shipping lines and most interplanetary cargo transport.
orbital colony	A nonterrestrial habitation, sometimes built freestanding in space and sometimes built on existing soil (e.g., asteroids and planetoids). The major orbital colonies are 49th Heaven, Allowell, Furtoid, Nova Ceti, and Patronell, but there are dozens of smaller colonies all over the solar system.

Osterman, Henry	Contemporary of Sheldon Surina and founder of the OCHRE Corporation. A famous iconoclast and recluse who zealously persecuted his enemies. Died under mysterious circumstances in 117.
Padron, Par	High executive of the Defense and Wellness Council from 153 until his death in 209. Nicknamed "the people's executive" because of his pro-democratic reforms.
Patronell	An orbital colony that circles Luna.
"perfection postponed"	A common phrase roughly translatable as "heaven forbid."
Pharisees	The disparate groups of fanatics that live around the areas once known as the Middle East. It is believed that several million people still practice many of the ancient religions in these remote places.
Pharisee Territories	Unconnectible lands occupied by the Pharisees.
Prepared, the	An order whose membership is only open to the elderly and the terminally ill. Its members are given special legal status and access to euthanasia procedures in the Dr. Plugenpatch databases that are otherwise banned.
Prime Committee	The central governing board that runs the affairs of the system. Much like the ancient United Nations, the Committee's functions are mainly diplomatic and administrative. All of the real power rests with the Defense and Wellness Council and the L-PRACGs.
Primo, Lucco	Founder of the Primo's bio/logic investment guide and one of the icons of capitalism and libertarianism during the Reawakening.

Primo's — The bio/logic investment guide that provides a series of ratings for programmers and their products. People all over the world rely on Primo's ratings as a gauge of reliability in bio/logics.

public directory — A storehouse of personal information used throughout the civilized world.

QuasiSuspension — A popular program that allows the user to schedule sleep and choose different levels of rest. Often used to ration out sleep in small doses and keep the user awake longer.

Reawakening — The period of intellectual renewal and discovery that began with Sheldon Surina's publication of his seminal paper on bio/logics. Continues to this day.

ROD — Routine On Demand. A simple bio/logic program created for a single (often wealthy) individual. Usually pronounced as one word ("rod").

Sigh, the — Virtual network devoted to sensual pleasure. Unlike the multi network, the Sigh does not allow interaction between real and virtual bodies.

Smith, Jesus Joshua — The first and most influential of the Three Jesuses. Led an exodus of faithful Christians and Moslems to the Pharisee Territories.

stretched stone — A rocklike building material that is remarkably strong and yet flexible as well.

subaether — A form of instantaneous transmission made possible by quantum entanglement.

Sudafrica — A populous area at the southern end of the African continent.

Surina, Marcus	Descendant of Prengal Surina and the "father of teleportation." Died in an orbital colony accident at the prime of his life, leaving TeleCo in shambles and prompting the Economic Plunge of the 310s.
Surina, Margaret	Daughter of Marcus Surina and the inventor of Multi-Real technology.
Surina, Prengal	Grandson of Sheldon Surina and discoverer of the universal law of physics, which is the cornerstone of all modern computing and engineering.
Surina, Sheldon	The father of bio/logics. Revived the ancient sciences of nanotechnology and paved the way for the drastic improvement of the human race through technology.
TeleCo	Quasi-governmental agency that runs all teleportation services, brought to prominence by Marcus Surina. Now tightly regulated by the Defense and Wellness Council.
teleportation	The process of instantaneous human travel over long distances. Technically, matter is not actually "transferred" during a teleportation, but rather telekinetically reconfigured.
Thassel, Kordez	Libertarian philosopher and founder of Creed Thassel.
Three Jesuses	Spiritual leaders who, in three separate movements, led pilgrimages of the religious faithful to found colonies of free religious worship in what are currently known as the Pharisee Territories.
Toradicus	High executive of the Defense and Wellness Council, known for bringing the L-PRACGs under central government control.

"Towards Perfection"   A greeting or farewell, originally derived from a saying of Sheldon Surina's.

treepaper   Ancient sheet of pulped wood for writing and printing with ink.

tube   The high-speed trains used in most civilized places on Earth for inter- and intra-city travel. The tube has become ubiquitous because its tracks are extremely cheap to build, easy to lay down, and unobtrusive in appearance.

TubeCo   The memecorp that runs the tube system. Now heavily subsidized by the Prime Committee.

unconnectible   Not able to connect to the resources on the Data Sea. A sometimes derogatory reference to the Islanders and the Pharisees, who shun modern technology. See also *connectible*.

universal law of physics   Scientific principle put forward by Prengal Surina that enables nearly limitless supplies of energy.

Vault   The network that makes financial transactions possible. Known for fanatical secrecy and paranoia, the administrators of the Vault pride themselves on never having suffered from a serious break-in.

viewscreen   A flat surface that can receive and display audio and visual transmissions from the Data Sea. Viewscreens are usually used for decoration in addition to entertainment.

West Texas   One of two former splinter states of New Alamo. See also *East Texas*.

Witt, Tobi Jae   Famous scientist and pioneer of artificial intelligence from before the Autonomous Revolt. She created the first

Autonomous Mind and died a violent death, though her killer was never identified.

workbench

A particular type of desk capable of projecting a Mind-Space bubble and allowing bio/logic programming.

xpression board

Musical instrument known for its versatility. Users create their own form and structure; thus no two xpression boards are the same.

Yu

The first modern orbital colony, financed and constructed by the Chinese. The destruction of Yu by the Autonomous Minds was the event that triggered the cataclysmic Autonomous Revolt.

APPENDIX B

HISTORICAL TIMELINE

The chronicling of modern history began with Sheldon Surina's publication of "Towards the Science of Bio/Logics and the New Direction for Humanity." Surina started the Reawakening, which ended the period of the Big Divide that began with the Autonomous Revolt. The publication of Surina's paper is considered to be the Zero Year of the Reawakening (YOR).

YOR	EVENT	
	Development of the precursors of the Data Sea on hardware-based machine networks.	
	The last pan-European collective alliance falls apart. The nation-states of Europe never again gain prominence on the world stage.	
	The predominant Arab nations form the Allahu Akbar Emirates to counter American and Chinese dominance.	ANTIQUITY
	Scientists make major advances in nanotechnology. Nanotechnology becomes commonplace for exterminating disease and regulating many bodily systems.	
	Final economic collapse of the United States of America. During the unrest that follows, the northeastern states form the Democratic American Collective (DAC), while the southern and western states form New Alamo.	
	Establishment of the first permanent city on Luna.	
	First orbital colony, Yu (named after the legendary founder of the first Chinese dynasty), launched by the Congressional China Assembly.	

	Yu is sabotaged and destroyed by the Autonomous Minds. **Beginning of the Autonomous Revolt.**	REVOLT
	End of the Autonomous Revolt. Much of the civilized world lies in ruins.	
	The Big Divide begins. A time of chaos and distrust of technology.	BIG DIVIDE
	The Ecumenical Council of New Alamo, seeking to establish order in a time of hunger and chaos, orders mass executions of its citizenry.	
	Rebellion in New Alamo splits the nation-state into West Texas and East Texas.	
	Birth of Sheldon Surina.	
	Birth of Henry Osterman.	
0	Sheldon Surina publishes his first manifesto on the science of bio/logics. **The Reawakening begins.**	REAWAKENING
10	Final dissolution of the New Alamo Ecumenical Council.	
10s–40s	The Three Jesuses lead pilgrimages of the faithful to Jerusalem. Rampaging Pharisees leave devastation in their wake.	
25	Henry Osterman founds the Osterman Company for Human Research and Engineering (OCHRE).	
35–37	Seeing potential ruination from the technological revolution that Sheldon Surina has engendered, the two Texan governments put a price on his head. Surina leaves the Gandhi University and goes into hiding.	
37	The president of West Texas is assassinated. The new president exonerates Sheldon Surina and calls off the manhunt for him. It is still many years before Surina can appear in public without intense security.	
39	Creed Élan is founded as a private philanthropic organization (though the term "creed" has not yet been coined).	

52	Dr. Plugenpatch is incorporated as a private enterprise. Henry Osterman and Sheldon Surina are among those on its original board.
60–100	Many of the great nation-states of antiquity dissolve as their primary functions (enforcing law, keeping the peace, encouraging trade) become irrelevant or more efficient to handle through distributed technology. People begin to form their own independent legal entities, or civic groups.
61	The Third Jesus leads a splinter group of radical Pharisees in building a new orbital colony (the first since the destruction of Yu). Though initially promising, 49th Heaven collapses within a generation. It reemerges to prominence a hundred years later as a sybaritic resort.
66	First fully functioning multi technology comes into existence. Sheldon Surina, though not the technology's inventor, makes vast engineering improvements. Within a decade, multi projections are ubiquitous among the wealthy.
70s–90s	Inspired by the apparent success of 49th Heaven, a rash of orbital colonies are funded and colonized. Space mania brings new funding and energy to ongoing efforts to colonize Mars.
80	Birth of Prengal Surina.
103	Major national and corporate interests join together with the vestiges of ancient nation-states to form the Prime Committee. The Committee is mainly seen as a bureaucratic organization whose task is to ensure public order and prevent another Autonomous Revolt.
107	The Prime Committee establishes the Defense and Wellness Council as a military and intelligence force. Its first high executive, Tul Jabbor, surprises the Prime Committee's corporate founders by expanding the Council's authority and in some cases turning on its sponsors (particularly OCHRE).

108	Creed Objectivv is founded by a reclusive mystic figure known as the Bodhisattva.
111	The Prime Committee undergoes a major effort to fund the development of multi technology throughout the system.
113	OCHRE becomes a target of the Prime Committee, which seeks to end the company's stranglehold on nanotechnology.
115	Dr. Plugenpatch agrees to special oversight and cooperation with the Defense and Wellness Council in order to avoid the same fate as OCHRE. The corporation becomes a hybrid governmental/private sector industry that forms the basis of medical treatment worldwide.
116	Death of Sheldon Surina. To honor his memory, Surina's successors build the compound at Andra Pradesh and found Creed Surina.
117	Tul Jabbor is assassinated. His killers are never found, but many suspect OCHRE. After a protracted legal battle, Henry Osterman dies under mysterious circumstances (some claim suicide). OCHRE battles over his successor for several years to come, then finally dissolves in 132.
122	Prengal Surina puts forth his universal law of physics.
130s	Major advances in hive birthing bring the technology to the public for the first time. A small minority that resists these advances begins emigrating to the Pacific Islands and Indonesia, where Luddites encourage isolation from the outside world. The remainder of the system comes to know them as Islanders. The Islander emigration continues for the next fifty years.
143	High Executive Toradicus begins a campaign to bring the L-PRACGs under Defense and Wellness Council control. He enlists Prengal Surina to lobby the L-PRACGs to construct a joint governmental framework with the Prime Committee. The Congress of L-PRACGs is founded.

146	The Islander Tolerance Act creates the Dogmatic Opposition.
150s	Teams working under Prengal Surina make startling advances in the control of gravity using maxims from the universal law of physics. Key members of these teams (including Prengal Surina) become the first board members of GravCo.
153	Par Padron is appointed high executive of the Defense and Wellness Council. He is nicknamed "the people's high executive" because of his actions to rein in the business community.
160s	The business of multi technology booms. By decade's end, most connectibles live within an hour of a multi facility.
162	Union Baseball adopts radical new rules to keep up with the times and to even the playing field among bio/logically enhanced players.
168	Death of the first bodhisattva of Creed Objectivv.
177	A coalition of business interests forms the Meme Cooperative to stave off the harsh populist reforms of Par Padron.
185	Death of Prengal Surina.
196	Libertarian rebels, funded and organized by the bio/logics industry titans, storm a handful of major cities in an attempt to overthrow the Prime Committee and the Defense and Wellness Council. Par Padron initiates martial law and puts down the disturbances.
200	The bio/logics industry attempts to pack the Prime Committee with its appointees and paid lobbyists. Par Padron pushes through a resolution declaring that the people (via the Congress of L-PRACGs) will always hold the majority of seats on the Committee.
209	Death of Par Padron.
220s–230s	A time of great economic and cultural stability worldwide, dubbed afterwards as the Golden Age. A resurgence in creedism results in the formation of the Creeds Coalition.

247	Birth of Marcus Surina.
250s	Almost all infants outside of the Pharisee and Islander territories are born and raised in hives. Life expectancies rise dramatically.
268	Creed Thassel is founded.
270	The first fiefcorp is established, and rules governing its structure are encoded by the Meme Cooperative. Most people see fiefcorps as a boon to society, helping the underprivileged gain skills and putting them on a track to social empowerment.
287	First successful tests of teleportation technology are conducted by a team that includes Marcus Surina. The extraordinary costs and energy involved have prohibited the widespread usage of teleportation to the present day.
290s–	The Great Boom, a time of economic prosperity, is
300s	ushered in, fed by the new fiefcorp sector and the promise of teleportation technology.
291	Lucco Primo establishes the Primo's bio/logic investment guide.
301	Birth of Margaret Surina.
302	Len Borda appointed high executive of the Defense and Wellness Council.
313	Marcus Surina dies in a shuttle accident in the orbital colonies.
310s–	The Economic Plunge of the 310s, a time of economic
320s	stagnation. Len Borda keeps the system afloat largely through the use of Prime Committee capital to fund research projects. Critics grumble about the return of the nation-state and centralized authority.
318	Rioting in Melbourne threatens the Prime Committee, but is put down by High Executive Borda.

327	Creed Thassel is nearly disbanded after scandal caused by the drudge Sen Sivv Sor's exposé on its membership practices.
331	Birth of Natch.
334	Warfare erupts between the Islanders and the Defense and Wellness Council. Although the official "war" lasts only a few years, unofficial skirmishes continue to the present day.
339	Margaret Surina founds the Surina Perfection Memecorp, and the drudges begin to whisper about a mysterious "Phoenix Project."
351	The world economy officially surpasses its previous peak, achieved in 313, before the death of Marcus Surina and the Economic Plunge.
359	**Present Day.**

APPENDIX C
ON THE SCIENCE OF BIO/LOGICS

Although Sheldon Surina has been credited with founding the discipline of bio/logics, he was not the first to try to use computational power to enhance the human body. Indeed, the science of nanotechnology had grown quite sophisticated in the years immediately preceding the Autonomous Revolt. But the revolt put an end to such experimentation. For many years, any attempt to explore the intersection of humans and machines was deemed an attempt to resurrect the Autonomous Minds. Dozens of promising scientists ended up dead or living in forced-labor camps because of their "radical" ideas.

Sheldon Surina's seminal paper "Towards the Science of Bio/Logics and a New Direction for Humanity" changed all that.

It is difficult to explain why Surina's ideas found acceptance when so many other similar suggestions ended up in the dustbin of history. Most students of the period have concluded that Surina's bio/logics system was different from its predecessors in one crucial aspect: its *humanocentric* approach emphasized personal choice and responsibility.

A THREE-LEGGED SYSTEM

Surina conceived of a system with equal roles for hardware, software, and information. Like a three-legged stool, removal of any of the legs would cause the system to collapse.

The hardware in question would consist of microscopic machines placed in strategic locations throughout the human body. These nanotechnological machines would contain a variety of standard tools for maintenance of human tissue, everything from routine measurement to precise surgery.

But in Surina's system, the machines themselves would be incapable of independent action. Their every movement would be controlled by programmable software that could be strictly controlled by the patient. Furthermore, Surina envisioned a competitive software industry arising to provide ever-improving versions of this controlling software.

The third indispensable leg of Surina's bio/logics system consisted of an independent storehouse of medical information. Software would then have a trusted source to consult for information that would affect the directions given to the hardware.

Surina's vision was remarkably prescient, and the bio/logics system in place today still abides by those original principles. The nanotechnological machines that Surina envisioned were pioneered by his protégé Henry Osterman and his OCHRE Corporation. Dr. Plugenpatch became the world's trusted repository of medical information. And of course, a highly competitive market for bio/logic software grew and continues to fuel the world economy to this day.

Of course, not all is as Surina envisioned it. In his paper "Towards the Science of Bio/Logics," Surina made free choice a prerequisite of a working system. He wanted users to be able to choose from a wide variety of nanotechnological systems, software programs, and information warehouses. According to Surina, free competition was crucial to encouraging innovation and preventing corruption. But Surina lived to see both the OCHRE Corporation and Dr. Plugenpatch achieve virtual monopolies in their respective fields, leaving only the software industry as a truly competitive field.

In addition, the strict separation of functions that Surina wanted has not always been maintained. The distinctions between the three legs of the system have begun to blur as the OCHRE Corporation's successors have imbued their bots with limited intelligence, and software programmers have embedded their own medical standards rather than rely on outside storehouses of information.

BIO/LOGIC PROGRAMMING

While the techniques of creating bio/logic programs have changed radically over the years, the principles remain the same.

Bio/logic software is a series of instructions a user can transmit to his or her OCHRE machines to perform a specific function. In Surina's day, programming was performed through the manipulation of a series of machine "languages," software was stored on miniature "chips" implanted within the body, and instructions were broadcast to the machines inside the body through radio waves.

Programming itself has evolved from a primitive linguistic model to today's more sophisticated visual model. This evolution enabled programmers to visualize logical structures instead of spelling them out. Advances in the science of holography allowed the invention of MindSpace, which allowed programmers to interact with their programs through a three-dimensional interface. The capabilities of MindSpace programming have been significantly expanded by the development of special tools for the medium, the bio/logic programming bars. A typical set of programming bars consists of twenty-six entities (marked A to Z after the Roman alphabet), with each bar containing three to six separate functions. Most MindSpace bubbles also recognize a common set of twelve hand gestures.

The data itself, once stored on plastic chips, is now stored in protected molecular chains scattered throughout the civilized world. Prengal Surina's universal law of physics and Aloretus Monk's discovery of subaether transmission have made it practical for programmers to store information on an atomic level virtually anywhere in the world.

THE FUTURE OF BIO/LOGICS

Libertarian elements of the government have been particularly active in promoting a renewal of competition in the hardware and information legs of Sheldon Surina's three-legged system. Proposals include privatizing Dr. Plugenpatch and breaking up the three main companies that have divided up the OCHRE spectrum between themselves. But detractors have pointed to the chaos of the bio/logic programming industry as reason to keep these industries heavily regulated and centralized.

The bulk of current bio/logic research is dedicated to improving the energy capacity of the human body. Users often encounter problems when bodily resources that run bio/logic programs are overtaxed, and some industry watchers predict severe resource limitations in the human body within the next twenty to thirty years.

APPENDIX D
ON THE SURINAS

The line of scientists, politicians, freethinkers, and programmers that began with Sheldon Surina is perhaps the greatest dynasty humankind has known since the Caesars. Not only did the Surinas lead the way out of the chaos of the Big Divide and give the world trust in technology again; they also enriched that world in ways no family had done before or has done since.

SHELDON SURINA (-41 TO 116)

Like most of his peers, Sheldon Surina was taught to shun the achievements of the scientists and programmers that led to the Autonomous Revolt. During Surina's formative years, the world was still feeling the aftershocks of that cataclysmic event and the disasters that followed it (although by this time, the world had regained a modicum of order, and New Alamo's fanaticism was already beginning to taper off). His parents sent him to the Gandhi University at Andra Pradesh for a spiritual education. It was during his long apprenticeship at the Gandhi University that Surina became enamored with the ancient wonders of biotechnology. Against the warnings of his proctors (who considered the sciences to be a heretical course of study), Sheldon embarked on a project to re-create the achievements of the biologists of antiquity.

When he was forty-one years old, Sheldon published his seminal work, "Towards the Science of Bio/Logics and a New Direction for Humanity." The first words of this manifesto were a shocking call to arms: "There is no problem that we cannot solve through scientific innovation." He then proceeded to outline a new discipline of science that would allow computer programs to interact with the systems of the human body. Surina called his new discipline "bio/logics."

The work caused a firestorm of controversy in the academic world, with many educators denouncing Surina as a heretic bent on causing another Autonomous Revolt. Within a decade, Surina had crafted the first working bio/logic program: HeartMonitor 1.0, which could make rational decisions about cardiological treatment on the fly. Using this and several other successful prototypes, Surina raised funds for the first bio/logic corporations. His investments in these firms eventually made him and many of his protégés phenomenally wealthy. One of his disciples, Henry Osterman, founder of the OCHRE Corporation, would be a lifelong collaborator (and sometime competitor).

Surina's growing fame and influence began to upset the balance of power among the fragile nation-states. Many of these states owed their survival to delicate antitechnology treaties designed to prevent another Autonomous Revolt. During the years 35 to 37, Surina became the target of numerous assassination plots hatched by the splinter East and West Texan governments. These threats largely ended with the overthrow of the West Texan regime in 37.

In the years that followed, Sheldon Surina had a hand in nearly every major technology to come down the pike. He created or co-created the key tools and practices of the bio/logic programming industry (including MindSpace and bio/logic programming bars). He made important contributions to the development of the multi network, and with Henry Osterman sat on the board of the original Dr. Plugenpatch company.

Growing fear of the power of bio/logic corporations led to the creation of the Prime Committee in the waning years of the Reawakening's first century. Sheldon Surina decried the Prime Committee as an "insidious evil" and became the world's leading opponent of centralized governmental authority. (Surina and Osterman had widely divergent views on this issue and eventually ended their friendship over the formation of the Defense and Wellness Council.)

Surina spent the opening years of the second century railing against the Council and the Committee and seeking their dissolution. A firm believer in individual empowerment and unbridled personal freedom, Surina believed that any centralized authority (no matter how limited) would lead to totalitarianism. The majority of public sentiment was against him, however, and in his last years Surina even began to advocate open rebellion and violence. He died in 116, a bitter man with waning political influence.

PRENGAL SURINA (80 TO 185)

Prengal Surina was never as tempestuous a figure as his grandfather Sheldon, but many have argued that his influence on modern society was even greater.

Because of the family's vast bio/logic fortune, Prengal was raised with great wealth and privilege in India. He followed in Sheldon's footsteps by attending the Gandhi University at Andra Pradesh, and eventually attained a permanent post on the faculty. Prengal tended to shy away from politics, however, despite the increasingly desperate urging of his grandfather and other anti-Prime Committee forces. Upon Sheldon's death, Prengal and his companion Ladaru organized Creed Surina in his honor, but disappointed many by insisting that the group be strictly apolitical.

At the age of forty-two, Prengal put forth what many consider to be the most significant scientific breakthrough of humanity since antiquity: the universal law of physics. Prengal's law neatly tied together the previously disparate fields of quantum and classical mechanics. By revealing the ways in which matter and energy are intimately connected throughout the universe—in ways that transcend space and time—Prengal made possible the fields of teleportation and antigravitation. Without the universal law of physics, multi projecting over great distances would be impossible.

Prengal Surina's breakthrough was poorly understood for many years. Unlike his grandfather, Prengal was not a charismatic figure who trumpeted his own accomplishments. As his work grew in stature and importance, however, the system began to view him with an almost mystical reverence.

When he did become involved in the political arena, it was only at the urging of his old friend, High Executive Toradicus. In direct contrast to his grandfather's beliefs, Prengal Surina became a spokesperson *for* centralizing power in the Prime Committee. The current system of L-PRACGs pledging support for the oversight of the Prime Committee largely owes its existence to the lobbying of Prengal Surina and the hard-nosed politics of Toradicus.

Prengal lived the last decades of his life in quiet seclusion at Andra Pradesh, remaining neutral in the great battles between big business and government during the term of High Executive Par Padron. He died in year 185 of the Reawakening.

MARCUS SURINA (247 TO 313)

Unlike his predecessors, Marcus Surina did not seek a life of scientific achievement. He spent much of his youth disavowing the wealth and "decadence" of the Surinas in Andra Pradesh and the creed that was his ancestor's namesake. Marcus became a drifter and adventurer out in the orbital colonies, where records were scarce. He had much wider experience in the world than either Sheldon or Marcus, and in his time he gambled, piloted starships, formed L-PRACGs, and ran a number of reputable and disreputable companies.

Marcus originally entered the science of teleportation as an investor. TeleCo was one of many pet projects he funded with Surina money. He had very little scientific training and only became involved in the development of the science after several of the principal players resigned from the project over frustrations with his management.

It was at that point that Marcus Surina experienced an epiphany of sorts and devoted himself to perfecting the science of teleportation. He made up for lost time by delving into the research and development processes with more single-mindedness than any of his predecessors. By the end of the century, Marcus had transformed himself from a playboy and dilettante to the leading scientist and entrepreneur of his age. His passion for teleportation fueled the fortunes of TeleCo and, indeed, the entire economy.

Marcus spent the last decade of his life in a feverish struggle to perfect teleportation. He became a public spokesperson and pitchman, not only for his own technology, but for the bio/logics industry in general. He engaged in a great public struggle with Len Borda, the newly appointed high executive of the Defense and Wellness Council, over the dangers of the project. Their dispute remained unresolved, however, when Marcus died suddenly (along with many of his top advisors) in a shuttle accident in the orbital colonies.

Rumor and innuendo attributed hundreds of illegitimate children to Marcus, who allegedly was an incessant womanizer. Most historians believe these claims to be wildly exaggerated. Whatever the truth of those claims, he left only one legitimate child and heir, a daughter, Margaret.

MARGARET SURINA (301–   )

The only child of Marcus Surina, Margaret has assumed the family mantle as bodhisattva of Creed Surina; the professorial chair at the Gandhi University held by every Surina since Sheldon; and head of the various family investments. She also founded the Surina Perfection Memecorp, but its aims and goals remain unknown at the present time.

APPENDIX E
ON THE MULTI NETWORK

Society has experimented with any number of virtual communities, from the primitive text environments of the World Wide Web to the sophisticated pleasure worlds of the Sigh. But none has achieved such widespread acceptance as the multi network.

A multi projection is a virtual body that "exists" in real space. While the multied body is only an illusion created by neural manipulation, it can interact with real ("meat") bodies in a way almost indistinguishable from physical human interaction. In order to achieve such verisimilitude, however, the architects of the multi network have had to limit many of the freedoms taken for granted in other virtual communities.

HOW IT WORKS

The multi network depends on two key components: (1) the trillions of microscopic bots that process and relay sensory information to the network, and (2) neural OCHREs that manipulate the mind into "seeing" the sights, "hearing" the sounds, and "feeling" the sensations of the network.

Similarly, those who interact with multi projections allow neural manipulation to trick the mind into believing the virtual bodies are present. Participation in the multi network is not optional in civilized society. Even unconnectibles such as Islanders and Pharisees are required to wear so-called "connectible collars" when not in their homelands so they can interact with multi projections.

Thanks to the advances in nanotechnology that have occurred since Henry Osterman's time, multi bots are lighter than air and only molecules thick. They carpet most of the Earth and populated colonies in concentrations high enough to provide sensory information almost anywhere a user would want to go, but still diffuse enough that their presence is undetectable to the naked eye.

Developments in subaether transmission have enabled multi to follow humanity to the moon, Mars, and the orbital colonies.

THE PHYSICS OF MULTI INTERACTION

Because multied bodies are merely illusions of the mind and do not have physical substance, their interactions with the physical world are governed by a strict set of unbreakable rules. Some rules simply repeat the constraints of nature (e.g., a real person cannot climb on top of a virtual body). Other rules are arbitrary decisions that have been hammered out over the years by a succession of governmental agencies.

The guiding principle of multi/meat interactions is that *they should be as "real" as possible.* In an ideal multi experience, it would be impossible to determine whether the user was present in the flesh or in multi. The multi network, unlike other networks, does not allow for any "improvements" on the human experience. Thus, a multied body contains all the warts and blemishes the actual human body does; multied bodies cannot fly, change shapes, or perform feats of inhuman strength; and they are clothed in the same garments as their real bodies.

Occasionally, things happen in the "real" world that cannot be reconciled in a virtual environment. One can throw a stone "through" a multi projection without incident. Larger discrepancies typically result in the automatic cutting of a multi connection.

As the ubiquity of the multi network has grown, society has largely adapted. Most doors and windows are capable of accepting and responding to multi commands. Auditoriums and meeting spaces generally have amenities for both types of audiences.

The verisimilitude of the multi network is what has kept it safe during the decades it has been in widespread use. The network has built-in safeguards that will automatically cut a connection in cases of extreme pain or duress. Because its rules are so rigid and the chance for mishap so small, the Defense and Wellness Council has fiercely blocked any attempts to liberalize the network rules or allow other virtual networks to participate in public space.

ENTERING AND EXITING THE NETWORK

Because of the high potential for danger in letting multi projections connect anywhere on the network, the network's governing bodies insisted early in its existence that entry points on the network be restricted.

Entrances must occur in specially designated "gateway zones." This is to prevent users from projecting to unauthorized locations, into the middle of a wall, or into some other obstruction. Most homes, businesses, and public places these days are equipped with gateway zones that allow apparition onto the multi network, but it is not uncommon for restricted or sensitive locations to limit gateway zones to a central location.

A user must be standing on a specially designated red tile square to enter the network. If that physical contact is interrupted, the connection is immediately cut. Given the obvious security risk of leaving one's body unattended, multi squares typically occur only in private residences or in heavily guarded public locations (multi facilities).

One can exit the multi network instantaneously from any spatial coordinate. Under pressure from the Prime Committee, the network administrators also developed a special device called a "disruptor" to allow authorities to cut multi connections. The Defense and Wellness

Council later augmented the basic disruptor design to allow certain bio/logic code to flow into a multi projection.

MULTI AND COMPUTING POWER

Multi technology relies on the fact that complete verisimilitude of experience is not necessary. Often the network can take advantage of common experiences stored within the brain and from them compile a representative sample. Take the example of a multied user walking barefoot on a field of grass. The network does not take up unnecessary bandwidth and computing power determining the position of each blade of grass and calculating its effects on the user's foot; it is deemed sufficient for the network to provide a *reasonable facsimile* of the sensation. Randomness algorithms ensure that the simulated sensations do not feel repetitious or calculated.

The network also maintains fluency and transmission speed by taking a number of practical shortcuts. For instance, the multi network does not relay visual information for anything the user is not focusing on.

Users of the multi network understand that their experience is only a simulation, and that occasionally the simulation will differ from reality in its details. As the technology has progressed, these differences have become smaller and smaller, to the point where the typical user cannot reliably distinguish between virtual environments and reality.

APPENDIX F

ON THE FIEFCORP SYSTEM

Rarely in the history of human enterprise has there been a more controversial entity than the fiefcorp. Conceived as a means to empower workers, many now complain that it has become an instrument of social ills.

HISTORY

Fiefcorps were made possible by the actions of Par Padron, who spent most of his tenure as Council high executive battling big business. Padron believed that governmental regulations and tax structures had come to favor larger companies, creating a climate in which smaller entrepreneurs could not succeed. Over the years, he succeeded in leveling the playing field among businesses and in democratizing the Prime Committee.

It was this latter action that triggered a populist resurgence on the Committee several decades later, and the subsequent votes to approve the business structure known as the fiefcorp. In order to spur innovation, fiefcorps were given substantial tax breaks during their initial decade of existence. In order to spur employment, the fiefcorp structure was modeled after the feudal master-and-apprentice relationship of ancient times.

Although the beginnings of the system were chaotic, the rapid formation, innovation, and dissolution of fiefcorps soon contributed to a beneficial effect known as "carbonization economics."

CARBONIZATION ECONOMICS

The short time window of reduced taxation, combined with low start-up costs, made fiefcorps a hotbed of innovation. Small companies were encouraged to come up with new ideas and bring them to market quickly. A fiefcorp master could bring in a number of apprentices, pay them only room and board to start, turn a very good profit in a few years, and then sell off his assets before taxes increased and start again. If the master needed additional funding to get the company off the ground, he could seek that money from the secondary market of capitalmen at relatively low interest rates.

With hundreds of thousands of fiefcorps formed, an economy based on efficiency and powerful ideas moved quickly. Pundits likened the effect to that of carbonized soda water, where bubbles quickly form, burst, and are replenished.

The rewards of running a successful fiefcorp were considerable. Profits from the greatest fiefcorps were extensive, and often allowed wily fiefcorp masters to leap into the more lucrative realm of real estate. But even in failure, the fiefcorp structure proved beneficial, because the labor market was constantly running a deficit of fresh talent. It was not unusual for people to found two or three failed companies before finding a winning formula.

ETHICAL PROBLEMS OF THE FIEFCORP

The biggest problem of a laissez-faire structure such as the fiefcorp system was its rampant lawlessness. Zest for profit often trumped rules of government, creed, and community. It was originally hoped that the low penalties for failure in a fiefcorp would discourage rule breaking, but this proved not to be true.

In an attempt to rein in the lawlessness of the fiefcorp sector, many in the industry turned to the Meme Cooperative. The Cooperative, founded a hundred years earlier by big business as a buffer to Par Padron's populist reforms, had since become mostly a lobbying organization to the Prime Committee and the L-PRACGs. Fiefcorps voluntarily ceded strict authority to the Cooperative to regulate their industry and act as a watchdog organization. Few believe that the Meme Cooperative has been successful in its mission, however.

Another third-party organization, Primo's, arose to provide an overseeing capacity to the fiefcorps. Founded by the fervent libertarian Lucco Primo in 291, the company's objective rating system has acted as a huge deterrent to fraudulent programming practices.

Still, many consider the problem of fiefcorp ethics a problem to this day. As a result, grumbling consumers typically turn to the L-PRACGs and the drudges for redress.

ACKNOWLEDGMENTS

The author would like to thank the following individuals for their contributions to this book: Lou Anders, Cindy Blank-Edelman, Bruce Bortz, Tobias Buckell, Jerome Edelman, Harrison Demchick, Kate Elliott, Deanna Hoak, J. D. Landis, Philip Mansour, Jill Maxick, Cat Rambo, and Anne Smith.

Most of all, the author would like to thank Victoria Blakeway Edelman, who made him take out Ferris.

ABOUT THE AUTHOR

DAVID LOUIS EDELMAN is a Web designer, programmer, and journalist. He lives with his wife, Victoria, near Washington, DC.

Over the past ten years, Mr. Edelman has programmed Web sites for the US Army and the FBI, taught software to the US Congress and the World Bank, written articles for the *Washington Post* and the *Baltimore Sun*, and directed the marketing departments of biometric and e-commerce companies.

Mr. Edelman was born in Birmingham, Alabama, in 1971 and grew up in Orange County, California. He received a BA in creative writing and journalism from Johns Hopkins University in 1993. *Infoquake* is his first novel.

Visit his Web site at www.davidlouisedelman.com.